the EX-MAS Holidays

the
EX-MAS
Holidays

ZOE ALLISON

Berkley Romance
New York

BERKLEY ROMANCE
Published by Berkley
An imprint of Penguin Random House LLC
penguinrandomhouse.com

Library of Congress Cataloging-in-Publication Data

Names: Allison, Zoe, author.
Title: The ex-mas holidays / Zoe Allison.
Description: First edition. | New York: Berkley Romance, 2023.
Identifiers: LCCN 2022060585 (print) | LCCN 2022060586 (ebook) |
ISBN 9780593550076 (trade paperback) | ISBN 9780593550083 (ebook)
Subjects: LCGFT: Romance fiction. | Novels.
Classification: LCC PR6101.L4577 E9 2023 (print) | LCC PR6101.L4577 (ebook) |
DDC 823/.92—dc23/eng/20230201
LC record available at https://lccn.loc.gov/2022060585
LC ebook record available at https://lccn.loc.gov/2022060586

First Edition: September 2023

Printed in the United States of America
1st Printing

Book design by Daniel Brount

For Mark, my best friend and biggest champion.
I love you more than all the book boyfriends
put together. And that's saying something.

the
EX-MAS
Holidays

Chapter ONE

"WHERE THE HELL ARE YOU, YOU FOOT-CRIPPLING LITTLE devils?"

Maya rummaged in the passenger-side footwell among various bags in order to find her heels, kicking off her trainers in favor of the more fitting party footwear.

Upon opening the car door to a blast of ice-cold air, she paused to put on her jacket before climbing out. *How is it possible for the temperature to drop about fifty bloody degrees when I've only traveled forty miles north?* Goodness knows how much colder it'd be when she continued on up the road later that evening.

As she strode out along the gentle incline of the driveway, she was distracted by the imposing size of the massive mansions on the cul-de-sac. Her feet went out from under her, and she only just managed to grab hold of a railing, narrowly preventing a fall onto her backside. "Shit!" Looking up, she checked that none of Kirsty's posh neighbors were around to hear her yelling that expletive. A glance back down confirmed the subtle shimmer of ice on the paving. "Bloody hell. Stupid winter weather."

A thought crossed her mind—was it a good idea to leave all her worldly possessions in the boot, outside, in the dark? *It's a nice area. Should be okay.*

There was something sad about the fact that her whole life fit in the back of her car. Sacrificing all the big items of furniture to Rich had seemed sensible when they divided it up—he was going to a new flat after all. *No point wasting money on storage when I'm going to be a sad twentysomething living in my childhood bedroom for the foreseeable future.* It's not as if there had been loads of stuff anyway. Their flat and ultimately their mortgage had been modest with her having chosen to work at a small accountancy firm and Rich opting to take on a finance role for a charity.

Though there had been a couple of items that had sentimental value, and were smaller. Such as the vintage Royal Albert afternoon tea plate that she would have loved to bring home in order for her and Liv to place scones upon it and pretend to take tea with Mr. Darcy and Mr. Bingley. But it had been a gift from Rich's mum, therefore Maya had relinquished it to him. Rich didn't even like afternoon tea, or scones. And he certainly wasn't partial to either Darcy or Bingley. But still, it was the right thing to do and, in any case, she was getting too old to be pretending that she was a character in a Jane Austen novel.

Maya picked her way to the front door, arms outstretched and legs akimbo, like the most inept trapeze artist in existence. There were a couple more slips, and she heartily wished that she'd kept those damned trainers on, but she'd come too far to turn back now.

"Come on, Maya. Grow a pair of ovaries." Fixing her gaze on the doorway, and wondering where this newfound habit of talking to herself had come from, she continued on her mission. Without further incident she managed to complete her quest, and arrived on the sanctity of the doorstep, in order to ring the bell.

Blowing out a relieved breath, she watched it puff into little clouds of condensation, misting up the beautiful stained glass window embedded in the door. The realization that she wouldn't know anybody at the party except for Kirsty hit, and she fiddled with her charm bracelet.

The door opened with a flood of warmth. "You made it." Kirsty grabbed hold of her in a tight hug.

"Hi," Maya said, her voice muffled by Kirsty's sequined shoulder. "You look fab. And your new house is fantastic."

Kirsty released her with a smile, transitioning into a curtsy. "Why, thank you." Straightening up, she winked. "Come in. That's everybody here now. And I do mean *everybody*."

Maya stepped inside to secure less slippery footing. Before she could ask why Kirsty had emphasized the *everybody*, she was ushered down the wide hallway and into a large living room. The surroundings resembled something out of a show home, all clean lines and glass.

Kirsty pointed to each of her friends in turn. "These are my neighbors Donna and Karen. And this is Isabelle and Una from work . . ." She went on, introducing Maya to around ten women.

Fixing a smile on her face, Maya attempted to cover the fact that the names were immediately slipping her mind like water through a sieve.

Kirsty held out her hands. "Let me take your coat."

Maya removed it, adjusting her gold off-the-shoulder top. "Can I help with anything in the kitchen?"

"Absolutely not," Kirsty said, giving her a mock-stern stare. "It's all in hand."

For some reason, that statement raised a raucous cheer from the small crowd of women, which almost made Maya jump. It was nice that everyone was able to relax and not be on kitchen duty, but she wasn't sure why it merited such an energetic response. What were they all on? Snowballs and Christmas cheer, most likely.

The others began chatting among themselves, and Kirsty touched Maya's arm. "What drink order can I put in for you?"

Maya wished she could get a hearty slug of whatever was fueling the rest of these women, but there was driving to be done, and disapproving fathers to be faced. "Just a Diet Coke, please. I'm not staying over."

"You're driving back to Glenavie tonight?" Kirsty asked.

Maya played with her charm bracelet, her stomach tightening. "I figured it was better to face the music sooner rather than later."

Kirsty embraced her, giving her a squeeze. "Hopefully you'll settle in quickly. But are you sure you can't stay? The roads are icy."

Maya shook her head, plastering a smile on her face. "I'm in the mindset to get there now."

Kirsty nodded. "You can backtrack at any time if you have a change of heart. Maybe you'll fancy joining in the fun a bit more once you see what I've got in store."

Maya raised her eyebrows. Kirsty certainly seemed rather cloak-and-dagger this evening.

"Have a seat," Kirsty said, with a wink. "I'll be back in a sec."

Maya sat on the massive, soft gray sofa next to a couple of the other guests. The room was so stylishly decorated that it was difficult to keep her envious eyes off all the furnishings. It was clearly a new build, and Kirsty had the place done out to the nines.

A smiling woman wearing a black jumpsuit shifted over to take Maya's hand in a shake. "I'm Isabelle."

Maya returned her smile. "Maya. Nice to meet you."

Isabelle sipped her wine as she nodded toward the large living room window. "I can't believe how cold it's getting."

"I know," the woman next to Isabelle piped up. "*I* can't believe that it's so soon until Christmas." She leaned across Isabelle to address Maya, her black tasseled top nearly dangling into Isabelle's drink. "Hi, I'm Una."

Maya shook Una's hand across Isabelle's front, nearly clothes-lining poor Isabelle in the process. "Great to meet you."

Una let out a loud sigh. "I haven't gotten *nearly* enough Christmas shopping done yet."

"Tell me about it," Isabelle replied, rolling her eyes. "I'm never going to get it done in time."

Maya's shoulders relaxed a little. Typical Scottish winter conversation made talking to new people easier. "Same. I've not even bought one present yet, because I'm in the middle of moving home. Literally. All my stuff is outside in the car." She stopped talking, aware that her mouth was running away with her.

"Really?" Isabelle asked, raising her eyebrows. "You're moving house tonight?"

"Yeah," Maya replied. She wished she had a drink in order to soothe her feelings of inadequacy—something stronger than the Diet Coke that Kirsty was fetching. She cleared her throat. "I'm moving home because I lost my job."

"Aw," Una said, reaching across Isabelle to take Maya's hand and nearly falling into Isabelle's lap. "Sorry to hear that. Especially at Christmas."

"Ah, it's fine," Maya said, waving her other hand and plastering on a grin. "Worse things happen at sea."

Why she was comparing her plight to a maritime incident, she had no idea. Since when did sailors lose their jobs, boyfriends, and flats, plus have to go home with their tails between their legs to face their disappointed fathers? Though, granted, Moby Dick probably *would* be worse. Or Jaws. Or Godzilla.

Isabelle leaned back, shooting Maya a sympathetic look. "But still. That must be very stressful. Where's home?"

"Glenavie," Maya replied, coming out of her sea monster ruminations. "Not too far from Glencoe."

"Ski country," Una said, a dreamy expression on her face. "Lovely. At least it'll be nice and Christmassy."

The image of her Highland hometown entered Maya's mind, adorned in twinkly Christmas lights and dusted with snow. Christmas in Glenavie was her favorite time of year. The idea of that infused a little comfort into her veins.

Kirsty reappeared with a couple of plates of nibbles, passing them around the room. "There's more stuff in the oven, so help yourselves. Oh, and, Maya, your drink's coming."

"No rush." Maya sat back to listen to her new acquaintances. It occurred to her that Kirsty had said her drink was "coming," so who was fetching it if not Kirsty?

She heard the door open behind her. The other women's voices rose by a number of decibels, plus an octave or two. Turning her head to find out what the kerfuffle was about, Maya was greeted by the sight of a firm and perfectly shaped naked male bottom across the huge floor space. A well-toned man had his back to her as he handed out drinks, not wearing a stitch of clothing except for a tiny apron around his waist, the strings of which were entwined with tinsel.

Maya laughed, finally realizing why Kirsty had been behaving in that "nudge-nudge, wink-wink" manner. Plus, why the women seemed drunk on more than just alcohol. They were also high on the sight of a hot naked man. She raised her eyebrows, turning back to Isabelle and Una. "Kirsty's hired one of those naked waiters, I see."

"Yes," said Isabelle, smiling. "He's been preparing and serving our drinks. What a treat."

Maya shook her head. "That's what she meant when I arrived. She was being all cryptic and like '*everybody*' is here."

Isabelle laughed. "She *is* rather pleased with herself."

"*I'm* rather pleased too," Una said, eyeing the man's back. "He's bloody gorgeous."

"I wouldn't know," Maya replied with a shrug and a smile. "I've not seen his face yet."

Una sighed. "The back of him is as appealing as the front." She placed her hand onto her forehead in a mock swoon. "Sandy-brown hair, ravishing amber eyes, and a sexy closely trimmed beard. My favorite."

Isabelle snorted. "Don't pretend that you've been looking at his face, Una. Not with that perfectly chiseled torso."

Una laughed.

Sandy-brown hair and ravishing amber eyes. Maya had known a man of that description before, minus the beard. Though she'd been eager to forget him, and that task had taken her a little while. The realization hit that, very soon, she might see him on a more regular basis. *Another reason to dread going back.*

Kirsty was gesturing to the naked waiter. "The Diet Coke is for the lady over there, on the sofa." Kirsty pointed toward Maya.

"Here you go," Una whispered. "Brace yourself."

Maya smiled, shaking her head. Who was this guy? Chris Hemsworth? She was sure he couldn't be *that* devastating.

The man turned. Maya's smile froze on her face, her jaw dropping as she took in his familiar, handsome features with a sinking heart. "*Sam?*"

His face fell, the creaminess of his cheeks staining pink. "Maya."

Chapter
TWO

THE CHATTER ACROSS THE ROOM CONTINUED, BUT MAYA'S SEC-tion fell silent. Kirsty, Isabelle, and Una stared at her, clearly confused as to how she knew hot-naked-guy.

She glanced around, double-checking that there were no secret cameras and that she wasn't on one of those prank TV shows. Unfortunately, it seemed real.

A million questions ran through her mind. The most pressing of which was *Why the hell are you naked in my mate's house?* Though it was closely followed by *Why did you lead me on, then dump me?* However, she didn't feel able to voice those queries, not in front of all these strangers. Especially when she hadn't seen him apart from in passing over the last eight years.

Maya cleared her throat. "Hi. You look . . ." *Naked? Hot AF?* "Well."

Sam raised an eyebrow, assessing her with a cool stare.

She shifted in her seat. Despite him not wearing a stitch apart from that tiny apron, it felt as if he had the upper hand, towering over her while she stayed put on the sofa. Maya tried to get up, but for a moment she wasn't sure that her legs would hold her.

"I *am* well, thanks," Sam replied, his face perfectly neutral. "And you?"

Bloody hell, this is beyond awkward. "Mm-hmm. Fine, fine." That minuscule apron was practically at her eyeline, and she couldn't bear it any longer, so she summoned the power to stand. However, she was then greeted by a better view of his naked torso and muscular arms, not to mention his amber eyes, which were still penetrating her inner being like some sort of alien mind probe.

"Anyway," Maya said, fixing her eyes on the doorway. "I've got to pee. Just had a long journey from Glasgow, you know? Tiny bladder and all that." She squeezed her eyes tight in discomfort as she walked across the room, closing the door behind her to pause at the bottom of the stairs. Feeling that it was safer to retreat up there, she climbed them, heading into the bathroom and shutting the door. She perched on the edge of the bath, taking a breath. This was worse than Moby Dick, Jaws, *or* Godzilla.

There was a knock at the door, and Kirsty stuck her head around it. "Are you okay? What's going on?"

Maya blew her fringe out of her eyes. "Don't ask."

Kirsty entered, taking a seat next to her on the uncomfortable porcelain. "How the hell do you know the naked waiter?"

Maya rubbed her temples. "Remember freshers' week, when I told you I'd not long been dumped by that guy at home?"

"Hmm," Kirsty said, frowning. "Not really."

"It was at that tequila night at the students' union."

Kirsty pursed her lips, clearly not recalling.

"I got off my head and sang 'Wrecking Ball' by Miley Cyrus at the karaoke and then cried to you about it in the toilets," Maya said, raising her eyebrows at the apparent revelation that Kirsty hadn't been paying attention to her display of teenage angst. Or perhaps that was a good thing, given how she'd murdered poor Miley's song.

"Oh, wait," Kirsty said, her eyes widening. "I *do* remember. That guy who was your best mate's twin brother?"

"Yep," Maya sighed.

"The one you were secretly in love with but he didn't know you existed?"

"Yes, yes. That's the one," Maya said quickly, trying to silence Kirsty's burgeoning stream of consciousness because, despite the passage of around eight years, it was still pretty gutting to remember the details.

"Oh!" Kirsty continued, raising her finger in triumph at her tequila-laden memory skills and seeming oblivious to Maya's discomfort. No doubt the current level of alcohol in her system was dampening her frontal lobe processes. "You ended up working together at the ski place, he suddenly decided he liked you, and you fooled around in the boot room a few times." Kirsty met Maya's eyes with a satisfied expression. "That guy?"

"Yes!" Maya said, rolling her eyes. "That guy."

Kirsty nodded. She stayed silent for a second, a frown spreading across her features. "What about that guy?"

Maya raised her eyebrows. "You've *got* to be kidding me." *How many cocktails has this woman consumed?*

"Ohh," Kirsty said, the alcohol-laden, slow-moving penny finally dropping. "Hot Naked Waiter Guy *is* that guy."

"*Yes,*" Maya said, waving her hands as if a major performance had finished.

"Blimey." Kirsty paused. "That's an extremely unfortunate coincidence."

No shit, Sherlock. Maya shook her head. "Though perhaps not for me, given my streak of crappy luck."

"Mm," Kirsty said. She hummed a few bars of Miley's "Wrecking Ball," then glanced over. "Sitting on this bath is tearing my arse to shreds."

Maya laughed despite herself. "Thanks for the sympathy, mate."

"Sorry," Kirsty said, standing and rubbing her bottom. "Come on. We'll chat some more in my room."

Kirsty took Maya's hand and led her out of the bathroom, across the upstairs landing, and into the primary bedroom, where she ushered Maya to sit on a plush chair.

Kirsty perched on a chaise longue. "What's the plan?"

Maya leaned back. "I'm going to live up here forever." She pointed across the room. "I'll sleep at the bottom of the bed and keep your and Paul's feet warm."

Kirsty raised her eyebrows. "That's the shittiest master plan I've ever heard. MI5 won't be calling you anytime soon."

"Nope. I could do with a job, though." Maya touched her charm bracelet, letting her fingers linger on the moon charm.

"Why the hell is he down here, working as a naked butler, if he lives up in Glenavie?" Kirsty asked.

Maya shrugged. "Beats me. I've barely seen him the last few years. But I'm sure he was still a ski instructor at the Glenavie resort. Liv's definitely mentioned it."

"Weird," Kirsty said, pursing her lips.

Maya huffed out her breath. "I still think the best plan is for me to stay here forever. I won't cause you any bother. Plus, it means I won't have to go home and get the you-need-to-decide-where-your-life-is-going lecture from Dad. Nor the ever-relevant TED talk 'Why Can't You Be More like Your Sister?'"

"Ugh," Kirsty said, wrinkling her nose. "He actually *said* that?"

Maya frowned, her stomach tightening. "No. But that's what he means when he goes on about all her achievements."

Kirsty groaned and rubbed her eyes, then quickly lifted her hands away. "Crap. I keep forgetting I've got all this eye makeup on. I'm going to look like a panda. Right. Here's plan B. I'll go and have a word with Sam in private, ask if he can leave early. It won't affect his fee."

Maya shook her head. "Don't. I'm not ruining your party. I'm sure everyone already thinks I'm a weirdo for leaving the room so abruptly."

"Nah. They were all too distracted by the drink and how hot the naked butler is." Kirsty paused, her eyes widening. "Oops. Sorry."

Maya groaned. "That's okay. I'm well aware of how attractive he is." The image of Sam standing there with all his muscles on display floated across her mind's eye, so she attempted to mentally push it down, but it kept popping back up like an unsinkable buoy.

Kirsty blew her breath out. "Anyway, the only ones who noticed were Isabelle and Una, and they don't think you're a weirdo." She smiled. "Maybe just a bit eccentric, and that you like to overshare your toilet habits."

Maya covered her face with her hands. "I forgot I said that."

Kirsty laughed. "Don't sweat it. It's not the most embarrassing thing that's happened tonight. Una was miming an enthusiastic pelvic thrust behind Sam's back earlier, and he turned around and caught her."

Maya snorted. "Classic Una."

Kirsty shot her a bemused smile. "You've only known her five minutes."

Maya waved her hand. "Yeah, but we're best pals now. She's the equivalent of the girl you meet in the toilets when you're out clubbing and she becomes your BFF for the night."

Kirsty laughed and Maya realized they couldn't stay there any longer. She was keeping Kirsty from her party. Time to put on her big-girl pants and reenter the room as if all were well. "Let's bite the bullet and head back down."

Kirsty stood. "Don't worry, I'm your moral support."

Maya followed her onto the landing. "We need to act casual and like nothing's wrong."

They descended the stairs.

Kirsty turned her head. "He'll know *something's* up. You've been in the loo for twenty minutes. He'll think either that you've been upset by seeing him, or that you weren't having a number *one* after all."

Maya let out a groan. "I don't know which of those is worse."

They stepped onto the downstairs landing, and Kirsty swaggered toward the living room door.

"Why are you walking like that?" Maya whispered.

"I'm being casual," Kirsty whispered back.

"Casual? More like constipated."

"Shh." Kirsty opened the door.

The chatter of the room greeted them, and Maya was reassured to find no one stopped talking to stare at her. Sam wasn't there—he must have gone back to the kitchen.

Lifting her drink from where it had been deposited on the coffee table, she rejoined Isabelle and Una.

"All right?" Isabelle asked as she sat down.

"Absolutely. Fine and dandy, thank you oh so very much." Maya squeezed her eyes shut briefly.

"That's good," Una said, taking up her natural position of practically lying in Isabelle's lap. "You dashed off in a hurry, and we were worried you were ill."

Maya laughed, aware that it sounded high pitched. "No, no, feeling great, thanks."

Isabelle sipped her wine with Una still leaning across her lap. Maya half expected Isabelle to start petting Una's head.

"You know the naked waiter?" Isabelle asked.

Maya swallowed. "Yeah. What a coincidence, eh?" She laughed and it still sounded squeaky. "He's my best friend Liv's twin brother. They're from my hometown and I wasn't expecting to see him here."

Una raised her eyebrows. "Or to see *so much* of him."

"Nope," Maya said, trying not to remember how hot he'd looked in that little apron. "Definitely not."

The door opened and the man himself entered.

Maya kept her eyes steadfastly on Una, hoping to God that she wouldn't be expected to recount any of what Una was saying because she couldn't take a word in. Out of the corner of her eye, she followed Sam's movements around the room as he handed out drinks and gave the ladies some chat. Something he'd always excelled at. *Bastard.*

Maya cleared her throat. "Does anyone need anything from the kitchen?"

"Ooh," Una said, handing over her empty wineglass. "I'll take a refill." The woman could clearly put it away.

Isabelle shook her head. "I'm fine." She glanced down at Maya's still-full glass of Diet Coke with a bemused expression.

Maya shot them a weak smile as she strode out of the room without casting her eyes on Sam's whereabouts.

On entering the large, open-plan kitchen, she placed the glasses onto the island, then rummaged in the fridge to lift out a half-full bottle of white wine. Taking it over to the island, she resisted the urge to glug it, and poured some for Una. The door opened and she snapped her gaze up, meeting Sam's amber eyes and nearly sloshing the wine out of the glass. *Ugh. I'd definitely prefer Moby Dick's company.*

"Hope you're not after my job," he said, busying himself next to her.

"Nope," Maya said quickly. "I can't pull off the tiny-apron-over-the-pubic-area look."

Sam paused to rake his gaze over her, eyebrow raised, and Maya wished she hadn't said that.

He turned back to his task. "Oh, I don't know about that."

Cheeky bugger. She supposed she *had* walked into that one. But it's not as if the thought of her naked had done anything for him in the past.

Maya screwed the top back onto the wine and glanced over, trying not to stare too much at his body. The silence was getting to her.

"Nice beard," she said, then winced. Was that the best she could come up with? Not "The nights are getting dark, aren't they?" or "It's really cold, isn't it?" or "Are you ready for Christmas?"

Sam smiled as he rubbed his fingers over where his sandy-brown, neatly groomed beard framed the pink of his lips. Maya tried not to let how sexy that gesture was affect her, and failed.

"You like it?"

She nodded, keeping her eyes on his face. "Suits you. How long have you had it?"

"About a year," Sam replied as he recommenced cocktail shaking. "Not seen you in a while, though."

God, this is surreal. "Nope."

Sam didn't seem fazed by being practically naked. But that wasn't a surprise, because he'd never been the sort to be easily intimidated. *Cocky git.*

Maya took the wine back to the fridge, then lifted her drinks. She turned to go, determined not to be the one who felt pressured into filling the silence.

"Hold on."

She stopped and turned, annoyed with herself for doing as he asked instead of ignoring him and his stupid tiny tinsel apron. "What?"

He glanced over as he poured the cocktail. "I need to ask you a favor."

A favor? You've some nerve.

Before she could answer, the door opened, and one of the women practically stumbled into the room. Maya shifted to prevent a collision.

"Hey," the woman slurred. Maya thought she'd been introduced as Donna. Or Doreen. Or Doris.

Probably-Donna sidled over to Sam, not even noticing Maya's presence. "Please, can I have a sloe comfortable screw against the wall? And I don't mean the cocktail." Donna burst into overenthusiastic laughter, and Maya struggled to keep the smile from her face.

Sam graciously humored Donna's drunken antics as he prepared her drink. He must have heard that joke a million times, but did a good job of pretending otherwise.

Maya edged closer to the door, wanting to make her escape, but aware that Sam had asked her to hold on. Wondering why she was even considering doing as he'd asked, she contemplated whether to sneak away. But then Sam ushered Donna toward the door, charming her out of the room.

He shut it, then closed the gap between the two of them—coming close enough that she inhaled a lungful of his scent. Crisp and fresh . . . suddenly she was back in the boot room at the ski resort, holding him close as he pushed her up against the wall and dragged his lips from her mouth onto her neck.

Maya tried to take shallow breaths so that she couldn't smell him, and stared at the ceiling in an effort not to look at his body.

"Maya."

"What?"

"You can look at me. It's not like you haven't seen me wearing as much in the Glenavie swimming pool."

She met his eyes, aware of the heat of his body close to hers against the backdrop of the cool kitchen. "Sam, you never had your actual *arse* out at the swimming pool. And we were probably about ten at the time."

He shrugged, clearly not affected by any of this. But why would he be? None of it had registered on his radar back then, never mind now.

Maya sipped her Coke, wishing to God that there were some rum in it. "Aren't you working at the ski resort anymore?"

"I am," Sam replied, running a hand through his sandy hair. "I just needed some extra money, and this is flexible, plus it pays well."

The tightening of his biceps distracted Maya for a moment. A rogue thought crossed her mind that she'd still love to run her fingers through his hair, despite his carelessness with her heart in the past. *Shut up, brain.*

She cleared her throat. "What favor did you want to ask? Because I need to get back to my friends." Arching an eyebrow, she attempted to appear badass and as if most of the people she was referring to weren't those she'd met only an hour ago.

He glanced down at where her top was revealing her shoulder. "I need you to keep it to yourself that I'm doing this job."

Maya frowned. "Why?"

"Just because."

Maya held his gaze for a few seconds, as if beating him in a staring competition would be some sort of victory. Sam looked away first, and she had to repress the urge to pump her fist in the air, which would have been foolish when she was holding two drinks.

He shifted away slightly. "I haven't told anyone I'm doing this job, that's why. I only take gigs far enough out of town that people I know won't be around." He looked at her as if she were breaking some sort of rule by being there.

Maya clenched the drinks a little more tightly. This was *her* friend's house. He was the one trespassing on her territory, not the other way around. She kept quiet, not wanting to give him the satisfaction of answering.

It had the desired effect—the balance of power seemed to stay in her corner, and he kept talking. "Catriona wouldn't like that I'm doing it. I don't want anyone to find out and tell her."

Aha. Catriona. That duplicitous cow. "Yeah," Maya said, acting as if this were the most boring conversation in history and that she wasn't affected by hearing that name. "That's fine, whatever. I need to get back to Kirsty now, so . . ."

She gestured at him to back off, and he raised an eyebrow, staying put.

"You need to back it up so I can get out of here. No turning round. I do not need to see your naked arse again."

He folded his arms, eyebrow still raised. "I've not had any complaints before."

She rolled her eyes. Bloody full of himself. He probably had this second job in order to fund some flash new car or designer gear or something equally shallow.

Sam smiled and took a couple of steps back, opening the door to allow her to exit the kitchen.

On entering the living room, Maya handed Una her drink, then made a beeline for Kirsty.

"So," Kirsty stage-whispered. "What happened in there?"

"Nothing," Maya muttered.

Kirsty narrowed her eyes, glancing over Maya's shoulder at where, she assumed, Sam must have reentered. "Did he mention what happened?"

Maya sipped her drink. "Nope. He could at least have apologized for humiliating me. But then again, he's had years to do that and he hasn't. So . . ." She shrugged.

Kirsty huffed out a breath. "I feel like docking his fee, but it's prepaid."

A needle of guilt stabbed at Maya's chest at the thought of Kirsty instigating any sort of sanction. Though she didn't know why, when she owed Sam nothing. "It's fine. Water under the bridge. He's forgotten about it, I've forgotten about it. And I'm bloody sure Catriona never even thought about it."

Kirsty gave her a hug. "I have a question," she said, pulling back to gesture across the room. "If this is the guy who dumped you for your friend because you weren't his type, then how come he can't take his eyes off you?"

Maya looked over her shoulder and found Sam staring right back at her.

Chapter
THREE

I T WAS PRETTY CHILLY IN THE DOWNSTAIRS TOILET, SO SAM didn't waste any time in pulling on his jeans and jumper.

Kirsty had said he could use one of the bedrooms to change again, but he'd felt weird about being up there now that he'd discovered she was Maya's friend. What if Maya was going to be sleeping in one of those rooms tonight? Imagining her getting undressed and climbing into the huge bed was a dangerous line of thought, one that had the opposite effect on his body to the cold ambient temperature.

Now that he'd realized Kirsty's link with Maya, he had become more aware of the opulence of his surroundings. The house could've been lifted straight from the pages of a catalog—all clean lines and monochrome palette. Not like his messy, hodgepodge place that could probably fit into this one twice over.

Sam checked his hair in the mirror, running a hand through to tousle it a little. Maya likely had a place just as huge in Glasgow, one that she'd share with that high-flying boyfriend of hers—Rich. Apt name for someone in his position. Sam rolled his eyes. He might as well have been called Richie Rich. Liv had said he was in finance or something, which was typical. Just the sort that Maya would go for, having made it clear in the past that a lowly ski instructor like Sam would be beneath her. Her dalliance with him must've been down to some sort of brief fantasy about wanting a bit of rough rather than a guy from her own middle-class background.

He closed his eyes in discomfort as he remembered turning to hand over that Diet Coke and being faced with Maya. He'd nearly dropped the damned thing, and that would've landed him in big trouble with Kirsty's expensive light gray plush carpeting. Why on earth did anyone pick carpets that color anyway? He was willing to bet that it was named something pretentious in the carpet store, like Elephant's Breath or Mist of the Wind. Surely brown or dark gray were more sensible shades to hide a multitude of sins.

Hopefully he'd managed to style out his discomfort by acting nonplussed when really his heart rate had been racing along faster than a cheetah on steroids washed down with Red Bull. Not that being partially clothed bothered him in general, otherwise he wouldn't do this job. But having his ex in the vicinity was another matter entirely.

Deciding that no amount of tousling was going to make him more attractive in Maya's eyes, he left the room to go find Kirsty. Under normal circumstances he'd head straight home. But for some reason, he had a hankering to check whether Kirsty needed any help with the clear-up. Denying to himself that reason was a mahogany-haired, chestnut-eyed, tawny-skinned beauty named Maya, he entered the kitchen. Kirsty was in there, tidying, with Maya's assistance. Their conversation tailed off as they glanced over and caught his presence.

He cleared his throat. "Can I give you a hand before I leave?"

Kirsty smiled. "Thanks, but that's okay. I've got my glamorous assistant here to help me."

Sam cast his gaze over Maya. The manner in which the neckline of her shiny gold top revealed her shoulder kept drawing his eye. An image flashed into his mind, of dragging his mouth over that very shoulder, savoring the taste of her skin on his lips. A burst of heat erupted in his core. "Lucky you," he said to Kirsty, before he could stop himself. *For fuck's sake, shut your bloody mouth.* That wasn't the first flirtatious comment he'd made toward Maya that evening, and they'd all had as much effect as speaking to a statue. There was no point in kidding himself that he was making those comments purely to rile her either, being acutely aware that he still found her very attractive—despite her past rejection. *Her* feelings on the matter clearly hadn't changed, judging by the manner in which she glanced away quickly and wouldn't meet his eyes.

Maya cleared her throat. "We're nearly finished here anyway."

Kirsty gave her a nudge. "You should set off now, I can cope. I don't want you driving when the temperature drops further."

Maya shot Kirsty a glance.

She must be driving back to Glasgow tonight, rather than staying over here.

Concern gathered in his mind at the thought of her traveling in the current conditions, despite the knowledge he'd be driving in it himself. Plus him having no business worrying about her welfare. "It's meant to freeze again overnight."

Maya raised her eyebrows. "It'll be fine." She paused. "Don't let me keep you."

He held her gaze for a couple of seconds, not sure how to feel about knowing that once he took his eyes off her, he might not see her again for another few years. "Maybe I'll see you around."

Maya hesitated for a beat. "Perhaps."

Kirsty cleared her throat. "I'll see you out, Sam."

Managing to tear his gaze away from Maya, he followed Kirsty out of the kitchen to the front door, where he put on his fur-collared parka and grabbed his bag. "Thanks, Kirsty. Hope you guys enjoy the rest of your night." The sound of laughter drifted through from the living room, and he smiled.

She returned his expression. "It'll probably be an all-nighter, they're a pretty raucous bunch."

Sam grasped the door handle. "Hope Donna understands my declining her offer to stick her tongue down my throat. I didn't think her husband, or my girlfriend, would approve."

Kirsty shrugged. "Sometimes rejection works out for the best. It's not always a bad thing."

Sam hesitated. Was that some kind of dig at him? Had Maya told Kirsty what had happened, and Kirsty was insinuating that Maya had been right to reject him? He opened the door, keen to get out of there. "Merry Christmas."

"Same to you."

Picking his way down the driveway, he noticed a sheen to the paving that hadn't been present on his arrival, so he trod carefully along the street toward his car. He'd been a little intimidated when he'd parked among all the high-end vehicles on the leafy avenue— his was the only banger in sight. Hopefully none of the posh residents in the neighborhood would assume he was a burglar casing the joint.

Jumping into the car, he dumped his bag and went to start it. Nothing happened. *Please, not again.* He waited a couple of seconds and gave it another shot, but still no luck. Resting his head back and looking up, he spoke to the heavens. "I've no idea why you hate me so much, but can't you give me a break? I've suffered enough this evening." Sam shook his head, glancing back down. "Why the hell am I talking to myself?"

He popped the bonnet and climbed out, heading for the front of the vehicle. The freezing cold touch of the car stung his fingers, and his breath formed puffs of condensation as he peered inside, shining his key ring torch on the traitorous engine. Fiddling around a little, he wondered what he'd do if it wouldn't start this time. He couldn't call anyone to pick him up because then he'd have to explain what he was doing out there. Unless he could create a believable story about what had brought him a few towns farther south from Glenavie, at eleven on a Friday night? "I fancied a random two-hour drive in my beat-up old car, despite it being icier than a polar bear's Christmas party"?

A return trip to the driver's side and a twist of the key confirmed that the hunk of junk was still deader than a dodo. He climbed back out and stood staring at the open bonnet, mulling over his options. Or lack thereof.

The sound of another vehicle approaching from behind became apparent, and he lifted his head, hoping it wasn't one of the residents here to inquire why such a dodgy heap was bringing down the tone of their estate, with its upmarket selection of Range Rovers, BMWs, and Audis. He couldn't see who was behind the wheel because he was blinded by their headlights. Someone climbed out and, as they moved forward, the light bounced off their shiny gold top.

Oh shit.

Maya walked over, glowing in the headlights like some sort of ethereal vision. Well, it was less of a walk and more like the gait of an intoxicated Bambi—at least she'd changed into trainers from those killer heels she'd had on earlier. Yeah, he'd taken in every last detail about what she was wearing, and how she'd worn it. Sam glanced skyward, his voice low. "This isn't what I meant when I asked you to give me a break."

Maya completed her slippery journey across the tarmac. "Okay?" Her expression was difficult to read.

He shifted his weight from one foot to another. "Not really. Bloody thing won't start."

Maya eyed the car, raising her eyebrows. Probably disgusted that it wasn't one of these shiny BMWs. "Does it normally give you trouble?"

He stifled a sigh. This evening was getting more mortifying by the minute, and that was despite their first meeting having involved him being stark naked except for a piece of cloth the size of a place mat. A large place mat, obviously. "Yeah. Usually, I can get it going again." He nudged the car with his foot, resentful of how it was showing him up. "But not this time."

Maya hugged her arms, and Sam wondered whether he should offer his parka. But he didn't want to do anything else that might come across as inappropriate.

"Is that why you need extra money?" she asked. "To buy a new car?"

Sam hesitated, running a hand through his hair and not meeting her eyes. "Something like that."

"Have you got breakdown cover?"

He grimaced. "Nope." *Nice one, Sam. You're such a catch.* Feeling inferior regarding material wealth wasn't something that had bothered him in a long time. At least, not since Maya.

"Hmm," Maya said, seeming to ponder the problem.

Sam wished she'd just leave him to his misery and zoom off back to Glasgow.

"You could call them and get the car registered, then ask them to come out? Or stay overnight in a hotel and do it in the morning?"

Sam rubbed his face. "I've got a kids' class to teach in the morning and I can't let them down. I suppose I could go with the roadside assistance option." He puffed out a breath. "I was just hoping to keep this last lot of money for the thing I'm saving for." He stopped talking in case he gave anything away. Not that it mattered if he told her what he was really doing with the money. She wasn't going to be around Glenavie anyway. But he didn't feel like divulging any more to this woman.

"The new car?" she asked.

"Yeah . . ." he said, glancing away. "That's right."

She'd likely think it pitiful that he might need to save for a vehicle. No doubt she could afford to buy one outright. Her family had always been what he thought of as two-holidays-a-year kind of people. Enough wealth to afford a summer break to some far-flung tropical paradise, plus a winter ski trip somewhere amazing like Whistler. Sam and his family had only ever managed a summer break elsewhere in Scotland. Not something he ever resented, but clearly there were those who looked down on such arrangements.

Sam had skied abroad on one occasion only, when they went on a school trip to Austria. His mum had saved for months and gone without herself in order to make it happen, and he'd been eternally grateful though agonizingly guilty about it.

Maya studied him, and it seemed as though she might finally give up and leave him to it. Her voice was a little subdued. "I can give you a lift home. That way you can teach your class in the morning, then decide what to do about the car later."

For a moment he didn't know what to say. An offer of assistance wasn't what he'd been expecting, especially when her objectionable attitude toward him had been on display thus far that evening. It *would* solve his situation, but it'd mean that she'd be going hours out of her way altogether—there and back again—before completing the journey to Glasgow. Unless she stayed at her parents' overnight and then went home in the morning. But surely if she didn't need to return that same night, then she'd be staying at Kirsty's.

He folded his arms and shook his head. "I can't put you out."

Maya hugged her arms a little more tightly, not meeting his eyes. "I'm going the exact same way as you. So, it's not putting me out."

Sam hesitated, trying to piece that statement together. "You're going home? To Glenavie?"

"Yeah," she said, glancing down at the ice-glazed tarmac.

She must be headed back for the weekend. Should he say yes, if she was going that way anyway? But the mere idea of that was excruciating.

"Maybe it's not out of your way," Sam said slowly, the words squeezing painfully past his vocal cords. "But I'm pretty sure being in my company for the two-hour drive isn't something you'd particularly relish."

She hesitated, then shot him a brief smile that didn't reach her eyes. "It's fine."

Sam looked at the car, then along the road. He had no other way of getting home tonight, not unless he wanted to call Catriona and risk her wrath. He ran a hand through his hair. "Okay." Trying not to audibly sigh, and attempting to infuse a little enthusiasm into his voice, he said, "Thanks."

Maya turned quickly, seeming keen to get back to the car. Perhaps because she was freezing. Or maybe because the thought of an imminent drive in his company was so repulsive to her, she had to get a brief reprieve from his presence. In any case, she must've misjudged the ice rink beneath their feet because she slipped, throwing her arms out in an attempt to steady herself.

Sam grabbed hold of her, hauling her into his chest before she could fall.

Maya grasped the furry lapels of his jacket, and as the momentum ceased, she was in his arms, clutching his clothing and staring into his eyes.

He was pinned by her soft gaze, like an animal in the headlights, his pulse a good deal faster than a few moments ago. As he inhaled her sweet scent, he was transported to summertime. Specifically, that summer where they'd had more than one clinch in the boot room at the ski resort. He could almost perceive the musty stillness of the space around them, feel the brush of her lips against his, taste her tongue in his mouth, and sense the soft touch of her skin beneath his fingers.

Maya cleared her throat, her voice quiet. "Thanks."

His airway felt constricted. "That's okay. Just make sure you're steady before I let you go."

Maya nodded, shifting her gaze away to extricate herself. She tested her footing. "I'll meet you in the car."

This time, she turned more slowly, gingerly making her way back to her vehicle.

Sam watched, aware that he should shut the bonnet and get his bag. But he had an overwhelming urge to ensure she reached her car without further incident. Shaking his head, he wondered why he felt protective over a woman who held him in such contempt. Although, if she still thought that he was so beneath her, why was she offering to help?

Finally, he managed to close the bonnet and quickly fetch his bag. "Thanks for nothing," he muttered to the dead automobile, before crossing the tarmac. Maybe Maya had offered to give him a hand because she felt sorry for him. He shuddered, a sick feeling swirling in his gut.

He opened her passenger door and stuck his head in, taken aback that her car was a decidedly normal hatchback rather than the high-end sort he'd been expecting. "Should I put this bag in the boot?"

Maya darted her gaze to the rear and then back to him. "The boot's full, I'm afraid."

Sam climbed in, placing the bag at his feet and closing the door. "No problem."

He took off his jacket, and as he leaned toward her to get his arm out, she moved away, touching her shoulder against the cold window and letting out an involuntary yelp.

For goodness' sake, I'm not that repulsive, surely?

She shot him a brief smile. "Buckle up."

Sam tried not to roll his eyes. He knew the drill for car travel. This wasn't his first rodeo. He rubbed his forehead. "This isn't what either of us was expecting this evening."

Maya kept her eyes on the road, her expression neutral. "Not really. I only expect to see my friends' brothers naked on Tuesdays."

Sam laughed before he could stop himself. As awkward as it was to be reminded of that fact, Maya making a joke of it did disarm the tension somewhat. "I meant sharing a car. But point taken."

A smile seemed to play at the corner of her mouth, but then it was gone. He'd always thought her smile to be the most beautiful he'd ever seen.

Sam ran a hand through his hair, feeling a little bolder. "Is it okay if we talk?" He gave her a side glance. "Or do you want me to remain silent for the whole journey?"

A short laugh escaped her lips, and he got the feeling that question was a little close to the bone. She cleared her throat. "Talking is fine."

Sam glanced over his shoulder, attempting to think of something neutral to say. "Is your boot so full because you're taking Christmas presents home?"

There was more than a moment's hesitation, and Sam wondered what on earth could be so controversial about that innocuous question.

"No. It's all my worldly possessions. I'm moving home for a bit."

The penny dropped. She'd been trying to keep from him that she was moving home on a more permanent basis. That was why she'd given Kirsty that funny look when they'd been discussing the journey prior to their departure. No doubt she didn't want him knowing in case he still held a torch for her, which was pretty conceited on her part.

Sam remained silent as Maya accelerated out of town onto the country road. The scenic mountain view was obscured by darkness, but he could just detect its statuesque outline, as if it were hiding behind an opaque gray curtain.

"Oh yeah?" he said, fiddling with the glove compartment and trying not to give any emotion away. If she thought that he'd feel anything about her coming home, then she was sorely mistaken. "Liv didn't mention it."

"It was kind of a last-minute thing. I was considering staying on after Rich and I broke up, but then I decided I'd move home and live with my parents instead." She shrugged, seeming to feign nonchalance.

"I *do* remember Liv saying that you'd lost your job." He paused, realizing it would be polite to convey some sort of condolence regarding that situation, and trying to avoid expressing any kind of opinion about her breakup. "Sorry to hear that."

Maya swallowed. "Well, you know. The firm went under. Sign of the times. But at least it's not as bad as Moby Dick."

Sam frowned. "Pardon?"

"Nothing." She shifted in her seat. "How're things at the ski resort? I've not been up there in ages."

He rubbed his eyes. "Fine." As if he'd disclose anything with her stuck-up attitude.

Maya glanced over. "Busy?"

"Yeah." Busy didn't cut it. Sometimes he felt as if he was going to snap in two under the recent pressure. He cleared his throat. "How's Hana?" That was a nice, neutral question at least.

"Great," Maya said, her voice flat. "She's the youngest partner in her law firm, and she and Rosie are engaged now, living in a massive mansion down in Thatched-Roof-Ville, southern England."

It might have been his imagination, but she sounded a little bitter about it. He eyed her. "Not a fan of thatched roofs, myself. Too much of a fire hazard if you ask me."

Another small smile played about her lips, and he took it as a tiny victory. "Indeed. What about your mum? She doing okay?"

"Yeah," he replied, with a cautious smile. "She and Angus are getting on well."

"He seems like a nice guy. I bumped into the two of them last time I was home."

"He is," Sam said, grateful that his mum had finally found a man who could be described that way, after being with his douche-bag father, followed by years alone. "She deserves someone nice." Family seemed like a safe topic to stay on. "Are your parents keeping okay?"

"Yeah, thanks. Same old."

"They'll be looking forward to having you home for a while."

She let out a brief laugh. "I think Dad's particularly looking forward to lecturing me about my lack of five-year plan to be the highest-flying accountant the world has ever seen."

A rueful smile tugged at his mouth. Dr. Omar Bashir was renowned for driving his daughters hard, ambition-wise. Omar had double standards where they were concerned, and what was good enough for everyone else was not good enough for his offspring. *Pretty sure I would've fallen into his "not good enough" category had Maya actually been interested in me.* "You know what parents are like, they never see us as adults. It'll still be the same when we're fifty."

"Yeah," Maya muttered. "They'll be lecturing us from their armchairs at the nursing home."

They managed to fill most of the silence by discussing other mutual acquaintances, with a bit of generic Christmas chat thrown in, and before too long they were entering the outskirts of Glenavie. The darkness of the country road gave way to bright street lighting, enhanced by the sparkly hue of Christmas lights. Sam breathed a sigh of relief that soon the journey would be over. The familiar granite villas with their warm and welcoming bay windows came into view, the sight of which always filled him with the comforting sense of coming home.

On the streets, there was a light sprinkling of snow, which hadn't been present farther south, and the cozy feeling was enhanced by the festive illuminations adorning both the streetlamps and the properties. They all twinkled in various hues of white, yellow, and orange. Some houses were bedecked in other primary colors, which at any other time might have appeared garish, but at this time of year, he loved it. The townsfolk tended to go all out for the festive season. Every year there was a competition for the best-lit house, hence the town-wide tradition of decorating for Christmas in late November—far earlier than the rest of the country. It was a Glenavie thing, and it was awesome. There really wasn't anywhere else he'd rather be, despite the likes of Maya looking down on it, and Catriona always going on at him about moving away to try the big-city life. Sam couldn't imagine anything worse.

Maya glanced over, her expression unexpectedly soft. "I always get this comforting feeling once I reach home. Especially at Christmas. I love seeing all the lights."

Sam raised his eyebrows. "Me too."

"I assume they're doing the Christmas lights competition this year?" Maya asked, craning her neck to look at the houses.

"Yeah," he replied, surprised by her interest and gesturing out the window toward the big house on the corner. "They still win every year." It was an old stone building, and each window was carefully dressed with rose-gold twinkly lights, matching those lining the rim of the roof. Each tree on the front lawn was draped symmetrically in the same shade of light.

"It *is* stunning," Maya said. "It's like something off a Christmas card."

Sam nodded. It was perfect, but that wasn't his thing. He preferred homely, welcoming, down to earth. He'd never choose somewhere beautiful but clinical like Kirsty's house over the likes of his smaller but cozier place. And he preferred the lights on the houses on his estate. They were fun and over the top rather than immaculate looking. But he wasn't surprised that Maya liked the huge, expensive, flawless big house on the corner. That was her all over.

"Okay," Maya said, clearing her throat. "You need to direct me now, because I don't know where you live."

Sam sat straighter. "Oh yeah. I forgot. Take the next left."

Maya followed his instructions as he guided her off the main road and through the housing estates. He was giving her an update on who was living where and doing what when it occurred to him that Maya wasn't the first to move away and then return. A few others around their age had already done the same for various reasons. It seemed like the curse of the millennials.

"Here it is," Sam said as they pulled up outside his row of semi-detached houses. The sick feeling began to swirl again. Would she look down on his area? Her parents lived a couple of estates over, in one of the grand older houses, and again, that wasn't something that had bothered him in a long time.

"This is lovely," Maya said, glancing around. "These weren't here the last time I was home."

Sam put on his jacket and lifted his bag. She was no doubt saying that to be polite. "Thanks for the lift."

"That's okay," Maya said, eyeing his movements with an almost wistful look on her face. Perhaps wishing tonight had never happened.

Opening the door, he figured it was best to leave it at that. They'd had an awkward enough evening as it was, and there really wasn't anything he could say to smooth that over. "Bye."

She gave him a wave. Then, as he made his way up to the front door, she pulled away, as if she didn't want to wait any longer before getting him out of her sight.

Chapter
FOUR

RUBBING HIS EYES, SAM TURNED ON THE COFFEE AND LEANED against the kitchen counter as the machine did its bubbly, noisy thing. The smooth, nutty scent infused the air, and he breathed it in, hoping that inhaling the caffeinated vapors might begin to kick-start his sleepy brain. He glanced at his watch, aware that this might need to be a coffee to go if he was to make it into work on time.

He wondered how much longer he could keep burning the candle at both ends. Vicky leaving the instructor team at short notice had them stretched thin. Well, it meant that Sam was overtaxed, as it was his duty to take up the slack as head instructor and protect his team. That, along with his latest promotion to assistant manager, had him thinking his success might be a poisoned chalice. Though it wasn't as if shouldering the burden was a new thing in his life, being a task he was used to ever since his arsehole of a dad buggered off to Jersey with a woman half his age. A heaviness developed in his chest as he recalled how helpless he'd felt back then. Sam had shifted into the role of protector and problem solver and he'd sensed Liv taking on board some of the mothering influence, because God knows it had been hard for their mum to do it all on her own. The twin siblings had subconsciously become part of each other's parenting team.

The butler thing wasn't helping his fatigue, but the reason behind taking on that job was also down to his instinct to be everyone's problem solver, even without being asked. And that drive wasn't something he could shake.

It wasn't as if Ben, the general manager, hadn't offered for him to step back a bit on the instructing when he took on more management. But Sam loved the slopes too much to become entirely office based. And so he had opted to amalgamate the two roles and hire a new instructor to pick up the slack. But now, with Vicky's departure, he was back to square one.

Wincing, he remembered the pulse-spiking mortification of locking eyes with Maya at that party the previous evening. It was like a bad dream come to life, walking into a room naked and finding your ex staring at you. Except, technically, she wasn't his ex. They hadn't gotten as far as becoming official before she'd unceremoniously rejected him. He should have seen it coming, realized that the Maya he'd fallen for wasn't the real her. Because prior to working together she'd been aloof and ignored him.

Though last night she had, annoyingly, looked as good as ever. And despite the passage of eight years, the sight of her still drove up his heart rate and awoke a fiery longing within him.

The coffee stopped hissing, and he poured some into his takeaway cup. Perhaps being abandoned by Maya wouldn't have stung so much if his dad hadn't done the same thing eighteen months beforehand. Or if he hadn't been infatuated with Maya like a pathetic puppy dog at the time. "Wanker," he muttered under his breath.

"Pardon?"

Sam snapped his gaze up to meet Catriona's hazel eyes. "Nothing."

She frowned, entering the kitchen and lifting the coffeepot to pour her own mugful. "You got home late last night."

"Yeah," he said, running a hand through his hair. "Arran's get-together went overtime."

He didn't relish lying. But he couldn't be arsed with the mouthful he'd get if she found out he'd been parading around half-naked in a room full of women. Well, maybe three-quarters naked. Perhaps four-fifths at a push.

Cat didn't reply, and his heart sank. She was clearly pissed off anyway, because he'd gotten home later than anticipated. His fault for hanging around there, kidding himself that he'd wanted to make sure he'd performed all his duties adequately when really it was so he could spend a little longer in the presence of a mahogany-haired beauty from his past. Perhaps if he'd known Maya was coming home for good, then he wouldn't have bothered. He was bound to see her around more of the time now. *Who am I kidding? I still would've stuck around last night if I'd known.* His insistence to himself that he didn't feel anything for her was becoming harder to maintain. In any case, the car had died, so he never would've managed to leave any earlier.

Watching Cat silently take a seat at the kitchen table, her mouth drawn into an "I'm annoyed with you, but I'm not going to admit it" line, he rubbed the back of his neck. The journey home had been awkward to say the least, so it was probably best if he didn't see much of Maya. She certainly hadn't seemed to have changed her tune about him.

He cleared his throat. Time to forget about Maya Bashir and

her glossy hair and alluring eyes—a task that he was clearly doomed to repeat in life—and head to work. He lifted his cup. "Can I borrow your car?"

Cat gave him a healthy dose of side-eye. "Why?"

"Mine broke down last night." He averted his gaze. "It's in the garage."

She sighed as if he'd taken a sledgehammer to the vehicle and sabotaged it on purpose. "For fuck's sake. When are you going to buy a new one?"

"When I can afford it." He let out a breath, trying not to make it too loud, because that was bound to piss her off further. "So can I borrow yours or not?"

"Ugh! Fine. The keys are on the hall table." She flipped her strawberry blond hair and grabbed her cup so forcefully that the coffee nearly sloshed out of it.

Sam headed for the door. "See you later." He was greeted by silence, and waited until he'd left the room before rolling his eyes.

Catriona's car was at least nicer to drive than his. Plus, it not breaking down every five seconds was a bonus.

Sam climbed in and started it, turning on the heating to defrost it a little before getting out to scrape the windows. After he climbed back in, he removed his jacket and woolly hat to begin the journey up to the ski resort, rolling his shoulders against the tension that had built up. Although he was unsure whether the stress response was down to running into Maya again or contending with Cat's moody ice queen act.

As he navigated a turn, he glanced along the road that led to Maya's parents' place, and wondered how she was getting on with Omar. If she'd lost her job without having something else lined up, Sam could imagine it wouldn't be met with a good reception. Even though it was hardly her fault—a lot of businesses were going under, so it wasn't as if the situation were under her control. Not unless she'd single-handedly created the economic crisis that was weighing heavily on the country.

Starting along the road into the mountains, he shook his head, attempting to get Maya out of the little camp she'd set up inside his mind, but the thought of her didn't shift. It was less of a camp and more an impenetrable fortress with iron gates and a patrolling dragon.

Sam glanced at the mountains. No matter how many times he admired the sparkling white, snowcapped peaks, they still took his breath away. Despite some people's opinion that his career wasn't worthwhile, to him, it was the best one in the world. He didn't even resent the fact that if his dad hadn't buggered off, then he might've gone to university and done something else rather than staying in Glenavie in order to keep watch over his mum and his sister. Because he loved what he did.

Pulling up in the ski resort car park, he put on his winter gear and headed to the center. Crossing the reception into the café, he went through the back foyer, where he took the stairs to his office in order to change into his skiwear. Being the assistant manager had some perks, and his own office was one of them.

Before he could head back out again, there was a knock at the door.

The general manager stuck his head round. "Are you decent?"

"Yeah, Ben. I wouldn't have unlocked the door otherwise." Sam flashed him a grin. "Not unless I'd wanted to scar you for life with the sight of me in a state of undress."

Ben smiled as he entered. "I've seen worse. Listen. Can I have a word with you after your class?"

Sam frowned, his jaw tightening. *What else is going wrong?* "Is everything okay?"

Ben glanced away. "Course. Just want to run something past you."

"Right." Sam eyed him, but Ben didn't elaborate. "I'll come find you after."

Ben shot him a smile. "Thanks."

He left the room, and Sam made his way out and onto the slopes to greet the kids' class.

❄ ❄ ❄

"COME ON, OLIVER. PIZZA, REMEMBER?" SAM RUBBED HIS FACE. The children's class was a massive pain in the arse.

He showed Oliver how to make a snowplow. Again. "It's like this, see? A V, like a slice of pizza."

"I'm hungry," said Oliver, scowling.

Sam sighed. "We're nearly done, and then your mum will be here to pick you up. Maybe you'll even get some real pizza for lunch."

Oliver threw his hands in the air and launched himself down the baby slope. "Pizza! Yeah!"

Unfortunately, he didn't follow through with making the pizza shape with his feet. Meaning he gathered too much momentum and careened into the rest of the kids, knocking them over like dominoes and resulting in a cacophony of crying.

Sam let out a slow breath. "I'm too old for this shit."

He skied down the slope to lift all the kids back onto their feet, then managed to make it through the last few minutes of the lesson. Fair enough, Vicky's fiancé had gotten a new job in Inverness, which had necessitated her move, but right now he was finding it hard not to curse her for leaving him in this mess.

Sam's thoughts flicked onto Maya and he almost let out a groan. Why couldn't he stop thinking about her when he hadn't done so in years? Apart from the odd time he'd seen her from a distance, which had led to a little spike in his heart rate followed by a day or so of reminiscing about the might-have-beens. But that was all. Though probably still too much for someone he'd had only a brief dalliance with back when they were eighteen years old. He was closer to thirty than his teens now.

Why had he started thinking about her in the first place? *Oh yes, the kids' class.* That had always been Maya's strength. A half-formed thought entered the back of his mind, relating to the fact that they had an instructor vacancy for the kids' class and Maya was back in town, jobless. Realizing that was the worst idea in the history of bad ideas, Sam quashed it, and set about rounding the kids up to take them back to the center. He huffed out his breath as he attempted to gather them together, catching a couple escaping back up the slope out of the corner of his eye. *This is like herding cats.*

Eventually, he managed to make it back inside, and to Ben's office.

Sam entered, taking off his jacket. "Come on, then. Hit me with it." He took a seat in front of Ben's desk, letting his body slump.

"With what?" Ben asked, glancing up and rubbing the side of his face.

Sam raised his eyebrow. "Don't try a gentle lead-in. I can tell when you're gearing up for a bombshell and I can't be bothered with sugarcoating. Spill it."

Ben sighed. His blue eyes looked tired, and Sam could swear there was more gray around his temples than there had been a few weeks ago.

"I think the accounts are messed up," Ben said. "The new firm we hired last tax year don't seem to be on the ball and whenever I chase them up, I don't hear back."

A knot gathered in Sam's stomach. This certainly wasn't his area of expertise, but it didn't feel like a good position to be in. "What does that mean, in real terms?"

Ben rubbed his face again. "I'm concerned that the business is going to owe more tax than we anticipated once the bill comes in."

"Shit," Sam said, a hollow feeling spreading through his chest. "Will there be enough to cover it?"

"I'm not sure," Ben replied, biting his lip.

Sam leaned back, running a hand through his hair, a million thoughts racing through his mind and none of them good.

Ben eyed him. "Listen. It's my problem to deal with. You've got enough on your plate. I just had to tell someone because it's been weighing on me."

Ben confiding in him wasn't a problem. They were the two longest-lasting employees at the resort and natural allies for moral support. Sam's instinct to try to fix things surfaced. The issue was, he just didn't have the skill set to solve this problem. A heaviness developed in his heart. "If there's anything I can do to help, just shout."

"Thanks, pal," Ben said, shooting him a weak smile. "But I'll think of something. Anyway, how are you coping with the instructor vacancy? You look tired."

Sam raised his eyebrows. "Thanks very much. You don't look so hot yourself."

Ben laughed. "I didn't mean it like that. We need to get a rocket up HR's arse to sort out the job advert. I'll chase them."

"Don't worry, I'll cope. You concentrate on this other thing." Sam pushed his chair back. "Do you want me to bring you a coffee?"

"That would be awesome."

Sam turned and left the office, heading down to the café and trying to breathe away the gathering weight in his chest.

❄ ❄ ❄

THE POT BEGAN TO BOIL OVER, AND SAM ONLY JUST CAUGHT IT before it flooded the hob, turning down the heat quickly and calling the pan a number of very rude names. He almost felt guilty for insulting an inanimate object. After all, it was his own fault that he couldn't concentrate.

Cat looked up from her phone. "You're going to burn that."

"Feel free to help," he muttered.

"Pardon?"

"Nothing."

Sam wondered why she spent the majority of her time at his place, when he clearly got on her nerves nowadays. Though it probably wasn't just nowadays. Their relationship had always been more on again, off again than the IT department's advice at work.

Managing to get dinner finished without further incident, he dished it up and took it over to the table. Cat finally put down her phone, and they started to eat.

Sam watched her across the table. "Is the food okay?"

"Yeah." She glanced up. "Did you sort your car?"

Cold flooded his system. He'd forgotten all about the car. Another problem to solve. But what could he do when it was stuck on a random housing estate a couple of hours away and he hadn't the means or the funds to get it brought to the Glenavie garage?

"No, not yet." He rubbed the back of his neck. "The garage hasn't gotten round to it."

"Bloody lazy," Cat said, shaking her head. "You need to chase them."

Sam cleared his throat. "Yeah." He stuffed some food into his mouth to avoid further questioning.

Cat picked up her phone, scrolling as she ate. Her face soured.

"Ugh. Have you seen these photos on Vicky's Insta? She looks awful. Can't pull off a smoky eye, that one."

Sam frowned as he chewed. A smoky eye? What did that even mean? Had someone puffed their cigarette into her face? Or had she gotten too close to a bonfire?

He swallowed his food. "Vicky always looks good to me."

Cat snapped her gaze up. "She *does*, does she?"

Wrong thing to say.

Cat scooped some food onto her fork, noisily scraping it across her plate as she went. "Maybe you should ask *Vicky* to eat dinner with you instead."

Sam kept quiet, wary of saying anything else that might land him in hot water.

"Just because she's got that rock on her finger, she thinks she's the bee's knees," Cat muttered.

"I thought she was meant to be your friend?" Sam cursed himself for speaking. Why couldn't he just shut his mouth, eat his dinner in silence, and keep out of trouble?

Cat rolled her eyes. "She *is* my friend, dummy."

I give up. Eyes down, Sam made sure he kept his gaze on his food for the rest of the meal. The problem was that the silence only left more room for his troubled thoughts—the broken-down car, the workload at the resort, Maya being back on the scene, the second job aging him faster than Dorian Gray glancing at his painting, and now Ben's tax bill bombshell.

Chapter
FIVE

"CAN YOU PASS THE MILK?" MAYA ASKED.

Her mum reached over and handed her the jug. "Here you go, sweetheart."

"So," her dad said, turning on the TV across the kitchen to display the news. "What's on the agenda for today?"

"Omar," her mum said, shooting him a death stare that would kill a lesser mortal. "At least let the girl eat her breakfast first."

He shrugged. "I'm just interested, Yvonne."

Maya stirred her tea, shrugging. "Oh, you know. Ending the recession, solving third world debt, stopping climate change, and achieving world peace." She tore into her toast for effect. "Then I'll see how I feel after lunch."

He had the decency to give her a small smile; then his serious face slid back into place. "I didn't hear job searching on that list."

Yvonne narrowed her blue eyes. "Omar."

"Just interested," he said, holding up his hands.

Maya let out a high-pitched laugh, fiddling with her charm bracelet and trying to ignore the tightening in her stomach. She reached over and tossed her dad some more toast. "Here you go. Put that in your mouth."

Omar raised an eyebrow, his gaze being drawn back to the news. "Is that an effort to shut me up?"

"No." Maya shook her head in an exaggerated manner. "Absolutely *not*." She glanced at her mum and nodded behind her dad's turned head, mouthing *yes*.

Yvonne let out a short laugh, and Omar turned to look at them, his dark eyes narrowed. Maya lifted her mug of tea to hide her expression, breathing away the constricted feeling in her gut.

He went back to watching the news, and Maya wiped a hand across her brow, mouthing *phew* across the table at Yvonne and eliciting a stifled noise from her mum in return.

Yvonne reached over to touch Maya's hand. "Have you heard from Elise? Are she and wee Jack coming home for Christmas?"

A cold prickle of sadness ran through Maya's veins, as if her blood had become infused with tiny icicles. "I think so. She said they were going to head up here a few weeks before Christmas, but she hadn't decided on a date yet."

Omar kept his eyes on the TV. "She's done well for herself, Elise. I like to think she followed in my footsteps after she did her work experience at our surgery."

Yvonne rolled her eyes. "Not *everything* is a reflection of you, sweetheart."

Omar sipped his tea. "I know. I'm not saying that."

Yvonne looked at Maya. "How's Elise coping? It must be six months now, since Harry died."

Maya nodded. "Yeah, around that. She's still signed off work. Last time I spoke to her, she was trying to make sense of how she'll get back to her job, plus take care of Jack on her own."

Omar shook his head. "A widow so young. It's terrible. She should come home so her parents can support her." He glanced at them. "We all can help out. I'd take her on at our surgery."

Maya studied her dad, her insides warming. As much as he was a pain in the arse, he did have a heart of gold when it came to rallying around others in the community. She just wished he'd champion her in the same way, but it was like he had double standards where his daughters were concerned.

"Right," Omar said, standing and kissing Maya's cheek, then Yvonne's. "I'm off to earn a living."

"Enjoy your clinic, Dad," Maya said, chewing on a mouthful of toast. "Don't let any of them cough on you, because I don't want to catch the flu before Christmas."

"I won't," Omar said as he left the room with a wave.

The front door shut, signaling his departure, and Maya sank into her chair, her shoulders relaxing.

Yvonne smiled. "He means well."

Maya huffed into her tea. For some reason, the unwelcome thought of Sam popped into her head, and she almost groaned. She'd thought about him on and off all the previous day, remembering how mortifying it'd been to see him and how he'd clearly not wanted to take her up on the offer of a lift. Her and her stupid Jiminy Cricket conscience. She should've scooted down in the driver's seat and snuck past him rather than stopping to help, but there was no way in a million years that she could've left him there, stranded. No matter how much she disliked him. And the conversation in the car had been like pulling teeth.

Even worse than the memory of mortification was the image of how good he'd looked. He was gorgeous clothed, but in a state of semi-undress? She tugged at her collar, suddenly feeling rather warm for a winter's afternoon in the Highlands. As he'd left the car, she was sure he'd caught her looking at him longingly, and so as soon as he'd climbed out, she had driven off in order to cover her embarrassment.

Surely Sunday should be her day of rest from ruminating over the ghosts of boyfriends past. Though he'd never been her boyfriend, just her tonsil-hockey partner. And the two of them had played a mean game. A game that he'd no longer wanted to participate in, and it'd been over before it really started.

A little flash of guilt entered her mind—she'd never told Liv what had happened between her and Sam. She'd been about to confess all—both her huge, yearslong crush and also their ski resort trysts. But then he'd dumped her and gone off with Cat and it didn't seem relevant anymore. In any case, Maya hadn't trusted herself to describe the situation to Sam's twin without calling him every expletive under the sun, and that wouldn't have been fair on Liv.

After that, Liv had fallen out with Cat, and Maya had gotten the feeling it could be to do with Liv not liking her friend being involved with her brother. So perhaps the whole thing had been a narrow escape. Except it had never felt that way.

"What's wrong?" Yvonne was frowning at her across the table as she drew her short blond hair into a ponytail.

"Nothing," Maya said quickly. "Just trying to think how I'm going to sort the whole 'third world debt, climate change, world peace' thing."

Yvonne raised her eyebrows, smiling. "You forgot ending the recession."

"Oh yeah," Maya said, lifting her mug to her mum. "I really should make a to-do list."

Yvonne laughed, then sipped her tea, eyeing Maya over the rim. "What's up? You always make a joke to get out of telling me when something's on your mind. And don't deny it, because you've been preoccupied ever since you arrived. Is it because of Rich?"

"Nah," Maya said, shrugging. "To be honest, the whole split has been perfectly amicable." She sighed. "No drama, no angst, no nothing. It all just fizzled out." She made a "pfft" sound and closed her fingers together, as if putting out a tiny candle. To be honest, she could describe the whole relationship that way. And pretty much all the others before it. No drama, no heat, no skin-tingling excitement. *Not since Sam.*

"The job issue? Is that it?" Yvonne asked.

"Er, yeah," Maya said. That was also playing on her mind, and she wasn't sure how much to give away. She couldn't tell her mum that she'd always hated her job and had never wanted to become an accountant. Not when her dad had paved the career path for her. "That *is* weighing on me." Maya swirled her tea, deciding that being vague was best. "I don't know what I want."

"Do you know what you *don't* want?"

Maya snapped her gaze up to meet Yvonne's. Had her mum guessed? "What I don't want?"

"That's right." Yvonne's blue gaze was almost penetrating. "Don't you want to be an accountant anymore?"

An ache developed in her stomach. Maybe she could tell her mum the truth? But she didn't want to disappoint her parents any further. Perhaps her mum would understand, but it might put her in a difficult position with Dad. She glanced away. "Of course I do."

There was a moment's silence before Yvonne answered. "Are you sure?"

Maya swallowed. "Yes."

Yvonne studied her for a couple of seconds. She cleared her throat. "By the way, I forgot to tell you that I ran into Ben at the supermarket last night."

Maya sipped her tea. "Big Boss Ben?"

Yvonne laughed. "I forgot you used to call him that."

Maya shot her a grin. "How is he?"

"He looked stressed, to be honest." Yvonne frowned. "They're short-staffed at the ski center, and it's taking its toll on Sam."

Maya tried to stop her treacherous ears from pricking up. "Oh?"

Yvonne nodded. "Sam's the assistant manager now, so he's been picking up the slack."

Something clicked in the back of Maya's mind. Sam had mentioned that he was teaching the Saturday-morning kids' class, when his realm had always been the advanced classes. He must be covering the junior lessons for this rota gap. Maya tried to feel triumphant that he was struggling where she excelled, but she couldn't muster anything but sympathy. *I'm such a pushover.*

It occurred to her that Sam had never mentioned his promotion either, when she'd asked him how the ski resort was. Strange, she'd have assumed his cocky, too-good-for-her attitude would've had him boasting about it.

"Anyway," Yvonne said. "I told Ben that you were back home for the foreseeable, and his eyes lit up brighter than the Christmas tree on the main green. Wouldn't surprise me if he called you about helping them out."

A flame of delight warmed Maya's heart at the thought of teaching at the resort again. It was the only job she'd ever really enjoyed and found fulfilling. Then she remembered that would mean working with Sam, plus how her dad would react, and her stomach tightened. She stamped on the flame. "I don't think that's a good idea."

"Really?" Yvonne put down her mug. "You used to love it there. And you enjoy teaching at Glencoe every winter. You could just help out for a bit, until they get something sorted?"

Maya wrinkled her nose. "I don't want to teach with Sam around. We don't get on." *And now I apparently can't be around him without undressing him with my eyes, which is a tad awkward.*

Yvonne frowned. "How come?"

"Because he's a cocky liar, that's why," Maya muttered. She paused. "Don't tell Liv I said that, by the way. She still thinks he's the best thing since sliced bread, after they shared a womb and all."

Yvonne smiled. "Cocky? He doesn't come across that way. Always seems very polite and kind."

Maya stuck her fingers into her mouth in a mock gag.

Yvonne raised her eyebrow. "I'm sensing this is some sort of woman-scorned situation."

"You guessed right," Maya said, stirring her tea unnecessarily aggressively. "But it was years ago. I didn't tell you at the time because I was a moody teenager who wouldn't be caught dead speaking to her mother about *feelings.*"

She put on a squeaky voice when she said the word *feelings*, and it drew a laugh from Yvonne.

"Anyway," Maya continued, "hardly a week later, I was off to Glasgow uni and it was forgotten among all the tequila and vodka shots." It had taken a lot more than that to forget him, but her mum didn't need to know that.

"Go on, then. Tell me what happened."

"Fine. But you can't tell anyone. Especially Liv, because she'd fall out with me."

Yvonne rolled her eyes. "Why would I tell anyone?" She paused. "Hold on, why would Liv mind?"

"*Because*," Maya said, feeling like it was the most obvious thing since she'd attempted to hide being pissed when she came home from the pub aged seventeen, "he's her brother. And she doesn't take kindly to her mates getting off with her brother."

"Aha," Yvonne said with a smile. "You snogged him, then."

"Ugh. Yes." Maya sipped her tea to take the bad taste out of her mouth. Though, at the time, his kisses had tasted pretty good. "We never used to hang around with the same crowds, so we didn't know each other despite having Liv in common. I fancied him but he was oblivious to my existence. I couldn't even pluck up the courage to speak to him. Then, when we worked together for that couple of months before I went to uni, we got closer. And . . . well, you know. Kissed in the boot room and stuff."

Maya didn't want to go into further details about the "and stuff." She figured her mum didn't need to know they'd had a couple more fumbles and had gotten to second base, with a definite plan outlined about when and where they'd meet to get to third, plus score a home run. Except that plan had been abandoned by Sam as soon as a better offer had come along. One with hazel eyes, a creamy complexion, and flowing strawberry blond hair.

"I still don't understand why you think Liv would mind," Yvonne said. "*You* didn't, when Hana used to go out with your friend Erica."

"The proof is in the pudding," Maya said, pointing her teaspoon. "Once Cat started going out with Sam, Liv stopped being mates with her."

"But so did you," Yvonne said, frowning.

"Yeah, but that was because Cat was meant to be my friend, then she stole Sam off me," Maya said, her voice rising. *Why am I getting worked up? It was a million years ago.* In any case, it wasn't possible to *steal* a person. They had to go willingly, which is exactly what Sam had done.

"I'm with you," Yvonne said, nodding slowly. "You'd begun something with Sam, then Cat got involved with him and they started going out, leaving you feeling rejected."

"Don't forget betrayed," Maya said, tearing into another piece of toast. Carbs healed all ills.

"*And* betrayed," Yvonne said.

"Plus, deceived," Maya said, her mouth full of toast.

Yvonne nodded, a smile on her lips. "Deceived. Noted."

Maya couldn't help but smile too. She finished chewing and swallowed. "Anyway. Needless to say, Cat and I stopped being friends over it. I'd confided in her that I'd liked him for ages. She was the only one I'd told because it was too awkward to tell Liv, and Elise had been away at medical school for a couple of years by then."

"What happened after the boot room kiss?" asked Yvonne.

Maya met her mum's eyes. "You know the nook?"

Yvonne smiled. "Ah yes. The old make-out spot behind the Tavern pub. You and your sister thought I didn't know about it, but us mums know everything." She tapped the side of her nose.

Maya ignored the icky feeling that Yvonne had known exactly what she and Hana had been up to at all times, and plowed on with her teenage tale of woe. "Sam and I were on the same night out at the Tavern, about a week before I was due to go to uni. Earlier that week we'd talked, and he'd asked me if I wanted to go to the nook with him that night and I'd said yes." Maya shot her mum a look. "You know."

Yvonne rolled her eyes. "For goodness' sake, girl. You can say it. How do you think you and your sister came to exist?"

Maya held up her hand. "Stop right there, no more info on that scenario please. I don't want my toast to make a reappearance. Fine. We were going to fool around a bit more and probably have sex. He'd fed me all this crap about how he wanted us to be each other's first." Maya rolled her eyes. "It was clearly a line. I'll bet he'd used it on loads of girls before me. Dickhead."

"You didn't meet after all?" Yvonne asked.

Maya blew her fringe out of her eyes. "We had a bit of a disagreement on the phone beforehand and it didn't get resolved because I . . ." She paused. "I had to end the call. But as far as I knew, our rendezvous was still on." She put on a French accent to say the word *rendezvous* and fluttered her lashes at Yvonne, which drew a laugh. But her heart rate was still rising.

"What was the disagreement about?"

Glancing away, Maya cleared her throat. "I can't really remember. Anyway. I arrived at the Tavern later on and was chatting to the ski girls. Then Cat came over, all solemn, and said that Sam had sent her to tell me that he wasn't interested anymore. I wasn't his type, he'd never see his twin sister's best mate like that, and he didn't want to go to the nook with me. Needless to say, I was bloody humiliated, so I scarpered."

Blowing out a big breath, Maya imagined that it was a fireball of her anger and humiliation that would send both Cat and Sam up in smoke. "I'd intended to go home to bed but ended up stewing about it. So, I decided to go back and confront him." She raised her eyebrows at her mum. "Which you know isn't like me."

A wry smile played on Yvonne's face.

As she opened her mouth to tell the end of the story, her voice caught and she stuttered for a moment. Her heart felt as if it was pumping rather hard. *What the hell is wrong with me? This is ancient history.* "As I approached the pub, I spotted Sam at the tree line, at the start of the path into the woods. But he wasn't on his own." She had to pause for a beat because her throat felt constricted. "He was with Cat, snogging her face off. They disappeared down the path. And everyone knows where that path leads."

Yvonne's eyes were wide. "The nook."

"Yep." Maya swallowed, her mouth awfully dry all of a sudden. She wet it by sipping her tea, and tried to will back the tears that were pricking her eyes. This wasn't something she'd thought about in years, never mind cried over. "One of the ski girls called me the next day, and told me the gossip that I'd missed. Including that Cat had been boasting about shagging Sam in the nook." She sighed, a colder sensation than her previous fiery breath. "I mean, he was a tosser for leading me on and making me think he actually liked me, but she was meant to be my friend. That's worse. She could've at least waited more than a couple of hours after he'd dumped me before jumping his bones. After all, I was off to Glasgow a week later and she could've been all over him then, without me being around to witness it."

Yvonne nodded. "That's tough. It really stings when female friends act like we only exist to be in competition over men." She eyed Maya. "Did they see you? When you went back to the pub?"

Maya puffed out a breath, and sipped her tea. "No. They were too *busy*. Anyway. It doesn't matter. The two of them are still together to this day. They were meant to be, and I was merely a blip on their radar. I'm over it." *Aren't I?* "But it doesn't mean I want to work with him again."

"Listen," Yvonne said, clearing the plates. "If you want my motherly advice, I'd say not to let a man stand in the way of what you want. If you'd enjoy a reprieve working at the ski resort, to help out your old boss and until something permanent in accounting comes along, then you go for it. It's not like you'd be teaching *with* Sam anyway. You'll each have your own separate classes."

Maya got up to help her mum tidy. "I'll think about it."

❄ ❄ ❄

MAYA STOOD OUTSIDE LIV'S FRONT DOOR, FEELING SMUG THAT this doorbell-ringing exercise was a lot less slippery than her Friday-night adventure, due to her trusty snow boots.

The door opened to reveal Liv's rosy-cheeked grin. Her dark waves swished as she pushed her glasses up her nose, magnifying her green eyes. "Miss Maya. How do you do?" She took a deep bow.

Maya curtsied. "Miss Olivia. May I say how fine you look this day?"

Liv clasped her hand to her chest, gesturing Maya inside. "Oh, thank you. You really are too much."

Maya grinned as she passed Liv into the hallway. They still enjoyed speaking to each other as if they were in a Jane Austen novel. *Probably because it's better than being in real life.* "What's happening with you?" she asked, following Liv into the kitchen and taking off her jacket. "Any sign of Mr. Darcy yet?"

"Nope," said Liv, grimacing as she headed to the kettle. "Still terminally single."

Maya sighed. She put on her best Austen voice. "I am sorry to say, Miss Olivia, that we are both a terrible burden on our poor parents."

"Yes, Miss Maya," Liv said, a solemn expression on her face. "I must sadly agree, that we are."

They both looked at each other, deadpan, and then Liv gave way first with a snort.

"Not a very ladylike laugh, Miss O." Maya grinned. "No wonder Darcy's keeping his distance."

"Shut it, you." Liv smiled as she brewed the tea. "Have you told Elise that you've come home?"

"Only briefly," said Maya, lifting their mugs from the side to take over to the table. "She's got much more important things to worry about."

Liv nodded, frowning. "Did you see her message in the Whats-App group?"

Maya shook her head, lifting out her phone. "No."

"It came during your drive over," Liv said, bringing the teapot and milk jug to the table.

Maya took a seat, opening the app to check. "She's coming home next weekend! Brilliant."

"Yes," Liv said, sitting across from her. "The three musketeers all together again. I can't wait to see wee Jack. I'll bet he's getting so big."

"I know," Maya said, thinking about the last time she'd seen Jack. He'd been only a few months old at his dad's funeral. A cold trickle went down her spine.

Liv grimaced. "Good job we got rid of the fourth musketeer. She didn't fit with the reference."

Maya almost gagged at the mention of Cat. Funny, she hadn't really thought about her during the last few years. Something about seeing Sam properly and having to have a conversation with him had brought all the old feelings back.

"Hmm," was all she could manage.

"You know she's been kicking up a stink about Sam coming to Mum's on Christmas Day?" Liv continued, not appearing to notice Maya's discomfort.

Under normal circumstances, Maya managed to hide it when-ever Liv complained about Cat or gave her an update on Sam, but it was more of a struggle not to put her fingers in her ears and go "la la la" this time.

Liv lifted the teapot to pour the steaming liquid into their cups. "I mean, it's not as if she isn't invited too, she just never wants to come. Plus, nobody's stopping her seeing *her* parents, and she and Sam can get together later on, after Christmas lunch is finished. Sam had Christmas dinner at theirs last year, so it's only fair that Mum gets to have him this year."

Maya took hold of the milk jug, concentrating on pouring it into the cups and giving them an overenthusiastic stir. She'd found it difficult to muster any sympathy for Sam in the past. He'd made his bed, with Catriona in it. So he could bloody well lie in it. Except, for some reason, now she *did* experience little needles of sympathy for him. Which was why she'd given him that lift. Why was she such a wimp?

She pushed Liv's mug toward her.

"Thanks," Liv said, lifting it. "Plus, she's always putting passive-aggressive comments on everyone's Insta posts. She's got so much internalized misogyny I think she must be an actual misogynist zipped up in a woman suit. If we took off her mask, Scooby-Doo-style, there'd be a ranty, angry man underneath."

Maya sipped her tea. With hindsight, Maya could see Cat always had been a "pick me" girl. She'd stab her best mate in the eye with a rusty spoon if it meant she'd get the briefest smirk from the most douchebaggy of douchebag guys.

Time to steer them onto a safer topic of conversation, which was her usual strategy when Liv spoke about Sam or Cat. A few interested noises, then change the subject. "Miss O, I really *must* say that you still make the most *divine* cup of tea."

"Why, thank you," said Liv, bowing in her chair. "A compliment indeed."

Maya tipped an imaginary cap, pleased that her trusty old tactic had worked.

Liv put down her cup. "What've you got planned for today?"

"Nothing," Maya said, rolling her eyes. "Much to Dad's disgust."

Liv touched Maya's hand. "It's probably just his way of showing he cares."

Maya wished he could find a more supportive way to do it. One that didn't make her feel like an inadequate loser. Whenever she'd dared to voice what she wanted when she was younger, if it didn't meet with Omar's high expectations, then she'd get a stern and disappointed response. No wonder she'd learned to hide her true desires in life.

"Hey, listen." Liv lifted her cup to gesture at Maya. "I've heard there's an opening at the ski center. They're down an instructor. And it's the junior class, your forte."

"Mm," Maya said, glancing at the window. "Mum told me."

"Why don't you go for it? You've never been bothered about accountancy. Do something that you enjoy for a change and see where the wind takes you." She moved her hand across the air in front of her, as if following the path of a sailboat.

Maya rolled her eyes. "Yeah, right. As if Dr. Bashir would go for that. He always told me that ski instructing was a holiday job for teenagers, or adults who couldn't get real jobs."

"Ouch." Liv winced. "Don't tell Sam that."

Maya stayed silent, pretending to herself that she wouldn't care if Sam's feelings were hurt and that she was a badass spurned woman, when really, she hated the thought of a comment like that getting back to him. Especially after those tense words they exchanged, albeit a long time ago. But he'd no doubt forgotten all about that.

She remembered his broken-down car and annoyingly felt nothing but sympathy that he had no transport. Why didn't he just use his butler money to sort it out?

Maya had caved the previous day and texted Kirsty, asking her to keep an eye on Sam's car. Why on earth she possessed this compulsion to do things for people who wouldn't spit on her if she were on fire, she'd never know. But despite that, guilt needled her chest at the thought that she could probably do more to help him.

Maya's phone buzzed, and she lifted it. "It's Big Boss Ben."

"Aha. His ears were burning."

Maya opened the message. "He's asking if I can help out with the kids' classes on a temporary contract." She put the phone down and sipped her tea.

Liv raised her eyebrows. "And? Don't leave me hanging."

Maya paused, hovering her mug at her lips. "And what?"

"What're you going to say?" Liv set her cup down with a clatter.

Maya hesitated. Working with Sam would be a massive pain in the arse. The guy was a cocky git, no matter how much he tried to pretend otherwise and no matter how much Maya loved his old housemate from the womb. *And* no matter that her stupid heart still fawned over how handsome he was, or that her lady bits had annoyingly tingled at the sight of him half-naked.

Although, working at the resort itself would be amazing. She allowed herself to sink contentedly into that thought, letting it surround her like the fluffiest of sweet cotton candy dreams. No more sitting at a boring desk, but out on the slopes, snow stinging her face and wind whipping through her hair as she cut through the fresh powder. It would give her mental well-being a much-needed boost. Plus, she'd get to work with Ben again, who was a legend, and his needing her help tugged at her heartstrings. Sam requiring her assistance also gave a hefty tug; however, she ignored that.

Her gut tightened. Dad wouldn't like it. Then again . . . he didn't need to know. Not yet anyway.

Liv smiled. "You're talking yourself round to it, aren't you?"

Maya couldn't help the smile playing about her lips. Leaning toward the decision of saying yes made her feel good, despite the

Sam-shaped reservations, and that was a good sign. "Maybe. I'll message BB Ben and say I'll meet him to discuss it." She sipped her tea.

"Go on, then," Liv said, gesturing across the table. "Don't leave the poor thing hanging."

Maya huffed out her breath. "You're such a bossy boots." She lifted her phone. "I'll bet your nursery kids think you're the bossiest teacher around." She quickly typed out a reply saying she'd be happy to meet and discuss.

"Too right," Liv replied, giving her a wink. "Boss bitch. That's me."

Maya laughed. As if anyone could ever think that lovely Liv was a bitch. Maya jumped when her phone buzzed immediately with a reply from Ben. "Blimey. He *is* keen." Opening it, she did a double take. "He wants to see me today."

Liv downed the last of her tea and pushed her chair back. "Drink up. Let's go there now."

Maya raised her eyebrow. "Right *now*?"

"Yeah," Liv replied, gesturing for her to hurry. "They've got the best scones *ever* in the café, and I've got a hankering for one."

Maya finished her tea and stood to follow Liv to the front door. "Are you telling me that the only reason you go to the resort is to eat scones in the café? I know you've not skied in about five years. And you were totally shit then."

Liv laughed as they left the house and headed for Maya's car. "That's right. Sorry, not sorry."

They got into the car and Maya started it. Knowing that she'd soon be at the resort caused a warm feeling to slide into her being. It was like drinking a really scrumptious hot chocolate, or perhaps a mulled wine. No, a hot chocolate with marshmallows infused with a bit of liqueur.

The journey up the snowy road into the mountains was as spectacular as ever—majestic, sparkling white peaks set against a bright blue sky. The scenery replenished Maya's heart with the joy that she'd been so desperately missing of late.

The light sprinkling of snow in town quickly gave way to deeper coverage as the altitude increased, and when they pulled into the ski center car park, a fresh dump of powder became apparent. Maya's heart sparked as she imagined the quality of the snow on the slopes, resolving to get onto them as soon as possible.

They climbed out into the cold, crisp air, and Maya appreciated the crunch of the snow beneath her boots as she glanced at Liv. "Will Sam be working today?" She clenched her fists in her pockets as she awaited the response.

"No," Liv replied, pausing to kick a pile of snow at Maya. "It's his day off."

A wave of relief mixed with a puzzling air of disappointment as Maya turned her head to avoid the smattering of snow from Liv's foot.

They entered the building, crossing the main foyer into the café and finding a seat. Maya glanced around, taking in the minor changes that had occurred since she was last there, and finding comfort in it largely being the same. Though she wasn't impressed that they didn't have their Christmas decorations up yet. *Scrooges.*

They took her favorite table, consisting of two squashy leather sofas across a low table in front of the real log fire. Maya picked up the menu. "Marvelous idea regarding the scones, Miss Olivia. A scone would be an absolute *delight.*"

"Wouldn't it just, Miss Maya?" Liv nodded sagely. "You simply *must* try the strawberry preserve and clotted cream. It is to *die* for."

Maya burst out laughing just as Ben rounded the corner, resembling the excited puppy that Maya had been imagining.

"Ladies." He scooped Maya into a bear hug as she stood to greet him. "Ms. Bashir. Am I glad to see you—my knight in shining armor."

He let go to look at her, and she flashed him a grin. "All right, Big Boss Ben? Still bossing it to the max?" She ruffled his dark, silver-tinged hair. "Grayer around the edges, I see."

Ben laughed. "Cheeky."

Maya shrugged. "Hey, it's no bad thing. Silver fox, that's you."

He smiled. "Really? Derek keeps suggesting that I should dye it."

Maya waved her hand. "Pfft. No offense, but your boyfriend knows nothing. You look both hot, and cool at the same time."

Ben grinned. He waved at one of the young members of the staff, and she came hurrying over. "Hi, Katie." He gestured to Maya and Liv. "What would you like?"

Liv smiled. "A flat white and a *scone* with *strawberry preserve* and *clotted cream*, please."

Maya started laughing and Liv joined in. Poor Katie appeared confused.

"Can I get the same, please?" Maya managed to blurt out through her laughter.

Ben gave them a bemused smile before turning back to Katie. "Just an Americano for me."

Katie nodded and hurried away, scribbling on her notepad.

"So," Ben said, rubbing his hands together. "When can you start, Maya?"

Maya raised her eyebrows. "That's a bit presumptuous. At least butter me up with the coffee and scone first."

"Come on," Ben said, smiling. "I can see the ski-instructing bug in your eyes. And I'll buy you a coffee every day."

Maya pursed her lips. "Every day, you say?"

"Yep."

"And a scone?"

"Yes."

"With *strawberry preserve* and *clotted cream?*"

Liv snorted.

"Yes. Whatever you want." Ben cocked his head and fluttered his eyelashes at her.

"Fine." Maya mock rolled her eyes, then leaned in to pinch his cheeks. "I'll start this week. I've nothing else on and it'll help me avoid Omar the Terrible."

Ben leaned back with a satisfied sigh. "Brilliant."

Katie appeared with their order. After she left, Maya and Liv took great delight in applying the cream and jam to their scones with their pinkies sticking out, speaking to each other in their Austen voices. Ben drank his Americano happily. Maya absorbed his satisfied glow, warmth infusing her that she'd been able to help a friend.

It occurred to her that helping always made her feel good, even though at times she had trouble saying no. Well, a lot of the time she had trouble saying no. But maybe she just needed to say no to the right people. *Like Dad.* The thought of that sent shivers down her spine, and not the good kind.

Maya nudged Ben. "So. BBB. What're you doing here on a Sunday? The big boss should be off the weekend, no?"

Ben glanced away, fiddling with his cup. "Just catching up on some admin."

Maya frowned, trying to assess the cloud that had passed over his features.

"Ooh," Liv said to Maya. "Do you want to go into town after this? There's a sale in your favorite jewelry shop. You can pick something for your Christmas present."

Maya shifted her eyes off Ben, still troubled by his change in demeanor. "Sounds great. You can choose something too."

"Nah, I've got enough jewelry. But I'll think of something you can spend your dough on for me."

"Right." Ben rose from his chair. "Duty calls. Maya, I'll send you all the details of the job plan, plus a digital contract. Can you start on Tuesday?"

"Coolio," Maya said, giving him a two-fingered salute. "No worries, Triple B."

Ben shook his head with a laugh, and gave them a wave as he left the area.

"He looks pretty stressed," Maya said to Liv in a low voice.

"Yeah. But you helping out will be a weight off."

"I dunno," Maya said as they stood and put on their jackets. "I feel like there's something else bothering him."

THE HIGH STREET WAS DUSTED WITH SNOW, AND THE LAMPPOSTS all carried their own individual Christmas lights in the shapes of holly leaves, Santas, snowmen, and Rudolphs. The shop fronts were lit up with festive displays, their doorways adorned with sprigs of mistletoe and holly.

Maya and Liv left the bookstore where they'd been browsing for a half hour, and Maya gave her a nudge. "Better watch who you shop with. There's mistletoe on nearly every doorway." She stuck her tongue out as if she were going to give Liv the mother of all French kisses.

Liv smiled, glancing away. "I wish."

They crossed the road to the jewelers, and Maya fingered her charm bracelet. This was where she'd bought it, aged sixteen.

As they entered, she let her touch linger on the moon charm. It too had come from this shop, though she hadn't been the one to buy it.

"Look," said Liv, distracting Maya from her thoughts.

Maya went over to join Liv at the charm section.

"Are there any you like?" Liv asked.

Maya examined the wares through the glass. "I'd quite like a Christmassy one."

She cast her eye over them, thinking about the tiny star charm that had been in this section when she was eighteen, and how she'd coveted both that one and the moon. But once she'd saved the money and come to the store to claim the star, it was gone. She'd never seen another one she liked as much.

Maya pointed through the glass. "How about that little robin? He's cute."

Liv bumped her shoulder. "Like you."

Maya shot her a disapproving stare. "I'm not cute. I'm ferocious, like a lion." She pretended to roar, then realized the shop assistant was giving her a funny look, so she stopped, heat rising in her cheeks.

"Ferocious my arse," Liv said, signaling to the assistant that they wanted something from the cabinet. "You're the most conflict-avoidant person I've ever met."

Maya kept quiet as the shop assistant arrived, and Liv got them to take out the robin charm, then paid for it at the desk.

They left the store, Liv pocketing the charm. "I'll wrap it for Christmas."

Maya opened her mouth to ask what Liv wanted for her present, but her voice caught before it reached her vocal cords. Sam and Cat were farther down the street, looking in a store window, hand in hand.

Maya took Liv's elbow, her heart rate accelerating. "I've just remembered I need to go back to the bookshop for something. Let's cross over."

Liv nodded. "Okay." She turned her head to check the traffic. "Oh, wait, there's Sam." She waved. "Sam!"

He looked up and smiled as he spotted his sister. Then his face fell as he took in Maya's presence.

Maya gritted her teeth as she followed Liv over to where Sam and Cat were standing. Cat appeared as if she were munching on a nest of wasps.

"Hi, guys," Liv said, giving Sam a hug and flashing Cat a smile. The smile appeared gracious enough, but Maya could detect a tightening in Liv's jaw as she performed the gesture.

"Look who's back in town for the foreseeable," Liv said as she put her arm around Maya's waist and squeezed.

Maya had, of course, seen Sam and Cat in similar instances over the years, albeit refreshingly brief, plus few and far between. But this time it stung worse than in the past. Perhaps that was down to having her first proper conversation with Sam a couple of evenings previously, or maybe it was due to him being practically naked for a large proportion of that time. But mainly, it must have been a result of her dredging up the past over the last couple of days, plus the fact that she was going to be here for a while. There was no escape back to Glasgow after a few days.

Sam eyed her with that cool stare.

Maya avoided his gaze. She hadn't mentioned to Liv that she'd run into him, because he'd asked her not to tell anyone. Though why she was cultivating his confidence she had no idea. *Perhaps because I can't say no.*

She snuck a very quick glance at him and regretted it because he looked cute in his dark gray woolly hat and red ski jacket. How dare he be so handsome, with his lovely amber eyes and sexy sandy beard? And anyway, he could at least be nice to her. After all, she *was* keeping his secret.

Cat snapped her gaze onto Maya's face, her eyes widening for a split second. "You're moving back here for good?"

Maya plastered on a smile. "Maybe. For the medium term anyway."

Cat stayed silent for a moment, keeping her gaze on Maya. "I don't know why you'd want to come back to this dead-end dump, after the big-city life."

Sam seemed to flinch.

Maya cleared her throat. "City life isn't all it's cracked up to be. I've always preferred the small, ski town life, myself."

Sam raised his eyebrows, and something about his expression made her skin tingle. Maya lifted her hand to catch her moon charm between her fingers, rubbing it.

Liv linked her arm with Maya's, addressing Sam and Cat. "What're you two up to today?"

"Bit of Christmas shopping," Sam said, glancing at Maya.

"And you need to sort your car," Cat said, shooting him a look. "We're having to use my car all the time because Sam's broke down again."

Maya met Sam's eyes, trying to fathom how much he'd told Cat.

He held her gaze for a second, and it seemed as if he were attempting to will her into not saying anything. As much as she didn't like the guy, Maya would never drop him in it. She stayed silent, listening in order to detect exactly what page Cat was on.

"It's been at the garage since Saturday morning," Cat continued. "They need to get it sorted, bloody lazy gits."

Maya glanced at Sam again. The car wasn't at the garage, it was still outside Kirsty's.

Sam seemed to shake his head almost imperceptibly, holding Maya's gaze.

Liv was frowning. "I don't think it's lazy. It's only been there since yesterday morning and today's Sunday, so they'll be closed. Give them a chance."

Cat shrugged. "It's just not good enough. They should've had it done by now." She gave Sam a withering look. "I told you that you should've bought something more upmarket. Like Vicky's boyfriend's Audi."

Liv squeezed Maya's arm a little too hard, and Maya was just starting to worry that she was going to cut off her circulation when Liv released her to reach out and tug Sam's sleeve. "Guess what? You're going to have the pleasure of Maya's company at the ski center. We've just been to see Ben, and she's going to teach the kids' classes until you get someone permanent. Make sure you act surprised when Ben tells you, though. I think he wanted to be the one to break the good news that you're off the hook from covering Vicky's classes."

One thing was for sure, Sam wasn't *acting* surprised right now. His eyes widened as he glanced at Maya, then back to Liv.

He cleared his throat, rubbing the back of his neck. "That's . . . great."

Cat shot him a disapproving look as he uttered the word *great*. She needn't have worried, because it was clear that he hardly meant it.

"When do you start?" he asked, his voice slightly strained.

"This week," Maya said, shifting from one foot to the other. "Ben seemed pretty desperate." She nudged Liv, keen to get out of the excruciating situation. "We'd better head to the bookstore."

"Hang on," Liv said to Sam, ignoring Maya. "How're you going to get to and from the resort this week, without a car?"

"Not quite figured that yet," Sam said. "Cat needs hers for work. I'm getting a lift with Ben tomorrow, then I'll see."

Liv looked at her, and Maya tried to send her a telepathic message. *Please don't say it, please don't say it.*

Liv shifted her gaze back to Sam. "Maybe Maya could give you a lift on Tuesday, and the other days she's in? Just until your car's ready?"

Maya closed her eyes for a second. *Bloody hell, Liv.*

Sam opened his mouth, darting his gaze from Liv to Maya, but staying silent.

Cat shook her head, a smile plastered on her face. "Oh, we don't want to put Maya out." She nudged Sam. "Do we, babe?"

Sam's voice was hoarse. "Of course not."

Maya eyed Cat for a second, and something snapped. Maybe she was crap at confrontation and would never voice how hurt or pissed off she was at these two. But one small passive-aggressive gesture couldn't do any harm.

"It's no problem." She met Sam's eyes, attempting to keep her voice neutral. "I can give you a lift. Just until your car's sorted."

Seeming unsure how to react, he swallowed. "Thanks. That'd be . . ." He glanced at Cat. "Good."

"Excellent," Liv said brightly. "I'll give Maya your number." She tugged Maya's arm. "Off to the bookshop?"

They moved away to cross the road, Maya catching Sam's gaze one last time before Cat dragged him down the street.

She followed Liv into the bookshop, standing by the first display and trying to think why in the name of all that was holy she'd agreed to that. Mind you, it wasn't as if she could've said, "No, I don't want to give your beloved brother a lift, because he's a complete arsehole." Especially in front of Sam. As much as that was her opinion, she wouldn't say it to his face.

Liv pulled off her hat. "Thanks for that, by the way. It'll be a big help to Sam. He's so stressed, and I don't want car trouble adding to his woes. Ben doesn't always go in at the same time, so that's not a regular option. But hopefully between you *and* Ben, Sam will be able to get lifts every day until the car's fixed."

A stab of sympathy caused Maya to look up. Only a tiny stab, though. Miniscule, in fact. "Sam's that stressed?"

Her mum had told her as much, but hearing it from Sam's twin was another matter.

"Yeah." Liv sifted through the books on the display table. "Covering the extra lessons, for one thing. You know the kids' class isn't his favorite." She rolled her eyes, smiling. "Plus the extra workload of the community project he heads up. And he's so tired lately. I think he's got too much on."

Community project? Maya glanced away, resisting the urge to ask more. No wonder Sam was tired—all of that, coupled with driving long distances of an evening to work at those parties.

Liv peered at the cover of a book. "There's also the charity sled race that he's organizing. That's a lot of work too."

Maya hesitated for a beat. "Sam organizes that?"

Liv nodded, studying the book with an innocent expression. "Not that he takes any credit."

Maya had heard about the race when she'd been home for Christmas the last couple of years, but had assumed Ben was behind it. Perhaps Sam wasn't *quite* as shallow and bigheaded as she'd thought.

Liv glanced up. "What did you want from in here?"

Maya frowned, trying to think what Liv meant. "Pardon?"

"You wanted to come back in here for something," Liv said, lifting another book to study the blurb on the back. "Remember?"

Maya recalled it had been her suggestion as a tactic to avoid speaking to Sam and Cat. So much for that plan.

"Oh, er . . ." She lifted the first book she laid eyes on and hid the cover from Liv when she realized she'd chosen *Talking About Erectile Dysfunction: It's Not That Hard.*

"This is the one. I'll just go pay for it." Moving over to the cashier with it stashed behind her back, she cursed herself for feeling anything but contempt for Sam.

Chapter
SIX

BEING ON THE SLOPES ALWAYS HELPED CLEAR SAM'S HEAD, AND taking his advanced classes down the black runs all day was just what the doctor ordered after spending so much time on the baby slope. As his last class ended in the late afternoon, the sound of laughter rang out from said area. Maya had the kids singing a song about pizza and chips as they nailed the actions heading down the slope.

At the end she gave them all a high five, making out that the last child had done it with such a force as to make her fall onto her back into a snowdrift, causing further peals of laughter from the children.

Sam smiled, watching her easy way with them. She had always excelled at engaging the kids and making them giggle. Though she was skilled at making everyone laugh, including him in the past. They'd forged a strong bond over that time they'd worked together aged eighteen, or at least it'd felt that way to him. During that couple of months, he'd been convinced that he'd had her previous, aloof manner all wrong. She'd known what to say to have him in stitches, a welcome relief when he'd been adjusting to life without his dad around. It had been one such joking-around session alone in the boot room that had morphed into a make-out session.

Sam shook his head to dispel those memories, and turned to complete his walk into the building. The ride into work with Maya had been stressful. He'd walked over to hers because he hadn't wanted to inconvenience her any further by having her pick him up. Plus, Cat was being weird about him getting a lift, so he'd figured it best to keep some distance between the two women. Him associating with any women consistently caused friction with Cat, but she seemed particularly pissed off.

Most of the ride had been spent in prickly silence. He'd commented on his surprise at her taking the job, and she'd seemed put out. But it *was* a surprise, him having assumed she wouldn't be interested when she was searching for a "real job" in accountancy. She'd then become defensive, admitting that she'd worked every winter at Glencoe. That had been a shock to him. He'd assumed she'd left this world behind when she left for university. The stony silence had then ensued until their arrival, and he'd thanked her for the lift. She'd made a pointed comment that she'd do anything for Liv. As if he needed reminding that Maya was only doing him any favors for his sister's sake.

Deciding to stop by Ben's office, he knocked on the door and entered. "How's it going?"

Ben sighed. "All right. Come in and take a load off."

Sam sat heavily onto a chair. "I take it you're no further forward with the accounts thing?"

Ben shook his head. "They aren't replying to my e-mails, and I get voice mail whenever I call."

He rubbed his chest in an attempt to rid the heavy feeling. "Can't we switch accountants?"

"It's too late in the tax year." Ben rubbed his forehead, then gave Sam a weak smile. "I'll sort it. Don't worry."

Sam nodded, staring through the window toward the whiteout and feeling as if the swirling in his gut matched that of the snow being spun by the wind outside.

"At least there's some good news, with Maya back on board?" Ben ventured. "Gets you off the hook with the kids' class."

Sam's pulse picked up at the sound of her name. He tried to keep his voice even and emotionless. "Yeah. Great news."

Ben shot him a frown, so Sam forced a smile onto his face. After all, it *was* good news that he didn't have to cover the children's classes any longer. It was just a shame that it was Maya who was doing it rather than someone who didn't dislike him, or that he hadn't gotten to second base with in the boot room.

Maya's other, non-making-out-related skills crossed his mind, and he eyed Ben for a moment, wondering if they should ask her to look at the accounts. But Sam didn't feel he could approach Maya for any more favors, and he doubted she'd be interested in helping. Teaching here was merely a distraction from the bigger fish she was no doubt frying.

Ben would sort it, and everything would be fine.

❄   ❄   ❄

THE COZINESS OF THE FIRESIDE TABLE CAUGHT SAM'S EYE AS HE waited in the queue to grab coffees for him and Ben. That was his favorite seat in the place, half-hidden in a small alcove near the big window that looked out onto the tree line at the edge of the slopes. A couple was sitting on one of the sofas, cuddled in together as they warmed up. For a moment the image of him and Maya snuggled by that fireside came to mind, and he shook his head to dispel it.

Ben appeared round the corner just as their order was ready.

"I was going to bring it up to you," Sam told him as Ben grabbed the drinks and gestured for Sam to sit at a nearby table.

"Thanks," Ben said. "But I just felt like I needed to get out of that damned office, you know?"

Sam did know. Being cooped up inside was not his cup of tea. And Ben had his head buried in the books more and more nowadays.

"Brilliant, here comes Maya," Ben said, causing Sam's pulse to pick up.

She approached their table, newly changed out of her ski gear and looking all fresh-faced, rosy cheeked, and utterly gorgeous. *For fuck's sake.* How come the passage of time made his ex even more attractive to him? Life wasn't fair.

She smiled at Ben, and Sam practically fucking melted at the sight of it. *God help me.* Then her smile dropped a little as she turned her gaze to him, and his jaw tightened. Even though they didn't get along, he liked putting a smile on her face. Not removing it.

"Hi, guys," she said in a neutral tone as she took a seat at the table. "Good day?"

Ben avoided looking at her. "Great, thanks." He shifted his eyes onto her with a smile. "And how was your first day?"

There it was. Her full-monty, megawatt smile. The one that told him she was genuinely full of joy and gave him joy in return. "It was so good!" Her voice was bright with enthusiasm, almost tinkling with it as if her vocal cords had been infused with Christmas bells. "I loved it." She sighed in a contented manner, leaning back. "It's amazing to be here again."

"And it's great to have you," Ben replied. "By the way, could you stay back a little before you head home? I need to run through some stuff with you. There are a few health and safety boxes we need to check off, including those related to the new facilities that weren't here during your previous employment."

The smile fell from her face, and Sam mourned its departure. "I, er . . ." She hesitated, seeming to wrestle for what she wanted to say. Clearly, it was "no" but Maya had always had an issue with that word. Funny, he'd assumed she would have gotten past her conflict-avoidant tendencies after she had the mother of all conflicts with him and then flounced off to university without a backward glance.

"The only thing is, I told my parents I'd be back for a certain time, and . . ." She trailed off, probably taking in the look of confusion on Ben's face as he wondered why a grown woman needed to be home to her parents by a deadline.

Sam suspected the reason was that Omar didn't yet know she was back teaching at the resort. Something he would no doubt still disapprove of.

His misplaced sense of protectiveness toward Maya rose up again, like an iron shield. "Don't worry, Ben, we've got it covered," he said, thinking on his feet. "Maya and I have time earmarked to cover all that stuff tomorrow."

Maya looked at him with a frown. "We do?" Her eyes widened as she cottoned on to what he was up to. "Oh yes, that's right. We *do*."

Sam had to work hard to prevent the corner of his mouth quirking up.

Ben shrugged. "Thanks, Sam."

Maya blessed him with a small smile. "Yeah, thanks, Sam."

It wasn't the full-monty, megawatt version, but it was enough.

❄   ❄   ❄

ON APPROACHING THE EXIT, MAYA WAS ALREADY WAITING, SO HE picked up the pace. "Sorry. I got engrossed in something." He'd been looking into how much it'd be to get some breakdown cover for his car, and also checking his schedule for the next butler gig, because he'd need transport when the time came.

"No problem," Maya said, turning to leave. He followed her out and into the car, where they buckled in. She cleared her throat. "Thanks for before, by the way. Covering for me, I mean. When Ben wanted me to stay behind."

"That's okay," he said, feeling self-conscious all of a sudden. He didn't want her to read too much into his looking out for her and think that he still had feelings for her. Because he didn't. Apart from thinking she was gorgeous, loving her smile, and having a misplaced sense of protectiveness toward her, that is.

He opted to change the subject. "Could you drop me off at Nico's gym?" He had a hankering for a workout, plus it was en route rather than Maya going all the way down to his place and then back again to get home.

"Yeah, that's fine," she replied as she pulled out of the car park. "How's Nico doing?"

"Good, thanks," Sam said. "Giving up law and opening the gym suited him."

Maya would likely disapprove of someone making such a career move, from professional to entrepreneur. Especially into fitness rather than a financial- or medical-related business.

Though, strangely, she was nodding with an interested expression. "It's really impressive that he made that transition. It's not easy to give up a big career, even if you don't like it."

There was a tone to her voice he couldn't place. As if she empathized with Nico's choice.

"His family weren't impressed," Sam said. "But he's made a success of it anyway."

Nico's dad was a lawyer and had been upset to say the least when his only son abandoned following in his footsteps to do something that he and his wife viewed as frivolous. Never mind that they had two daughters in addition, whose professions they didn't seem to mind, as long as they had gotten married and provided grandkids for them. Pretty sexist in Sam's eyes.

As he watched Maya, a cloud seemed to pass over her face as he described Nico's parents' reaction.

But then it was gone, replaced by a bright smile. "Ah well. Parents. Can't live with them, can't pretend they've got early onset dementia and stick them in a home."

Sam managed a smile in return.

The rest of the drive passed in silence. Maya didn't seem to have the energy for any further small talk, and neither did he.

Once they arrived at the gym, Sam quickly climbed out. "Thanks. I'll give you some fuel money for all of this."

Her face fell. "I don't want anything."

A sick feeling swirled in his gut. He was the one accustomed to being leaned on, not the other way around. And he certainly wasn't used to relying on people who couldn't stand him and whom he disliked in return. *But do I really dislike her? Or do I just wish that I did?* His jaw tensed. He didn't need her pity regarding his lack of funds. "Don't do me any favors. I can pay my way where this is concerned."

Maya frowned. "That's not what I meant."

His patience sapped by the stress of his day, he shrugged. "I'll give you some money later in the week."

He shut the car door and headed into the gym. He'd expected to hear her roaring off behind him, but for some reason she stayed put.

Ignoring the situation, and the seed of guilt that had sown itself into his mind regarding his being short with her, Sam went through the turnstile into the gym and made for the changing rooms.

Working out was another activity that helped clear his mind, and he'd often come here whenever he had a disagreement with Cat. It occurred to him that they were arguing pretty much every week at the moment, and that was a sign that things were gearing along the usual path of her having a massive blowout and dumping him.

After he'd finished and showered, he went in search of Nico. He'd be in his office at this time of day doing some admin.

Sam knocked on the door and heard Nico call, "Yeah?"

Opening it and sticking his head around the side, he flashed a grin. "All right, arsehole?"

Nico laughed and stood. "Come in, you total ballbag."

Sam crossed the room into Nico's hug and as usual felt as if he was being cuddled by a bear. The man was huge, and despite Sam viewing himself as being lean and muscular, being near Nico made him feel like a pre–Super Soldier Serum Captain America. Nico could give the Rock a run for his money.

"Have a seat," Nico said, moving behind his desk. "Want a coffee?"

"Go on, then," Sam replied as Nico went to the high-tech coffee machine behind him. "Can't say no to a hot guy like you, can I?"

Nico grinned. "Pretty hot yourself, Holland. Remember it's you that's the naked butler, not me."

"Shh," Sam said, glancing over his shoulder.

Nico rolled his eyes as the coffee machine hummed to life. "Stop acting all James Bond. No one can hear us in my office."

Sam shook his head. "It was you that told me about it, so don't act all innocent. I know about your previous naked-butlering days. I'm the apprentice here, and you're the Jedi master."

Nico passed Sam his drink, lifting his own. The espresso cup looked tiny in his large hands. He took a seat across from Sam. "So, why do you need the money? You're the assistant manager now, so I would've thought you'd be set."

Sam sipped his coffee. "It's not for me, it's for someone else. And my first pay packet for the promotion doesn't come in until the end of the month."

Nico frowned. "Who's the money for, then?"

Sam met Nico's charcoal-gray eyes. "They don't want me to say, because they're too proud."

Nico raised his eyebrows. "I can guess who you mean. But I'll keep quiet." He leaned over the desk. "Maybe I could give him something too, to help out? Plus take the pressure off you."

Sam set his cup down. "Don't. He'll be upset and think I've asked you to. I've not told him that I've taken on an extra job to provide the cash. He thinks that I've some spare after my promotion, and he keeps note of everything I give him so he can pay me back later."

Nico nodded. "If you need me to, I can give you some money and then you could pass it to him as if it's from you? Then you wouldn't need to continue with your second job."

The thought was tempting. Sam rubbed his chest as the heavy sensation gathered. He couldn't reconcile himself with getting someone else to shoulder the burden. He had taken it on as his responsibility. "Thanks, man. But there's nearly enough now, for the equipment he needs to buy."

Nico leaned back to lift his cup again. "How's it going with Cat?" He paused to meet Sam's eyes. "Not great, I assume. If you're back here again."

Sam let out a breath. "Yeah. Not great."

Nico eyed him. "Don't take this the wrong way"—his voice was gentle—"but why do you take her back every time she asks? It's always the same pattern. She finishes it, then asks you back as if she's doing you a favor, and you say yes."

Sam hesitated, attempting to fathom the answer to the question that he often asked himself. At first, Cat had been so loving toward him, acting as if she sympathized about his dad leaving and Maya dumping him. Over time, she'd become his emotional crutch.

Nico smiled. "You can be on your own, you know. You'd survive."

Sam swallowed. Being rejected was the one scenario he *couldn't* cope with, and the thought of that happening with him and Cat made him nauseated. It was safer to ease the pain by accepting her offer to come back to him. Especially when she'd start being really nice to him again. It would seem as if they were going back to how things had been, and he'd feel that if he just trod carefully enough, that's how they'd stay. Plus, the fact they'd been together on and off since they were eighteen meant staying with Cat was familiar and, somehow, comforting. "Easy for you to say, with your commitment-phobic bachelor life."

Nico shrugged. "It's a choice. I'm better off on my own."

Sam couldn't understand that. It wasn't that he disliked his own company. He enjoyed having time to himself. But only ever having a string of short-term relationships? That wasn't his thing, and he'd never understood why it was Nico's.

"Anyway," Sam said, finishing his drink. "I'd better head, I'm walking home and I don't want to be too late because she'll be pissed off."

Nico raised his eyebrows. "Walking? Did the car conk out again?"

Sam stood. "Yeah. It's a pain in the arse."

Nico got up. "How did you get down here from work?"

Sam turned toward the doorway. "I got a lift off Maya."

"Maya Bashir? I didn't know she was in town. Back a little early for Christmas, isn't she?"

Sam grasped the door handle and turned to face Nico. "She's back for a while. Lost her job. Now she's helping Ben out for a bit by covering Vicky's classes."

Nico nudged his arm. "Good news for you. Those classes were doing your head in."

Sam smiled. The person taking the classes was now also doing his head in.

He hadn't told Nico about what'd happened with Maya in the past. Nor anyone else for that matter, except for their other best friend, Arran. Sam had kept their involvement on the down low in case anything had gotten back to Maya's dad before they were ready to tell him. And then, after it ended, there seemed little point in talking about it. Mainly because it hurt too much, but also due to him being with Cat.

Arran had known that Sam liked Maya, being from the same class at school, unlike Nico, who'd been a couple of years ahead, and away at law school by then. Sam had confided in Arran regarding their couple of trysts, and then how it'd ended.

Sam had had an inkling that her being from a doctor's family who lived in a big house could be an issue, when he was from a single-parent broken home and had no intention of going off to university and leaving his mum and sister on their own. And maybe if Cat hadn't kept reminding him of his inadequacy by criticizing that choice, he might've gotten over it by now.

Nico rubbed his chin. "I always felt a bit of an affinity with the

Bashir girls, us both having Middle Eastern dads. Same pressure to be *professional*."

Something niggled at the back of Sam's mind—the way in which Maya had sounded empathetic to Nico's issues with his parents' disapproval. But Maya had been as keen as they had to have a *real job* in accountancy. That was the difference.

Sam nodded, eager to end the conversation because he was becoming more confused where Maya was concerned. "I'll see you later in the week." He opened the door and waved to Nico as he left the gym.

Pulling his coat around him and zipping it, Sam struck out for home. He loved walking the streets at this time of year. The cold was bracing, and it was an excellent excuse to look at all the Christmas lights.

There were a few more up tonight, and he took in each house along the route, mentally scoring them as if he were the judge of the Christmas lights competition. When he neared home, he paused to admire his favorite. It had lights dripping from every window and dangling from the gutters. There was an inflatable Santa on the roof, complete with sleigh and a full complement of reindeer. Each bush and tree in the front garden was draped in lights from every color of the rainbow, and there was a huge LED Christmas tree on the front lawn, surrounded by inflatable penguins. Sam smiled. If he had his way, *they'd* win the competition, not the big, posh, perfect-looking house with no character. This place was fun and festive, rather than being all about the aesthetics. And to him, that embodied the spirit of Christmas.

Turning to head down the street, he completed his journey home. As he reached the doorstep and took out his keys, he checked the time and realized it was later than he'd thought. He'd texted Cat and let her know he was going to the gym and to sort herself out for dinner rather than waiting for him, but that wouldn't matter with Cat. She'd still be annoyed.

With a sinking feeling, he opened the door, expecting to be greeted by stony silence. He removed his outerwear, walking along the small hallway into the kitchen, where he could hear her moving around. A delicious, tomatoey-oregano smell greeted him.

"Hi," Cat said brightly, coming over and giving him a kiss. She went back to the oven and opened it.

Sam hesitated. He hadn't expected this scenario, but it was a welcome one. "Have you made lasagna? It smells awesome."

"Yeah, I know it's your favorite," she said, closing the oven door. "Not as good as the authentic one that Nico's mum makes, but it'll do. I'm afraid I don't have the Italian genes."

Sam grabbed them some plates and set the table, warmth infusing his soul. "It'll more than do. I love your version and I'm starving."

Cat smiled as Sam dished it up for them. She fetched them a couple of glasses and poured some wine, then sat across from him as they tucked in.

"Mm," Sam said, tension drifting from his shoulders. "This is amazing, thank you."

She sipped her drink. "You're welcome." She paused, placing her glass back down. "How was work?"

Sam frowned. Cat didn't normally ask him how work was. She said that skiing was boring and cold. "Fine, thanks. I was glad not to have to take the kids' class this afternoon. It's been difficult to get back in time from my advanced lesson ready for it starting."

"Oh yeah?" she said, not seeming to be listening. "And did you survive your lifts with Maya?"

Sam hesitated, his pulse picking up. "It was okay. We didn't say much."

Cat nodded. "Remember how she used to criticize working at the ski resort and say it wasn't a real job, despite working there herself?" Cat shook her head. "And now she's back there again. Still a hypocrite."

Sam nodded, taking another forkful of his food and choosing to stay silent.

Chapter
SEVEN

MAYA OPENED AND CLOSED HER DRAWERS NOISILY AS SHE PUT her clothing away, remembering how she'd let Sam rile her when she'd dropped him at the gym the evening before last. She'd had to sit in the car park for a couple of minutes to recover before setting off. Then, the rides to and from work the previous day had been pretty much deathly silent.

How dare he act all high and mighty just because she'd declined his offer of fuel money? She'd only said no because it would be unfair to take it when she was going in the same direction as him, not out of pity or whatever it was he'd gone on about. The journey would be no different and cost an equal amount whether he was in the car or not, so it hadn't seemed fair. Plus, taking his money when he was trying to save for that new car wouldn't be something she'd feel comfortable with. Despite her suspicion that he probably only had to save because he'd want to get something flash to show off in. She slammed a drawer. "Tosser."

"Maya? Everything all right?" Yvonne called up the stairs.

Oops. Better stop making it sound like World War III was raging in her bedroom.

"Yeah, sorry, Mum," she called back.

Sitting on the bed, she took a deep breath. Sam had also been snide about her coming back to work at the resort, as if she weren't worthy of the task. Probably because she was a woman. She'd had men be dicks about her abilities before, in both accountancy and skiing. *Sexist prick.*

The confusing thing was, it had seemed as if he was looking out for her when he'd interjected to save her explaining to Ben why she couldn't stay late on her first day. But she must have misinterpreted his intentions, because after that he'd gone back to being a dickhead. He'd clearly had his heart set on getting to the gym that evening, and that was why he'd done it.

An idea flashed into her mind. One that would mean she'd be able to get out of giving him lifts sooner rather than later. As long as the garage could revive his car. But would doing it get her into trouble with him, when he clearly didn't want any favors?

Maya blew out her breath. Who cared what he thought? He didn't rank highly with her either, so what did his opinion matter? Ignoring the thought that his opinion *did* still matter to her a little, she took out her phone. In any case, the other issue was that Kirsty had messaged to say that the well-to-do neighborhood watch on her street had been curtain twitching and messaging on their estate's WhatsApp group to ask about the old car that had been sitting there constantly for a few nights, with no comings or goings. They wanted to know whom it belonged to, under the guise of neighborhood safety, but Maya would bet they also didn't like the look of it on their posh street. *Snobby bastards.*

Pretending that Sam's car getting reported to some vehicle-related authority and towed away didn't matter to her, she dialed her breakdown company. "Hi there. I just wondered if I can add my . . . boyfriend's car to my breakdown insurance? We don't live at the same address though . . . great. Thank you. Yes, here are the details . . ."

She gave them Sam's information and the location of his vehicle, arranging for it to be collected and taken to the garage in Glenavie and then getting the fee for his cover added onto her direct debit. As she ended the call, there was a stab of panic that she'd done the wrong thing, but then relief set in that it would mean less car sharing, and she smiled like the smuggest Cheshire cat that had gotten all of the cream plus every dairy item on the entire farm. The notion that she'd done something to help Sam also provided a little warmth to her soul, but she ignored that, and set about earning her keep around the house on her day off.

❄ ❄ ❄

MAYA PULLED ON HER SWIMSUIT AND FIXED HER HAIR INTO A messy bun. She'd been determined to try out the new facilities ever since Sam's rather brusque tour on her second morning here.

They were housed in a new building tacked onto the side of the ski center, accessed via the back foyer off the slopes. There were three separate changing areas—female, male, and unisex—and each of those led into the space containing a hydrotherapy pool, a sauna, and a steam room.

A genius idea of Ben's. She rolled her shoulders, eager to get into the steam room and soothe the muscles that were aching in a kind of satisfying manner from her newfound job. The thought of having to go back to sitting behind a desk made her shudder.

She eyed the hydrotherapy pool on the way past. One day, when she had more time, she'd need to try that out too. Crossing the area, she grasped the steam room door and opened it, stepping into a warm cloud of eucalyptus.

Blinking against the wet heat of the air, she found her way through the steam to the nearest edge of the tiled bench that ran around the rather spacious room. She couldn't even see the far end of it through the steam, but she was pretty sure no one else was present. It was a bit too early in the day for these facilities to be busy.

Just as she settled onto her seat and breathed a satisfied sigh, a male voice cut through the cloud. "Hey."

Oh shit. There was no mistaking Sam's husky tone. She peered through the moisture and made out his rather impressive, swim-short-clad form, laid out along the bench opposite with an arm tucked behind his head.

Her pulse quickened. What was it with her newfound tendency to accidentally bump into her ex while he was partially clothed? Did the universe have it in for her? Oh, hey, Maya, just as you're going through the most stressful period in your life, here's your nearly naked hot ex to remind you of what you missed out on. *Thanks for nothing, universe.*

"Hey," she replied, painfully aware that her eyes were adjusting a bit too efficiently and revealing the manner in which his wet hair fell onto his forehead in appealing dark tendrils. His skin was glistening with beads of moisture that clung to the muscular contours of his chest, arms, and legs.

There was a tightening low in her belly, which had no business being there and that she tried her damnedest to ignore. Then she realized that this time, she *too* was wearing less clothing than would be ideal in front of her ex, and she touched the strap of her swimsuit self-consciously.

Sam's gaze appeared drawn to the movement of her fingers, his jaw clenching. He blinked, swinging his legs down to sit facing her and leaning his forearms on his knees. The muscles in his arms bulged as he kept his eyes on the floor at her feet, his voice gruff. "How's your morning going?"

Her own voice came out a little squeaky. "Fine. Just thought I'd pop in here quickly to try it out."

He glanced up, looking at her from under his brows with his wet hair falling onto his face, and for a moment she thought she was going to slide off her seat and melt into the warm water pooling on the floor. *Why are you doing this to me?* she asked her misguided libido.

Sam sat a little straighter, shifting his eyes onto the wall somewhere near her head. *He can't even look at me. I suppose that means he doesn't have as much trouble keeping his eyes off me in a state of undress as I do him.*

He ran a hand through the slick of his hair. "You should try the hydrotherapy pool too. It works wonders for aching muscles."

"Will do," she said, openly studying every ridge of *his* muscles while his gaze was preoccupied with the wall tiling.

"Anyway," he said, bringing his eyes onto her just as she snapped hers up to his face, narrowly avoiding getting caught staring. "I'd better head."

She nodded, getting the impression that he glanced down her body for a second. Then he swallowed hard, and stood up quickly.

He strode to the door, taking hold of the handle. "See you later."

"Yep," she replied. "Later."

Sam hesitated for a moment, as if wrestling with something. Then he opened the door and was gone.

❄ ❄ ❄

SITTING IN THE SKI CENTER CAFÉ AT LUNCH, MAYA STIRRED HER coffee as she scrolled through the lesson plan on her tablet. She had a few new ideas to keep the kids engaged, and was on a roll with her class.

Unable to keep the smile from her face, she pondered that she hadn't even completed a full week and being there was already mending her broken soul. Pity working at a desk doing accounting didn't make her feel like that.

Sighing, she lifted her mug. She'd confided in her mum about taking the post, but sworn her to secrecy in case Dad got pissed off that she was distracting herself from her job search. Omar hadn't suspected as yet, being out at work all day during the week and home late. But Maya was aware that she'd need to speak to him sooner rather than later, because he was bound to find out otherwise. She'd just have to emphasize that it was only a short-term thing until she found something else in her field.

Movement caught the corner of her eye, and she lifted her gaze to find that Sam was approaching. Her heart spiraled downward. Wasn't it enough that she had to put up with his bad attitude on the way to and from work, without having to speak to the guy during the working day? And she'd already had that cringeworthy run-in at the steam room this morning to contend with.

The unwelcome memory of him sitting partially clothed and dripping wet entered her mind, and she frowned into her coffee as she stirred it vigorously.

He was still wearing his ski boots, and it irked her that everyone else moved awkwardly like a stormtrooper in them, while Sam managed to pull off a cool kind of swagger. If she were honest, then she would have described his gait as sexy, but even thinking that annoyed the hell out of her.

Sam took a seat beside her, appearing distracted and running a hand through his hair.

"No, that's okay, the seat isn't taken," she said, unable to keep the sarcasm from her voice.

"What?" he said, meeting her gaze as if he hadn't even heard what she'd said.

Maya rolled her eyes. "Nothing."

She hadn't had the guts to admit to him that she'd arranged to get his car towed to the Glenavie garage. But she'd need to soon, because once it arrived the next day, they'd phone him about it. However, it was difficult to open the conversation when they were barely talking. Speaking of which, why was he here sitting next to her?

Sam let out a breath, which sounded as if he'd been holding it since the age of the dinosaurs. "Ben says that I have to interview you."

Maya hesitated. "Pardon?"

Sam huffed out another breath. "Ben says that—"

"Yeah," Maya said, her pulse spiking. "I heard you. I just don't get it."

He ran a hand through his hair again, and Maya wished she could stop watching him whenever he did that.

"Apparently, even though it's a short-term thing, HR say we need an interview for everything to be aboveboard. And it's part of my remit as the head of the instructing team."

Maya tried not to curl her lip. Having any sort of longer conversation with him, over and above their brief, tense exchanges, was a painful thought. "Can we do it now? Seeing as we're in each other's company already."

He shook his head. "I haven't got time." He let out another short, sharp breath, and Maya wondered if he'd been pumped full of air right before this conversation. "My working day is chock-full for the foreseeable because there's so much left to do for the charity sled race."

Ugh. That's right. Throw in that you're organizing a charity thing to make me feel bad. Maya tried to physically kick herself under the table for feeling impressed by his altruism.

"What's that wobbling the table?" he asked, moving to peer underneath.

"Nothing," Maya said quickly. "What do you want to do? About the interview?"

He met her eyes, and she could tell that whatever he was about to say pained him. "Can we meet after work?"

Maya hesitated. She didn't relish the idea, but she couldn't say no, for Ben's sake. Not if the interview was needed to keep things aboveboard. "Fine. When?"

"Tonight? Get it out of the way?"

He clearly didn't want it hanging over him for any longer than was necessary. Finally, something they could agree upon. "Where?"

Sam looked as though he hadn't thought that part through. "We can stay here after hours, do it in my office? Or I suppose we could meet at the pub. I'm meant to be meeting Arran there anyway."

Maya thought quickly. Being alone with him in his office was not an attractive prospect. She wasn't keen on meeting him out and about either, but at least there would be other people around. Plus, she could have a drink afterward, or perhaps even during, in order to soothe her nerves. "Let's meet at the pub. Which one are you going to? And I assume the Arran you're meeting is Arran Adebayo, from school?"

"Yeah, that's right." He glanced away. "We're meeting at the Tavern."

The scene of the crime. Maya narrowed her eyes. Fine. It wasn't as if she hadn't been there multiple times since that night, she just hadn't been there at the same time as Sam. But it was water under the bridge, ancient history, all forgotten. "Done. I'll meet you at eight."

"Great." Sam scraped his chair back. "See you later. I'll make sure I'm not late to meet you at the car tonight." He walked off.

Like he's doing me a bloody favor just by not being late. Maya let out a "humph" and lifted her coffee. Though she supposed he *was* busy, organizing charity events and the like. But that thought just made her feel guilty for being annoyed with him.

❄ ❄ ❄

"YOU'VE NOT EATEN MUCH, SWEETHEART," YVONNE SAID.

Maya pushed her food around the plate. "Sorry. I had a big lunch." She pondered the salad she'd eaten earlier, with the intention that'd she'd be gorging herself on her mum's steak pie later on. But now her appetite had vanished due to her nerves about meeting Sam. *Bloody Sam and his steak-pie-sabotaging ways.*

Omar clicked off the TV. "I spoke to Hana earlier. She told me that you were working at the ski center." He gave Maya a pointed look.

Maya's pulse spiked, her breath catching in her throat. She had asked her sister not to say anything. But Hana clearly couldn't resist getting one over on her by snitching to their dad. Her sister didn't even need to curry favor in his eyes, because she was already shiny and perfect.

"This had better not hamper your search for a real job," Omar said, eyeing her.

Her gut squeezed painfully. The way that he said *real job* stung. He'd made it clear in his lectures over the years that ski instructing was not a proper career in his eyes. Maya had persuaded him to let her do the instructing course at age seventeen, and then, once there was a vacancy, get a part-time job at the resort under Ben. But Omar had been firm that it wasn't something he'd consider backing beyond that, and he expected her to go to university and qualify for a vocational, professional career. His only approved subjects were medicine, law, or finance related.

Only once, she'd cautiously floated the idea to her dad of delaying university and working a gap year at the resort. It had not gone down well, and was a mistake she never repeated. After that she'd never been able to voice to anybody else how much she loved instructing and that her innermost desire was to stay on at the resort and not go to uni at all. A lifetime of having her wishes stomped on by her father had taught her to keep quiet.

So she'd made the decision to abandon it as a choice, in order to pursue accountancy. The career she'd only chosen to please her father. Though she hadn't been able to bring herself to relinquish instructing altogether, which was why she'd worked at Glencoe on the side.

Yvonne leaned on the table, bringing herself closer to Omar. "I told her to do it. As a favor to Ben, and Sam. They needed someone at short notice, and it's only temporary until something comes up elsewhere." She gave him a hard stare. "It's not as if loads of people are hiring anyway. Not just before Christmas. She can search properly in the New Year."

Omar was silent for a moment. "A favor to Sam?"

Maya swallowed, her mouth dry. *Shit.* "It's for Ben, really."

Her dad was studying her. "I don't want us to experience the same issues that Sam caused in the past."

She shook her head quickly, avoiding her mum's quizzical gaze.

"I want you to be settled, Maya," Omar continued. "Just look at your sister."

Ugh, here we go.

"Hana is a partner in the firm, the youngest they've ever had," Omar continued. "She and Rosie are engaged to be married and have a beautiful house together."

Maya didn't know why he had to say the same things over and over. She *knew* all of that stuff about Hana; she was her sister for goodness' sake. And having it shoved down her throat at regular intervals wasn't something she needed—now or ever.

"You need more ambition," Omar said, not showing any signs of stopping soon. "Working for such a small company was a mistake, no wonder they went under. You always have this misguided sense of altruism. Like you have to help the underdog." He shook his head. "Backing the underdog gets you nowhere in life. A big firm is where it's at. Like Hana's."

Maya plastered a smile onto her face, trying to control her heart rate. "Don't panic, they'll perfect the human-cloning process any day now, and then you'll be able to get a carbon copy of Hana to replace me with." She stood to clear her plate, her hands trembling. "I'll live in the attic like Mr. Rochester's wife. All I'll need is a bit of Mum's steak pie now and again, and I'll be set." She scraped her plate into the bin and put it in the dishwasher, heading for the kitchen door.

"Sweetheart," Yvonne called after her.

Maya continued walking. "I've got to go and meet . . . someone for an interview. I won't be long."

She pulled on her jacket and boots at the front door. *Too right I won't be long. This evening is shitty enough without Sam making it even more of a shit fest.*

Closing the door behind her, she set off. Sam had insisted on meeting her at the crossroads to walk to the Tavern together, something about not wanting her to walk alone in the dark. *At what point did he become concerned with my welfare?* She seemed to recall him expressing some reservation regarding her driving in the icy conditions when they'd been at Kirsty's as well, but she pushed that thought aside.

Glancing at the houses lining the street, she opted to distract herself with all of the amazing lights. She loved them, and the more over the top the better. That's what Christmas was all about. Why on earth did that big house on the corner win the competition every year? It was beautiful, but so boring. It didn't capture the fun of Christmas. Especially the childhood aspect of it. Give her inflatable Santas and lights from every color of the rainbow any day.

Rounding the corner, she spotted Sam waiting for her at the crossroads, and her tiny bubble of Christmas joy burst into green, Grinch-like confetti.

She closed the gap between them and gave him a nod as he fell into step beside her.

"Hi," he said. "Thanks for this."

"Sure," she replied, her voice flat.

Sam frowned. "You okay?"

Maya let out a breath. She shouldn't say anything to her mortal enemy. But it was all so fresh in her mind, and there was no one else around to talk to. "Yeah. Just bloody Dad."

Sam walked alongside her in silence for a moment. "And here I was thinking it was merely my company that had you down in the dumps this evening."

She managed a smile. "Nah. You're small potatoes, mate."

He laughed, which surprised her somewhat. Being aware that she still had the ability to elicit that response from him, even during that first car ride from Kirsty's, helped her relax a little.

"Want to talk about it?" he asked, shoving his hands into his pockets.

Hesitating, she pondered that question. She did want to get it off her chest, though she'd infinitely rather it were his twin sister here, or anyone else for that matter. But Liv was at her karate class and beggars couldn't be choosers, because it wasn't as if there were anyone else to confide in either. Elise had much bigger issues, and bloody Hana could go and suck it. Plus, this was something Sam could empathize with, working at the resort himself. "He found out that I'm teaching at the resort and he doesn't like it."

Sam's face was neutral. "He thinks it's going to distract you from searching for a real job."

Her heart sank. *Shit. He does remember.* She'd been so preoccupied that she hadn't considered that this could be dangerous ground, given that the subject had caused friction between them in the past. And their destination this evening—the Tavern—was the same as on the night of said disagreement. *Talk about a bad omen.* She kept quiet, neither confirming nor denying Sam's statement.

His voice was even. "Sorry to hear that you argued."

She nodded, aware that she should change the subject, but for some reason was unable to. "It felt like when I was younger, with him belittling my choices and crushing my dreams. It's only a temporary thing until I get another job, but he still made me feel like shit." She paused, aware that she was saying too much, but the words were tumbling out and she couldn't stop them. "And he went on about Hana again and how perfect she is. How I should be more like her."

Sam seemed to be listening intently. "Crushing your dreams?"

"Yeah. It was always the same with him."

Glancing over, his expression was unreadable. "I remember you being unsure about whether to pursue accountancy." He cleared his throat. "But then you reconciled yourself with the idea."

I had no choice but to reconcile myself with it. Because of Dad. Sam had been the only person she'd confided her career doubts in before she went to uni. Not only her doubts, in fact, but her true desires—not to go to uni at all but become a ski instructor instead. He'd been a natural ally, as a fellow ski instructor. Sam had encouraged her to speak to her dad, and it had *not* gone down well.

Sam had really seemed to listen back then, though she'd subsequently assumed it was merely an act on his behalf.

She shrugged. "I made my bed with accounting, so I'm lying in it. Dunno why he has to make everything into a big deal."

He shot her a wry smile. "Any accountancy jobs on the horizon?"

"Not yet. I'll find something, though."

They approached the Tavern, and Maya's eye was caught by the huge Christmas tree outside, adorned in blue, green, and yellow lights. "Aw, they've got their tree up. I love it. They just need an inflatable Santa or something and they'd be all set." Good job it was there to distract her gaze from the tree line, where she'd witnessed the gut-wrenching sight of Sam and Cat's deception.

He held the door for her as they entered. The pub was split over two levels, with a ground-floor and first-floor bar. Their generation had always preferred the first floor. Sam tugged off his hat as they ascended the stairs. "You like the Christmas inflatables?"

"Yeah," Maya said, unzipping her jacket. "The more over the top, the better. If I had my way, one of those houses with lights from every color of the rainbow and all of the inflatables possible would win the competition."

Sam threw her a bemused look as they secured a table. "Really? I had you pegged for a big-house-on-the-corner fan."

"Nah," she replied, taking a seat across from him. "Too predictable."

Sam shot her a smile. "I agree. It isn't my cup of tea. I've got a few contenders on my list for the crown."

Maya raised her eyebrows. "You have? Which ones?"

"I'll show you on the lights competition Facebook page. But first, I owe you a drink. Probably more than one, for all of the lifts. What would you like?"

That sounded awfully like he was being courteous. "Bottle of beer please. Doesn't matter which one."

He headed for the bar, and Maya looked around. Being here with him brought back long-faded memories, of standing there across the room when Cat told her Sam was backtracking on his involvement with her. Maya had glanced over, and he'd been laughing with his mates. As if it were insignificant.

It still pissed her off when she thought of it, but they had only been teens at the time. Communication skills hadn't been her forte then either, so he hadn't been the only one who possessed that flaw. *And perhaps they still aren't my strong area.* As her inability to admit to her father what she wanted—or rather didn't want—in life illustrated.

Sam appeared through the crowd with two bottles, sliding one across the table to her as he took a seat. He pulled a pen and a form out of his jacket where it was hanging on the seat behind him. "Let's get this thing done."

Maya grasped her beer, aware that, so far, the evening hadn't been quite as hideous as she'd been expecting.

Sam filled in some of the blanks, including her date of birth, address, and qualifications. She smiled. "I don't even need to be here. You could've done this all on your own."

He looked up and flashed her a grin. "That's the basics. We just have to run through a couple of safety scenarios."

Maya took a swig from her bottle. "Hit me."

He read them out, and she answered easily. Then he asked her the details of the classes she'd taught at Glencoe, and the names of her references. Before too long, he was recapping his pen. "That was the easiest interview I've ever done. Probably could've fitted it in at work after all."

Maya laughed. "Now you bloody tell me."

He shot her a sheepish expression. "Sorry. At least you got a drink out of it."

"True," she said, leaning back. "I might have one more for the road, though. Saves me returning home too soon to face Dad's wrath." She stood. "Can I get you one?"

"Yeah," he replied, a smile on his lips. "But then I'll have to get you another because I can't have you being one up on me."

She rolled her eyes. "Whatever."

Sam laughed as she moved off to the bar.

Once she had the fresh bottles, she came back to the table. Sam was frowning at his phone.

"What's wrong?"

He put the phone down, and accepted his beer. "Thanks. It's Arran. He can't make it."

"That's a shame," she said, taking her seat. "Is he okay?"

"Yeah. His ex called and asked him to take their little boy, Jayce, at the last minute."

Maya nodded, remembering Liv mention Arran and his son in the past. "Hold on," she said. "His ex? I thought Liv said he was getting married this summer?"

Sam grimaced. "He was. But she called it off a few weeks beforehand."

"Ouch." Maya winced, trying to imagine what that must feel like. Pretty shitty, she'd bet. "How is he?"

"Okay," Sam said, seeming surprised that she was asking. "Getting there. He was made redundant from his painting and decorating job earlier this year though, so it's not been a good one for him."

Maya made a mental note to stop being a selfish cow and feeling sorry for herself regarding her own single status and jobless situation. At least she and Rich hadn't been engaged and it'd been a mutual breakup. Plus, they didn't have any kids. "Poor Arran. What's he doing now?"

Sam hesitated for a second. "He's getting a new art studio off the ground. It's always been his dream, but he'd been scared to take the risk. Then he got his redundancy package and he figured it was now or never."

Now or never. Does that apply to me, too?

Maya cleared her throat. "I remember he was awesome at art when we were at school." She shot him a smile. "Unlike me and my rubbish skills. I couldn't even draw a stick man."

Sam laughed. "I do remember that house you painted a picture of, which looked more like a potato."

Maya coughed on her beer. "Below the belt, Holland. I'm sensitive about my lack of artistic prowess."

He shrugged, still smiling. "You were a whiz at math, so you'll get no sympathy from me."

"Humph," she said, pretending to be affronted as she sipped her beer. Then she remembered what he'd said earlier on. "Hey, you promised to show me your short list on the lights competition page."

His eyes widened, and she tried to ignore how appealing his apparent excitement was.

He pulled out his phone and gestured for her to come around the table to sit next to him. She did so, trying not to lean in too closely and get a whiff of that evocative scent of his as he showed her the screen.

"I've liked the pics of all my favorites," he told her.

Taking the phone, she scrolled through, noticing a pattern among all the ones he'd liked. They were precisely the ones she would also choose, which was both unexpected and weird.

"You've got a good group here." She glanced up. "I didn't think I'd agree with your selection. But you have excellent taste."

Accepting the phone back, he laughed. "You're surprised that I have good taste?"

Figuring it was best to mind how she answered, given that his taste had included choosing her friend over her, she hesitated. "I thought that you'd prefer the classic aesthetic."

Shaking his head, he leaned in. "No way. I like to root for the underdog. The rookie. The new kid on the block."

The underdog. Maya remembered her father disparaging her for backing the exact same kind of contender, and met Sam's gaze for a moment. He really was throwing her this evening. She glanced away, fiddling with her charm bracelet.

The movement of her fingers seemed to catch his eye, and he reached down to take her wrist. Maya almost flinched. But not because his touch was unpleasant, far from it.

Sam fingered the bracelet. "You still wear this."

Maya held her breath, hoping that he hadn't spotted the charm. He turned her wrist to reveal the tiny moon, running his fingertip over it.

His voice was quiet. "And you kept the one I gave you—I mean, *we* gave you. For your eighteenth."

Maya's mouth went dry. It had been her birthday a few weeks before she'd left for university, after the two of them had started working together, but before they'd had their little trysts in the boot room. She'd told him how she liked the moon and the star charms in the jewelry store. Sam had turned up to her birthday drinks with the moon charm inside a little black jewelry box and presented it to her, a gift from the whole ski team.

"You know me," Maya said, trying to keep things light. "I always loved anything to do with the moon and the stars. Think I was a werewolf in a previous life."

Sam met her gaze. "I remember." He held on to her wrist for another couple of seconds, causing her heart to trip over itself. Then he appeared to come to his senses and released her in favor of his bottle. He lifted it and took a long drink.

Maya followed suit, figuring that reminding him how he'd once liked her or, at least, pretended to like her, wasn't a good idea.

They finished their drinks, and she wondered whether she should call it a night after that awkward moment, but the thought that her dad might still be awake made her hesitate.

Sam gave her a nudge. "One for the road?"

What the hell. I'm used to being awkward in his presence now.

"Okay," she replied. "Last one, then I'm going home to face whatever terrible fate awaits me."

He gave her a smile as he lifted the empties to take back to the bar.

Maya glanced at the moon charm. It was her favorite because she'd coveted it, and the star one, for ages. Plus, it was gifted from all her old work colleagues and had nostalgic value. But deep down it meant more than that. It carried extra significance because Sam had given it to her. Something that she hadn't been keen on admitting to herself in the past.

He arrived with the drinks, taking a seat and clinking his bottle against hers. "I'll walk you home after this one."

Maya shook her head. "You stay. I'll be fine on my own."

"Nope. Sorry." His mouth was set in a firm line. "It's against my moral code not to."

Maya smiled, wondering if he ever cursed his moral code the way she did hers. Walking home the woman he'd felt up a couple of times before deciding her friend was a better option likely wasn't an idea he'd be keen on, if not for said pesky moral code.

"When did you tell your dad about the job?" Sam asked. "Tonight?"

Maya shook her head. "I didn't tell him. Hana, the massive traitor who's going to lose her head when I see her, told him."

He raised his eyebrows. "She broke your confidence?"

"Yep." Maya took a long swig of her beer while Sam winced.

"Oof. That's got to sting."

"Yeah," she sighed. "It's like his attitude has created this competition between us. I try to avoid it, but I'm aware that I'm jealous of her achievements and I've got this inferiority complex where she's concerned."

Sam nodded. "And she perpetuates it?"

"Yep. Every time I confide in her, she finds a way to use it against me." Maya pulled at the corner of the label on her beer. "I should have learned by now not to trust her with anything."

Sam was watching her. "That must feel like shit. Liv is really good at keeping my confidence."

"You're lucky," Maya said, meeting his eyes. "Though I'm not sure if this is more a female thing. Being in competition over a dad's affection."

Immediately she regretted saying that, because a father's affection was something that neither Sam nor Liv knew about. "I'm sorry," she said, closing her eyes briefly. "I didn't think before I said that."

Sam studied her for a moment, as if he were surprised that she would've clocked the reference. "That's okay. I don't mind."

He certainly was being very gracious. Perhaps he was trying to make up for his past wrongs.

Maya looked away. "How come you haven't confided in Liv about your butler thing? I'm sure she wouldn't tell Cat."

Sam hesitated for a moment. "Because I'm keeping someone else's confidence. If it was my own secret, I'd tell her. But it's not, and when someone asks me not to say anything to anyone, I take that seriously."

For goodness' sake. Couldn't he stop acting all altruistic and noble for a second? He was making her feel bad for disliking him. *Because I do dislike him . . . don't I?*

She gave him a nod, too confused to speak.

He leaned back a little. "Are you going to talk to your sister about how you feel?"

Maya blew her fringe out of her eyes. "Probably not."

"Why?"

She raised an eyebrow. "Because I'm totally shit at confrontation. That's why I've never spoken to my dad about hating my career." Perhaps she shouldn't have said that. It was a little too honest.

Sam opened his mouth, then paused. "You actually hate it?"

"With a passion." She swigged from her bottle like a lush, then eyed him. "Do not tell *anybody* that, by the way. If it gets back to Dad, I'm toast."

He smiled. "I just told you what a great secret keeper I am, remember?"

"Oh yeah. You'll need to prove it then, or I'll have your guts for garters." Though for some reason, she already felt as if she could trust him. Her instinct was informing her he was genuine, which heightened her confusion, because she'd felt that way before and he'd left her humiliated.

He gave her a two-fingered salute. "Noted."

They drained the last of their drinks, and Maya checked the time. "Should be safe to return now."

She stood to go fetch her jacket from the other chair. "You really don't have to come, not if you don't want to."

He shook his head, putting on his parka. "I want to make sure you get home okay, if that's all right with you. Especially when it was my idea to come here."

Maya nodded, afraid to say anything else, because she found that sentiment a little moving. She turned to lead them down the stairs, wondering whether she'd always been this much of a sap or if it'd been a more recent development.

They headed outside, and Maya glanced toward where the tree line was decorated in sparkly fairy lights. Emboldened by the alcohol, she asked, "Is the nook still there?"

Sam glanced at the woods, then set his sights ahead as they began to walk, his voice strained. "Yeah."

"Do teenagers still go there to make out?" *Why am I talking about this? What's wrong with me?*

"Nah." He cleared his throat. "They conduct all of their business on Snapchat as far as I can tell."

Maya opted to change the subject, because she shouldn't have mentioned the nook in the first place. "Is Ben okay? He seems stressed."

Sam glanced at her. "I think he's got a lot on."

Maya nodded, still feeling as if it were more than that. "Are you sure that's all it is? Because I've met him for a coffee every day I've been in this week, and he seems really distracted."

Sam was silent for a second, so she glanced over. He was watching the ground as they walked. "I've not noticed. But I'm getting a lift with him tomorrow, so I'll ask."

"Can you let me know if there's anything I can do to help, with whatever it is?"

Sam looked up, a strange expression on his face. "Of course."

They made their way to the crossroads and then down the hill into the housing estates. He stopped at the point that they'd have to cross over, and looked at her. "Do you want to see something before we go to yours?"

"What?" she asked.

"My favorite house," Sam said. "Their lights entry isn't on the Facebook page yet."

Maya's curiosity got the better of her. "Go on, then."

Sam smiled, and she followed him farther down the hill, and around the corner until they weren't far from his place.

"Check this out." He pointed along the street, and the whole area was lit up like Blackpool Illuminations.

Maya had never seen so many houses on one street go all out before. However, it was still apparent which property Sam was referring to. A smile spread across her face as she took it in. Inflatable Santa, penguins and all. "That is genius."

"Right?" Sam said, standing next to her to admire it.

"Good choice, Mr. Holland," Maya said as they turned to retrace their steps. "You should apply to be a judge, and sway the vote."

Sucking his breath in through his teeth, he shook his head as they crossed the street. "That's a hard panel to get on. You need to be a mover and a shaker in town."

Maya shrugged. "You're the assistant manager at the ski resort. Doesn't that hold any sway?"

He shot her a weird look. "Doubt it."

They neared a little closer to Maya's estate, and she noticed how, disappointingly, the lights became more sedate as they went. "My parents' area is so boring compared to yours."

Sam glanced over. "I have to admit, I thought your taste in lights would have been the opposite to mine."

"Why's that?" Maya asked as her house loomed into view.

He shrugged. "The houses around your way go for a more conservative look. Plus, Cat hates all the inflatables and stuff. She thinks it's tacky."

Maya clenched her jaw. *What's Cat's opinion got to do with mine?* Their tastes had never run the same. Not since Sam anyway.

Her pulse spiked as she remembered anew the humiliation she'd felt that night, when she'd trusted him, and Cat. A little bit like how she'd been beginning to trust him again now. Surely that was a mistake, when he'd proven in the past that her instincts toward him were all wrong? And wasn't it insensitive that he was assuming she wouldn't like something just because Catriona didn't? Plus, he was being hypocritical by insinuating that she preferred a classic aesthetic with regard to these decorations, when *he* was the one who'd dumped Maya and her nonclassical looks for a more traditionally Scottish-appearing woman. It had been clear that was what Cat was getting at when she'd relayed that Sam had said Maya wasn't his type. She clenched her fists in her pockets.

Sam must've sensed that he'd said something to piss her off, because he remained silent for the remainder of the short walk.

As they approached her house, the wave of hurtful memories swelled. They stopped at the bottom of her driveway, and before he could speak, she did. "By the way. You'll get a call from the Glenavie garage tomorrow."

He frowned. "I will?"

"Yeah. I contacted my breakdown service and pretended that you were my boyfriend, got you added onto my cover. They're picking your car up tomorrow and towing it to the garage." His eyes widened, and he opened his mouth, but she got in first. "Before you have another go at me for trying to help, I didn't do it for your benefit. The sooner your car is fixed, the sooner we won't have to travel in the same vehicle anymore." She turned to head along the driveway. "Thanks for the drink, and walking me home."

Opening the door, she went inside and shut it behind her, leaving him standing on the driveway, apparently speechless.

Chapter
EIGHT

"SAM?"

He looked up, meeting his mum's gaze across the kitchen table, aware that she'd asked him something. But he had no idea what she had said.

He cleared his throat. "Sorry?"

Tara smiled. "You seem a million miles away. Is everything all right?"

Depends on your definition of all right. If it meant being terrified that the ski resort might be in serious difficulty, feeling the burden of responsibility toward a friend who needed financial support, his girlfriend probably being on course to dump him *again*, plus that he was generally knackered, then yes. He was all right.

Although Cat's usual pattern of behavior *had* changed. She'd gone from being generally pissed off to like she was buttering him up for something.

A cold nausea swirled its way into his stomach. What if she was planning on trying the "we should move away from Glenavie" conversation again? Sam had always known this was the place for him, and enduring the same debate on at least a yearly basis was pretty soul destroying.

The other person playing on his mind was Maya. He hadn't seen her at the resort earlier that day. She must have been avoiding him.

He thought back to the previous evening. They'd been getting along pretty well, until he'd mentioned Cat. But why should Maya be bothered about her? Cat certainly gave the impression they didn't get along, what with all of her barbed comments about how Maya thought she was too good for the rest of them, going off to university and becoming an accountant. Those were opinions he'd shared for a long time, fueled by his argument with Maya and her subsequent cold rejection of him.

But recently, things didn't seem to fit. They got along so well at times, though, granted, in other moments they rubbed each other the wrong way. However, she was really funny, and he couldn't help but laugh at her quips, plus she seemed so empathetic toward other people.

She'd also taken him off guard when she said that she preferred the small ski-town life and hated being an accountant. Even that she loved all the same over-the-top Christmas decorations as him.

None of it fitted with the picture he'd painted of Maya in his head. It did sit more evenly with Liv's opinion of her, but in the past he'd put that down to bias, because best friends overlook each other's flaws.

The biggest thing he couldn't get over was the fact she'd kept that moon charm. Did it mean something to her that he'd gifted it? Or had she kept it only because she'd loved the trinket so much? After all, she'd been admiring it for a while before he'd bought it.

He'd organized and purchased it, but the rest of the ski team had put in for it too. That would be why Maya didn't associate the charm with him.

Right at that inopportune moment, the memory of seeing her walk into the steam room popped into his head, and he nearly groaned out loud. It was like his brain had it on priority replay. A few times a day it would appear out of nowhere like a really annoying but mind-meltingly hot advertisement.

He'd struggled so hard to keep his eyes off how her tawny-brown skin had glistened and the way her swimsuit hugged her curves. But he had failed spectacularly and so had no choice but to extricate himself from the situation, his brain screaming, *Mayday!* and pressing the imaginary ejector seat button.

He rubbed his beard, glancing up and realizing that he still hadn't answered his mother, who was giving him a patient look. "Sorry, Mum. I've got a few things on my mind."

Tara touched his hand. "You seem as if the weight of the world is on your shoulders."

"That's because his girlfriend is an almighty pain in the arse," Liv called from the kitchen. She crossed the open-plan area toward the table, carrying the pot of stew. "Tuck in."

Sam eyed her, but she avoided his gaze, and he could tell that she'd made her previous comment without thinking.

Lifting the lid, Tara stirred the pot. "This is lovely. But I feel guilty that you've come round to mine for dinner and done the cooking yourself."

Liv kissed the top of their mother's head. "You cooked every night for us when we lived here. Now it's your turn to put your feet up. Anyway," she said, taking a seat next to Tara and across from Sam, "I love cooking."

Tara dished the food onto their plates, and Sam shot Liv a look.

Liv raised an eyebrow. "Why are you giving me a death stare?"

"You know why. Stop slagging off Cat."

He took a mouthful of food and had to stop himself from groaning at how good it was, not wanting to give Liv the satisfaction.

"I only speak the truth," Liv muttered, concentrating on her food.

Sam rolled his eyes. Liv hadn't been friends with Cat for years, and he suspected that could be down to him being too open with his twin sister about Cat's mood swings. Their relationship pattern didn't help either. Cat had finished things about five times, but it was never for that long before she backtracked. Though, thinking about it, he realized she never apologized for her behavior. It was more as if she were doing him a favor by asking him back. And he supposed it felt as if she was.

In time, Sam had realized he should be less candid about Cat around his sister. It had been difficult when they were so close. Often Liv would know what was going on, even if he didn't verbalize it. And as much as he told Liv off for any little comments regarding his relationship, deep down he knew that she only wanted what was best for him. Not that she was correct in her opinion of Cat, however. It was hard to explain to people on the outside that when it was good, it was really nice. He felt settled, and safe. As if cocooned in a frayed but familiar blanket.

Swallowing another mouthful of stew, he gave Liv a grudging look. "This is really good."

Liv flashed him a grin. "I know."

He shook his head, unable to suppress a smile.

Liv sipped her water. "How's Maya getting on at the ski resort?"

Even hearing her name made his pulse pick up. "Fine, I think. We don't see that much of each other." *Except for the other day in the steam room, where we saw a whole lot of each other.*

"Is she back at the resort?" Tara asked. "I didn't realize. Ben must be ecstatic."

"And Sam," Liv replied, raising her eyebrows at him.

Sam paused chewing to look at her. "What do you mean?"

Liv shrugged. "You don't have to cover the kids' class any longer." She eyed him as she lifted her glass. "What else would I mean?"

Sam narrowed his eyes, but Liv just met his gaze in a steadfast, innocent manner. He'd never admitted to her that he and Maya had been on the brink of starting something, because it had been over before it began. Then, once it had ended, he didn't feel able to talk about it without being negative about Maya, and that wouldn't have been fair to Liv.

Shifting his gaze onto Tara, he nodded toward the empty chair. "Where's Angus?"

"He's out with his friends. I deliberately didn't invite him."

Sam's pulse stepped up a notch. "Why not?"

Tara glanced up. "Don't panic, not for any bad reason."

His shoulders relaxed. For a moment he'd thought she was going to say things with Angus were heading south.

"I wanted the two of you to myself," Tara continued. "To discuss something."

Sam glanced at Liv and could tell she too was none the wiser.

Tara smiled. "I've asked Angus to move in here with me. But I wanted to check that you were both okay with it."

She'd hardly got the last few words out when Liv squealed and threw her arms around her. Tara laughed, glancing over to assess Sam's reaction.

He smiled, pleased for his mum, but concerned all the same. What if Angus left? The stakes were higher if they were living together. If he were honest with himself, that was why he'd fallen short of buying a place with Cat. She'd suggested it, but he'd put off the decision. Which was dumb, because she pretty much lived at his place rather than at her parents', but somehow not making it official felt as if he were keeping himself safe.

His mum was looking at him as Liv settled back into her seat. Taking his hand, she gave it a squeeze. "Are you okay, love?"

Guilt needled him that he was raining on her parade. He forced his smile wider, nodding. "I'm really happy for you guys."

Tara raised her eyebrows. "But?"

Sam glanced at Liv, who gave him a reassuring smile. He cleared his throat, feeling like the ultimate party pooper killjoy Grinch Who Stole Christmas. "Is it a good idea? Do you think you guys are . . . steady enough?"

Tara gave him another squeeze. "We are, sweetheart. But you know what? If anything ever did go wrong, I'd be okay."

She held his gaze, and for a moment he felt as if he might well up.

He swallowed, and Liv took hold of his other hand across the table. Then he realized that his mum and sister were holding hands too so that the Hollands were like three sides of a triangle.

Tara glanced at Liv with a smile. "You guys need to stop worrying about me. I'm a grown woman. It's my job to worry about you two, not the other way around. And, Sam." He met his mother's eyes as she continued. "Someone leaving isn't the worst thing that can happen. Sometimes, it's for the best."

They both looked at him for a moment, and he sensed that comment was some sort of intervention. One he didn't feel ready to hear. Instead, he nodded and let go of their hands, turning back to his food and telling himself that was because it was getting cold.

❄ ❄ ❄

SAM WAVED AT HIS COLLEAGUE ROWAN AS HE TOOK OFF HIS SKI helmet. The cool air soothed the heat that had built up inside, and he tipped his face up to the sun, appreciating that he got to be out on this mountain every day and even got paid for it.

The sound of someone carving through the powder made him turn, and there was no mistaking Maya's form approaching down the black run he'd just completed. No mistaking to him anyway. His brain sure had imprinted every detail of her to a worryingly exact degree.

She slowed, glancing over through her goggles and doing a small double take as she realized he was standing there. He knew he should probably ski away now rather than risk any tense conversation on the slope in front of the students, but for some reason his legs were stuck and he couldn't take his eyes off her.

Coming to a stop, she removed her goggles and helmet and shook out her hair, the sun catching it and creating a glossy sheen that made him want to reach out and touch it.

This was their first meeting since the fallout after the interview at the Tavern, him having gotten another lift in with Ben that morning.

She looked at him, and despite the lack of a smile, it still sent a firebolt into his core. He swallowed, trying to think of something neutral to say, but all coherent thought exited his brain, slamming the door as it went.

After a couple more seconds of empty-brain syndrome, he opened his mouth. *I should thank her for getting my car towed to the garage.*

Just then, something—or someone—whacked into Maya from

the slope side, throwing her forward into him with such a force that he went flying onto his back.

It took a few seconds to compute what had happened, and as he tried, it became apparent that he was on his back with his ex lying right on top of him, her face buried in his neck.

The mayday signal was sounding loudly in his brain as it associated every touch of her body with the visual from the steam room. And that was even through skiwear.

He became aware of someone shouting, "Sorry!" as their voice faded into the distance and he saw an out-of-control skier completing their chaotic course to the end of the run and going into the soft barrier at the end, where Rowan was on hand to check on them.

He turned his attention back to the sensation of Maya's warm breath on his neck and the scent of her soft hair scattered across his face. The feel of her made his skin crackle with electricity, and the memory of her pressing against him in the boot room surfaced—as real and delicious as if it were yesterday.

His heart was beating so forcefully in his chest that he was afraid she might feel it in hers. "Okay?" he managed to ask in a gruff voice.

Maya shifted on top of him. "Yeah." She lifted her head, avoiding his eyes and appearing mortified. "Sorry. I didn't see them."

He shook his head. "Me neither. Are you hurt?"

She was pushing herself to her feet, having planted a hand at either side of him. Sam realized that both of their skis had unattached with the impact. "I'm fine," she told him, standing up and giving him a glance. "You?" She held out a hand to help him up, which he declined because making contact with her again felt like too much when he was already overwhelmed.

He got to his feet. "Fine."

She eyed him, and he got the distinct impression she'd taken his decline of her hand as a slight. But before he could say anything more, she turned to grab her skis and clomped off through the snow.

❄ ❄ ❄

CAT TUGGED HIM CLOSER TO REST HIS HEAD ON HER CHEST, PULL-ing the fleecy blanket over them as they watched TV.

Sam put his arms around her waist, appreciating the coziness in the living room against the backdrop of the cold winter night outside. If it could just be like this all of the time, or if Cat could be this version of herself for at least half the time, he'd be so happy.

Perhaps now, it was going to be different. He'd thought her familiar pattern of behavior had been recurring, but then it hadn't. She'd surprised him. It might be that her surprising him would continue, in a good way.

She stroked his hair. "How was work?"

It was nice that she was showing an interest in his job too. "Fine, thanks." He closed his eyes, the movement of her fingers through his hair making him content and sleepy.

"Did you get a lift with Ben today?"

"Yeah." He felt as if he might drift off to sleep.

"Bet that was a relief, not to have to travel with Maya."

That comment threw off his sleepy groove a little as he tried not to remember the feel of Maya lying on top of him in the snow earlier. "Mm-hmm."

She kissed the top of his head. "At least the garage is working on your car now. Soon you won't have to see her at all, once that's back on the road and she returns to her snooty career."

The tension began to flow back into his shoulders. For some

reason, the idea of Maya's imminent departure didn't make him happy. Plus, it brought back the knowledge that Maya had come to his rescue regarding his car, and he didn't know how to feel about the kindness. On one hand, he was embarrassed that she'd come to his aid again. But moreover, he was grateful to her, though a little confused about why she'd done it. Fair enough, she didn't want to car share anymore because they still found each other's company prickly, but she kept showing this generous nature that he'd forgotten existed.

Cat began to massage his scalp, and he let out a contented breath as the tension reversed again to flow out of him.

"Remember years ago, when you two had a bit of a thing?"

Sam sighed as the flow about turned yet again. It was up and down more times than a yo-yo.

"And remember how you guys argued because she slagged off your job? Pretty hypocritical, when *she* worked there at the time. *Not a real job* my arse."

Sam stayed silent, partly in the hope that Cat might think he'd fallen asleep and stop talking about Maya so that he could lull himself back into sleepiness. But also, because remembering that fallout was still painful. Plus what Cat was saying didn't ring true with the Maya he'd gotten to know a little over the past week.

"Anyway." Cat's voice was lower, soothing. "I know how hard you're working at the moment. I hope having her around isn't making it too much worse."

In an attempt to achieve some peace, and hopefully end this one-sided conversation, he shook his head against her chest. "It's fine."

Chapter
NINE

THE BELL ON THE TEAROOM DOOR JINGLED, AND MAYA LOOKED up from her and Liv's table in the corner, jumping up and nearly sending their plate of scones and teapot flying. "She's here!" She practically ran between the tables and threw her arms around both a stunned-looking Elise and a smiling Jack, who was on Elise's hip.

"What a lovely greeting!" Elise said as Maya pulled back to meet her gaze.

Maya's heart clenched. Despite Elise wearing a smile, her normally bright blue eyes projected a dull appearance, reinforced by the dark circles underneath. Her blond hair was scraped into a ponytail, leaving a pinched look to her face where a rosy glow would usually have been present.

Liv arrived at Maya's elbow to give Elise and Jack a hug. "Come and sit. We've got a table in the corner with a high chair."

They led Elise to their round table, and Maya reached out to take Jack while Elise removed her jacket.

Addressing Jack, she gave him a big smile. "Come on, handsome. Let's get you a treat."

"What about me?" Elise complained as she took a seat. "Don't I get a treat?"

"You can also have one, if you behave yourself," Maya replied with a wink.

Elise laughed, watching Maya get Jack settled in his high chair.

"Tea?" Maya asked, trying not to let the sadness infuse her bones. Even Elise's laugh hadn't lit up her eyes.

"Yes please," Elise said, glancing around the room, which was done out in a cozy Christmas manner, with mismatching tables and comfy chairs. Each table sported a central decoration made of dark green holly and ivy leaves studded with bright red berries and glossy brown pine cones. A wreath strewn with twinkly white lights made its way around the cornicing, and Christmas music tinkled quietly in the background. "This place is gorgeous. How long has it been here?"

"About six months," Liv replied. "We ordered the special Christmas tea. And the scones are cranberry, cinnamon, and orange."

Elise's eyes widened as she admired the scone Liv had placed onto her plate. "That looks, and sounds, amazing."

"We aren't too sure what's in the Christmas tea, though," Maya told her as she passed the milk. "Could be apple spice, or possibly juice squeezed from an elf."

Liv nodded sagely. "Or perhaps a sprinkling from Santa's beard."

Elise arched an eyebrow as she stared into her cup. "Not sure you're selling this, guys."

"Ach, it's fine," Maya told her, waving a hand. "No elves were harmed in the making of this production."

Elise chuckled.

"Are you going to stay on, Elise?" Maya asked. "Or just here for Christmas?"

Elise sipped from her cup. "I've decided to stay." She sighed. "I feel like a bit of a failure, but there you go."

Liv took her hand. "A failure? You're anything but."

Maya frowned, watching the two of them across the table. "Why do you feel that way?"

Elise glanced at Jack. "I should be able to manage, loads of single parents do." She nudged Liv. "Just look at your mum, she's bloody awesome."

Liv reached across and hugged her. "It's hardly the same. Coming out of a toxic relationship and being a widow are completely different. Plus, Sam and I were older."

"Don't be so hard on yourself," Maya said, studying Elise with that now-familiar clench in her heart. "You have to do what feels right, whatever helps you cope."

Elise blinked, her eyes shining.

Maya grabbed a packet of tissues from her bag and handed it over.

Elise took one and dabbed her eyes. Maya was expecting her voice to be wobbly, but it came out firm. Perhaps a little too firm. "Thank you. I appreciate you both." A weak smile crossed her face. "That's one of the reasons I want to come back. Being among family and friends feels right. And as much as my friends in Edinburgh are great, they were Harry's friends too. I feel like I need my own people." She shook her head. "I know that sounds stupid."

"Not at all," Liv said quietly. "It makes perfect sense."

"Anyway," Elise continued, taking a breath and clasping her hands together. "I figured we could stay with Mum and Dad until I sort out a place of my own. And maybe I can do some ad hoc shifts in various places, find a practice I like."

Maya smiled, her heart lifting from where it had thus far taken up residence around her feet. "Don't let Dr. B hear you say that. He's determined to poach you for his practice."

Elise laughed. "I'd love to work with them. They were great when I did my work experience."

Liv reached over to squeeze Elise's hand. "Don't rush yourself, though. We know what you're like, expecting to run before you can walk."

Elise shook her head. "I'll try not to. It'll take a while to find my feet, especially because I can't rely on Mum and Dad too much for childcare. Mum's suffering really badly with her joints, and Dad . . . well. Childcare is *not* his forte." She rolled her eyes. "Mum says he never even changed my nappy when I was a baby."

Liv huffed out a breath. "Sounds like my dad."

Maya eyed them both. Even though Omar did her head in, he'd always been an attentive father. Not one of these types who called looking after his own children "babysitting" and couldn't cope with longer than a couple of hours alone with his offspring.

Elise shot her a smile. "How are you doing, Maya? Seems we're all coming home to roost. I'm sorry the firm didn't survive."

"Yeah," Maya said, shrugging. "You know. That's the way the cookie crumbles. Unfortunately, my whole bag of cookies seems rather brittle just now." Guilt needled her chest, and she reached over to touch Elise's hand. "But it's not significant."

Elise raised her eyebrow. "Don't give me that crap about how your problems don't matter just because you think other people's are worse." She gestured between Liv and herself. "We know you've been miserable. And you need to do something about it."

Maya raised her eyebrows as Liv nodded in agreement. "Methinks you two have been talking about me."

Liv shrugged. "Course we have."

"*Well,*" Maya said, using her poshest voice and lifting her cup with her pinkie sticking out. "I am *most* offended, Miss O and Miss E. I hereby officially turn my back on you both." She swiveled around in her chair so that her back was facing them, to the sound of their laughter.

"Come on," Elise said. "You know it's only because we love you."

Maya let out a "humph" and swiveled back round again, flashing a smile, pleased that she'd managed to deflect the conversation with a joke.

Liv sipped her drink. "Have you had it out with Hana yet?"

Maya grimaced like she'd licked a lemon.

"Or your dad?" Elise asked.

Maya screwed her face even tighter, as if she'd swallowed a whole bag full of lemons.

Elise shot her one of her "looks." The "I'm a doctor, and you need to listen to my wisdom" look. "You need to tell them both how you feel. Otherwise, it's going to continue to fester."

Maya hid her face behind her mug. "I don't mind a bit of festering. Festering is safe. Nobody's feelings get hurt."

"Except yours," Liv said.

"That, I can cope with," Maya replied, sipping her tea and renewing her determination to ignore the situation. In the same manner she'd been avoiding her parents after Omar's barbed comment about Sam the other night. "Ooh, this is tasty. I might buy a packet to take home to Mum." She ignored the look that passed between Liv and Elise, and focused on her cup.

※ ※ ※

SINKING DEEPER INTO THE WARM WATER, MAYA RELISHED THE feel of the bubbles soothing her tired muscles. She closed her eyes and let her arms float up to the surface, imagining that the bubbles were lifting away all of her cares.

The ambient lighting and background hum of the hydrotherapy pool was calming, quieting her mind until she arrived at the edge of a sleeplike trance. Echoes of the day played through her thoughts—the kids in her class having fun as they honed their technique. Having a laugh with her new colleagues in the café . . .

She became aware of someone climbing into the pool at the opposite side, and wondered if Rowan, one of the other instructors and a new friend, had come to join her. But before she could open her eyes to find out, a familiar, pulse-kicking piney-fresh scent infused her nostrils.

Sam.

She peeked through one eye. It was indeed him, and his eyes were on her. *Oh fuck.*

Heat rose in her face as she remembered the mortification of their most recent encounter, when she'd been sent flying and had ended up in a heap on top of him. She had been acutely aware of the hardness of his body under hers and couldn't get out of there fast enough.

Although, in terms of silver linings, Maya was grateful that on this occasion, her body was fully submerged rather than being on display like when she'd walked in on him in the steam room.

He gave her a wry smile. "I considered turning around and leaving again when I saw you were in the pool."

She arched an eyebrow. "Oh yeah?"

He nodded. "But then I figured that we need to talk."

She sank even lower into the water. "I'm not sure I like the sound of that."

Sam let out a low chuckle that stirred something deep in her belly. "Don't worry. All I wanted to say was thanks."

Maya brought her head out of the water to assess him, like a suspicious meerkat popping up to nose at its surroundings. "Thanks? What for?"

He lifted his arms onto the sides of the pool, muscles on display as the bubbles washed over his chest, and she worked hard not to stare. "For arranging my car to get towed to the garage. You saved me a big headache."

She watched him for a moment, absorbing the sincerity in his voice.

It was difficult to work him out. They'd seemed to get along pretty well at the pub the other night, at least until he'd tried to compare her with bloody Cat. Not what she wanted to hear, especially after her last comparison with Catriona had left her unable to compete. Maya had never had an overt problem with self-confidence, but growing up, she had been aware that the definition of Scottish beauty didn't appear to include her tawny skin tone and dark features. There were never any women of a similar mixed-race heritage to her in magazines or on TV.

She'd never thought she'd have a chance with Sam. His previous girlfriends had fitted the kind of aesthetic that Cat exuded, with fair hair and skin. So when he'd reversed course with Maya and gone for Cat instead, she'd realized that she should've expected it.

She glanced down at the pool surface, sitting straighter so that her shoulders came above the waterline and trying to hide the blush that she could feel heating her cheeks.

"I know that your motivation was to get the sanctity of your commute back," he told her. "But I still appreciate it."

Maya looked up, and he was wearing a sort of wistful expression. "Well," she said reluctantly. "I suppose I kind of did it for you too." She paused. "A tiny bit."

He smiled, and she admired the way it lit up his amber eyes. "How tiny?"

She lifted her hand and indicated about a millimeter between thumb and forefinger, making him laugh. He had the most amazing, deep, rumbling laugh that made her soul hum. She realized that she'd missed hearing it over the past few days, since experiencing it multiple times that evening they'd shared in the pub.

"I'll take that," he told her with a smile.

Whenever they had a conversation rather than a mere exchange of snippy remarks, he came across as empathetic, like his sister. That was incongruent with the manner in which he'd shattered her heart when she was an impressionable teen. At the pub he'd listened and taken on board what she'd said about her dad, and Hana. Plus, he organized this charity race every year and undertook the community work that Liv had mentioned. There was also the naked-butler thing. She'd assumed it was an extension of his ego, but he was doing it in order to help someone else out.

All in all, despite their most recent tense exchange, he seemed more like the Sam she'd worked alongside and gotten cozy with. The one who'd paid attention to their conversations and had arranged a really thoughtful gift for her eighteenth birthday, rather than the man who'd sent her friend over to shatter her heart, then bedded that same friend, all in a single evening. Though she was unsure if it could be called bedded, when they'd done it in the foliage of the nook. Bushed? Shrubbed?

"You're welcome," she told him, opting to accept his sentiment as sincere. "Glad to help."

His demeanor seemed to relax, and she got the feeling he might have been building up to saying all of that. Deciding that this time it was her turn to make a swift exit, especially since she was struggling not to ogle him in the water, she pushed herself to standing. "I'll leave you in peace to enjoy the pool. See you later."

He nodded, his gaze trailing down her body for a second, and then on a slow blink coming back up to her face.

She climbed out, feeling as if his eyes were on her the whole way, but unable to bring herself to turn back around to check.

❄ ❄ ❄

AT THE END OF THE DAY, SAM WAS IN THE MAIN FOYER, WAITING for her. Ben had to stay late, and so they had already arranged she would take Sam home that day.

She closed the gap across the foyer. "Hi. All set?"

"Yep. Good to go," he said, holding the door for her. "I assume all the Christmas decor is your doing?" He gestured toward the bright red tinsel she'd painstakingly wrapped around the metal banisters leading up to the main entrance.

"Yep," she replied proudly. "The lack of festivity was giving me anxiety, so I raided the store cupboard." She had erected a tree in the café's alcove, another in the back foyer, and strung lights everywhere she could reach. Including around the fireplace—her pièce de résistance.

They headed out and across the car park. "I appreciate it," Sam told her with a smile. "As a fellow Christmas lights fan."

They climbed into her car, and she started it. Then she made to get back out to scrape the windshield. But he stopped her.

"No," he said, taking the scraper from her. "You stay in here. I'll do it." He climbed out, making a start on the job.

Taken aback by another display of good grace, she watched him for a second, until the buzz of her phone distracted her. A message from Hana flashed on the screen.

Have you apologized to Dad yet,
for going behind his back?

A cold, heavy weight settled into her stomach, and she dropped the phone into her drinks holder.

Going behind his back? It was hardly that. She'd agreed to help Ben because he'd needed her, and it's not as if she had anything else on just now. Christ, she hadn't even broken it to Dad or Hana, or Mum for that matter, that she hated accountancy. What would their reaction be if she did?

Maya blinked against the prickling sensation in her eyes. This was what she got for trying to confide in her big sister.

The door opened and Sam climbed in. "All done."

Maya rubbed her eyes, her throat constricting. She tried to keep her voice even but it came out wobbly. "Thank you."

Sam turned, his face falling. "Hey, what's wrong?"

Plastering on a smile, she avoided his eyes and infused a false brightness into her tone. "Nothing. Let's head out."

"Wait," Sam said, touching her hand. The brief sensation of his fingers on her skin sent heat coursing along her arm, and she hesitated, glancing up into his eyes.

"Why don't you take a minute before we go? You don't have to tell me what it is if you don't want to. We can just sit here for a bit." He gave her a smile. "I *would* offer to drive, but I'm not insured on your car, and if I bump it, I'm sure I'd go even further down in your estimation."

Maya managed a more genuine smile, the lump in her throat becoming a little less painful. "Okay. Thank you." She leaned back for a moment and became aware that, despite his assumptions, she *did* want to confide in him. Perhaps it was because she'd already told him a bit of the story, or maybe it was that, again, he was in the wrong place at the wrong time. "I got a message from Hana." She couldn't bring herself to voice what it said, so she gave him her phone, fiddling with her charm bracelet as he read it.

Sam frowned as he read. "That's a really shitty thing to say."

He glanced into her eyes, and she could tell he genuinely thought so, rather than just saying what she wanted to hear.

Maya shook her head. "I'm jealous of you."

He handed the phone over, still frowning. "Of me? Why?"

"Because you've got the most amazing sister in the world." Guilt needled her at saying that. She loved Hana, of course she did. But this constant battle over their father's affections was too much to bear. Especially when there *was* no battle. Hana was the outright winner, always achieving what Omar wanted. Plus, Maya had no interest in even being in the fight in the first place. She was content for Hana to be the winner, if it meant that she could be allowed to do what made her happy, and for her sister to back her up rather than sticking the knife in when Maya was vulnerable.

Sam gave her a gentle smile, leaning his head back against the headrest to study her and eliciting a soothing warmth in her heart. For a moment she was transported back to how attentive teenage Sam had been to her woes. Maya had also listened to what he'd divulged, about his dad. His opening up to her had felt like a special privilege, and she'd never told anybody what he'd said, about feeling rejected. Not even Liv. Although it was clearly a deep-rooted issue that they'd only begun to touch upon, when he'd then backtracked on wanting anything to do with her.

A thought niggled at the back of Maya's mind. Something to do with the Sam of the present day resembling the one whom she'd trusted with her innermost thoughts, the one whom she had been planning on a mutual exchange of intimacy with. For the first time since moving away to Glasgow, she questioned what had changed for him that night. Apart from their disagreement.

At the time she'd put it down to adolescent misjudgment, telling herself that boys had one-track minds and lied to get what they wanted. Sure, some of them did, and she had assumed she'd been duped by one of them. But this man, the one that she'd scratched the surface of over the past couple of weeks, didn't seem the sort to do that. And what would he have to gain now, by pretending to be something that he wasn't? Perhaps what he'd done back then was in some way down to his parental trauma. Maybe it'd made him do weird things. Not an excuse for his behavior, but an explanation at least.

"Liv is pretty amazing," Sam said, rubbing his fingers over his beard. "But don't tell her I said that. She'll get a big head."

Maya let out a laugh that sounded fairly close to being a sob.

"I'm sorry that Hana let you down." The look in his eyes was intense, and it made her feel like she'd hatched a swarm of butterflies in her stomach. "It's so much worse when it's family who does that," he continued.

Maya's mouth went dry. He was tuning in to her with empathy. The emotional intensity of the situation dialed up a few notches because not only did she know the history of his own experience with family betrayal, but he'd also given her his personal insights. "I'm sorry."

He frowned. "What for?"

She swallowed in an attempt to create an oasis in the Sahara desert of her mouth. "I'm being insensitive. About your dad."

He raised his eyebrows. "No, you're not. But thanks for thinking of it."

Maya managed a smile and a gulp of air.

Sam started to lift his hand, then hesitated, before continuing to reach over and take hers. "My dad buggered off without a backward glance. If I'd been given the chance to speak to him, tell him how he'd hurt me, and my mum and sister, then I would have. But we don't hear from him from one year to the next."

The touch of his hand and the power of his words were combining to do strange things to her insides. Strange, but not unpleasant.

"Hana is still in your life, and so is your dad. Maybe you should speak to them. Starting with Hana. Be honest about the way they make you feel."

She couldn't take her eyes off his. He was mesmerizing, and randomly it made her think of the chocolate fountain her friend had hired for a birthday party. Maya had sat staring at the liquid flow for about twenty minutes with a resulting warm and tingly sensation. Sam was certainly giving off a sweet, warm vibe at this precise moment. *And I remember him tasting warm and sweet too.*

She cleared her throat, giving his hand a squeeze and letting go. "Thank you. It's really kind of you to listen, and I appreciate your advice." She pulled away through the car park. "You always gave good advice."

Sam settled into his seat. "And you were always a good listener."

Smiling, she started down the hill road. "Even when I'd make a joke about everything?"

Sam laughed. "Yeah. I appreciated your jokes. No one else managed to lift me from my melancholy moods with a laugh like you did."

Maya's smile spread further as they continued their journey along the snowy mountain pass, her insides warm and fuzzy as if she'd been drinking straight out of that chocolate fountain.

✳ ✳ ✳

LIFTING THE PHONE FOR THE TENTH TIME, MAYA STARED AT IT. Calling Hana was even harder than she'd expected. After what Sam had said, she'd ruminated over it all evening, driven by the realization that she should be grateful for the ability to have it out with Hana when Sam and Liv had never gotten the opportunity with their dad. Plus, Elise would never have the chance to speak to Harry ever again. What if something happened to Hana, and Maya hadn't ever tried to salvage their relationship?

Her finger hovered over the call button, and then she set the phone down again. "Argh! Why am I the biggest wimp in the history of the universe?" She folded her arms. "I'm also talking to myself again."

Eyeing the phone, she decided that a text might be a better baby step. Normally when this sort of thing occurred, she'd leave it a couple of days, then message Hana a funny meme. Bypassing her humor defense mechanism and addressing the issue was uncharted territory.

After typing and deleting a number of times, she finally pressed send.

> I don't feel I should have to apologize for helping out Ben when he needed me. Nor for spending a little time, between jobs, doing something I love which benefits the children in Glenavie.

Her heart spasmed in hefty palpitations as she placed the phone onto her bedside table. When it didn't immediately buzz with a reply, she opened it again. The message was confirmed as read. *Oh my*

God, this is torture. Wishing she could become an ostrich and keep her head firmly buried in the sand, she lay back on the bed.

Still nothing. Should she text again and apologize for sending the message? *Stop wimping out. Hold firm.*

Another few minutes passed. Perhaps she should go and speak to her mum, ask her what to do. But she didn't want to upset her by letting her know that she was at odds with Hana. Liv would be out at her karate class, and there was no way Maya was going to bother Elise with this. As she sat up straight, a thought occurred to her. Maybe she could message Sam. She bit her thumbnail. Was that inappropriate? But he was the one who had suggested she contact Hana, so surely it wasn't?

After holding out a little longer, her heart couldn't take it anymore. Lifting the phone, she messaged him.

> Sorry to bother you. Need some advice. Texted Hana
> to say I don't think I have anything to apologize for.
> I can see she's read it but nothing back. Should I
> message again? Or call? Or take it back?

Setting the phone down again, she suffered a resurgence of palpitations after texting the last person in the world whom she thought she'd be going to for advice.

She waited a few minutes, but there was no reply from Sam either. Resisting the urge to check if it was marked as read, she placed the phone into her pocket and went downstairs to have a cup of tea with her mum. It was best not to get the phone out until it buzzed with a reply from somebody, otherwise she'd end up staring at it all evening.

Chapter
TEN

SAM RANG THE DOORBELL, WONDERING WHETHER MAYA HAD bitten the bullet and called Hana the previous evening.

The door opened and she stepped out, looking gorgeous in a woolly bobble hat with her dark locks flowing over her shoulders. Sam glanced away. He had no business thinking that she was gorgeous.

"Morning." She shut the door, and they crossed the driveway to her car. Her voice was extra bright—the way it sounded when she was trying to cover that she was upset about something.

Wondering how he could read the tone of her voice when they hardly knew each other, he climbed into the passenger seat. She must have spoken to Hana. That'd be why she sounded funny. "You okay? Did you speak to your sister?"

Maya shot him a frown as she started the car. "I texted her." She paused as she began to back out of the driveway. "Didn't you get my message?"

Sam sat straighter. "You messaged me?"

She continued to frown as they drove through the estate. "Yeah. To ask your advice about it."

Shaking his head, he took out his phone. One thing was for sure. If Maya had asked for his advice, he would've given it, no questions asked. Although he didn't want to examine the reasons why he felt so adamant about that.

He opened his messages, but there was nothing from Maya. "It's not here. Maybe it didn't send?"

Maya stopped at a junction and pulled hers out. She speedily flicked through it and passed it over. Sure enough, the message was marked as delivered on her phone. He read it quickly. "That's weird. Maybe it's still bouncing around the satellites."

Maya laughed, continuing their journey. "Yeah. It'll probably arrive at Christmas. *Next* year."

He smiled as he placed her phone down. "What happened in the end?"

"Nothing." She sighed. "Ghosted. Now what do I do?"

Feeling privileged that she was asking his opinion on the matter, Sam thought for a moment. It was clearly difficult for her to get involved in any sort of conflict. But she was going to worry about it unless she did. "Why don't you set a time limit on it? If she hasn't replied by a certain point, then you contact her again."

Maya nodded. "Text, or call?"

"Calling is more intimidating, but sometimes it's easier to get stuff off your chest that way. Big conversations get kind of stilted via text."

She was nodding, an intense expression on her face. He remembered that look from when they were younger. It was how he'd known that she was really tuning in to what he was saying, concentrating hard and not making any of her usual quips. At the time, he'd been either giving her advice, or confiding in her about his dad. At that point it had been eighteen months since his father's disappearing act, and it all still felt very raw. Maya had been a natural confidante, not only because they'd gotten on so well, but because she'd already known the intricacies of the story from Liv.

She glanced over. "Thank you. I appreciate it."

Sam smiled, warmth infusing him. "Sorry your message didn't get through. I would've answered if it had."

Maya returned his smile. "No worries. It's something for you to look forward to when it arrives. Next Christmas." She gave him a wink that set his skin on fire. "Hey, did you hear when your car might come back?"

"Next week hopefully," Sam said with a weird mix of relief and disappointment. "Only thing is I've got another butler gig this weekend. I'll need to see if I can borrow Cat's car."

"How will you do that, if she doesn't know about the job?"

He let out a breath. "Not sure about that yet."

"Maybe you can borrow Liv's car. I know you don't want to tell anyone what the dosh is for, but I'm sure she'd understand, whatever it is. Plus, she's a good secret keeper." She smiled. "*Almost* as good as you."

Sam laughed. "She's second to me in everything, including age, because I popped out three minutes before her." He ran a hand through his hair. "I'd like to tell her, but the person in question wouldn't want me to. So . . ."

Maya nodded. "I understand."

That statement made him warm and fuzzy. Enough to go out on a limb. "Listen. You remember how you asked me to tell you if I had any info about Ben and his gray-hair-inducing stress levels?"

"Yeah. What's the lowdown?"

"I've actually known about this for a week or so, but I wasn't sure whether to say anything." He paused.

"Come on, Holland. Spit it out."

Sam smiled, even though talking about the tax thing gave him palpitations. Goodness knows what it was doing to Ben's ticker. "Ben thinks there's been a miscalculation on the tax return, but the accountants are ghosting him whenever he contacts them. He's worried that there won't be enough funds to pay the tax bill, if it's heftier than anticipated."

Maya frowned. "No wonder he's stressed. Why didn't he come to me?"

"I'm not sure. I haven't spoken to him about getting you involved, I didn't want to put you in a difficult position."

She shook her head. "It's an easy position. I'm going to look at the accounts, and sort it out for him."

He realized that he trusted Maya to do exactly that. And maybe he was beginning to trust her beyond her accounting skills. "You've got no idea how relieved I am to hear you say that."

She gave him a two-fingered salute as they entered the car park. "No problem, Holland. I'm the most boring superhero in the world. Superaccountant."

Sam laughed. "I don't think I could ever describe you as boring."

Maya shot him a smile that gave him an electric feeling.

"Oh, I nearly forgot," she said, turning to him as she parked.

Why are her eyes so amazing?

"Big Boss Ben wants me to help you with your sled race thingy." She paused, seeming to assess his reaction, and continuing when he smiled. "As long as that's okay. Don't wanna steal your thunder with my accounting superpowers." She gave him another one of those winks, and Sam wondered how it was possible for a jokey gesture to borderline turn him on.

Pushing aside his natural instinct to shoulder the burden

alone because he liked the warm feeling that Maya's assistance now seemed to give him, he nodded. "That would be awesome. If you can spare the time." He unbuckled and they both climbed out of the car.

"Absolutely," Maya replied as they crossed the car park. "I'm technically unemployed, so I've all the time in the world."

** ** **

BEN REACTED AS PREDICTED WHEN SAM TOLD HIM THAT MAYA wanted to look over the accounts. The weight had visibly risen from his shoulders and drifted off into the stratosphere. When Sam had queried why he hadn't come out and asked Maya himself, Ben said he didn't want to overstep when he'd practically twisted her arm to come and work with them already.

Sam came off the slopes, following his class toward the terrace that led into the building. He took a glance toward the baby slope, as was now customary for him at the end of the day. He'd stopped kidding himself that it was to check how his old class was getting on, when it was really because he wanted to get an eyeful of their instructor. They were finishing and he paused to watch.

One of the kids waved at him—Oliver. Sam waved back, wondering if the kid had ever gotten to eat that pizza he'd been craving. Maya turned her head to see whom Oliver was waving at and clocked Sam. She said something to her class and then gestured for him to come over.

"Hey," Maya said as he approached. "The kids here think they can direct us against each other in a pizza and chips race." The children started cheering, and Maya had to quieten them down.

Sam cast his eyes around the group and came to rest on Maya, smiling. "How would this race work?"

Maya pointed at one of the children. "Emily and her team will direct me, and Oliver and his team will direct you. We have to do what they say—if your team captain shouts *pizza*, then you snowplow, and if they shout *chips*, then it's straight skis." She flashed him a grin. "What say you, Samuel Leonard Holland?"

Oliver and his team started laughing. "Your middle name's Leonard!"

Sam raised his eyebrow at Maya, a smile tugging at his mouth. "Below the belt, Bashir."

She shrugged, tapping the side of her nose. "I'm psyching you out. *Tactics.*"

Sam laughed. "I'm not sure I want to be on the receiving end of your tactics."

"Too late." Maya put her thumb on the end of her nose and wiggled her fingers at him, inducing more laughter from the children. "Right! Stay in your two groups. Captains shout the instructions and do the mime for pizza, or chips. Come on, Leonard." Maya turned and started up the baby slope, skis over her shoulder, before he could respond.

"Hey!" He hurried as much as he could in his cumbersome ski boots and caught her. "You're in for it, Bashir."

She laughed. "That's what you think. Okay, this is a good spot."

They clipped into their skis and Sam eyed her, trying to stop thinking about how good she looked, even layered in skiwear. He attempted to avoid the memory of how good she looked in a swimsuit too, and failed.

She was grinning widely, which made him suspicious. "What've you got up your sleeve?" he asked.

She put on a singsong voice. "Wouldn't you like to know."

Gesturing down the slope, she signaled to the captains to begin their instructions. Emily shouted *chips* and Oliver called *pizza*, and Sam immediately caught on to what was happening. Yelling *chips* over and over, Emily and her team waved their hands in the air as Maya shot ahead, her hair streaming behind her. Oliver and his team kept shouting *pizza* and collapsing with laughter as Sam trailed behind, forced to keep the brakes on by his own "team."

Finally, he came to a stop in front of Maya, who was standing watching him with her arms folded.

He flashed her a smile. "Cheat."

"I don't know *what* you mean." She tossed her hair over her shoulder as the kids chattered in excitement. "Class dismissed! See you next time."

They dispersed under Maya's watchful eye. She leaned toward him. "Thanks for playing along."

He nudged her arm. "I didn't exactly have the lowdown before the game started."

She gave him a smile, pushing up his heart rate. "Come on. You wouldn't have wanted to spoil the kids' fun, would you?"

Returning her expression, he shook his head. "The kids' fun, or yours?"

She waved her hand. "To-may-to, to-mah-to."

Sam laughed. "Just you wait. When you least expect it, revenge is mine."

Maya joined in laughing with him, and for a minute, Sam forgot that they'd ever been at loggerheads.

They started to walk toward the center, skis over their shoulders, and he decided to ask her yet another favor. He was getting used to this alien territory of asking others for help rather than shouldering everything himself. Or perhaps, he was only used to it with Maya. "Would it be okay if we make a stop on the way home? I need to drop something off at Arran's. I meant to do it last week, but the car's been dead and he lives a little way out of town, between here and Glenavie."

"Sure," Maya said. "It'd be nice to see him. Do you need to do anything else before we leave, or can we get changed and go?"

"I'm all set."

"Excellent. See you in five, Leonard." She gave him a wave as she headed for the women's changing rooms.

❄ ❄ ❄

WEAVING THEIR WAY DOWN THE MOUNTAIN ROAD, SAM HAD TO hold his sides because Maya was about to split them with laughter. "Oh my God! I'd nearly forgotten that story."

Maya held one hand in the air as she drove. "How could you forget? The guy was butt naked on skis!"

Sam rubbed his eyes. Reminiscing about what went down when they were teens on the slopes was a tonic. He couldn't detect that tension in his shoulders anymore, plus the perpetual heaviness in his stomach had dissipated since Maya had gotten on the case with the accounts.

If he were honest with himself, he couldn't even remember the last time Cat and he had laughed together.

Smiling, Maya shook her head. "I love being back here."

He studied the contented look on her face, his heart warming in response. "In Glenavie, or at the resort?"

"Both." She glanced over. "Triple B seemed pleased when I saw him earlier. He's sending me the accounts later on."

"Thanks so much for doing that," Sam replied, eyeing her. "I know it's for Ben's benefit and not mine, but I really am grateful."

"No problem, Sammy boy. It's for both of you, and everyone at the resort of course. Is it a right or a left here?"

"Right." There was no point in denying that he liked the idea of her wanting to do things for him.

"Is this the house that Arran shared with his ex?" Maya asked as they drew nearer to their destination.

"No. They had to sell so he could get a smaller place. He's converted the garage into an art studio."

"That sounds cool." Her eyes widened. "Hey, do you think he'd mind if I came in for a look?"

"I'm sure he'd love it."

Discussing his friends with enthusiasm was another thing lacking in his relationship with Cat. Sam was so proud of Arran, but whenever he spoke to Catriona about it, she made her uninterest clear. Sam rubbed his temple. Thinking about the faults in his relationship was unfair on Cat.

Maya maneuvered the final turn, and they arrived at Arran's place, at the end of a small cul-de-sac. They climbed out and headed to the front door, where Sam rang the doorbell.

He glanced at Maya as she took off her hat and pulled her hair into a ponytail. Her earrings caught his attention. One was a tiny crescent moon and the other a star. "Nice earrings."

Maya fingered them both. "Thanks."

"Very you," he said softly. He held her gaze as she smiled shyly, color rising in her cheeks.

The door opened and Arran answered. "Hey, Sam. Maya—long time no see." He gave each of them a hug as they entered the house.

Sam had messaged Arran before they'd set off to say that Maya was giving him a lift over. He'd already told Arran about Maya's return and had a feeling he'd read something into it, being the only friend in whom Sam had confided about their past. Sam had informed him that nothing was going on except some car sharing. He'd also explained to Arran that he didn't even like Maya and the feeling was more than mutual; however, Sam was seriously doubting himself, on both those counts.

Arran took them along the hallway into the kitchen and offered them a hot drink, which they accepted.

Sam took a seat at the breakfast bar with Maya next to him. "How're things in the studio?"

"Good," Arran said. "I'm having a go at a self-portrait. If it's passable, I might start painting other people."

Sam rolled his eyes. "*Passable*? Your stuff is amazing."

Arran smiled and shrugged. He handed them their mugs and lifted his own.

Sam sipped his tea. "Can we show Maya?"

Arran nodded. "Sure. Walk this way."

They stood and followed him out into the hallway, then took a door off it into the converted garage. There was a large window facing the street, and the walls were lined with canvases. Maya walked over to the stunning landscapes that were on display, holding her mug. "My goodness. These are spectacular."

"Right?" Sam drew level with her, her reaction creating a warm happiness within him. "That's what I keep telling him."

Maya moved on to the next one, and he followed.

"Does Liv know about this?" she asked. "She'd love it. You know how she likes to promote small businesses."

Arran smiled. "Yeah, she's one of my biggest supporters, aside from her darling brother here."

Maya smiled, and seemed to shake her head slightly.

Sam walked across the room to check out Arran's self-portrait. As expected, it was brilliant. He'd captured his handsome features, copper-brown skin and dark coiled hair perfectly. "Mate. This is fantastic."

Maya came to stand next to him. "Oh my God, Arran. This is perfect."

Arran rubbed the back of his neck. "Thank you."

Maya's mouth was open as she studied it. "Where do you advertise yourself?"

"The usual. Website, Facebook, Twitter, Insta. Local flyers."

Maya nodded, casting her gaze right around the room.

Sam cleared his throat. "I'm just going to borrow Arran for a sec in private, if you want to carry on checking out his stuff."

"Is that okay?" Maya asked Arran.

"Absolutely," he replied.

Sam led Arran out of the room, and they went back into the kitchen. "Here you go. I had a bit more spare cash lying about. A bonus from Ben." He handed over his latest lot of butler money, but Arran hesitated.

"I dunno, man. You've given me loads already, and I feel guilty for ever telling you I was turned down for that bank loan."

Sam pressed it into his palm. "You need those new paints. Get them with this. What else do you need?"

Arran blinked. "Just that work light. But I can manage, honestly."

Sam shook his head. "I'll get you the dosh for the light. Then we're quits." He smiled. "I won't take no for an answer."

Arran looked at the cash in his hand for a second, then set his drink down to reach out and hug Sam. "I appreciate this. Might even be close to admitting that you're not a complete tosser."

The comfort of Arran's hug infused his soul, and Sam laughed as he released him. "Wow. Praise indeed."

Arran pocketed the money. "You're getting all this back, as soon as I'm on my feet." He shot Sam a smile. "By the way, what's the deal with Maya? You guys sure don't look like people who hate each other."

Sam glanced at the tiled floor. "I think we've found some common ground." He met Arran's eyes. "She's a lot more fun than I remember. And friendlier. And kinder."

Arran raised his eyebrows. "Basically, all the things you thought she was, before she said that she'd never be interested in an unambitious ski instructor who didn't want to leave Glenavie?"

"Yeah, pretty much," Sam muttered. The words still stung. Even from someone else's mouth.

Arran shook his head. "It was a bit weird, though."

Sam sipped his tea in an attempt to take away the bad taste. "What was?"

"It just . . . didn't seem like something Maya would say."

Sam shrugged, setting down his mug and turning to head back to the studio because talking about this still hurt. "Well, she did. Her actual words were that she was going to study accountancy, because ski instructing wasn't a real job. But the past is the past." Something niggled at the back of his mind as he walked along the hallway, but he ignored it, keen not to go over painful memories.

He entered the studio, followed by Arran. "All set, Maya?"

"Yeah," she said, seeming distracted by the paintings. She pointed at one of the landscapes. "I like this one best."

His heart rate stepped up a notch. She'd singled out his favorite. He would've bought it by now if he'd had enough cash. There was no way in hell he'd let Arran give it to him for mates' rates. "I love that one."

Maya turned to meet his eyes. "You do?"

Sam nodded. "I know the spot it was painted from. I took a photo of it for Arran because it's my favorite view in Glenavie."

She looked back at the painting, smiling.

He glanced across the room at where Arran was tidying some equipment, then shifted closer to Maya. "I'm not surprised you like it. It is a night scene after all. The moon and stars are really clear."

As she turned to face him, something was shining in her liquid brown eyes. It made his breath catch.

She cleared her throat. "I'd love to see the real view. If you wouldn't mind pointing it out sometime."

Sam's mouth went dry, and he swallowed. "Sure."

"Oh," Arran said loudly, crossing the room to his desk. "I nearly forgot." He made a show of opening a drawer and lifting a ledger, then pulled out the money Sam had just handed over.

Sam frowned. *What's he doing?*

Arran opened the book and picked up a pen. "I need to make note of this cash that Sam's given me. I like to keep track of it all so I know exactly how much I'm indebted to him. Can't have him lording it over me for too long." He flashed them a smile and scribbled in the ledger.

Maya lifted her gaze to Sam's and raised her eyebrows.

Sam didn't know how to react, so he just shrugged. "Okay, let's get going." He ran a hand through his hair. "I don't want to hold up my chauffeur for longer than necessary."

He led them out of the studio, and Maya nudged his arm as they moved down the hallway. "Chauffeur, eh? I hope this means you'll be providing me with one of those jaunty little caps. And some aviator shades."

"I'll get you some for Christmas," Sam replied, shooting her a grin. "It'll be a good look for you."

They left the house, and Sam gave Arran a quizzical expression as he hugged him goodbye. Arran winked in response, waving as they climbed into the car.

Maya glanced over as she pulled away down the road. "What was that flashing the cash and writing in the ledger all about?"

Sam shook his head, tapping out a text to Arran asking that very question. "It's weird, because he told me not to tell anyone that I was lending to him."

"I'm assuming this is where your butlering dosh has been going?"

"That's right. Though I didn't tell him I was doing the butlering. He wouldn't accept the money if he knew I'd taken on a second job for it. Plus, the fewer people that know the better."

"Because of Cat?" Her voice always sounded a little flat whenever she said Cat's name.

"Yeah. Nico knows, and you. No one else, because I figure then there's more chance of it getting back to her. But also because I'd feel guilty if too many people knew when she doesn't."

Maya was silent for a moment, and Sam's phone buzzed with a message from Arran.

> I'm trying to big you up, pal. Maybe she's
> changed her mind about ditching you.
> I'm doing what I can to help my buddy.

Sam put the phone away. It didn't feel right to reply that Maya had made her feelings clear in the past, when the woman was sitting right next to him. He'd speak to Arran about it later.

"What're you going to do about your butler gig at the weekend?" Maya asked. "Have you got transport?"

Sam rubbed his neck. "Not yet. I looked at the bus route through that way but it'd mean either getting there two hours early or two hours late."

Maya frowned. "No other cars to borrow?"

"I'm not insured on anyone else's." He shook his head. "And there's no way I'd try to get insured on Nico's. It'd cost a fortune with his flash Porsche."

"How much longer do you need to keep doing it?"

"Probably just a couple more gigs, to get Arran this light he needs for the studio. Then he should be set. And after that, I'll be getting my pay rise anyway."

She was silent for a second. "I'll drive you."

At first, he didn't know what to say. He waited for the familiar sick feeling to surface, the one he detected whenever he felt inadequate. But it didn't. "I can't ask you to do that."

"Aha, well. You're not asking, are you? I'm *offering*." She tapped the side of her nose. "Big difference, pal."

An infusion of warmth filled his chest. "You've already done a lot for me. I know I came across badly before, but I really am grateful that you arranged for my car to be towed, and I'll pay you back whatever I owe for that."

"Don't sweat it. There's no rush. To be honest I don't even want the money back anyway." She abruptly stopped talking, shooting him a glance.

She's worried I'm going to react negatively. It occurred to him that his previous reaction might've come across as his being a dick about a woman providing assistance. But that hadn't been why his pride was hurt. It was because it was *this* woman, the one who had thought him not good enough, and his concern had been that he'd been coming off as confirming his inadequacy.

However, she hadn't behaved as if she looked down on him,

more like she wanted to help a friend. And yet they weren't even friends. *Although, the past couple of days, it's felt like we are.* "If you give me a lift at the weekend, then I'm definitely giving you fuel money. And I'm buying you a drink. Maybe at the after event for the sled race?"

Maya held her hand out as she drove. "You drive a hard bargain."

Sam took her hand in a quick shake. Even that brief touch sent a ripple of flame over his skin. Distracted for a moment, he realized too late that they'd missed the turnoff for her parents' and were on their way to his house. The warmth from Maya's touch turned icy. "Just drop me here. I don't want you going farther out of your way."

"I'll take you home, we're only two minutes away."

Sam's pulse spiked. "Here's fine. There won't be anywhere to stop outside my place. The street gets busy."

She glanced over, then began to maneuver to pull in, and he could tell that she knew the real reason. If Cat saw Maya dropping him off, it'd put her in a bad mood all night. It had been out of sight, out of mind to an extent, if Sam walked to Maya's and back again.

They came to a stop and he climbed out, sticking his head back through the door. "Thanks again for helping with my transport woes."

"No problem. Thanks for your sibling-related advice."

He gave her a wave. "Let me know how it goes."

Closing the car door, he headed along the road, giving her another wave as she pulled away, and already looking forward to seeing her again.

"Cat?" he called as he entered the house. "You home?" There was no answer. Sam took off his outerwear and dropped his phone and keys onto the kitchen table, before heading into the downstairs cloakroom. As he washed up, he tried to fathom how he felt about Maya, but it was too complicated. In any case, it didn't matter what his feelings were, she wasn't interested, and moreover, he had a girlfriend. Thinking about other women wasn't on.

Opening the cloakroom door, he glanced into the kitchen. Cat was at the table, quickly putting down his phone. He frowned, walking into the room. "Hey. I didn't realize you were in."

Cat stood, flashing him a bright smile. "I was upstairs." She gave him a big hug. "How was your day?"

"Fine, thanks." He glanced at the table. "Were you looking through my phone?"

She made a dismissive noise. "Of course not."

"Why did you have it in your hand just now?" he asked, studying her.

Cat wandered into the kitchen. "I thought it was mine, that's all. Then I lifted it and saw your screen saver of the ski slope and realized. What do you want for dinner?"

Her explanation didn't quite hit the mark, and it bothered him. He tried to fathom how he might get the real answer out of her, but he was acutely aware that she was in a good mood, and pushing her on this kind of stuff would end up in a blowout. So he resigned himself to leave it for now, and helped her prepare dinner.

Chapter
ELEVEN

MAYA GAVE HERSELF A PEP TALK. "COME ON, MAYA. PRESS THE call button. It's only your sister." She nearly chickened out, thinking that she might text instead. But then she remembered Sam's advice—big conversations were best done verbally. She pressed call and it rang out. Just as she was trying to decide whether to leave a message, Hana answered, her voice flat.

Maya tried to infuse extra light into her voice. "All right, sis? What's going down in England-shire?"

Hana sighed. "You know. Work, bills. The usual."

There was a few seconds' silence, and Maya's heart rate stepped up. This was already awful. No wonder she normally shied away from this sort of crap. "You don't sound yourself."

"I'm really stressed, Maya. You wouldn't understand."

A cold heaviness entered her stomach. *Wouldn't understand? I've just lost my job and my relationship and I'm back home living with our parents, one of whom thinks I'm the biggest loser out there.*

"That's a little unfair." Maya let out a breath. That statement had taken all of her courage, and she had about as much as the cowardly lion to begin with.

"I don't have time to talk about it now. I'll need to call you back."

Relief that this conversation would soon be over mixed with the disappointment that the tension was going to be prolonged left Maya feeling hollow. "Okay."

They ended the call, and she fell back onto her bed. "Ugh. Speaking to people *sucks*."

Deciding to go and off-load to Liv, Maya grabbed her bag and headed down the stairs.

❄ ❄ ❄

LIV APPROACHED AROUND THE CORNER, AND MAYA GOT OUT OF her car. Liv did a double take. "Miss Maya. Are you stalking me?"

"Yep. I've been tailing you for days. You need to stop frequenting such dodgy establishments."

Liv smiled. "I assume you're coming in?"

"Please." She followed Liv into her house. "How was nursery school today?"

"Great. Apart from one of the boys getting his foot stuck down the toilet and we had to call the fire brigade."

Maya had to stand still for a moment as she laughed. "Why did he have his foot in the bog?"

Liv rolled her eyes. "Goodness knows. But he's fine now."

Taking off her jacket as they entered the kitchen, Maya placed it onto the back of a chair. "Not having to walk around with a toilet on one's foot does make for a more successful life."

"Indeed," Liv replied, putting the kettle on. "For one thing, it'd be awfully unbalanced."

Maya fetched out a couple of mugs. "I suppose plan B could have been to put a toilet on his other foot. Create some symmetry."

Liv laughed as she clearly imagined the boy waddling along the street with a lavatory attached to each leg.

They took their drinks to the table, where Liv shot Maya a look. "Spill it."

Maya paused. "What, the tea?"

"Yeah. Well, no. Not literally. Spill what's on your mind."

Maya blew her fringe out of her eyes. "I called Hana."

Liv paused, mug en route to her mouth. "And?"

Shrugging, Maya lifted her cup. "And nothing. She fobbed me off, didn't even mention the message. Said she was stressed."

Liv frowned. "That's a shame. She's dragging it out."

"I know." Maya sipped her tea. "I don't like having proper conversations. I don't want to do it anymore." Every time she decided that confronting people was the answer, this sort of thing happened. Like when she'd gone back to the Tavern that night and witnessed the soul-raking sight of the guy she had been in love with kissing her close friend. Avoiding conflict was a much happier option.

"Maybe give her a bit more time, then contact her again."

"I'll see."

Maya eyed Liv. She'd been thinking a lot about Sam, especially since that rigmarole the previous evening whereby he'd created an excuse to get dropped off out of Cat's sight. He clearly didn't want Cat seeing her, which was weird. Cat knew Maya was giving him a lift, and in any case, why would she mind? Sure, there was no love lost between the two of them, but it wasn't relevant. Plus it was strange that he was keeping secrets from his girlfriend about his other job. It's not like he was a spy or a hit man.

Maya cleared her throat. "Sam and I stopped by Arran's on the way home last night."

Liv's eyes lit up as bright as the neighborhood houses all decked out for the holiday. "You did?"

Maya smiled, taking in that reaction. "Yeah. His studio's fantastic."

Her eyes were infused with a definite sparkle. "I know, right? I love his stuff, he's so talented."

Maya sipped her tea, feigning nonchalance. "He's handsome, isn't he?"

Liv smiled. "Yeah."

Maya gave her a nudge. "You've still got a thing for him."

Liv pushed her glasses up her nose. "Maybe I still like him. But he was always with Jess, and now they've split but it's left him kind of broken and he doesn't seem interested." She paused. "I'm not sure if he's uninterested in relationships in general, or just uninterested in *me*."

Maya shook her head. "It can't be that he's not interested in you. You're hot AF."

Liv smiled, and sipped her tea, avoiding Maya's gaze. "How's that brother of mine doing?"

"Funny you should ask," Maya said, setting down her cup and eliciting raised eyebrows from Liv. Maya was aware that whenever Liv mentioned Sam, she normally wouldn't engage. But things were changing. "What's the deal with him and Cat? I've worked out that he doesn't want me picking him or dropping him off from home because he doesn't want her to see. And their relationship seems odd . . ." Pausing, she thought for a moment. She didn't want to break Sam's confidence about the butler job. "Like he keeps things from her. Because he's afraid of her reaction."

Liv paused, her eyes widening. Then she clattered her cup onto the table and leaned in. "I'm so glad you said that. Yes. That's them all over. The whole relationship is up and down like a journey over the Rockies, and Cat's the driver."

Maya took a breath, absorbing the fast rate of Liv's speech. Liv was clearly relieved to be speaking about this, and with a guilty jolt, Maya realized that Liv must have been trying to get this off her chest on numerous occasions in the past. But Maya would merely make a couple of half-hearted interested noises and then change the subject—all because of her stupid pride and anger that Sam had abandoned her in favor of Cat. *What a shitty friend I've been.* "Go on."

"She manipulates him into doing what she wants and gaslights him if he notices anything," Liv continued, gripping her mug. "She's really selfish and self-absorbed, but it's as if he's blind to it. I think she's a narcissist."

Maya raised her eyebrows, her pulse picking up. "Have you said anything?"

Liv shook her head. "Not in years. I learned my lesson back when I sat him down and tried to tell him how it was from the outside looking in, but he wouldn't have it. He didn't speak to me for a week. Then I realized I had to keep quiet or it might come between us, and then there'd be no voice of reason at all in his ear." Liv's eyes were shining, and Maya felt worse than ever that she hadn't let her talk about it before.

Reaching over, she squeezed Liv's hand. "What did you say?"

Liv took a breath. "That it was an unhealthy relationship. I explained that he didn't have a frame of reference and that's why he perhaps couldn't see it, because they've been together since they were eighteen."

Maya nodded. Whatever had happened between her and Sam

in the past didn't matter anymore. And as much as she'd wanted him to suffer in his relationship with Cat at the time, she didn't feel that way any longer. Weirdly, she just wanted him to be happy. "Is there anything I can do to help?"

Liv shook her head. "All any of us can do is support him. Offer a sympathetic ear. Then hopefully, one day, he'll see the light."

❄   ❄   ❄

WAITING ROUND THE CORNER FROM SAM'S HOUSE, MAYA FELT LIKE she was in a spy movie. She scooted down in her seat, watching the odd person walk past and pretending that she was tailing them. "The name's Bond. Maya Bond. I'm a rubbish spy who tells the enemy their full name the very instant she meets them."

The passenger door opened just as she finished her sentence and Sam shot her a bemused smile. "What're you doing?"

She scrambled to sit straight. "Nothing. Definitely not pretending to be a spy."

He climbed in with a laugh. "Who're you spying on?"

Maya narrowed her eyes and gestured along the street. "See the guy in the overcoat? Suspicious. What's he got under there?"

Sam leaned over, and she held her breath because he always smelled so good and it made certain areas a bit tingly.

"Probably a huge woolly jumper." He leaned back, buckling in. "On account that it's like, minus five outside."

Maya shot him a look. "Party pooper." She started the engine as he flashed her a grin. "Right. Stick the address in the satnav, old boy, and let's be on our way." She eyed him with a raised brow as he typed it in. "Are you wearing that tiny apron under your jeans?"

Sam stopped typing in order to laugh. "Stop imagining what I've got on under my clothes, you perv."

Maya pulled away with a shrug. "It's not my fault that you

assaulted my eyeballs when I was innocently sitting on my friend's sofa the other week."

He was smiling. "Many apologies for such a terrible sensory experience."

With a sigh, she placed the back of her hand onto her forehead. "Sadly, I cannot unsee what I have seen." She made the sign of the cross, and Sam laughed hard. The ability to elicit that response from him was something she didn't want to relinquish. Especially when, from what Liv had said, laughs sounded a bit sparse in his relationship with Cat. Maya just wished she didn't find him so attractive because it was a lost cause. Lost at sea, many years ago, never to be seen again. And probably scoffed by Moby Dick for good measure.

Seeing him in his naked-butler outfit (if you could call a tiny apron an "outfit") certainly had not been a "terrible sensory experience." Plus, despite the associated embarrassment, she'd enjoyed seeing the spectacle of him another couple of times since then— courtesy of the excellent hydrotherapy-spa suite. *God bless Ben.*

She shot Sam a side glance. He was taking out a bottle of water and starting to sip it. Suppressing a grin, she kept her eyes forward. "Have you got your balls?"

He coughed on the water, nearly spitting it out in the process. "*What?*"

"You know," she said, staring ahead and keeping a straight face. "The shiny little ones I gave you to put on your apron."

Sam raised his eyebrows. "The *baubles* you mean?"

She shrugged. "Balls. Baubles. Same diff."

He laughed. "I've got them, thanks. They're a nice festive touch."

"As long as no one's *literally* touching," Maya waggled her eyebrows at him.

He shook his head, smiling. "It happens."

"Does it?" Maya screwed her face up. "Ew."

"Hey," he said, arching a brow. "The idea of touching me can't be *that* gross."

Shoving aside that idea before she got overexcited, Maya shook her head. "I don't mean *that*. I mean it's out of order for random women to touch you."

"Ah, okay. I don't need to be affronted." He settled back into his seat. "Don't worry, it's usually only a pinch on the bum, and at least tonight I've got a bodyguard with me. Did you bring your super-hero outfit?"

"In the back," she replied without missing a beat. "Super-accountant, that's me. If there's any trouble, just call and I'll come running in with some mental arithmetic that'll make their eye-balls spin."

He chuckled, and even that platonic response made her heart swell and skin come alive with delicious sensitivity.

They continued to chat through the entire journey, and every time Maya glanced over, his gaze was already on her, a smile warming his face and his amber eyes sparkling like the rose-gold lights on the big house on the corner.

✳ ✳ ✳

IT DIDN'T TAKE LONG BEFORE THEY WERE PULLING UP OUTSIDE the address in question, and Maya peered through the windshield. "I'm going to take a little drive so the car doesn't cool down too quickly, then I'll come back here to wait for you."

Sam nodded, putting on his jacket. "Won't you get bored?"

"Nah. I've got a book with me. My to-be-read pile is higher than the levels of my dad's disappointment."

Sam paused. "Did Hana call back?"

Her heart sank at the sound of her sister's name. "Nope."

"Bummer. And what about Dr. B? Have you spoken to him?"

Maya grimaced, closed her eyes, and remained silent.

Sam nudged her arm. "Talk to him. It won't be as bad as you think."

Maya opened one eye to look at him. "Yes. It will." *He should know that, after the last time he encouraged me to speak to Dad. But then I suppose I never got a chance to explain how it went.* "I'm not speaking to anyone about my authentic feelings ever again."

He was giving her his soft "I'm listening" smile, and it made her heart do a weird melty thing.

"Anyway, you'd better get in there, or hordes of women will be disappointed," she said, averting her gaze.

He made to exit the vehicle.

"Wait."

He turned back, and Maya grinned. "Tell them to keep the curtains open so I can get an eyeful."

Sam laughed and climbed out, then stuck his head back in and said, "Perv," before shutting the door.

She stuck her tongue out at him as he walked off, then blew him a kiss. He pretended to catch it and put it in the pocket of his parka, a smile playing at the corner of his mouth.

❄ ❄ ❄

THERE WAS MOVEMENT IN HER PERIPHERAL VISION, AND AS SHE raised her gaze, Sam appeared from the house, making his way toward the car.

He climbed in and Maya gave him a smile. "How did it go?"

Sam huffed out a breath as he buckled his seat belt. "I nearly called you for backup. The Christmas spirit possessed some of them a little too heavily."

"Uh-oh," Maya said, starting the engine. "It's a dangerous profession."

"You can say that again."

Glancing over as she pulled away, she shot him a grin. "Sam L. Holland. Ski instructor by day, naked butler by night."

Shaking his head, he gave her a smile. "I still need to get you back for outing my middle name to your class."

"You'll never get me. I'm too wily," Maya replied, guiding them onto the country road toward Glenavie.

"Just you wait. When you least expect it, that's when I'll strike." He yawned, rubbing his eyes.

Maya eyed him for a second, remembering what Liv had said about his taking on too much and how she worried he was tired and stressed. And Liv didn't even know about this second job.

Thinking of Arran and his studio plus his little boy, Maya pondered that Sam always seemed to take on everyone else's burden. He had to be the problem solver, the fixer for those around him. "Close your eyes and have a rest."

"That'd be rude," he replied, settling back into his seat. "I can't leave my chauffeur with no chat."

Maya smiled. "It's fine. I endured your rubbish chat all the way here, so it'll be a delight to have some peace on the way home."

"Hey," Sam said, grinning. "How dare you. There was a house full of women tonight who *loved* my banter."

"Yeah, right," Maya said, sniggering. "*That's* not what they loved."

They both laughed, though Sam's ended up in another yawn.

"Seriously," Maya said. "Get some sleep. I really don't mind."

"Maybe just for a second." He closed his eyes.

After a few minutes, Maya snuck a glance at him and could tell he'd dropped off. She watched the road, mindful to avoid any pot-holes so as not to disturb her sleeping passenger.

Sleeping beauty.

The evening shadows cast definition over his cheekbones and accentuated the duskiness of his beard, a contrast to his fair skin. His lips were full and soft looking. Though Maya knew they were also soft *feeling*, because she'd experienced them up close in the past.

Burning the candle at both ends was doing him no good. But it wasn't her place to comment; they hardly knew each other. And a short time ago, they hadn't even been friends. It struck her how quickly, and deeply, they'd reconnected. And that was despite more than one false start.

Their bond of friendship might even be deepening past what it had been as teenagers. Perhaps because it had been built on a foundation of old conflict. Maybe that made for sturdier bonds.

When they arrived back home, Maya contemplated taking him right to his driveway so he could get straight to bed. But Liv had said that any attempts to go against his instincts regarding Cat wouldn't be met with a favorable response. So she pulled in a little way from his place as usual.

When he didn't naturally waken once the movement of the vehicle had ceased, she gave him a gentle shake. He opened his eyes with a start. "Are we nearly there?" He glanced around, his eyes clouded with sleep.

"We're at yours," Maya said gently.

Sam sat up, stretching. "I didn't realize I'd dropped off for so long."

She caught him peering out of the window with a frown on his face, no doubt checking that they weren't too close to the property, because he relaxed again once he clocked that they were a little away along the street. "Thank you. You're an absolute star."

"No problem. Just remember I still need that chauffeur hat and shades."

He reached into his pocket and took out some cash. "Here you go. This should cover your uniform."

Maya frowned. "What's that for?"

"Fuel money," he replied, trying to get her to take it. "As our deal stipulated."

She shook her head. "I don't want it."

Sam took her hand and forced the cash into her palm. "Tough. That was the deal, and I would've had to spend the same if I'd taken my own car."

"Fine." She sighed. "You're so stubborn."

Sam grinned, and it made her pulse accelerate. "So are you." He opened the door, then paused. Leaning back toward her, he kissed her cheek.

A wave of heat spread across her skin.

"Thanks again," he said quietly. "See you next week."

She watched him walk down the street and turn onto his driveway, very aware that she'd need to tread carefully. The bond of friendship might be deepening for them both, but for her it carried with it a very strong sense of attraction, along with the longing that had lain dormant for the past eight years. And another heartbreak at Sam Holland's hands was the last thing she needed.

❄ ❄ ❄

THE SUN WAS BRIGHT IN THE AFTERNOON SKY AS MAYA ASSEMbled the intermediate class at the bottom of the slope, ready to ascend the chairlift for the last run of their session. One of the other instructors had called in sick, and no one else was free to cover. So, when Rowan had approached her in a panic about it, Maya had stepped up.

"Okay, everyone onto the lift and we'll meet at the top of the red slope. Remember the pointers I gave you on the last run, and I'll check you all out on the way down." She gave them a wink. "In a manner of speaking."

There was laughter from the group, which morphed into chatter as they joined the queue for the lift.

One of the students cut away from the rest in order to stand next to her at the front. He lifted his goggles, revealing a lovely pair of blue eyes, which he accentuated with a gorgeous smile. "This class is fantastic. You're a great teacher."

Maya flipped her hair. "Why, thank you. Brodie, isn't it?"

He nodded, his smile widening.

"I usually teach the kids' class, because they're more my mental age."

Brodie laughed. "Will you be covering all week?"

"Not sure yet. Depends on whether Aileen recovers."

"I hope not." His eyes widened. "Shit. I didn't mean that the way it sounded."

Maya raised her eyebrow. "Poor Aileen. Don't jinx her recovery."

He shot her a "yikes" expression and she laughed.

"I wish her well. I'd just like it if you could take the class a bit longer, that's all. I've learned so much today."

Pride swelled in her chest. She loved helping people develop their skiing. It was fun, mindful, exhilarating, and relaxing all rolled into one.

The two of them climbed off the lift and skied around the corner to the top of the run. It stretched before them, the sun glittering off the sparkling white path ahead.

Maya pulled her goggles down as the rest of the class arrived. "Wipeouts, assemble!"

She always got her classes to name themselves, and this lot had picked the name Wipeouts after a couple of spectacular crashes from the two cockiest guys in the collective.

"Okay, team. With great *powder*, comes great responsibility! Remember your pointers, and *go*."

They started off, the main wipeout culprits in the lead.

Carving through the class on the way down, she focused on each one in turn, calling out encouragement and constructive criticism on the way. With the wind whipping through her hair, the sun warming her face, and absorbing the excitement from her students, Maya felt freer than she had in years.

Toward the end of the run, she turned and skied backward ahead of the students, eliciting a cheer from the group as they came to stop at the bottom.

Maya took off her helmet and goggles to shake everybody's hand as they left. All of them thanked her, and she received hugs from a couple of the women. Even the two cocky guys were on good form, giving her a high five on the way past. Sometimes she had trouble with those male personalities in the group, thinking that they knew more than her due to their possession of a pair of testicles. Luckily, she hadn't had to utilize any of her heckler put-downs with these guys. She could do it if required; it was a lot easier than confronting those she loved. But as with any sort of conflict, it gave her palpitations. Another reason that she preferred the kids' groups.

With a sigh, she wished that she could do this full-time and forever. The thought of that coupled with the idea of never having to return to her desk brought her so much delight she could almost taste it. But she couldn't face alienating her father, and her sister by default, in choosing a career they didn't approve of.

Lost in those thoughts as she wandered over to the terrace, it took her a moment to realize someone was calling her name. Looking up, she spotted Brodie waving her over to one of the outside tables. "Can I get you a coffee? If you've time before your next class?"

Maya checked her watch. "Sure. I've got time."

She stuck her skis in the snow at the edge of the terrace and took a seat next to him, sliding off her gloves. Katie came past and they ordered a couple of coffees.

Maya turned to face her student. "So, Brodie. What's the lowdown? The word on the street?"

He laughed. "Word is, you're the best ski instructor in town."

Flashing him a grin, she leaned back. "Seriously. How's it going? Are you enjoying it?"

"It's amazing."

He had that light in his eyes, the one that only came from carving through perfect powder. "I moved here earlier in the year and knew the basics, but figured I'd need to up my game to get the most out of being a Glenavie resident."

"Absolutely." She held a hand aloft for him to high-five, and he took the opportunity. "Where did you live before?"

"Glasgow."

"Hey," she said, spreading her palms. "Same."

"You're kidding?" He raised his eyebrows. "I figured you'd be a Highland woman, born and bred."

She winked. "I am. But I was away pretending to be a city woman for a bit. Turns out I was pretty shit at it, so now I'm back home with my tail between my legs."

Laughing, he shook his head. "What took you to Glasgow?"

"Work. I was a boring accountant in another life."

He appeared bemused. "I can't imagine you behind a desk."

"No." Maya sighed. "Me neither. Zat is ze problem."

"Ah. Okay." He nodded. "The office didn't suit you."

The thought of her office created a hollow feeling inside. "Nope."

Katie arrived with their drinks, and Maya took her usual opportunity to surreptitiously press a fiver into her palm. Katie smiled, her cheeks coloring a little, and Maya gave her a wink.

She turned back to Brodie. "Why the move on your part?"

"I managed a ski store in Glasgow. I applied for the transfer when a new branch opened here, because I fancied a change of scene."

"Good choice." She lifted her cup to sip from it. "Do you know many folks in town?"

"A couple," he replied, fiddling with a sugar packet. "I'm still getting to know people."

Maya leaned an elbow on the table. "You should come to the sled race, and the after-party. There'll be loads of folks I can introduce you to."

Brodie smiled, and it lit up his eyes. "I'd love that. Thank you."

It occurred to Maya that she needed to get on the case with Sam regarding the sled race. She'd gotten distracted by the accounts, and time was ticking to the charity event. It was unclear what still needed to be done.

Brodie leaned across the table. "You know the lead instructor? The guy with the beard?"

"Sam," Maya replied, thinking what a coincidence it was that she'd just been thinking about him. Although, she did spend a disproportionate amount of time with him on her mind lately. "What about him?"

"Is he your boyfriend?" Brodie asked, his voice low.

A tingling sensation rippled over her skin at the thought. But there was no chance of that ever being the case. "No. Why?"

Brodie frowned a little. "Because he's over there by the bottom of the slope, watching us and giving me the evil eye."

Maya suppressed the urge to snap her head around, and instead leaned back slowly, then turned. Sam was standing a few yards away, surrounded by his class as they chatted to him, and he did keep glancing in their direction.

"Are you sure? It doesn't seem as if he's giving us any dirty looks."

Brodie shrugged. "Maybe I misinterpreted. Anyway, the race thing sounds great. I'll be there."

"Excellent." Maya finished her drink. "Duty calls. I'm off to join those of my mental age. But I'll see you tomorrow, if Aileen still isn't up to it."

Brodie gave her a wave. "Later, teach."

Maya snuck a glance at Sam as she stood. He did appear to be frowning a little, until he caught her eye and she gave him a wave. At which point he smiled and waved back.

❄ ❄ ❄

PUSHING OPEN THE DOUBLE DOORS FROM THE CAFÉ, MAYA CROSSED over to where Sam was leaning against the vending machine, arms folded.

"All set?" she asked as she drew level with him.

"Yep." He strolled over and held the door for her, following her out. "Rowan told me you came to the rescue while I was on the slopes. Sorry that you got saddled with the extra class."

"No worries." She opened the car and they climbed in. "I really enjoyed it. I'll cover again tomorrow if Aileen can't make it."

Sam was silent for a moment as she started the car and pulled out of the car park. "Are you sure? I can do it if not, it's my remit after all."

She shook her head, unable to keep the smile from her face or the enthusiasm from her voice. "I loved it. It was amazing." She sighed. "It feels so good to be back out there, teaching. You know?"

Running a hand through his hair in a familiar way, he smiled. "I know."

Maya met his eyes, and a silent understanding passed between them, reminding her they were kindred spirits when it came to this stuff. She swallowed as she glanced away. Perhaps she was starting to believe that they were kindred spirits in general too, but that was a dangerous train of thought. "Tomorrow we need to look at the race plans. Time's getting on."

"That'd be great," Sam replied, his eyes lighting up. "There's an issue with one of the prizes, and I could use your help with that."

"No worries. Let's meet in the afternoon, before I start the kids' class."

"Awesome." He sighed. "I hope the race comes off okay. I wanted it to be bigger and better this year, but I'm worried it'll go in the opposite direction because I've spread myself too thin."

Maya glanced over, touching his hand. Which she then regretted because every time she made contact with him, it felt like she'd been electrocuted. In a good, but intense way. "It'll be fine. We'll sort it. I was telling one of the students about it today—Brodie. He's going to come."

"Oh yeah?" His voice was a tad flat. "Is that the guy you were having coffee with?"

"Yeah, that was him. He manages one of the ski shops in town. The new one."

He fiddled with the glove compartment. "Cool."

They completed the journey to the usual spot where Maya had dropped him off after the butler gig. "I'll pick you up here, tomorrow morning."

"Thanks." He hesitated, glancing down the street, then brushed his lips against her cheek.

For a second, she couldn't catch her breath. She had to consciously pull herself together.

"See you tomorrow," he said, and he was out of the car before she managed to respond.

Chapter
TWELVE

HANGING UP THE PHONE WITH THE GARAGE, SAM BREATHED a sigh of relief that the car was fixed and would be ready for pickup early the next morning. But when he pondered that it meant the drive home that evening would be his last ride with Maya, a stab of disappointment quickly followed.

Rubbing the back of his neck, he realized he'd be sorry to lose their little nuggets of time. He got the feeling that she would too. But it couldn't last forever, and at least he'd still get to see her at work. Somehow, that was cold comfort. He lifted his wrist to check the time and registered they were due to meet soon. His pulse kicked with excitement.

Standing and grabbing his jacket and laptop case, he made his way downstairs and through the back foyer onto the terrace, scanning the area for her coming off the slopes from the class she was covering again for Aileen. He didn't know what he would've done without Maya's assistance over the past few weeks. Probably have had a nervous breakdown.

Signaling Katie on her way past, he ordered them a couple of hot chocolates. Maya was a fan of the café's signature hot chocolate piled high with marshmallows and cream.

On a whim, he asked Katie to bring their order to the fireside table in the alcove. He'd discovered it was Maya's favorite place to sit too. Another thing they had in common.

He smiled, thinking about just how many similarities they shared and how lucky he was to have her as a friend again. Perhaps an even closer friendship than they'd originally had, and that was something he'd never thought would be the case.

He spotted her arriving at the bottom of the slope, followed closely by that Brodie guy. Something swirled sickeningly in his stomach.

The realization that, deep down, he wanted more than friendship with Maya rose up, and guilt overwhelmed him. That was why he was jealous at the thought of her becoming romantically involved with someone else.

I don't have any right to be jealous. She's a friend, not my girlfriend. Stop being a dick. He swallowed in an attempt to dislodge the feeling, but it didn't work.

Brodie was lifting his hand to Maya's arm, and Sam realized there was a large tear in her ski jacket. Maya smiled at Brodie, and nodded as he moved away. Then she spoke to her other students, doling out hugs and high fives.

Eventually she turned and saw him, a big smile spreading across her face, which sent a wave of heat through his being.

She crossed the snow toward him, her skis over her shoulder and her dark hair fluttering in the breeze.

Maya arrived on the terrace and gave him a hug. He breathed her in, and those delicious memories of their teenage trysts permeated his brain. The feel of her soft, full lips on his. How she'd moaned when he'd slipped his hand under her top, then whispered to him that she didn't want him to stop. And he wouldn't have, if they hadn't been interrupted by a colleague.

Sam released her. Shortly after that encounter, she'd made it very clear that she *did* want him to stop. Permanently.

He cleared his throat. "Katie's taking our hot chocolates into the alcove."

Her face brightened with that megawatt smile he loved so much. "Hot chocolate in the alcove. My favorite." She turned to lead the way into the building.

"I know," he said quietly, following on.

As they entered, Sam marveled at how festive Maya had made the place look. A tree glittering with red and gold tinsel and baubles sat in the corner opposite the fireplace, and twinkly white lights were draped around a garland made of holly that sat atop the mantel. Across from the table and adjacent to the fireside wall, the floor-to-ceiling window looked out onto crisp white snow bordered by the evergreen tree line.

Maya took a seat on one of the squashy leather sofas, removing her jacket. He went to follow suit across the other side, but she waved him over and patted the seat next to her. "Makes it easier to see the laptop screen."

For a moment his heart had lifted that she wanted him to sit next to her, but it was only for convenience. Still, he wasn't complaining about being close to her.

He sat down, taking off his coat and pulling out his laptop. "How did the class go?"

"Good. Except for this." She pointed to the flap of material that was dangling from the arm of her jacket.

"What happened?" Sam asked with a frown. The jacket was ruined.

"Bear attack," Maya deadpanned. Sam burst out laughing and she shot him a smile. "Not really. 'Twas an erroneous tree."

"A tree, eh?" He raised his eyebrows. "Altercations with plant life, is it?"

She shrugged. "You should see the other guy. Bleeding bark all over the shop."

Sam smiled, studying her and wishing she didn't make him feel like this. He couldn't remember a woman who had made him laugh, or fall, as hard.

Clearing his throat, he opened the web page with all the details of the events. Maya leaned in, and he had to be careful not to breathe her in too deeply lest he end up back in that boot room in his mind's eye.

Katie came over with their hot chocolates, and Sam pushed a tip into her hand, eliciting a blush of her cheeks. As she departed, he caught Maya smiling at him before she glanced away. "What's the issue with the race prizes?" she asked, eyeing the laptop screen. "This looks spot-on, mate."

"Here," he said, pointing to the second prize. "It's fallen through. We need another one."

"Oh, I see," Maya replied as she scanned further down the list. "Ooh, a month's free gym membership. Good old Nico."

"Yep. Hence the issue. These are all favors from friends, and I've run out of friends."

"Aw," she said, lifting her gaze to his and giving him an unexpected kiss on the cheek. Heat rose in his face.

"I'll be your friend," she told him with a wink.

Heat began to rise elsewhere in his body, so he swallowed hard and glanced away. "Thanks, pal." *"Pals" don't react like that to a mere kiss on the cheek.*

Maya was frowning into the middle distance. "Shall I ask Brodie if his ski shop can donate anything? He said he'd give me a discount on a new jacket, so I can ask him then. Which reminds me." She turned to look at him. "Can we stop off in town on the way home? I want to get the jacket before tomorrow."

Sam smiled. "You don't need to ask permission, Maya. You're the one giving *me* a lift."

She gave a mock sniff. "I'm merely being a courteous friend."

Bumping her shoulder, he smiled. "And I appreciate it. But it's fine." Something occurred to him. "By the way, the garage called. My car will be ready tomorrow, so no more chauffeuring for you."

Her face fell for a second before she seemed to catch herself, and smiled. "Aw. Does this mean I'll have to turn in the hat and shades?"

Had that really been a flash of disappointment on her face? Was it possible she might miss their chats in the car as much as he would? He gave her a solemn look. "Yes. I'm afraid that the uniform must be forfeited."

She rubbed her eyes as if wiping away imaginary tears.

"Aw," he said, pretending to join in, brushing his thumb over her cheek and then regretting it because it was followed by an overpowering urge to kiss her. He shifted away again. "I'll let you keep the gear a little longer."

Her expression seemed tentative. "Maybe . . ." She glanced away. "Maybe we can still car share, sometimes. Just until Ben finds someone permanent."

"Yeah," he said, smiling even though imagining her leaving the resort made his heart sink right down to his snow boots. "I'd like that."

Maya fingered the keys on his laptop. "Anyway. Shall I ask Brodie about donating something when I see him later?"

Sam stopped himself from going with his gut reaction, which was to shout no inappropriately loudly, because he was aware that his motivations behind that response were far from honorable. *Don't be a tosser.*

He thought for a moment, and realized that it wouldn't be a great option anyway. "I would've said yes, but we already have some ski gear on the prize list."

"Ah, bugger," she said, eyeing the screen. "So we do."

"We could keep it as a reserve option, though," Sam said, feeling bad that she was disappointed not to have solved the issue. "If we can't think of anything different."

Maya stared out of the window again, and a smile spread over her face.

"What is it?" he asked, admiring the way in which the crackling fire cast a soft orangey glow over her beautiful face, making her lovely smile impossibly more appealing.

"I've got it." She brought her gaze back onto him, and it was as if a light were being shone in his direction. "We can use one of Arran's landscapes. It's perfect, because they're of the Glenavie mountains, where the race is taking place. Plus he's a local artist, *and*"—she pointed at him in emphasis—"it'll be good publicity for his business."

Sam nodded. It *was* a brilliant idea, but, as much as he hated to admit it, there was a stumbling block. "I love it. The only thing is I don't have the cash to stump for a painting, and I'm not asking him to donate it. Not when he's just getting off the ground."

Maya waved her hand. "Course not. That's why *I'm* going to buy it. Then I'll donate it to the race."

The breath caught in his throat as he looked at her. "That's so generous."

She wrinkled her nose, and it made him want to kiss it. "Not at all. I want to help. It makes me feel good."

Sam touched her hand. "Can you afford it? After losing your job? And you've only just started here."

She shrugged. "It's fine. I've got savings, plus the money from selling the flat I had with Rich. He compensated me for all the furniture because he moved into his own place and I'm living rent-free with the parentals."

Sam sensed the weight of the problem lifting from his shoulders. It seemed she had that effect on him.

The Maya effect.

Then he realized that she'd said *flat*, when he'd expected the two of them to have had some huge mansion in the posh end of Glasgow.

"Message Arran now and get him to put one aside for us," Maya said. She paused. "Not our favorite one, though."

Sam took out his phone, glancing up. He liked that she'd said *our* favorite. "No? You want that one for yourself?"

She glanced away. "Yeah. That's right."

Sam sent the message to Arran. "Done."

Rubbing her hands together, Maya leaned back. "Excellent. I'll go fetch it tomorrow and give him the cash." She smiled. "I might take Liv with me. She needs to choose a Christmas present."

She lifted her mug to sip her hot chocolate, and when she finished, there was a blob of cream on the end of her nose. Before he could stop himself, Sam reached out to wipe it off with his thumb. She molded her gaze with his, her chestnut eyes wide. Without thinking, he popped his thumb into his mouth to quickly suck the cream off. Her eyes seemed to grow even wider as she watched him, a light blush coloring her cheeks.

He shifted in his seat, painfully aware of her proximity and regretting his actions in case they had come off as inappropriate.

Maya smiled, taking another sip. "This really is the best hot chocolate."

She didn't seem to have taken offense, so he relaxed again, trying not to stare too hard as she licked the remnants of her drink from her lips.

❄ ❄ ❄

"GUESS WHAT?"

Sam looked at Maya as she drove the mountain pass, the mischievous expression on her face making him feel like he was on fire. "What?"

She smiled. "That's not a guess. It's a question."

He laughed. "You need to give me a clue so I'm guessing in the right ballpark of all the possible contexts in the known universe."

Pausing, she pursed her lips. "Good point. It's to do with the sled race prize list."

"But we sorted that already," he said, grinning. "We're the A team, remember?"

"True. But I reckon I've thought of a way to enhance it further."

"In addition to Arran's prize?"

"Yes."

Sam studied her as she drove, trying to work her out. There was a smile playing on her face. "An extra prize?"

Raising her eyebrows, she shot him a side glance. "Yep."

"Intriguing. What is it?"

"I can't tell you yet."

He burst out laughing. "All that buildup, and you can't tell me?"

Maya bit her lip, and it did unspeakable things to his body. "I need to make a phone call tonight. Then I'll tell you tomorrow, if it comes off."

"I'm going to be on tenterhooks all night."

"Argh. Sorry." She winced. "I shouldn't have said anything."

He leaned his elbow onto the door, resting his head on his hand to study her. "That's okay. It'll give me something to look forward to."

They arrived in town and Maya parked. "Do you want to come with me?"

Sam was tempted. He loved a browse in a ski shop—what skier didn't? But he realized that he had some sort of conflict of interest where Brodie was concerned, and he didn't trust himself to be around if Maya wanted to ask the guy out or something. The idea of that left a cold heaviness in his stomach. However, ignoring that and not letting it affect his actions and spoil anything for Maya was the right thing to do.

"That's okay. I want to have a nosy in the deli across the street." Sam gave her a wave as he headed across the road and into the store. He wanted to choose something for his mum's Christmas present. Searching around, he decided to get her an artisan hamper made up.

The shop assistant helped him select an order, and he paid a deposit for it, with a plan to come collect it at a later date. As he left the shop, it occurred to him that he'd have his own car by then. At least that meant no more scoring lifts and feeling guilty about it. Although he'd stopped feeling guilty pretty quickly about Maya's lift to the butler gig last weekend, because he'd enjoyed it so much and could tell she had too.

Smiling, he glanced up. Maya was standing in the doorway of

the ski shop, holding a bag. She must've gotten her jacket. He was about to wave, when Brodie appeared next to her and gestured above their heads.

They were standing under mistletoe.

Sam's heart sank as Maya smiled and leaned over to give Brodie a kiss on the lips, and Sam felt as if it would never rise back into his chest again.

*   *   *

PUSHING HIS FOOD AROUND ON HIS PLATE, SAM INADVERTENTLY made a screeching noise with his fork. He snapped up his gaze to meet Cat's disapproving expression. "Sorry."

She shook her head and went back to her dinner. "How was work?"

"Okay. We're on a better track with the sled race."

"That's good."

Her tone indicated she wasn't really listening to the answer, and he wondered why she kept asking him the same questions of an evening. He knew what was coming next.

"Did you talk to Maya?"

Usually, he'd have said no in order to save the third degree. But he didn't have the patience that evening. Perhaps it was something to do with watching Maya kiss Brodie, even though he had no right to feel anything about that particular situation. "We shared a ride to work and back. Of course we talked."

She lifted her gaze, eyes narrowed. "About what?"

Dropping his fork, he rubbed his eyes. "The weather. Skiing. The sled race. Why?"

Her tone was flat. "Because I want to know, that's why."

He opted not to say anything. Years of experience had taught him when to stay quiet.

"She's manipulative and a liar. Just look at how she hurt you in the past."

He was struggling more than usual to stay in his safe cocoon of silence. "Cat, she can't manipulate or hurt me when we're only discussing skiing." He was aware that they'd discussed more than that, confided more than that. But he'd sensed she was genuine, and he'd listened to her issues as much as she had his.

"That's what she wants you to think."

Lifting his gaze to meet hers, he shook his head. "Why don't you give her a chance? We've all changed since we were eighteen."

The expression on her face told him that had been the wrong thing to say.

She pressed her lips into a line as thin as tracing paper, her eyes rivaling the narrowness of her mouth. "What's she told you?"

His heart rate spiked. "Nothing. She just confided some stuff about her family."

"Some bullshit about her sister?"

Sam opened his mouth to reply, then hesitated. *That was a very good guess.* The niggle from a few nights ago reappeared in his mind, when he'd seen Cat looking at his phone and she'd made an excuse, coupled with the missing text from Maya, which still hadn't arrived despite his bouncing-around-the-satellites theory.

The text that was about Maya's sister.

Sam spoke slowly, having to force the words through his constricted throat. "Have you been going through my messages? And *deleting* them?"

There was a moment's pause. Then Cat shoved her chair back so hard that he startled.

"How *dare* you accuse me of that. That is the lowest thing I've ever heard in my life." She grabbed her plate and took it over to the kitchen, scraping it into the food bin so violently that Sam was concerned for the welfare of the crockery. "I have never been so insulted in my life. I wouldn't treat my worst enemy the way that you treat me. I don't know why I put up with it." She practically threw the plate into the sink, and Sam winced, convinced it must've smashed. "Everybody else thinks so too. My family, friends. I've told them all what you're like, and they say I can do better and they don't know why I stay with you. You keep me tied to this dead-end town when I could be out in a big city somewhere, living the high life, finding a guy who can treat me well and lavish things on me. All you do is hold me back. You've no ambition."

It was the sort of monologue she went into whenever she had one of her blowouts, and it would end with him apologizing and asking her not to leave. But it would always fuel her determination to do just that, and she'd go—not returning for a few days.

But this time he didn't have the energy. "Why don't you go to your mum's, then."

She stared at him, seemingly in disbelief that he wasn't playing along. Darting her eyes across the room, she opened her mouth, then closed it again. "I'm going to bed. You can sleep in the spare room." With an about turn, she stalked out of the kitchen and slammed the door behind her.

"It would be my pleasure," Sam muttered.

Chapter

THIRTEEN

MAYA CROSSED THROUGH THE SKI CENTER AND UP THE STAIRS toward Sam's office. By rights she shouldn't have been in the building. Aileen was back, and Maya wasn't teaching until the next day, but she was too excited not to give Sam this news in person.

Knocking on his door, she listened for an answer, her pulse picking up. She thought she heard him say, "Yeah," so she opened it.

He was there, sitting behind his desk, and the sight of him made her heart trip.

"Guess what?" she said, smiling as she entered. He looked up, and there were dark circles under his eyes.

Maya shut the door behind her, the wind taken out of her sails. "You okay?"

He rubbed his eyes. "I didn't sleep well."

There was a tension in the room that she hadn't expected. She eased into a seat, her excitement extinguished. "Are you unwell? Maybe you've got what Aileen had."

Shaking his head, he gave her a weak smile, but it only served to heighten her anxiety. "I'm fine."

He didn't elaborate, and Maya was thrown for a moment. Did he want her to ask more? Or was he hoping she'd go away? Her gut instinct was to make her excuses and leave.

But something stopped her—the way that Liv had described her worries about her twin brother. Maya couldn't abandon him without first making an effort.

She remembered the ride home from town the previous evening; he'd been a little subdued then. Had something happened when he was in that deli? Had he gotten a message? But he'd denied anything was wrong when she'd asked him.

Swallowing, she took a breath. "Do you want to talk? It seemed like you weren't yourself on the ride home yesterday."

His jaw tensed, and he rubbed his temples. "Everything's fine."

"Are you sure? Because I really think that—"

"Maya. I said it's fine. So it's fine."

He hadn't raised his voice, but there was a razor-sharp edge that she'd not heard him use in a long time. Not since those tense words they'd exchanged prior to him ending it with her. The sound of his tone pricked at her eyes and she blinked, a lump rising in her throat.

She stood, trying to keep the wobble from her voice. "I'll leave you to it." Crossing the room, she opened the door and shut it behind her, closing her eyes tight to keep the tears in.

❄ ❄ ❄

MAYA GRINNED AS SHE DROVE. "I THINK WE'VE FOUND YOUR Darcy." She and Liv had just paid a visit to Arran's studio, to purchase the painting for the sled race prize. She'd chosen a day scene near the slopes because she'd been transfixed by the manner in which Arran had caught the sun glinting off the snow, feeling as if she could step into the painting, Mary Poppins–style, and carve her way down the trail.

Maya had asked Liv along to choose a painting for Christmas. With the ulterior motive of getting Liv a visit with Arran of course. Regular cupid, she was.

"Don't," Liv replied, looking out the window. "He's not interested."

"He seemed very interested to me." Arran hadn't seemed able to keep his eyes off Liv, watching her as she carried his son, Jayce, around the studio, with the wee one making regular grabs for her glasses. Maya had been furiously taking notes in her mental cupid notebook. It was full to the brim, and she'd need to buy a new one from the imaginary notebook store. "Anyway, you can't wait around for Darcy to come to you, you need to grab him by the waistcoat."

"He's just friendly, and that's how he is with everyone." Liv pushed her glasses up her nose. "He was so in love with Jess and a bit lost when she finished it. I think he still half hopes she might come back."

Maya glanced over, taking in the expression on Liv's face. It was sad, but also something else. Wary?

While they had been at the studio, Arran had also sung Sam's praises, waxing lyrical about the community project that Sam created a few years back. The scheme was aimed at helping less-privileged kids access skiing by subsidizing lessons and providing free skiwear. Maya had already heard about it from Liv and a few others at the resort, though nothing from Sam himself. It wasn't as if she needed to hear anything else that would make him more attractive in her eyes, but it had done so nonetheless. All the more gut-wrenching that he wasn't interested in her in that manner.

Sometimes, she let herself think that he was. Such as when he listened to her so intently and offered her sage advice. Or by the fireside yesterday, when there were a couple of moments that she'd foolishly thought he might want to kiss her. However, those perceptions were merely what she wanted to see, rather than what was really going on in front of her.

The sight of Sam sucking that cream off his thumb had burned onto her brain, and she'd had to fight off thoughts regarding what else she'd love to experience him doing with that mouth.

Maya had bought a third painting from Arran, the night scene that she and Sam both coveted, and was fast becoming Arran's largest patron. But she hadn't yet decided what she was going to do with it. A half-formed, silly thought had floated the other day about giving it to Sam for Christmas. Now she wasn't so sure, partly because of their tense exchange earlier but mainly because it was a big gift for someone who was only a friend, and she didn't want to give away how she felt about him. However, she loved the landscape and could always keep it for herself if gifting it to Sam didn't feel right. She hadn't treated herself to anything for a long time.

Clearing her throat, Liv glanced over. "What's happening with Hana?"

Maya grimaced. "I've not tried to call or text again."

Liv nodded. "And your dad?"

"Kind of been avoiding each other."

"Hmm."

"Hmm, indeed," Maya said.

"Do you think you should call Hana? Tell her you need to discuss it?"

The idea of that made her shudder. "I don't know."

Liv sighed. "Families, eh? Pain in the arse."

Maya remembered how exhausted Sam had appeared earlier,

and it pained her more than the memory of the edge to his voice. "Have you spoken to Sam recently?"

"Not this week. Why?"

Maya cleared her throat. "He looked tired today. And he was . . . a little short."

Liv frowned. "He gets like that if they've had an argument."

"Right," Maya replied, unsure what else to say.

"I'll call him," Liv said. "But usually, he won't give me any detail. I think he's afraid to say too much because he knows what my opinion of her is. My fault for being too candid in the past."

Maya glanced over as they arrived at Liv's, wishing she could do something to help, but feeling powerless.

Liv leaned over to kiss Maya's cheek. "Thank you for the trip to see a handsome man's wares."

"You're welcome."

Liv left the car with a wave, and Maya sat for a moment, feeling stressed by all the difficulties around her and wishing she could solve their current problems as easily as she did math.

❄ ❄ ❄

DINNER WAS TENSE AGAIN, WITH YVONNE CHATTING TO EACH OF them in turn and attempting to get Maya and Omar to engage with each other, but neither taking her up on it. Maya felt bad that her mum was desperate to mend the family rifts. Especially when it wasn't that long until Christmas.

The first to finish, Maya jumped to her feet. "I'll do the cleanup tonight. You guys have a rest." She began clearing the plates.

Omar finally raised his eyes from the medical magazine he'd been reading over dinner, to address Maya. "I've sent you an e-mail, with some firms you can send your CV to."

It felt like a heavy boulder dropped on her, causing her to freeze as she loaded the dishwasher, before she forced her body to keep moving. "Have they got openings?"

"No, but it doesn't hurt to get your details in so they have you in mind for the future."

Maya's mouth went dry. The future scenario of being trapped behind a desk seemed especially bleak compared to skiing the slopes. "Okay, Dad."

She finished her task as quickly as possible, then made her excuses before leaving the room. Yvonne flashed her a sympathetic look as she departed.

Taking the stairs two at a time, she shut herself in her room, lying down on the bed. Apart from the little oasis of joy with Liv at Arran's studio, it had been rather a shitty day.

Her phone buzzed with a message, and for a moment her heart rose into her mouth. *What if it's Hana, having another go at me?*

She lifted it to find it was from Sam.

I owe you an apology for being a dick
earlier. I'd like to say sorry in person,
if you don't mind me coming over.

Maya hovered her finger over the phone for a second, but the decision was already made.

Sure. Free whenever you are.

Thanks. On my way.

Maya let out a breath, unsure how to navigate this situation. She blew her fringe out of her eyes. He could've just apologized on the phone, but the fact that he wanted to do it face-to-face was touching.

There was a knock at her bedroom door, and she opened it to see Yvonne standing there. "Can I have a word?"

"Sure." She gestured her mum in. "What's up, buttercup?"

Smiling, Yvonne sat on the bed. "Do you really want to send those CVs out? Or did you only agree to it to please your father?"

The hair on the back of Maya's neck pricked up. "No, I want to do it," she said quickly.

Yvonne raised her eyebrows, but Maya got in there before she could ask more. "Sam'll be here in a minute. We need to discuss something."

"Oh yes? What's going on with you guys?"

"I don't know, to be honest. We're kind of friends now." She paused to sit next to her mum. "Scratch that, we are actual friends. It's just a bit of a rocky road."

Yvonne nodded. "I noticed your dad was a bit funny the other day, when I mentioned you working at the resort as a favor to Sam. But later on, when I asked him why, he changed the subject."

Glancing down, Maya rubbed her toe over the carpet. "Dad used to think Sam was a bad influence, back when I started at the ski center."

"How come? He didn't know about your involvement?"

"No, he didn't. It was a misunderstanding, really. I enjoyed working there and wondered . . ." She hesitated, choosing her words carefully. "Whether I might like to pursue it as a career, rather than going to uni. Sam encouraged me to speak to Dad about it, and I did. But . . . Dad and I both decided it was best that I continue with the plan for an accountancy career. None of it was Sam's influence, he was just trying to help me voice my feelings."

She was aware it was a heavily edited version of the truth. But if she told her mum the exact details, then it would be easy for Yvonne to put two and two together. And she didn't want to put her mum in a difficult position with her dad.

The discussion with her dad had, in fact, been more of a blowout, which had taken place on the date of the Tavern night out. Maya had tried to explain that she wanted to consider deferring university and staying on at the resort. She hadn't even suggested that the situation be permanent. But Omar had still come down hard, rubbishing her plan and reducing her to an ashamed child. She'd made the mistake of mentioning Sam's support, and her dad had taken it the wrong way, accusing Sam of interfering and being a negative influence, when the idea was purely Maya's construction and Sam had merely suggested that she voice it.

Omar had towered over her as she'd called Sam to say that she'd changed her mind about the idea, that she was going through with accountancy after all because ski instructing wasn't a real job. Sam had taken that personally, which she'd felt bad about, but also resentful that he was making it about him. They'd exchanged a few tense words before she'd ended the call, because it had been overwhelmingly stressful with her dad in earshot. Not that Sam had known Omar was there. She couldn't tell him that at the time, and then she'd never gotten the chance.

Maya had assumed they'd smooth it over at the pub later that evening. But in the end, those had ended up being the last words they'd spoken before she left for university a week later.

She closed her eyes for a moment, the painful memories washing over her. She *had* tried to go back and speak to Sam, to explain what had really happened. And to apologize, even though she'd been upset that he'd taken what she'd said as a slight when it wasn't about him, and they hadn't even been her words but those of her father.

But then she'd been confronted by the sight of Sam making out with her friend and concluded that he was a total knob. And that, as they say, was that.

But none of it mattered now. Eight years had passed, and Sam was a different person. Bygones were bygones, and confronting the past only brought pain, so it was best ignored and not spoken about again. *Though maybe I should've tried harder to explain to Dad that Sam was only trying to help.* At the time, she'd been too convinced of Sam's lack of integrity once the sight of him with Cat had shattered the remaining fragments of her broken heart.

The doorbell sounded, bringing her out of the rumination and saving her from any further elaborations. "That'll be Sam."

Yvonne took her hand with a squeeze, then left the room, and Maya practically ran down the stairs, shouting, "It's for me!" for her father's benefit. Not that he showed any signs of emerging from the living room, where he was no doubt buried in that bloody medical journal. Yawn.

As she reached the door, she realized her heart was tripping along rather fast, and it wasn't only from the exertion of her light-speed descent from the first floor.

Despite expecting him, she was thrown by the sight of Sam. He still appeared tired, but his tousled hair looked ripe for running her fingers through, and the burnt-orange jumper showing under the open zip of his jacket brought out the intensity of his amber eyes.

She managed a smile and gestured him inside, trying not to stare at the way his jeans hugged the contours of his muscular thighs. "Here," she said, "I'll take your jacket."

As she took it from him, their fingers brushed right as his gaze locked with hers, and an electrifying pulse coursed through her body.

"Thanks," Sam said, bending to remove his boots.

"Come upstairs." Maya started in that direction with him following.

Sam paused as he caught sight of Yvonne in the kitchen. "Hey, Mrs. B."

"Hi, Sam," she replied. "And it's Yvonne."

"Hi, Yvonne," he called back as he ascended the stairs behind Maya.

She led him into her room, giving him the seat by her desk, while she hovered at the door. "Do you want a tea or a coffee?"

Sam smiled. "I'm fine, thanks."

Maya sat on the bed across from him. "How was your day?"

He ran a hand through his hair. "Pretty shit. But that was my own fault. I feel really bad about how I spoke to you earlier."

Her mouth dry, she shook her head. "It's okay."

"No, it's not. I'm really sorry." He sighed. "I didn't sleep well last night because I was in the spare room and I can't get comfy in there."

She nodded, wanting to ask why he'd slept there, but remembering what Liv had said about how he'd keep the details to himself if there'd been an argument with Cat. "Could you not get comfy because it's like a graveyard for all your old crap? That's what our spare room was like at the flat I shared with Rich."

Sam laughed. "Yeah, pretty much. I think we might find Atlantis in there, one day."

Maya smiled.

"Anyway," he continued. "I was in a foul mood and you caught me at the wrong time. Especially since . . ." He tailed off, glancing away.

"Since what?" she asked gently.

He swallowed, and met her gaze. "Since Cat and I had a big

row last night. That's why I was relegated to the spare room, aka the general dumping ground." He shot her a smile.

Maya winced. "I'm sorry."

"Don't be . . ." He rubbed his face. "It's me who's apologizing to you here."

"Did the argument with Cat start in the deli?" Maya asked, remembering his quiet mood after they'd met back at the car.

He frowned. "The deli? No, why?"

Maya blew her fringe out of her eyes. "You seemed a lot quieter after I'd gotten my new jacket at Brodie's place."

A dark expression passed over his face, but he covered it with a weak smile. "No, it was later on."

Maya wasn't sure how hard she should try to delve into it. She wanted to support him but was aware how cagey he tended to be. He'd also already confided more than it seemed Liv would have anticipated. Was that because he viewed Maya as neutral ground, rather than being too close to the subject as family?

"Listen," she said as he glanced up to meet her eyes. "If you ever want, or need, to talk about anything, you can speak to me, okay? I won't judge, and I certainly won't tell anyone else. Just think of me as a sounding board."

He held her gaze with an intense look in his eyes, and it seemed as if he was struggling to decide whether to say anything more. But then he appeared to check himself. "I really appreciate that, Maya. And thanks for overlooking me being a tosser this morning."

"Well, you know." She shot him a grin. "You're *still* a tosser. But what can we do?"

Sam laughed, and it gave her a warm feeling after he'd seemed so miserable earlier. Suddenly, Maya remembered the good news she'd wanted to give him that morning. She'd forgotten after the wind had been knocked out of her sails.

Infused with anticipation, she stood, clapping her hands together.

Sam raised his eyebrows. "What?"

"Oh my God, I just remembered what I needed to tell you." Her voice felt squeaky with excitement, and a smile spread over Sam's face as he watched her.

Trying not to speak too quickly, she continued. "I've organized that other prize I told you about. It's going to have to take top billing, because it's *good*." She said the word *good* in a deep voice, and the sound of it brought him to his feet.

"What is it?"

"Okay," Maya said, unable to keep still as she shifted her weight from one foot to the other. "You remember my friend Kirsty? The one whose house you were naked in?"

Sam laughed, taking a step toward her. "How could I forget?"

"Her husband, Paul, works for a record company. They've got Iona Mac signed with them."

Sam raised his eyebrows. "Iona Mac, as in the biggest pop star in Scotland?"

"No," Maya said, waggling her finger. "The biggest pop star in *Britain*, according to the charts."

Sam took another step closer, his eyes becoming wider by the minute. "You need to conclude this story right now, before I die of anticipation."

Maya couldn't help letting out a little squeal. "Paul's got us six free tickets with backstage passes to Iona's Glasgow gig in January!"

Sam's mouth dropped open, and he stared at her for a second. "Oh my God!" He closed the gap between them and enveloped her in a hug, lifting her right off the ground. "I can't believe it! That's awesome."

He squeezed her tightly, and she found her face buried in his hair, breathing in his scent. As he set her down to meet her gaze, that scene from years ago, in the boot room, was right there. She could almost reach out and touch it.

"Maya, you are bloody amazing." He leaned to kiss her cheek, slow to let his lips leave her skin, and once he did, he held her face close to his. "Thank you so much. For everything. I don't even know *how* to thank you for all the stuff you've done for me, apart from saying it a million times. Thank you, thank you, thank you."

Her pulse throbbed in her ears as she got lost in his eyes. "You'll need to say it another nine hundred and ninety-nine thousand, nine hundred and ninety-seven times if you're to hit the million mark."

He laughed softly. The urge to kiss him permeated her soul, but she shoved it down—he only saw her as a friend, plus he had a girlfriend. Albeit a toxic one; however, that was his choice.

But if he only sees me as a friend, why is he still holding my face and looking into my eyes as if he wants to kiss me too?

"Maya!" They jumped apart as Yvonne's voice sounded up the stairs. "Do you guys want any tea?"

Maya swallowed, looking at Sam. "Tea?"

He smiled, color streaking his cheeks as he ran a hand through his hair. "That's okay. I'd better head back before Cat wonders where I am."

The sound of Cat's name took some of the shine from Maya's high. She opted not to ask where he'd told Cat he was going.

She cleared her throat. "I'm free after my junior class tomorrow morning, if you're able to meet to finalize the arrangements for the sled race?"

"Yes. Thank you." He followed her out of the room and down the stairs. "I think I'm going to be thanking you every day for the rest of my life."

Maya called through to Yvonne that no tea was required, watching him pull on his boots and thinking that being in contact with him every day for the rest of their lives was something she quite liked the sound of.

The many other, more X-rated ways in which he might thank her began to crowd her thoughts—all of them containing very accurate detail of his body thanks to what she had witnessed at Kirsty's and also in the spa suite.

Heat rose in her face as he looked up to flash her a smile, and she shoved those thoughts out of her mind quickly before she made a fool of herself.

Chapter
FOURTEEN

THE KIDS SEEMED TO BE HAVING LOADS OF FUN, CHUCKING snow at each other. Sam smiled as he watched them from the terrace, noticing that Maya was lobbing snow with them. She seemed so happy working at the resort, and, not for the first time, he imagined what it would be like if she stayed on permanently. The idea of it made him feel as if he had electricity coursing through his system.

After taking a seat with his laptop, he ordered them some coffees and waited for her to finish, having decided that being by the fireside with her was best avoided in case he got any more romantic ideas. In any case, it had been occupied.

How did the mere act of watching her laugh and smile make him so happy? All of it was adding up. He loved her company and she made him feel so relaxed. She was always there for him when he needed her, and allowed him to be there for her even if they hadn't been getting on as well. That he'd been eaten with jealousy at witnessing her kiss Brodie. Sam winced as he remembered his reaction and how it had, in some part, contributed to his surliness with her the previous morning. Granted, his response was mainly down to Cat-related stress and sleep deprivation, but he couldn't deny that jealousy was mixed in there. What a shitty thing to do on his part. She was free to kiss anyone she liked, and it was none of his business.

He rubbed his eyes as he remembered how much he'd wanted her to kiss *him* the previous evening, in her bedroom. Shaking his head, he felt like the worst person in the world. Jealous about his friend living her own life. Thinking about kissing his friend when he had a girlfriend. Albeit one who not only refused to share a bed with him, but had fucked off to her parents' house and was ignoring him. But that was no excuse for his treacherous thoughts.

The coffees arrived shortly before the woman herself, who walked over and removed her helmet with a shake of her hair that left him so weak at the knees he was relieved he was sitting. She brushed her lips against his cheek as she took a seat next to him, and it sent a wave of heat flaming over his skin.

"Right, Leonard. Where are we at?"

He smiled. Her teasing was so goddamned sexy. That was how they'd ended up against the wall of the boot room in days gone by. Maya had pinched something of his and wouldn't give it back until he'd admitted that she'd had the best technique on a slalom run they'd just finished. She'd held whatever it was—he couldn't remember what, he hadn't even cared at the time; he'd just been enjoying the game—above her head so that he'd had to reach to get it, his body pressing against hers in the process. One thing had led to another and . . .

Maya nudged him. "Come on, slow coach. Get the tech fired up."

Sam shook his head, realizing his heart was tripping along pretty fast. "Sorry. Here we go."

Opening the fresh version of the web page that he'd had Rowan spruce that morning, he showed her the changes they'd made to the prize list, with the gig tickets at the top.

Maya rubbed her hands together. "Awesome. We should e-mail the existing entrants to let them know about the changes to the prize list. We also need to go big on advertising the new list, because it might draw more people in."

He nodded. "I'll get some fresh flyers made and we'll put them in the local shops and noticeboards."

"No. I'll do it. You deserve a reprieve. What about the equipment and staffing on the day?"

"Sorted," Sam said, absorbing the heartwarming sensation of her protecting him from the burden. "Except that Vicky was included in the numbers, so we're a person down."

Maya shot him an open-mouthed look, pointing to herself in an affronted manner. "What am I, chopped liver?"

Smiling, he nudged her arm. "One didn't want to *assume*."

She blew out a breath. "I am fully invested in this mother, so *assume* away. What about the after event?"

"All set. We've booked the top room at the Tavern. It went down well last year." He smiled. "People were more generous with the raffle ticket uptake in a premises with an alcohol license, compared to when we used to have it in the ski café."

"Clever," Maya said, lifting her coffee to her mouth. "Sounds like we're on track?"

"Yeah," Sam replied, realizing that it was pretty much sorted, now that the headache of the missing prize was solved. Plus, it was even better with the brand-new, massive top prize. He couldn't resist leaning over to kiss her cheek.

She raised her eyebrows, and he thought he detected a little blush appearing on her face. "What was that for?"

"General awesomeness." He gave her a wink, and the color seemed to heighten on her cheeks. *She's so adorable.*

Maya cleared her throat. "Is it okay if I take this coffee and go use your office for a bit? I want to have another look at Ben's accounts, and I don't like doing it in the staff room with all the comings and goings and potential reading over my shoulder."

"Of course. But you shouldn't be staying on after your lesson. Why don't you head off and relax? You deserve it." Guilt needled him that he'd gotten her roped into all this extra work. Especially when she was worried about her own problems and family tension with her sister and father.

She smiled. "Nah. I'm nearly done, and I want to get it finished so that Ben can get it off his worry list."

Sam eyed her, his hope rising. "Off the worry list—as in, there's nothing to worry about?"

Maya waggled her hand to and fro. "Hopefully nothing big. I think he's right about the miscalculation and that the resort owes more than anticipated."

Sam's heart plummeted, and it must've shown on his face, because she took his hand. Her touch created a soothing sensation, which counteracted the sinking feeling.

"Don't panic." She gave him a squeeze. "I don't think the damage will be much worse than Ben had originally been told, and should be within means."

Sighing with relief, he squeezed back and held on to her fingers, letting them entwine with his and appreciating how her touch made his skin come alive. "When will you know for sure?"

Maya rubbed her thumb over the tips of his fingers, nudging up his heart rate. "Today, I reckon. I'm on a mission to get it done this afternoon. Then you can both get your beauty sleep."

She let go of his hand to stand, and he immediately felt the loss of her touch.

"Are you saying that I need beauty sleep?" he said, flashing her a smile.

Maya eyed him as she lifted her cup to take with her. "Nah. You're pretty cute."

He expected her to do her usual jokey wink, but she didn't. Color streaked her cheeks in the brightest flush yet as she walked off.

❄ ❄ ❄

HEADING INTO THE BACK FOYER, SAM PLACED HIS SKIS INTO A locker and switched his ski boots for snow boots. Then he went upstairs to see how Maya was getting on.

Cat popped into his mind with an accompanying sinking feeling, and he wondered how long she was going to continue to avoid him after he'd messaged saying they needed to talk. He wanted to discuss his suspicions regarding her going through his phone, plus deleting texts, but she was ghosting him. The problem was she had a habit of deflecting any heat off herself and onto him, and he now realized she was rather skilled at it. Normally he'd end up apologizing and feeling like the bad guy.

Shoving Cat out of his brain, he gave a quick knock and opened his office door.

Maya glanced up, and meeting her gaze made every nerve in his body spark.

"Any joy, Superaccountant?" He closed the door and took in her big smile as he walked over.

"Yep. Just finishing up. We'd better get Ben, it's looking good."

A rush of relief buoyed his spirits. "Like you thought?"

"A little better, actually."

Her smile widened as he gestured for her to stand.

"What is it?" she asked, getting to her feet.

Sam folded her into his arms, breathing in the soothing, exhilarating scent of her. "Just need to give you this."

Maya sank her head onto his chest, wrapping her arms around his waist, and it felt so good. She fitted against him perfectly, and he tried in vain to fight the feeling that they fitted together in more ways than just physically. Maya was a problem solver—like him—and having someone around to shoulder that burden with him was like a breath of fresh air. He didn't even have to ask half the time; she was just there. Supporting, sorting, getting the job done. Nothing like the Maya he'd painted a picture of all these years.

But was *it me who formed that image? Or did Maya walk out on me, and then Cat was the one who painted the picture after that?*

Perhaps he hadn't been, and never would be, good enough boyfriend material for Maya. In fact, there was no *perhaps* about it—she was too good for him. Plus, he was involved in a messy relationship, and even if that was on course to end soon, Maya was probably about to embark upon something with Brodie—who Sam had to admit seemed like a decent guy when he'd spoken to him in passing. But all of that didn't mean Sam and Maya couldn't be friends. There was no point in letting a past rejection get in the way of genuine friendship, otherwise it made him as toxic as the likes of his dad.

He eased his hold on her, but she didn't let him go for another couple of seconds, and once she did, she gave him the softest smile, which made his heart soar. "Come on," he said. "Let's go tell Ben."

❄   ❄   ❄

THE CHAIRLIFT RATTLED UP THE MOUNTAIN, AND FOR SOME REA-son Sam couldn't stop looking at his ski-clad feet with Maya's dangling next to them. He liked seeing that view again, after eight years of drought where her company on the mountain was concerned.

She was smiling as she watched the scenery. "No matter how many times I'm up here, it still takes my breath away," she said, turning to grace him with the full beam of her smile. "You know what I mean?"

"Yeah," he said, absorbing the soft warmth of her brown eyes. "I know exactly what you mean."

The lift arrived at the top of the slopes and they skied off, waiting a few yards away for Rowan and Aileen to join them from the chairlift behind. The four of them had decided to do a celebratory but competitive run down the mountain before leaving for the day.

This kind of thing was right up Maya's alley, and he could see the zealous glint in her eyes as she pulled her goggles onto her face. As soon as the woman was on the slopes, it was all about speed and winning for her, hence her sabotage of him in the pizza and chips race. He smiled at the memory.

"Right," Rowan told the group as she rubbed her hands together like some kind of maniacal genius. "You know the drill. Choose your run, first one at the terrace wins."

They were on the anterior side of the mountain, where the runs ended at the back terrace of the ski center. Choosing which run to take was a fine art. Some were more direct, but others lent themselves to the gathering of higher speeds. Sam had a sneaking suspicion that Rowan would take her favorite red run, and Aileen one of the blacks.

He rested his eyes on Maya. Which would she choose? He had a feeling that, like him, she might be inclined to go for an off-piste route.

"Ready?" Aileen asked them all, and the group gave her a mix of nods and thumbs-ups. Except for Maya, who shouted, "Hell yeah," and caused them all to laugh. Sam grinned. *Probably another one of her psyching out "tactics."*

"Count down from three, then we go from here," Aileen said. "Right . . . three, two, one, go!"

Everyone pushed off, Rowan heading for red and Aileen for black, as Sam had predicted.

He and Maya set off toward the same run. Another black. Sam's intention was to cross the tree line on the right-hand side and take an off-piste route that would be a little quicker than sticking on the main route.

He accelerated down the slope, heading in that direction, and noticed that Maya was veering off toward the opposite side—making for the tree line on the left. So his suspicion that she too would choose off-piste had been correct.

Suddenly, a nag of paranoia struck his gut. Her route sported a sheer cliff face just above it, with higher wind exposure. Those factors along with the recent heavy dump of snow made for a bigger avalanche risk in that area. *Stop being overprotective. Maya will know that. She's experienced.*

He continued on his path for a few more seconds, the irrational fear escalating and driving up his heart rate. *Fuck it.* He veered left across the slope and through the tree line after her.

As he emerged, he spotted her farther down the route, oblivious to his presence and tackling the slope like the pro she was. A sense of foolishness overcame him, but he stuck with his choice. He'd choose feeling foolish over worrying about her any day of the week.

It appeared that she hadn't noticed him tailing her; she seemed too zoned in on her path. As sneaky as it felt, he opted to stay a few yards behind in order to keep watch without having to explain himself. He hoped that she hadn't clocked the fact that he'd been headed in a different direction a few moments before. Though if she did, perhaps she might put it down to his being a bit of a cheat, rather than suspecting he wanted to look out for her.

The line of trees to their right whizzed past, and for a moment the anxiety he'd experienced melted away, leaving only the exhilaration of skiing off-piste behind his favorite ski buddy.

He admired her form as she carved a path ahead of him, feeling as if he could watch her all day. She was graceful yet ruthlessly fast on skis, and although he knew he could catch up with her, he would have to work pretty hard to do so.

She was clearly engrossed in her descent and preoccupied with her goal, because she still hadn't noticed him. It was only a matter of time before she did, however, and he was aware he'd need to style it out with an excuse when the time came. And there was no point in fooling himself that he was only looking out for her as a friend, when the real story was he had it bad for her.

Fuck. I really do have it bad.

That thought hit him right in the heart, to the point that it took him a second to register the low-pitched rumble behind them, like a small aircraft passing above. A brief turn of his head confirmed snow starting to tumble down the rock face. *I fucking knew it.*

His reflexes kicking in and his pulse ramping up, Sam crouched, keeping his skis straight and poles out behind him, increasing his velocity as he closed the gap between him and Maya. It took a matter of seconds, and yet it felt like hours.

"Maya!" he shouted as he drew alongside her left. She did a double take, opening her mouth to say something.

Sam gestured to the tree line on the right. "Get in there, now!"

She could clearly read him like a book because she immediately veered off to the right, no questions asked, making it into the trees before even turning her head to look at the burgeoning tumble of snow behind them.

He stayed behind her to ensure she got to safety first, and they both came to an abrupt stop.

Maya grabbed hold of a tree trunk, flashing him an urgent look. "Sam! Grab a tree."

He wasn't taking any chances. Not where Maya was concerned. Rather than grabbing his own tree, he positioned himself behind her, covering her with his body and taking hold of the tree above her head, shielding her face with his arm.

The rumble became louder, and the tumble appeared in his eyeline, about a hundred yards away to the right, where they'd been skiing a few moments before.

"Sam," Maya gasped, concern in her voice. She tried to move her arm to take hold of his, as if she wanted to secure his safety.

"Don't," he told her, speaking into her ear as he pressed her against the tree. "Hold on to the tree. I've got you." She halted her movements, but he felt the touch of her fingers on the underside of his arm.

They both fell silent, closing their mouths in case any snow veered off the slope and into the trees toward them. Sam watched the snow tumble, then slow, and then settle, creating a loose surface over the off-piste area nearby but not coming toward the cover of the trees.

For a couple more seconds, he held her there, absorbing the rise and fall of her shoulders against his chest as she breathed deeply. Relief that she was safe mixed with the white-hot heat of holding her close.

Eventually, Maya loosened her grip on the tree, and he eased back a couple of feet to let her turn to face him. Shoving her goggles up onto her helmet, she slid forward on the snow to wrap her arms around his waist and press her face into his chest. "I don't know whether to thank you or punch you in the face."

Sam held her tightly. "Hmm. I'd probably prefer the first option." He flashed her a smile as she lifted her head to look at him.

"You should've grabbed your own tree," she told him, her tone accusatory as she searched his eyes. "It would've been safer for you."

"Yeah, well. Yours was closer," he said with a shrug, lifting up his goggles and trying to keep his gaze off the neighboring tree that he'd skied past in order to get to hers.

"Thanks for the heads-up," she said, her voice softening again. "I didn't hear it until after you told me to get in here." She winced. "Bit too focused on winning."

"Really?" he said, raising his eyebrows. "That doesn't sound like you."

Maya punched his arm. "Shut it. You're just as competitive."

Yeah. Except, apparently, when it comes to simping over you. Then I'd lose any race, anytime.

"No problem," he said, trying not to imagine what might've happened if he hadn't followed her and the unlikely scenario that she didn't realize the avalanche was coming in time to avoid it.

She eyed him curiously. "How come you were following me anyway? I thought I saw you heading toward the other side of the slope."

Ah shit. He glanced away. "Just trying to be sneaky." He brought his eyes back to hers. "Like you in that pizza and chips race with the kids."

She arched an eyebrow. "Very underhand, Leonard."

Sam shot her a grin. "I learned from the best."

Maya smiled warmly, before the expression suddenly fell from her features. "Shit! Rowan and Aileen are going to win." She hurriedly pulled her goggles onto her face. "Come on!" She turned and skied off through the trees onto the black slope.

Sam followed her down, a solitary pairing on the run as they carved their way toward the finish line, and he felt as if they were the only two people in the world. By the end, he'd almost forgotten that it was a race because he'd been enjoying himself so much in the moment. The two of them skied off the end of the run toward the terrace simultaneously, and he got the sense that Maya had felt the same.

Aileen was there already, arms folded and wearing a smug smile. Sam spotted Rowan approaching at speed from the opposite direction, determined to get second place. Maya shot him a look, and both of them pushed off faster, each grabbing at the other one's arm in an attempt to gain advantage and achieve second place.

Just as it looked as if they might claim joint second, Maya gave him an overenthusiastic tug to the sleeve, and her ski accidentally caught with his, causing them both to slow and her to tip sideways, where he caught hold of her.

Both of them laughing at their schoolkid antics, he steadied her as she came about to face him, and he absorbed the beautiful way her laughter lit up her face. Over her head, he saw Rowan joining Aileen at the terrace in second place, and the pair high-fiving.

"I hate to tell you this," he said, grinning. "But we're joint last."

Maya smiled. "I'm standing in front of you, so I'm kind of third and you're last."

He rolled his eyes. "Typical."

She chuckled. "Ah well. Perhaps I don't mind being joint last with you."

A fiery warmth built in his heart. "Same."

Pushing back to turn toward the others, she gave him a wink. "Anyway. Serves you right for trying to cheat by following me. You might've been first otherwise."

"Yeah," he replied, following her. "Serves me right."

Chapter
FIFTEEN

THE KETTLE SIGNALED THE COMPLETION OF ITS TASK, AND MAYA leaned against the kitchen wall, phone in hand. The previous day, she'd spoken to Elise, who'd told her she had to call Hana. *"Because nobody knows better than me that time is short."*

Elise was right, but it didn't make the job any easier.

Placing the phone into her pocket with a sigh, she poured hot water onto her tea bag, breathing in the steamy, fragrant scent. The doorbell rang, and she frowned. "Who's that?"

Wondering why she'd asked that question to an empty house, she walked down the hallway to answer the door. When she opened it to find Hana on the other side, it seemed as if the universe was trying to tell her something. Something that made her heart accelerate and froze her to the spot.

"Out of the way," Hana said, bustling past with a small wheeled suitcase, her dark bob bouncing around her face. "It's freezing. I keep forgetting how bloody cold it is up here."

Maya stood to the side, peering out toward the driveway in confusion. "Where's Rosie?"

"Back home," Hana called down the hall.

Maya shut the door, following her into the kitchen. "What's going on? We weren't expecting you for a few more weeks. And why isn't Rosie with you?"

Hana was taking off her jacket. "Where're Mum and Dad?"

"At work," Maya said, watching her. Hana still didn't elaborate. "So . . . are you going to tell me what's happening?"

"Nothing. I just decided to come ahead a little early." Hana went to the kettle. "Is this boiled?"

"Yeah." Maya walked over. "Here, I'll make you one." Busying herself with the task, she watched her sister out of the corner of her eye. Hana took a seat and rubbed her face, staring out the window.

Maya brought the tea over. Hana nodded toward the garden, and the little property sitting at the end, which housed Yvonne's physio business. "Is Mum coming in soon?"

Maya nodded. "She should finish around four."

Hana took her mug. "Thanks."

Maya sat across from her sister, mug in hand. Here was the ideal opportunity to do what Elise and Liv, and Sam for that matter, had encouraged her to. But her mouth was dry and she didn't know where to start. "Is everything okay?"

Hana brought her gaze to meet hers. "Why?"

Maya shifted in her seat. "Because you're here early. Plus, you sounded stressed on the phone."

Hana sipped her tea, appearing to tighten her grip on the mug. "I *am* stressed."

Maya waited for Hana to elaborate, but she didn't. "What about?"

"What do you think?" Hana snapped. "I work in the biggest law firm in my region. I've got so much work on, it's coming out of my ears, and *nobody* seems to appreciate the pressure I'm under.

Not you, not Rosie." She shook her head. "Though I wouldn't expect you to understand, flouncing around on the bloody slopes all day without a care in the world."

Maya tightened her grip on her mug, that same cold, heavy sensation that usually accompanied a conversation with her sister sinking into her. "Without a care in the world? I lost my job and split with my boyfriend."

Hana rolled her eyes, and the tension in Maya's jaw mounted. "You were always moaning about that job, and you didn't seem bothered when you and Rich broke up anyway."

The knife of betrayal dug into Maya's ribs as her sister belittled her life, once again. Fair enough Hana was stressed at work, but that wasn't Maya's fault. She put her mug down, her temper beginning to crack. "Why did you tell Dad about my instructor job when I'd asked you to keep it to yourself?"

Hana gave her a hard stare. "It's unfair of you to go against his wishes like that. After all he's done for you? It was so hard for his family to make their way in Scotland as immigrants, and he only wants what's best for us. You're throwing that back in his face larking around at that stupid ski resort."

Maya took a breath in an attempt to combat the tightening sensation in her throat. She tried to keep the wobble out of her voice, and failed. "You're making me sound really selfish."

"That's because you are."

The words speared Maya's heart. It wasn't only that the sentiment was hurtful but that she suspected her sister was correct. Going after what she wanted in life *was* selfish. If she took the path she desired, she was doing what was best for her, rather than her family.

Swallowing hard, she got to her feet. Her knees felt loose, like they mightn't hold her weight. "I need to be somewhere."

Leaving the room quickly, she noted that Hana didn't try to stop her, or say anything at all. After speedily pulling on her jacket and boots, she grabbed her woolly hat and gloves to step outside into the winter afternoon twilight, shutting the door behind her and taking a lungful of icy cold air.

Having no idea where she should go, but feeling she needed to walk, she set off onto the pavement and along the street.

After wandering around for a few minutes, trying to distract herself with the Christmas lights, she took out her phone and called Liv. It rang out and went to voice mail, so Maya hung up. She hovered her thumb over Elise's number. Calling Elise might be selfish when she had such big issues going on. Although, it *had* been her advice to get into a discussion with Hana.

Not knowing what was self-centered and what was reasonable anymore, she took her finger away from Elise's number and sat on a low wall, staring across the road into the darkness.

Her phoned buzzed with a message from Sam.

> BB Ben is so stoked about the accounts thing that he's talking about giving us both a bonus.

At least there was some good news in the world. Sam deserved a bonus.

> Brilliant. There's no one more deserving than you.

> Yeah there is. You.

Maya's thumb seemed to type of its own free will, her stream of consciousness directly galvanizing it without her rational mind censoring her thoughts.

I'm too selfish.

What?! You're the least selfish person I know.

Maya sat for a moment, realizing she'd typed on impulse and unsure what to say next. She didn't want to rain on his parade. That would be even more self-centered of her.

The phone began to ring, and it was him. Maya cleared her throat, trying to reinforce her voice before answering. "Hey, Leonard. How goes it?"

"What's wrong?"

Her voice wobbled. "Nothing."

His tone was soft. "Maya."

She swallowed the lump in her throat. "Hana arrived home unexpectedly." Her voice broke. "She says that I lark around without a care in the world and it's selfish of me to work at the resort when Dad had to work so hard as the son of an immigrant family."

There was a second's silence. "Are you at home?"

"No. I'm sitting on a wall two streets down from ours, freezing my arse off. I didn't want to be in the house with her."

"I'm coming to get you."

Panic rose in her chest at the thought of him putting himself out, plus what would he say to Cat? "Sam, don't—"

"Stay there. I'll be two minutes." He hung up.

"Shit." Maya glanced around, hoping there were no schoolchildren within earshot. She huffed out her breath, feeling like the most pathetic specimen in the world. "For goodness' sake," she muttered. "You're going to get Sam in trouble now. Selfish again."

Maybe once he arrived, she could insist she was fine and send him home.

A few minutes later, some headlights approached, and she recognized the car that had died on Kirsty's street a few weeks ago.

Standing and realizing that her bottom had gone numb, she waddled painfully over to open the passenger door.

She leaned down and popped her head in. "I almost didn't recognize this car with the engine running."

He smiled, and she felt as if the sight of that might heal all her ills. Nearly.

"Get in," he said.

"It's fine," Maya replied, staying put. "I overreacted. I'm just going to head home."

Sam raised his eyebrows. "Get in the car. I'm taking you somewhere."

She sighed. "Okay, okay. But I really am fine." Climbing inside, she removed her hat and gloves.

He eyed her as she buckled in, then set out toward the crossroads. Maya stayed quiet, unable to trust her voice not to break and give way to tears.

Sam took them through town and up the hill road, the Tavern looming into view with its big sparkly tree.

"The pub?" Maya asked, raising her eyebrows. "I suppose I could do with a drink."

Sam parked. "We're not going inside."

He climbed out of the car and she followed suit, frowning as he lifted something from the boot.

"What's that?"

"A waterproof sheet."

"What for?"

"Sitting on." He gave her a smile and held out his hand.

She studied him curiously for a second, then took it. Despite both their hands being gloved, it still sent tingles up her arm. Sam led her toward the fairy-light-adorned tree line, and onto the little path that led through the woods, turning on the torch on his keys.

"Hey," she said, raising her eyebrows. "I hope you're not leading me into the nook to have your wicked way with me."

Sam laughed. "That's not where we're going."

Course not. There's no way you want to be there with me. She shoved the memory of him and Cat on the path together from her mind.

As they made their way along, the familiar cluster of foliage that was the nook came into view. Maya smiled as she remembered being in there with a guy when she was younger. Not one as attractive as Sam, but it had been exciting at the time.

Back then, the area had been tamed into the shape of a den in which amorous teens had found private shelter. But now years of disuse had caused it to grow out of its previous shape, and it resembled an overgrown bush. *Feels a bit like me. Overgrown and messy.*

Sam glanced over as they passed it by, continuing along the path through the woods. "Okay?"

"Yeah," Maya said, picking her way along next to him. "I just wish I knew where we were going."

"You'll see."

Eventually they emerged from the trees onto a snowy field, and Maya was struck by how clear the sky was. Every star could be picked out precisely.

"Oh my goodness." She stopped for a second to study the heavens, holding her breath in awe.

"Right?" Sam said, smiling. He squeezed her hand. "Come on. We're nearly there."

Crunching through the snow over the field, Maya could see

that it led to the downward slope of the hill, which overlooked a little valley in the mountains.

As they neared the start of the slope, Sam stopped and rolled out the waterproof sheet onto the soft snow. "Have a seat."

Maya climbed onto it and he joined her. Gazing upward, she saw a perfect view of the moon and stars above the valley. The familiarity of the scene clicked into place, and she sucked in her breath. "This is the view in Arran's painting." The one she had secretly stashed in her room and that she still didn't know whether to keep or to give to Sam. She glanced over and he was smiling.

"That's right."

Holding his gaze, a large smile spread over her face. "I love it."

Sam moved his gloved hand over to hers, covering it, and they both looked up again.

"It's spectacular," Maya whispered, afraid that speaking too loudly might break the spell of the place.

"Try this." He lay down on the sheet, patting the space next to him, and Maya followed suit.

The velvety black sky domed above them, dotted with specks of silver and gold, the moon hanging full as the centerpiece.

Sam took her hand again, and she sighed. "Thank you for bringing me here."

His voice was low and smooth. "You're welcome."

They lay there for a few moments, Maya taking in the patterns of light and feeling like the weight was drifting from her into the heavens. The warm sensation of Sam's emotional rescue, along with the memory of his physical protection from the avalanche, made her feel as if she were wrapped in a comforting cocoon.

Finally, Sam spoke. "You aren't selfish, Maya."

Her breath caught, and she hesitated for a moment. Then she shifted a little closer to him on the sheet, sensing him doing the same, until their sides were touching and their entwined hands rested on where their thighs were in contact. "But Hana says that Dad worked hard to create this path of self-sufficiency for us. So that we wouldn't have to struggle. And that I'm flaunting it in his face." She swallowed. "It's not fair for me to consider dumping all of that."

Sam was silent for a second. "You want to dump accountancy?"

He seemed surprised to hear it. Maya turned her head so she could look at him, and he matched her posture, meeting her eyes. She nodded, her woolly hat rustling on the plastic sheeting and cutting into the silence. "It's crossed my mind, since I started working at the resort. But I can't do it."

Sam turned his body to face her. "You've never thought that accountancy was for you, have you?"

His eyes seemed to draw her in. She could swear he had magnets in there. "No."

"What do you want to do instead?"

Maya opened her mouth, still afraid to voice it. Sam shuffled a little closer, as if closing the gap between them would make it easier for her to get the words out.

"I want to stay on at the resort," she said quietly.

Something shifted in his gaze, and he lifted his other hand to brush her hair from her face. "There's nothing wrong with that. You can be self-sufficient *and* be a ski instructor. Plus, you can be happy. You aren't doing any harm by wanting that, Maya. And you shouldn't feel guilty about it."

Looking into his eyes, she could believe anything he said. *That's what got me into trouble before.* She glanced away. "I wish I could make them see that."

He smiled. "We'll think of something."

Maya nodded, enjoying the warm fuzzy feeling of Sam insinuating they were a team. "Anyway. Enough about me and my non-sense. What's going down with you?" She paused. "Out of the general dumping ground yet?"

He let out a short laugh. "I think the general dumping ground is where I always am, whether or not I sleep in my own room."

She squeezed his hand and he reciprocated. "Want to talk about it?" She fell silent, expecting him to say no.

"Yeah. I do. I feel like it's driving me crazy."

She held on to his hand tightly.

Sam sighed. "We argued because I think she's been going through my phone. Even deleting my messages."

Deleting his messages . . . She shot him a frown.

He met her eyes. "Yes. That's what I reckon happened to your text, the one that never arrived."

"Wow," Maya said, trying to tone down her response so that she didn't put him offside. "That is out of order."

"I know."

But the intonation of his voice indicated he wasn't sure, as if he needed it validated.

Maya kept her gaze meshed with his. "Going through your partner's phone without permission is wrong. Full stop. And deleting their messages is unforgivable."

She hoped saying that wouldn't cause him to pull away, the way he'd done with Liv in the past. Her shoulders relaxed as his face took on a relieved expression.

"Did she apologize for it?" she asked.

Sam appeared to think for a moment. "No. She didn't admit it at all. Just started yelling at me about what a terrible person I was to accuse her, and that everybody knew it, plus no one knows why she stays with me because I hold her back."

He seemed about to say more, but then he stopped.

"But . . . she didn't deny it?"

He opened his mouth, then glanced away. "No. She didn't." Frowning, he met her eyes again. "Though I hadn't even appreciated that until you asked."

Maya turned fully onto her side so that she was facing him directly. "Sam. That's called gaslighting."

He shuffled over to mirror her. "What do you mean?"

Her instinct was to be cautious after he was short with her the other morning. But taking a hit was something she could cope with if it helped him recognize toxic behaviors, so she plowed on. "It's a form of emotional abuse, whereby the partner who's the perpetrator makes the other one question their thoughts or suspicions. And deflecting from themselves when they've done something wrong—making the other person think *they're* in the wrong instead—is an example of that behavior."

Sam looked away, and Maya's heart rate picked up. Perhaps she'd been too blunt, made him angry with her.

He swallowed. "Shit." Meeting her gaze again, he nodded. "That's the sort of stuff my dad used to pull with Mum."

The sledgehammer hit that Sam's relationship situation was related to his experience with his dad, and she wondered how she hadn't seen it before. Sam was his mum in this scenario, and Cat his father. In addition, Sam's abandonment issues and fear of rejection, which fueled him staying with Cat, were a result of his dad's behavior toward the family.

She squeezed his hand, guilty that she'd blamed him for choosing Cat in the past when the real issue was he'd fallen in with someone toxic who was the worst person for him given his history and vulnerabilities. Although Maya hadn't known that at the time—she'd been friends with Cat up until that point and was only now realizing the extent of the woman's toxicity.

Sam rolled onto his back, keeping hold of Maya's hand as he gazed at the sky again. Maya appreciated the chance to have him so near her for a few seconds, then went onto her back, thinking she should keep a distance, and joined him in the stargazing.

She kept silent, aware that he'd had enough revelations for one evening. One step at a time.

WAITING ON THE CORNER, SAM CRANED HIS NECK TO SEE IF Maya was approaching. When she'd suggested making a walking route out of all their favorite contenders for the Christmas lights competition, he'd been delighted. A little Christmas cheer was just what the doctor ordered.

Until now Sam would have avoided getting close with any female acquaintances in order to maintain a stress-free existence. He'd socialize with Vicky and his other female colleagues while at work but then keep his distance—only seeing them when Cat was with him. But that wasn't an option with Maya. Cat wouldn't be up for hanging out, and the idea of *not* seeing Maya was abhorrent.

The issue of the deleted text passed through his mind. During his lunch break he'd googled *gaslighting*, and it had led to some reading on the kinds of personalities that used it. He'd also called in to see his mum and surreptitiously mentioned it to her. Angus had been there, and Sam had taken Angus up on his offer to leave the room while Sam had a chat with her. He felt bad for chasing Angus out of what was now his own living room. But Sam still couldn't fully trust Angus not to bolt from their lives and so was wary of involving him in Sam's vulnerabilities.

Tara had known what gaslighting was, commenting that she'd seen it in action with the twins' father. If his mum had questioned any of his dad's bad behavior, his dad made it look as if she were being unreasonable. *Nagging* and *overemotional* were some of the terms he'd used. He'd also used a lot of *paranoid* and *jealous* when Tara had suspected him of cheating.

The case was becoming more concrete by the minute and what he had to do, even more clear. But Cat was still avoiding him, staying at her mum's and leaving all of his messages—telling her they needed to sit down and talk—unanswered. Perhaps he should just turn up at her parents' house unannounced? Though the idea of them being around for the discussion left him cold.

Salvation from his dark thoughts arrived when Maya strolled round the corner through the snow, carrying two cups and looking gorgeous in her down jacket and woolly hat. She was the only person he knew who could practically saunter in snow. Everyone else crunched along with a high step, resembling a horse performing dressage.

He'd been taken aback to hear that she wanted to be a ski instructor full-time, after the derogatory things she'd said about his career choice in the past. He hadn't voiced his surprise the previous evening, when they'd been stargazing, because it would've been selfish to harp on the past when they'd been talking about her issues with her family. They'd both changed a lot since they were teenagers, and Maya had no doubt moved past the snobbish career ideas her father had instilled in her when she was younger.

Flashing him a grin, she closed the distance between them and kissed his cheek, sending a surge of heat through his body despite the freezing temperature.

"Here," she said, handing him a cup. "Can't have a Christmas lights walk without hot chocolate and marshmallows."

A smile spread over his face. "Awesome, thank you."

He took a sip, and the velvety chocolate flowed over his tongue, laced with the sweet stickiness of the half-melted marshmallows. "Oh my God," he practically groaned. "That's as good as the one in the ski café."

"Right?" Maya said as they started to walk. She gave him a wink. "Multitalented, that's me. Numbers, hot drinks, cheating at pizza and chips races . . ."

Sam laughed. "I still haven't forgiven you for that, by the way. Or for telling the kids my middle name's Leonard." He nudged her arm. "Revenge is still in the offing."

Maya shrugged, sipping her drink. "I'm glad I don't have a middle name. It used to annoy me when I was younger, but now I realize it can't be used as blackmail material."

"There are still plenty of other ways I can get back at you," he said, enjoying the expression she flashed him—it was clearly meant to be withering, but on her, it just looked cute.

"Here's the first one," Maya said, tugging his sleeve to halt him in his tracks. She rummaged in her jacket pocket to take out a couple of pieces of card and handed him one, then got a pen out and gave him that too.

Sam studied the card. She'd noted down all the houses on their route, with an area to the side for them to be marked out of five.

Warmth unfurled in his chest. "You made us scorecards?" She was so cool and brilliant.

"Yes. We get to pretend that we're big Glenavie movers and shakers, on the judging panel for the lights competition. Right. This one's got those icicle-shaped ones. I love it."

Sam nodded, taking in the display and scribbling a number.

"Maybe on the way around we should decide what ideas we'd pinch, if we had our own house to decorate." *If we had our own house? Way to be inappropriate.* He glanced over but she was smiling, so hopefully he hadn't made her uncomfortable with that comment.

"Great idea. I'd want icicle lights."

"Icicle lights," he murmured, scribbling it on the other side of his card. "Noted."

They set off for the next house.

"Why don't you decorate your house for real?" Maya asked. "I tried to convince my parents, but Dad didn't go for it."

Sam shook his head as he sipped the sweet warmth of his drink. "Cat doesn't like them. Reckons they're tacky."

Maya was silent for a second. "Yeah. I remember you saying that."

Sam glanced over, aware that the last time he'd mentioned it, it had been to compare Cat's opinion with what he'd assumed Maya's to be, and it hadn't gone down well. He cleared his throat. "Here's house number two."

"Ooh, inflatable Santa." Maya put on a singsong voice. "Bonus points." She gestured to his card. "Write that on our list."

Sam gave her a salute. "No problem." He scribbled *inflatable Santa* underneath *icicle lights*.

They both noted their scores, discussing the merits of the display as if it were a serious judging process, then moved on, and it was as if Sam's soul were lightening with every passing minute.

As they neared number three, he gave her a nudge. "Not to bring down the mood, but what's happening with Hana?"

Maya made a mock gag. "Nothing. She's being cool and distant with me. And still won't elaborate about why she turned up on the doorstep unannounced from England."

Sam raised his eyebrows. "Thatched roof burned down?"

Maya laughed, and he appreciated the way the sound of it infused him with a warm glow.

"Who knows. Perhaps her perfect life was too perfect so she needed to create some drama." Pausing, she sipped her drink. "Actually, that's unfair. She works really hard and is clearly very stressed."

Sam smiled at the way she automatically empathized with people's positions, even when they didn't seem able to do the same for her. "What about your mum and dad? Have they spoken to her?"

"Nope. In my family there are a lot of elephant-in-the-room situations. Everyone knows it's there, but no one speaks about it so as not to rock the boat." She sighed. "It's like an imaginary circus in my house, tiptoeing around all the invisible pachyderms."

Sam gave her a sideways glance. Conflict avoidance must have been the reason she hadn't communicated directly to him that she didn't want to continue seeing him when they were younger. Sending someone else as messenger had been easier when she disliked direct confrontation. But that was irrelevant now, and he certainly wasn't going to mention it and spoil their blossoming friendship. Especially when she needed his support.

"Mum tries to get us to talk, but even she ends up skirting around the subject." She shrugged. "And I've sent those CVs that Dad wanted me to. Because I can't admit to him that it isn't what *I* want."

Sam circled her shoulders as they continued on their walk, wishing he could fix it all for her.

Altogether the light walk took over an hour, and Sam relished every moment, trying to ignore the feeling that he didn't want their time together to end.

He'd deliberately engineered it so he could walk her back to hers rather than the other way around. He didn't want her going back alone when it was late.

Maya leaned in as they reached her driveway, meaning he was enveloped in her scent. It always did terrible things to his heart rate.

"Let's compare notes." She held her card next to his, scanning them. "We're pretty much in tune here. We'd make awesome judges." Shifting away again, she sniffed. "How dare they not let us on the panel."

Sam smiled. "To be fair, we haven't asked. And it's too late now."

"Ooh." Her eyes widened. "Next year, shall we ask if we can join it? They can only say no, right?"

Sam's heart swelled at the thought that she might still be around, and in his life as his friend, in a year's time. "Let's do it."

Maya did a little dance in the snow, making him laugh.

"Awe-some," she sang, then hugged him. "Keep your scorecard so we can see how our votes compare against the real results."

He gave her a squeeze, realizing that snow was falling. "Will do." He eased back to look at her, the fluttering flakes of snow clinging to the dark of her eyelashes and forming tiny beads of moisture on her lips that he desperately wanted to kiss off.

She released him slowly, and he handed back her cup. "Thanks for the hot chocolate."

Giving him a wink, she headed along the driveway, doing a twirl in the falling snow as she went. "You are very welcome, Samuel Leonard Holland."

Chapter
SEVENTEEN

IT WASN'T THAT SHE WAS PROUD OF AVOIDING HER SISTER, BUT Maya certainly was pleased about it. She'd hardly seen her family in an effort to avoid any more arguments.

Planning for the sled race had taken over her days and nights, and Maya had thrown herself into not only that, but all aspects of work, and had ended up eating most of her meals at the café, each evening hanging out with whoever was working late and grabbing some food with them. She'd even been coming in on her days off, much to Ben's delight.

Sam had encouraged her to go home and at least speak to her mother, but Maya didn't even feel able to do that—not wanting to be "selfish" in pitting her mum against her dad and sister.

Sam had told her that Cat was staying at her mum's and not speaking to him. Maya wondered whether that signaled the death knell of their relationship, or if it was just another one of their many bumps in the road. From what she'd heard, their relationship had suffered much drama and multiple large blowouts along the way.

But she couldn't help feeling that this time must be different, what with Sam's revelation about Cat's underhanded behavior.

Not that Sam seeing the light and separating from Cat's toxicity would mean Maya would expect him to suddenly be interested in her—she was painfully aware that they were just friends. But it would make his life more content, and Liv could stop worrying about him. The idea of both those things made Maya very happy.

By the time the Sunday of the race rolled around, Maya was living and breathing the resort, and she loved it.

Skiing to the top of the short, green run that was to serve as the race venue, she surveyed the hill, making sure all the markers were in place. The bright white slope swept down before her, glittering invitingly, begging her to cut into the fresh and pristine powder.

The sun sparkled off the surface and warmed her face against the cold, yet gentle, winter breeze. She pulled her goggles over her eyes, setting off down the side of the slope in order to check it from the bottom. Her skis sliced satisfyingly into the snow, the sensation infusing her soul with joy.

Sam appeared at the bottom of the slope as she had a few more yards to go. Smiling, she carved into the powder and came to a standstill next to him, deliberately spraying him with a soft shower of snow.

He laughed, brushing himself off. "You'd better watch it."

Maya took off her goggles and helmet. "Oh, I will." She skied away a little, toward the terrace, then turned to flash him a grin. "Or *will* I?"

Sam laughed hard at that point, and Maya enjoyed the way his face lit up. Maybe he'd never break away from Cat, but perhaps he could find some way to improve their relationship. And in the meantime, Maya would be there to make him laugh.

Sam strolled over to where she was checking the finish line markers. He leaned in. "Shall we test it out before the contenders arrive?"

A burst of excitement gathered in her belly, rising into her chest. "Great idea."

Maya unbuckled her skis and stuck them in the snow, grabbing her snow boots from the terrace and changing into them while Sam crunched through the powder to fetch two brightly colored plastic sleds from the pile at the bottom of the slope.

They picked their way up the side of the run to stand at the top, sleds under their arms. Maya surveyed the area, working out the fastest route down.

Sam had chosen his spot and was settling into his red sled. "Don't think that you're going to beat me."

Maya decided on her starting point, aware that her competitive streak was taking over. "I don't *think* I'm going to beat you. I *know* I am."

Sam smiled. "Not a chance."

Maya shook her head, climbing into her bright blue sled. She was going to win, no matter what it took.

"Ready?" he called.

"Yes," she said, grinning. "But are *you*?"

"Stop trying to psych me out, Bashir."

Maya laughed.

"Okay," Sam called. "Three, two, one, go!"

Maya shoved herself off, immediately taking the most aerodynamic form possible and keeping her course on the fastest route. She glanced to the side, where she could see Sam was neck and neck with her.

In determination, she shifted slightly, increasing her speed and pulling away. Delight flooded through her, and she zoned in harder on her course.

Maya careened the last few yards, sailing over the finish line with a whoop. "Yes!" she shouted, clambering out of the sled. "In your face, Holland!"

She looked up, wondering why she couldn't hear him cursing in his signature manner whenever she beat him at anything.

Her heart rose into her mouth as she spotted his prone form lying at the side of the track. Nausea socked her gut, sending her heart rate rocketing and galvanizing her into a sprint.

"Sam!" she shouted, closing the gap between them within seconds.

He was lying on his front, his face turned away from her. She threw herself down, grabbing his arm and shaking it. "Sam?"

She took his other arm and hauled him onto his back, leaning down to study his face and check he was breathing.

"Ha!" he shouted, opening his eyes and coming to life, causing an adrenaline spike that made her snap back and grab her chest.

He began laughing so hard that he had to hold his stomach. "Got you!"

Maya was frozen on the spot, kneeling next to him with her heart still hammering. Her jaw dropped. "You little—"

"Your face." Sam sat up, still laughing. "I told you I'd get my revenge when you least expected it."

Annoyed that he'd gotten one over on her, and panicked her to boot, Maya grabbed a handful of snow and threw it at him.

He lifted his arms to block it. "Oh no you don't."

She went to stand in order to make a run for it, but he grabbed her and launched her onto her back, pinning her in place and reaching for some snow, which she could tell was going down her jumper unless she got free.

As he shifted his weight, Maya threw him off balance, knocking him away from her. She grabbed her own handful of snow and stuffed it down the front of his jacket before he could react.

"Aah!" he shouted, jumping to his feet and trying to untuck his clothes to get it out. "Oh my God, it's so cold!"

Maya backed off a few yards to what she thought was a safe distance. She couldn't keep the grin off her face. "Duh. It's snow, Leonard."

He snapped his head up to meet her gaze, his amber eyes narrowed but sparkling. "Oh, you are in for it now."

Sam started to run at her and she screamed, sprinting away toward the center. But it was a cumbersome movement in ski gear, and she felt as if she were running through treacle.

Sam caught up and grabbed her from behind, lifting her off her feet as he kept walking toward the building.

"Put me down!" she shouted.

"I will," he said, his warm breath tickling her ear and sending a shiver along her spine. "But then you're helping me to find a bloody jumper before this race starts. I'm soaked to the skin."

They reached the terrace and he set her down, grabbing her hand to tug her inside. She looked at him as they crossed the threshold, and he was grinning broadly.

"You started it," she said, smiling back.

"No, *you* started it," he said as they made their way across the back foyer. "By setting me up in that pizza and chips race with the kids. *And* telling them my middle name." He let go of her hand to open the door to the stairwell.

They approached the stairs, and Maya shoved his arm.

He gave her a shove in return as they climbed.

Upon reaching the top, she went to shove him again, but he quickly opened his office door and stepped in, avoiding her touch. "Ha," he said, flashing her the sexiest smile she'd ever seen. "Right. Check all of the drawers. I must've got a T-shirt or a jumper in here somewhere."

"*Me* check?" Maya said, heading for the desk. "What're *you* going to do?"

"Get this wet stuff off, of course. I'm freezing."

He started pulling off his upper clothing, and Maya's pulse throbbed. She'd seen him topless before and she wasn't sure she could handle it again.

She kept her eyes off him as he undressed, searching the drawers until she found a top in one of them. She lifted it, trying to figure out how to pass it over without looking at him.

"Come on, Maya. I'm catching my death here."

Maya glanced over and he was wiping his wet chest with his T-shirt, trying to soak up the moisture. She was frozen in place for a second, watching him rub the glistening beads of water from his skin with a burning ache in her belly.

He glanced up and she wrenched her eyes off him, holding out the top and keeping her gaze averted.

Sam took it from her. "Thanks." He turned his head, following her eyeline toward the wall. "What're you looking at?"

"Nothing. I'm trying to preserve your dignity," she said, continuing to stare at the wall.

He laughed. "You saw me wearing much less than this at Kirsty's house. And in the spa."

"I know. But still. In your office is different."

She could tell he'd finished dressing, so she brought her eyes back onto him, but the force of meeting his gaze threw her for a moment. She cleared her throat. "Let's go get this party started."

Leading him out of the office and back down the stairs, she tried to pretend that her escalating feelings for him didn't exist.

Out on the terrace, the rest of the team had gathered, ready to begin the race. Sam directed everybody to their stations, and shortly after, the contestants arrived. Each one signed up at the desk they'd erected on the terrace, and took a race number, which they attached to their front and back.

Maya herded the spectators behind the barriers, finding Liv and Elise and making sure they had good spots at the front of the crowd, and perhaps also near to Arran, who was standing with Nico. Cupid was still doing her duty.

Eventually the racers were led to the top of the run. They'd drawn in a good number, especially once word got around regarding the new top prize. A large amount of sponsorship money had come in already, and that would only increase once the final amount was in, plus whatever they raised at the after-party.

Pride swelled in Maya's chest at what Sam, and the rest of their colleagues at the resort, had achieved. Especially when the money was going to the children's hospice.

Maya stood at her position on the finish line, shifting her weight from one foot to the other in anticipation. She signaled across to Rowan, who was posted on the other side, and Rowan gave her a nod.

Maya raised her arm to let the staff at the top of the hill know they were ready.

Sam took his place next to her. Once she and Rowan had conferred to agree on the winners and passed him their numbers, he would announce it over his megaphone.

The staff at the top fired the starting pistol, and the racers set off.

The contestants came racing down the hill, a few careening off to the side and falling off their sleds after only a few yards.

Sam leaned toward her ear, his breath warming her cheek and creating a fiery wave of heat across her skin. "Amateurs."

Maya smiled, making a mammoth effort to keep her eyes on the racers and off Sam. The first three reached the line to roars of delight from the crowd, and Maya jotted their numbers. A few seconds later, another batch arrived.

They waited until the last few stragglers had passed the finish line, then Rowan sprinted across to confer with Maya. Their numbers matched.

Maya passed Sam the sheet.

"What does this even say?" He peered at it. "I didn't realize doctor's handwriting was hereditary."

Maya smacked his arm. "None of your cheek, Leonard."

He winked at her, lifting his megaphone to make the announcement.

There was much rejoicing from the victors, and Rowan gave Maya a high five. They went to congratulate the winners, standing around a little while to chat to everyone.

"Well done, Maya," Elise said, giving her a hug. "What a brilliant cause, and that top prize is fantastic." She kissed her cheek.

Liv came in next for a hug. "Give me that other cheek." She planted a very noisy kiss on the other side.

Maya screwed her face up and pretended that she didn't love it. A tiny spear of sadness pierced her being that her family weren't here, joining in, and neither would they show any pride in what had been achieved. A little voice told her a big part of that was because she'd refused to speak to them all week and hadn't even told her dad and Hana what day the race was on. Though they could easily have looked it up on the resort website. At least her mum had asked to come, but Maya had dissuaded her.

Gesturing toward Arran and Nico, Maya waved them over. "What about these lovely gentlemen, and their fabulous prizes?"

Arran kissed Maya's cheek. "My prize was donated by *you*, so stop trying to deflect the credit."

Nico laughed, sweeping in. "Hey, Maya. Long time no see." He gave her a wink. "I *did* donate my own prize, so . . ."

He flashed Arran a grin, and Arran punched his arm, then shook his hand and winced in the pretense that Nico's deltoid had injured it. Though, to be fair, it probably had. The guy was built like a tank.

Liv was laughing at Nico's antics, but Elise didn't appear impressed.

Maya gestured toward the car park. "I'll see you guys at the pub. I'm just going to help with the clear-up."

The four of them left Maya in order to go and greet Sam, who was surrounded by the winners and their supporters. He flashed Maya a smile as she waved and headed up the run to help collect the markers.

Once Maya emerged into the car park, Sam was leaning against his car, waiting for her. They'd opted to travel in together that morning, and he'd leave his car at the pub so they could both have a drink. Then they'd swing by on the way into work the next morning, in order to collect it.

Maya reached him. "Don't scratch your paintwork with your leaning against the car in a sexy manner."

They climbed in.

Sam buckled his seat belt, smiling. "You think I'm sexy?"

"Nope," she fired back, her pulse ramping up. "I mean you *think* you are."

He slapped a hand over his heart. "Ouch."

Maya laughed as he took them out of the car park and onto the road toward the pub.

Sam glanced over. "I didn't see Brodie in the crowd. Is he still coming?"

"Yeah," Maya said, rummaging in her bag to check she had her purse to purchase some raffle tickets. "He had to go into the shop today, but he'll be at the after event."

"Cool," Sam said, his voice a little flat. He paused. "What's happening with you guys?"

"How do you mean?" Where was that damned purse? If she couldn't find it, then they'd need to swing by hers to fetch it, because she wanted a wad of tickets. Unless she could borrow off Liv or Elise.

"Are you guys seeing each other?"

"Aha. There it is." She lifted out the purse. "Are we what?"

He hesitated. "Seeing each other."

For a moment she had to think what he meant. "Brodie and me? We're just friends. I'm not really looking to date again yet."

Maya thought for a moment, not really sure why she felt that way. It wasn't as if she was heartbroken over Rich; she hardly thought about him at all. So why *wasn't* she interested in dating anyone?

"I just assumed, after that kiss under the mistletoe . . ." Sam shot her a smile, though for some reason it didn't reach his eyes.

Maya swallowed as she realized the reason she wasn't interested in Brodie, or anyone else for that matter, was the feelings she harbored for Sam. Feelings that she didn't want to examine the depth of because she'd end up hurt. He still had a girlfriend, even if she refused to speak to him.

She plastered a smile onto her face, sobered by those thoughts. "It was just a peck. Didn't mean anything."

They pulled into the car park and headed for the top floor. There were cheers from the crowd as Sam entered, and he was swept into more hugs and slaps on the back.

Smiling, Maya headed to the table that Liv and Elise were at, sitting with Arran and Nico, plus Ben and a few others from the ski team. There was a bottle of beer waiting for her, and she took a seat, listening to the chat at the table and watching Sam work the room. He was handed beer after beer, and seemed to be doing a sterling job of sinking them.

Nico leaned over. "Hopefully Sam won't be slurring too much by the time he takes to the microphone for his speech and prize giving."

"I know," Maya said, keeping her eyes on Sam. "They'd better bring the gig forward before the guy keels over." She glanced down at their bottles. "Speaking of which, it's my round. Same again?"

Nico nodded. "Please."

Maya stood. "Everyone want another?" There was a chorus of yeses, and Maya headed first toward the raffle table to purchase a huge pile of tickets, and then the bar to get a trayful of fresh drinks.

Just as she reached the table with the tray and was handing them out, Sam got onto the makeshift stage at the side of the room, and someone tapped their glass loudly for quiet.

Maya took her seat as a chorus of shushes filled the air and everyone fell silent to listen.

Sam cleared his throat. "I want to thank you all for giving up your Sunday in order to make the fourth annual Glenavie sled race such a success. We've raised a lot of money so far for a truly excellent cause." He pointed to a picture of the children's hospice on the screen behind him.

Maya leaned over to Nico. "Surprisingly nonslurred."

He grinned.

Sam continued. "I particularly want to thank the ski team, who gave up their time to run the event today. Especially Maya, who's hiding over there, not wanting to take any of the credit."

Everyone looked at her, so she tried to duck behind Nico.

"Oh no you don't," Nico said loudly, shifting to the side.

She received a round of applause and a big cheer, heat rising in her face as she gave the room an awkward wave.

Sam smiled, meeting Maya's gaze. "Maya donated one of the prizes, a fabulous oil painting by our very own Arran Adebayo." He pointed toward Arran, and their table led a large cheer, with Arran giving a wave to the room. "Plus, Maya also organized our top prize, through her contacts."

There was another cheer; then Sam started to run down the winners, last to first, and gave each of the prize donors a shoutout. When it got to Nico's prize, he stood and took a bow, with more than one admiring glance from the ladies in the room. Except Elise, who rolled her eyes.

"And finally," Sam announced. "The first prize is . . . six tickets to see Glasgow's own Iona Mac perform in her home city, along with backstage passes."

The room erupted, and the winner of the prize jumped out of their seat in delight.

Maya couldn't keep the grin off her face as the winner threw their arms around Sam. She raised her bottle to the table and clinked it with the others', taking a drink.

The chat started again, and Maya began to feel fatigued after the day's activities. Watching Sam for a little while, she noticed that he'd managed to sink a few more bottles, judging by the little pile in the corner by the stage.

Eventually, she glanced over her shoulder, and spotted Brodie at the bar. "Back in a sec," she told the others, and got up to make her way over.

"You made it," she said as she approached.

Brodie kissed her cheek. "Sorry I'm so late, couldn't get away. Looks like it went well?"

"It was awesome. All went smoothly. No broken bones, which is a bonus."

"Absolutely," Brodie said, clinking his bottle with hers. "What's next for you? Are you staying on at the resort?"

Maya pursed her lips. "Not sure. I need to assess the situation."

"Sounds very precise." He shot her a smile.

She shrugged. "I'm an accountant by trade. We're a precise bunch."

"Good point." Brodie lifted his gaze behind her. "Here comes the man of the moment."

Maya turned just as Sam drew level with her, circling her shoulders and kissing her cheek.

She sensed that he was a little unsteady as she put her arm around his waist. "All right, Leonard?"

"Yep." He gave her a squeeze, glancing at Brodie. "Hey, Brodie."

Maya might have been imagining it, but it seemed like there was an edge to Sam's voice.

"Congrats," Brodie said, flashing him a smile. "I hear the day was a success."

"S'all down to my savior, here," Sam replied, tugging Maya closer into his side. He might not have been slurring before, but he was now.

"I don't know about that," Maya said. "It would have come off, with or without me. You'd gotten most of it done by the time I came on board."

Sam's words ran together, threaded into one long string by the alcohol. "But it wouldn't have been as good without your grand prize."

He gave her another squeeze.

Brodie nodded. "I can't believe you got those tickets, Maya. They're like gold dust."

Maya smiled. "What can I say? I've got the contacts."

Brodie laughed, and Sam brought her in to kiss her forehead, swaying a little.

Brodie raised his eyebrows.

Maya glanced at Sam. His eyes were glazed. "Are you a little tipsy, perchance?"

Sam held his thumb and index finger up, indicating a tiny amount. "A wee bit."

Brodie smiled. "He deserves to celebrate." He took a drink. "Have you two worked together awhile?"

"No," Maya said, looking at Sam. "What's it been? Few weeks?"

Sam frowned, his features taking on the expression more slowly than if he were sober. "Yeah, but we worked together before. When we were teenagers."

Maya nodded, lifting her drink to her lips.

"Is that how you first met?" Brodie asked.

Sam shook his head, swaying away from Maya and then back again with the movement. "We were at school together," he said as Maya sipped her drink. "Then we worked together. And then"—he took a big, exaggerated breath—"she broke my heart in this very bar. But I've forgiven her for that now." Sam pulled her in again to kiss her forehead.

Maya's pulse spiked as she pushed her hand against his chest to look him in the eyes. He blinked slowly.

What the hell was he playing at? She glanced over at Brodie, who was watching them with raised eyebrows. Clearing her throat, Maya gave a high-pitched laugh. "That is *not* what happened."

Sam shrugged, dangling his hand over her shoulder. "Yeah, 'tis. But it's water under the bridge now."

Maya's heart rate accelerated as she met Brodie's gaze. She was pissed off with Sam, making up crap like that. But what made it worse was him doing it in front of her new friend.

She swallowed. "Brodie, do you want to come meet my other friends?"

Clearly reading that Maya wanted to end the conversation, Brodie nodded. "That'd be great, thanks." He shifted away out of earshot, no doubt as a courtesy to Maya.

Maya took Sam's arm from her shoulders. "You wait here," she muttered. "I want a word with you."

He frowned, seeming oblivious. "A word 'bout what?"

Narrowing her eyes, she kept her voice low, but didn't manage to keep the waver out of it. "About you making shit up in front of people, that's what. I know you've had a bit to drink, but it's not fair to lie."

Sam raised his eyebrows. "Wasn't a lie."

She balled her free hand into a fist, trying to control her spiraling emotions. "Yes, it was. Me breaking your heart? Try the other way around."

Shooting him a hard stare, Maya moved off to catch Brodie and take his elbow. She steered him away.

He leaned in as they walked. "What was that all about?"

"I have no idea," she whispered, glancing back at Sam, who was watching them, a frown on his face. "He must be more drunk than I thought. I might have to get him home early."

"He was acting pretty possessive over you," Brodie said as they crossed the room. "Like he was marking his territory."

She shook her head. "We're just friends."

"I think you need to tell *him* that, not me."

They reached the table.

"Hey, guys," Maya said. "This is my friend Brodie." She pointed at everyone in turn. "This is Liv, Elise, Arran, Nico, Rowan, Ben . . ." She introduced a couple more people, then gave Brodie her seat next to Nico, who engaged him in conversation. Then she excused herself to go back to the bar, intent upon giving Sam the grilling of his life.

As she pushed her way through the crowds, she spotted him—with his face attached to Catriona's. Maya halted in her tracks, the memory of seeing them in the same clinch eight years ago at the tree line outside seizing her.

Earlier today Sam had told her that he still hadn't heard from Cat, and that she normally had no interest in the event. Maya hadn't laid eyes on her at any point during the proceedings up until now. Therefore, she must have just arrived, and immediately suckered herself to Sam's face like a strawberry blond octopus.

Backing into the crowd, Maya tried to dissolve away. She reached the table and took a seat across from Brodie and Nico, next to Liv, grabbing her beer and taking a very large slug. She didn't have to worry about Sam anymore—he had his girlfriend to take care of him.

Chapter
EIGHTEEN

SAM ROLLED OVER IN BED AND GROANED, LIFTING A HAND TO his head. *Fucking hell.* Every tiny movement made his whole brain throb.

Opening his eyes a crack, he spied the bedside clock and realized that he'd need to get up for his afternoon class soon. A glance across the bed confirmed that it was empty. He couldn't remember much about the previous evening, but he had a vague recollection of Cat arriving, much to his surprise. He couldn't recall them talking much, if at all. She'd only seemed interested in making out with him at the bar, and he hadn't had the wherewithal to suggest otherwise. The rest of the night was a haze. He'd have to try to get hold of her later to arrange to talk, and hopefully, her presence last night would mean she'd engage with it this time.

Shit. He was meant to have been up earlier, in order to get a lift with Maya to fetch his car from the Tavern. Groaning again, he reached over and grabbed his phone. Squinting at the screen, he felt as if his head were about to split in two. *I am never drinking again.*

There were a couple of missed calls from Maya, plus a message.

We need to talk.

Sam frowned, then realized it really hurt his head, so he tried to relax his face, wishing he had a few syringes of Botox to inject in case he inadvertently made any more painful expressions.

What did *they* have to talk about? The race? No, everything was tied up with that. He tried to think, but even that was painful. Reaching across to his bedside drawer, he felt around for some painkillers and swallowed a couple with the glass of water that could have been sitting there for a week, but he didn't care.

❋ ❋ ❋

REACHING THE END OF THE BLACK RUN, SAM WONDERED HOW he'd made it through the lesson with only half an operating brain. He hadn't even been able to wear his goggles because the pressure they exerted on his face was too much, but without them the low winter sun had hurt his eyes. He'd resorted to sunglasses and re-signed himself to everyone thinking he was a poser.

Lifting off his helmet, his head felt a thousand times lighter. Time to locate Maya and find out what she wanted to talk about, because he hadn't managed to see her yet. After he'd taken the first lot of painkillers, he'd fallen back to sleep, then had only awoken just in time to walk to his car and make it here for his class.

He headed into the center, wondering where she'd be. She didn't have any classes on a Monday, but there were numerous jobs she'd voluntarily taken on, and had been coming in every day. She was working too hard and clearly avoiding speaking to her family. Frowning, he decided he needed to do more to support her.

As he entered the café, Rowan walked toward him, and he gave her a wave. "Hey, have you seen Maya?"

"Yeah," Rowan replied, nodding her head toward the main foyer with a smile. "She's in the boot room. Got a bee in her bonnet about how things are organized."

Sam shook his head, grinning. "Thanks."

Sounded about right. Maya would have this place in top shape by the time she left. As he crossed into the main foyer, the grin fell from his face, his heart gone icy cold at the thought of her leaving.

Sam opened the door to the boot room. It was nice and dark in there, soothing his eyes.

He realized he still had on his sunglasses. Taking them off, he wandered through the aisles. "Maya?"

Her voice rang out, sounding flatter than usual. "Down here."

As he rounded a corner, she was there, sitting cross-legged on the floor, a massive pile of boots in front of her.

"What're you doing?" he asked.

"Making a new system." She stretched, glancing at him. Her eyes appeared wary for some reason. "I pinched an idea from Glencoe."

Sam took off his jacket and sat next to her. "I am so hungover you wouldn't believe it." He unbuckled his ski boots.

"I'm not surprised. You drank half the bar last night." Her voice still sounded weird. Like her usual brightness had been sucked out. Maybe she was hungover too.

The idea of alcohol pained him. "I'm never drinking again." He removed the boots and smiled at her. Her face was pinched, and it caused his smile to slip. Something major was up. "Are you okay?"

She studied him. Her tone was flat, blunt. "You don't remember, do you?"

Sam rubbed his beard, trying to fathom what she meant. "Remember what?"

"Last night." She glared at him. "What you said to Brodie at the bar."

Sam frowned, trying to recall. Things had gotten a little hazy after the prize giving, and he only had snatches of memory.

He must've looked blank because Maya gave him a nudge. "You kept hugging me and kissing my forehead and stuff in front of Brodie."

His gut churned. He remembered seeing Maya with Brodie. He'd gone over there and acted like a possessive arse over a woman who wasn't even his.

"Oh God." He rubbed his temples, squeezing his eyes shut. "I do remember that. I'm sorry, did I ruin things for you guys?" Why the hell had he done that? He hadn't been able to stop himself from questioning her about Brodie on the way to the Tavern either, and he hadn't even had a drink then.

Maya shook her head. "You didn't ruin anything. I told you before, we're just friends. I explained to him after our little peck that I wasn't interested in anything else." She gave him a pointed look. "However. If I *did* want to be anything more than friends with him, then it wouldn't be any of your business."

Sam closed his eyes in extreme discomfort. "I know. I'm sorry."

"Then why were you acting like that?"

Opening his eyes again, he wasn't sure what to say. He certainly didn't want to admit that he'd been jealous. "Just being overprotective because you're my friend."

She was studying him, her dark eyes practically boring into his soul. "But you said that you thought Brodie was a good guy."

Sam fiddled with the clasp of his ski boot, unsure how to get out of this one. "I don't know him that well. So maybe when I got a drink in me, I decided to make sure he was good enough for you."

He kept his gaze off hers, in case she saw through his lie with her bewitching, probing eyes.

"And is that why you made up that story? About me breaking your heart? What's that got to do with being protective?"

Frowning, Sam finally met her gaze. The memory of saying that materialized, as did Maya's strange reaction afterward. "I didn't make that up. It's what happened."

Maya opened her mouth, then closed it again. There was a hard edge to her tone. "That's pretty heartless, Sam."

He raised his eyebrows, his pulse kicking up. "Heartless?" Maya was the one who'd been heartless. Fair enough she was different now, and the past was the past. But she could at least own it.

"Yeah," she said, meeting his gaze and frowning, like she couldn't understand why he would've been upset. "Sam, I know it was ages ago and it means nothing now. But back then, I *really* liked you." She took a breath, her voice unsteady. "And I thought that you liked *me*."

Sam shook his head. It was beginning to thump again, and his heart was tripping over itself. "I *did* like you, of course I did. More than liked, in fact." He hesitated, then decided there was no point in hiding it. "I was in love with you, Maya."

She was staring at him now, and it was unnerving how all of this seemed to be news to her. Looking away, he knew he shouldn't continue, but it was as if the effects of his hangover were blocking his usual inhibitions. "I wanted us to make things official, and I was going to ask you that night. To be my girlfriend, I mean. But then we argued and you sent Cat to tell me that you'd changed your mind and couldn't get seriously involved with a lowly ski instructor when you were off to university to become an accountant."

He shrugged, trying to play down how much it hurt to say it out loud, even after all this time. "I'm sorry that I acted like an arsehole with Brodie, and I'll apologize to him too. There's no excuse for it. But what I said about the heartbreak was true." He stopped talking because his mouth had run away with him once all the feelings had come tumbling out. He couldn't believe that he'd admitted he used to be in love with her.

Maya didn't reply, so he glanced up. The color had drained from her face, and for a moment he thought she might keel over.

"Hey," he said, shifting closer, his heart plummeting that he'd hurt her feelings by admitting how deeply it'd affected him. "It's fine now. We all say stuff that's a bit undiplomatic at that age."

Maya still didn't speak. Nausea balled in his stomach, and this time he couldn't blame the hangover.

Maya swallowed, her voice catching. "Cat said that to you? That I wasn't interested? Because you were a *ski instructor*?"

Searching her face, he nodded, his nausea escalating.

She was blinking hard, fighting tears, and the sight of it cut into his heart.

She took a deep breath. "And you believed her. Of course you did, she was one of my best friends at the time."

The penny dropped, and he thought he might actually vomit.

"Wait—are you telling me . . ." His voice tailed off because he couldn't bring himself to say it.

Maya nodded, gulping in air. "Catriona lied." Her voice was barely a whisper. "I *never* said that. I was planning on going with you to the nook. And for the record, I would've said yes to being your girlfriend."

She paused to wipe her face because tears were falling, and Sam's heart pounded painfully.

"Cat came to *me*," she continued. "And it must've been before she told you that lie, because I was watching you laugh with your mates across the bar at the time. She was all solemn and apologetic, even gave me a hug." Maya closed her eyes. "She told me that you'd asked her to come and break it to me, as my friend. That you'd changed your mind. You could never see me as anything but your sister's best friend, and you didn't want to keep in touch when I went to uni."

If Sam had been punched in the gut with a sledgehammer, it would've been less painful. Winded, he sat there for a moment, frozen to the spot as reality hit and years of infinite possibilities played out in his mind, all involving what would have happened if Catriona hadn't sabotaged them.

Maya touched his hand. Her face was wet with tears. "Shit. That fallout we had on the phone beforehand . . . it must've sown the seed that I thought your career wasn't good enough. But I was only parroting what my dad made me say. He was standing over me at the time." She gulped in more air. "Do you believe me?"

The strength of their connection vibrated with a profound intensity, and Sam knew with every fiber of his being that Maya was telling the truth. He reached out to tug her into his chest, kissing the top of her head and wiping her face with his thumb, then using his jumper when that didn't do a good enough job. "Of course I believe you."

She let out a little sob and buried her face in his chest. The lump in his throat throbbed, sending painful pricks of emotion into his eyes. Sam rested his cheek on top of her head, unable to bear the thought of letting her go. "Fuck. I should've known that was your dad talking, not you. I let my paranoid inferiority complex get in the way. I should have supported you, not taken it personally."

They sat in silence for a minute. He couldn't bring himself to voice what was going through his head, and he sensed she felt the same.

Eventually, she lifted her hand to play with the V-neck of his jumper. "I came back to the pub, to confront you and try to sort out what happened on the phone. But I saw you . . ." She paused and took a deep breath. "Kissing her on the path to the nook, and it was the worst thing I'd ever witnessed. The next day, I heard that you'd slept with her. I'd thought my heart was already broken by then, but boy, was I wrong."

Sam tensed as that last part of the story hit home—how it would've looked to Maya. Like he'd dumped her and immediately taken up with her friend. The idea of it knifed right into his heart. "Holy shit." He squeezed his eyes shut, as if that might in turn force the agonizing thoughts from his mind. "I'm so sorry. She was there to pick up the pieces and I let her. Out of heartbreak but, if I'm honest, also spite." He tightened his arms around her. "Fucking hell. You must've thought I was the mother of all arseholes."

"Yeah," she whispered against his jumper. "Pretty much." She paused. "Though maybe more the granddaddy of all arseholes."

Despite the situation, Sam couldn't help but laugh, and Maya joined in with a quiet chuckle. He absorbed the vibration through his chest, trying to soak it in in order to ease his pain.

She wiped her face with her sleeve, sitting up to meet his gaze. "And you must have thought I was a snobby bitch."

"Well. I was an idiot for ever thinking badly of you." Sam gathered his sleeve in his fist to finally rub her cheeks clean. "No more tears. I won't have you crying over me anymore."

She pursed her lips, and he had to resist the urge to kiss them. "I've kind of never cried over you, if you think about it. Only over Catriona."

The sound of her name made him grit his teeth. "Good point."

Maya glanced away, fingering her charm bracelet and running her thumb over the moon he'd given her. His beautiful, funny girl, who'd loved the moon and the stars and who'd stolen his heart.

Sam stood, determination setting in.

Maya snapped her gaze up as he pulled on his jacket and lifted his ski boots. "Where are you going?"

He bent to kiss the top of her head, pausing briefly to inhale her scent and bolster his intentions. "I need to speak to Cat, and this time I'm not taking no for an answer. I'll call you later."

"Okay," she said, an anxious edge to her voice.

"Don't worry," he called as he left the area to go in search of his snow boots. "Everything's going to be fine."

❄ ❄ ❄

PACING THE ROOM, SAM CHECKED HIS WATCH. HE'D MESSAGED Cat, making her believe that he was preparing them dinner as if it were a peace offering. On impulse, he lifted his phone to video call Liv. She connected immediately, and he could see in her eyes that Maya had already contacted her. "All right, bro?"

"Did Maya call you?"

She frowned. "Yeah. I'm so sorry about what happened."

He ran a hand through his hair. "I'm the one who's sorry. I should've fucking listened to you."

"It's okay, Sam. You trusted her and she manipulated you. That's not your fault."

His heart ached. "What about Maya? She ended up hurt because of my naivety."

Liv shook her head. "Being naive isn't a crime, Sam. In any case, Catriona's had us all fooled at some point. Me included."

"But you saw through her a lot more quickly than me," he muttered.

"It's different when you're *outside* the narcissist's bubble," Liv said. "On the inside, you're subjected to trauma bonding. It's how they tether you to them, emotionally." She took a breath. "Have you spoken to her?"

He glanced down the hallway toward the front door. "Not yet. I'm waiting for her now."

Liv bit her lip. "Remember that she won't admit it. She'll try to lie her way out."

"I know," Sam said on a sigh. "I just need to tell her that I know, and make sure it hits home that it's over between us. Forever."

Liv was silent for a second, and when he met her gaze, there was relief in her eyes. "I'm so glad to have you back."

Sam sat heavily on one of the kitchen chairs. "I've always been here, Liv."

"Not really." She winced. "We had to walk on eggshells with you a lot of the time. Mum and me. We didn't want to alienate you by criticizing her."

"Ugh." Sam rubbed his forehead, trying to massage away the pain of imagining his mother and sister tiptoeing around him. "I'm sorry. What a mess."

Liv sighed. "If only I'd found out about what happened between you and Maya in the past. If I'd questioned you both a little more, then I would've worked out the lie." Her eyes were sad. "But you were both too polite to tell me."

Sam laughed despite himself. "Neither of us wanted to slag off the other one to you. So maybe we still secretly cared about each other the whole time."

Liv smiled softly.

He brought the screen closer. "Do you want to do something at the weekend? We could ask Maya, Arran, Nico, Elise."

Her eyes lit up. "I'd love that."

The front door opened, signaling Cat's arrival. "Cool. I need to go now, but I'll call you after."

She nodded. "Good luck. Love you."

"Love you too."

Cat walked in as he ended the call, her face screwed up. "Who the hell are you talking to?"

She'd clearly heard him telling his sister that he loved her, and had jumped to conclusions. All contemplation of a gentle lead-in went out the window. "My fucking *sister*. That's who."

Cat paused, flicking her hair. "Well. There's no need to swear." She moved into the kitchen. "What are we having for dinner?"

Sam got to his feet, his fists clenched and pulse ramping up. "There's every need to fucking swear, and we're having nothing for dinner."

She narrowed her eyes. "What do you mean?"

"I *mean*, I know what you did. What you've been trying to cover up ever since Maya arrived back in town—by poisoning me against her, deleting her messages, trying to get me not to speak to her. All in an effort to cover the lie you've been spinning for years."

Sam spotted it, the slight widening of her eyes as she realized he was onto her, before her mask fell back into place.

His jaw tightened as he remembered the sight of Maya's tears. "When we were eighteen. You pretended to Maya that I didn't want to meet with her and I wasn't interested. Then you lied to me with all that crap about how she was finished with me because I wasn't good enough. The truth is, *you're* the one who thinks I'm not good enough, not Maya. And you knew I was insecure about it."

Cat stared at him, but then she glanced away quickly before answering. Another tell. Not that he needed one to know the truth.

"I can't believe this," Cat said slowly. "How *could* you? How could you believe her over me? Your own girlfriend?"

Sam rolled his eyes, considering walking out. But this was *his* house. She should be the one to leave. Plus, who knows what she'd do if he left her there alone? Probably cut up all his clothes and find some dog shit to smear over everything.

She must have taken in his uninterested response, because her voice faltered where normally she would've gained momentum. "I can't believe how you treat me. It's emotional abuse, that's what it is. Everyone thinks so—"

"Ugh." He threw his hands in the air. "This is like a broken record. Yeah, I know. Everyone thinks I'm a twat. Whatever. I want you to leave. I'm sick of all your shit, and I can't believe I've wasted years on you. I actually *am* a massive twat where that's concerned."

She was silent for a moment, seeming thrown. Then she tossed her hair. "Bollocks to that, because *I'm* leaving *you*. Right now. So don't try to stop me."

Sam shifted ahead of her to the kitchen doorway before she could get there, then along the hallway and opened the front door. "No problem. Off you fuck. I'll pack your stuff and leave it on the doorstep tomorrow."

Grabbing her coat, she stormed past him.

"Hold on," he said as she whipped her head round. "Give me your keys."

She pointed furiously into the hallway, where they were lying on the table, then continued to stomp away through the snow to her car.

Sam slammed the door behind her, leaning against it. "Good riddance."

Chapter
NINETEEN

B EN WAS TALKING, BUT MAYA WAS FINDING IT HARD TO CON-
centrate. She couldn't resist glancing behind him across the
terrace, where Sam was speaking to his students. He kept meeting
her eyes, and each time it sent these little pulses of electricity into
her core.

They'd spoken the previous evening, but Cat had gotten home
later than anticipated and then Sam had debriefed with Liv first.
He'd sounded exhausted by the time he'd called Maya, a mixture
of physical and emotional hangover. The conversation had merely
consisted of a factual account of his dealing with Cat, and then
Maya had told him to get some sleep, promising that they'd talk
more the next day.

The revelation that their estrangement for the past eight years
had been based on a lie had seemed unbelievable at first, but each
passing minute made it more and more obvious. Of course Cat had
lied, the evil bitch traitor from hell. Why on earth hadn't Maya
worked that out? She'd been so sure of Sam's nature, and she'd
trusted him. But at the time she'd also had faith in Cat and had

thought all along that Sam being interested in her was too good to be true. So, when everything fell apart, it had been easy to think that it *was* too good to be true. Especially after their tiff on the phone and the trauma of seeing Cat and Sam together.

The knowledge that her desire to avoid conflict had prevented her from discovering the truth about a former friend's betrayal and subsequently lost her the love of her life was too painful to digest all at once.

Taking a deep breath, she tried to concentrate on what Big Boss Ben was saying.

"What do you think?" he said.

Maya opened her mouth, then closed it again. "I'm really sorry, Triple B, but I wasn't listening."

Ben raised his eyebrows, then followed the direction of her gaze over to where she was borderline staring at Sam again. "Oh, I see."

Maya blew her fringe out of her eyes. "See what?"

Ben smiled, shaking his head. "It's about time something happened between you guys. You're worse than bloody Ross and Rachel off *Friends*."

"Shh. He might hear you. Nothing's happened between us. He only split with his girlfriend yesterday. I'm giving him some space."

"For goodness' sake, woman," Ben said, glancing back at where Sam was now borderline staring at Maya. "The guy clearly wants the opposite of space where you're concerned. He wants you all up in his personal space ASAP."

"B Double B, you need to shut it now and tell me what you were saying. You know, when I wasn't listening," Maya said, working hard not to glance back over at Sam for the millionth time in five minutes.

Ben rolled his eyes, then turned and waved Sam over.

"What're you doing?" Maya whispered.

"Don't panic. The thing you weren't listening to might involve him, so you both might as well not listen to me at the same time."

Sam arrived, moving around Ben to stand next to Maya, his hand practically brushing against hers. "What's up?"

"Unbelievable sexual tension, that's what," Ben muttered.

Maya's eyes widened.

"What?" Sam said.

"Nothing," Ben replied. "Right. I've got an American tourist who wants some one-to-one lessons. She's requested, and I quote, 'either the cool mixed-race girl with the dark hair or the hot guy with the beard.' So, which of you wants to do it?"

Maya started laughing before she could answer, and Sam shot her a grin.

"Maya," Ben said. "Is that an offer?"

"Yeah." She shrugged, still smiling. "I can do it. Unless it clashes with my classes."

"Oh, wait," Ben said, checking his phone. "Good point. The times she's asked for *do* clash . . . but Sam can do it." He looked up. "That okay?"

"Yeah, fine." Sam shifted a little closer to Maya, the back of his hand touching hers and making her shiver.

Maya glanced at him. "You're a pushover. You need to learn to say no."

He shot her a smile. "So do you."

Ben rolled his eyes. "I need a coffee."

He went to head back inside, and Sam called after him. "When does she start?"

"This afternoon," Ben replied over his shoulder. "She'll be here in an hour, name's Emma. I'll send you the rest of the timetable."

"In an hour?" Maya said. "Bloody keen. On her part, and Ben's. She must be paying a fortune for the private lessons."

He turned to face her. "I know." The sight of him up close made her breath catch. "Have you got time for a coffee?"

Maya winced. "I said I'd help Rowan with something, otherwise I would have. What about after this lesson with the tourist? You'll only be an hour, right?"

Sam lifted a hand to pull a piece of fluff out of her hair, slowly trailing his fingers through the strands and creating an electrifying sensation throughout her body. "Sounds about right. Meet you here in a couple of hours?"

Maya swallowed, her mouth dry. "I'll probably be finished a little earlier, so I'll come and catch the end of your lesson."

He smiled and kissed her cheek before making his way back over to the people he'd been speaking to. Maya had to take a moment to compose herself from the spine-tingling sensation of the brush of his lips, before dragging herself off the terrace to go meet Rowan.

❄ ❄ ❄

MAYA SURVEYED THE AREA. SHE'D ASSUMED THE TOURIST WOULD be a beginner and therefore be on the baby slope with Sam. Hearing a squeal, she craned her neck, spotting them in the beginners' area, and settled into her seat to watch.

The student looked a little older than them. It also seemed she had the hots for Sam, judging by the way she kept throwing her arms around him to come to a stop rather than using an actual snowplow. She nearly knocked him off his feet at one point, and Maya started laughing, then clapped a hand over her mouth when a few people turned to look at her.

Sniggering, she spied on them for the rest of the lesson. It almost seemed as if Emma were a little more capable than she let on, but was putting on a damsel-in-distress act in order to play up to Sam.

They finished, and Sam made to leave but Emma took his arm, leaning in closer to say something in his ear. He smiled and shook his head, but she held on to him, seemingly in an attempt to convince him about whatever she'd asked.

"Uh-oh, Sammy boy," Maya said to herself. "You've got a limpet there."

Sam glanced over, clearly trying to find an escape. He spotted Maya, and she gave him a wave with a massive open-mouthed smile that clearly indicated she was enjoying his discomfort.

He turned back to Emma and pointed toward Maya, saying something that made Emma drop her hand and glance over.

Maya stopped waving. *Uh-oh. Methinks I'm being roped into whatever this is.*

Sam was coming toward her, with Emma staying put in the background, watching.

Maya stood to lean against the side of the terrace, wondering what on earth was going on.

Sam pulled off his helmet and goggles, unzipping the front of his jacket as he arrived, and climbing onto the terrace to stand in front of her. He put his stuff onto the table, and circled her waist.

"Just go with it," he said in a low voice. "I had to tell her you were my girlfriend to get away."

Her pulse accelerated. There was no point in pretending to herself that she minded. Far from it. "You told her what?"

"Shh. Please." He glanced over his shoulder. "I'm bloody black and blue from her throwing herself at me. Just play along so I don't get jumped next lesson."

Like she needed any convincing. Maya put her arms around his neck to draw him closer. His scent was like pine trees on a crisp winter's day and conjured the exhilaration of whizzing through an off-piste pine forest. She quickly glanced past him. "Oh my God, she's still watching. What the actual? Is she a bunny-boiling stalker?"

Sam bent his head closer, rubbing his nose against hers, and for a moment Maya almost forgot that it was pretend.

"I don't know," he whispered. "But I'm a bit scared."

"*You're* scared? It's *me* she's going to come for in my sleep," she whispered back.

He smiled. "I'll protect you."

Maya arched a brow. "In my *sleep*? You wouldn't be there."

His smile spread more widely, and heat rose in her face.

Sam bent his head to kiss her cheek. "You're adorable when you blush."

"I'm not blushing," she murmured, her skin tingling from his kiss. "It's just the cold."

"Yeah, right."

"Shut it, Leonard, or I'm leaving you with stalker Emma."

"Is she still there?"

"Yes." She let out a breath. "For goodness' sake, we're going to be stuck here forever."

Sam raised his eyebrows. "Stuck in a clinch with you? I can think of worse things."

A warm sensation flooded her system. "Oh yeah?"

"Mm-hmm."

"Well, I think we're going to have to think bigger, because she's not budging."

"What did you have in mind?"

She only hesitated for a split second. "A fake kiss."

"What's a *fake* kiss?"

"It's like a real kiss, but we're just doing it for Emma's benefit."

"Okay. So basically, you're going to kiss me."

"Yeah. That okay?"

"Fine by me."

"You sure?"

A smile tugged at his mouth. "Just kiss me, Maya."

Her heart hammering, Maya pushed her fingers into his hair, pleased that she'd already taken off her gloves so that she could feel the soft strands between her fingers. She'd been imagining running her fingers through his sandy locks for ages.

Drawing his head down, she slowly brushed her mouth against his, the contact immediately creating a burst of heat in her chest, which sent electricity coursing through her circulation. The familiar softness of his lips contrasted with the new grazing sensation of his beard, which hadn't featured the last time they'd found themselves like this.

Maya had intended to leave it at that, but now that she was this close in his embrace, she didn't want to stop. Neither did he, judging by the way he tightened his arms around her, pulling her in to deepen the kiss in a way that signaled to her he'd been wanting this for as long as she had.

A low ache developed in her belly, pulsing with every shift of his mouth over hers. All intentions that this was fake went out the window, and Maya even forgot that they were in a public area, where people they knew could be watching.

Sam broke off for a second, his eyes heavy lidded and lips rosy from their kiss. "Is she still there?"

He sounded like he was hoping she would be, even leaning back in before Maya had answered.

A quick glance confirmed that Emma was gone. But Maya let his lips meet hers again, murmuring, "Still there," and feeling not at all bad about the white lie. She wrapped her arms around his neck, welcoming the hard press of his body against hers as he dipped in his tongue. The sensation of it caused liquid fire to pool within her, traveling all the way to the tips of her fingers and down to her toes.

Maya broke off to rest her forehead against his, her pulse throbbing. "I think I'm a fan of the beard."

Kissing her nose, Sam smiled. "Not had a bearded kiss before?"

"Nope. Unless you count Bowser."

He lifted a hand to trace her lower lip with his thumb, sending goose bumps tingling across her skin. "I'm definitely not counting my mum's old dog."

Maya shrugged, having to force herself not to bite the tip of his thumb. She wished to God that they weren't in a public area. "I dunno. He gave pretty good kisses."

Raising his eyebrows, Sam leaned in to brush his lips against hers. "I hope I can measure up."

Maya grasped the front of his jumper. "I'd better double-check. For science."

She drew him in, this time sliding her tongue in a little, and hoping that they weren't going to get arrested for public indecency.

Sam responded, his breath hitching, and it sent a sweet thrill into her core. He ran a hand down to rest on the small of her back as he pushed his tongue against hers, his fingers grazing dangerously close to her bottom.

Breaking off, he glanced behind her, heat glittering in his gaze. "Okay. There're definitely people watching now, and some of them might be the parents of your kids' class. So I'd better cool it."

Brushing his cheek with her fingers, Maya smiled. "I've got a confession."

His eyes were sparkling like the sun glinting off the snow. "What?"

"Emma's been gone for about ten years. I made out she was still there in order to keep kissing you."

Sam arched a brow, and it gave her jelly legs. "That's disgraceful behavior."

She shrugged, still smiling. "Sorry, not sorry."

Grinning, he leaned round to whisper in her ear, the sensation of his breath making her skin prickle with delicious sensitivity. "I know she wasn't there. I saw her out of the corner of my eye, going into the center."

Still wearing a smile, he took her hands in his and pressed his lips to them. "Your hands are cold." He placed them onto his chest and drew his open jacket around them. "Can I pick you up tonight? We can go to our stargazing spot."

A burst of delight flowed through her. "I'd love that."

Sam leaned in to kiss her cheek. "Bring a blanket."

❄ ❄ ❄

SHIFTING HER WEIGHT FROM ONE FOOT TO THE OTHER, MAYA looked at her watch, then peered out of the small window in the front door.

Yvonne entered the hallway from the kitchen. "Maya, you've been dancing around in the porch for ten minutes. What's going on?"

Glancing back at the door, Maya tried to keep her feet planted. "Sam's coming to collect me."

A smile spread over her mum's face. She came down the hallway. "Is this a date?" she whispered.

Maya glanced at the living room door. Omar and Hana were in there. "I don't know," she whispered back.

Yvonne peered out of the little window. "Why don't you know? He's broken up with Cat and everything that happened was a misunderstanding."

"Not a misunderstanding. A lie."

"Okay, a lie. But not from either of you. So . . ." Yvonne gave Maya a knowing look.

"Ugh, Mother," Maya said, rolling her eyes. "Stop."

Yvonne laughed, then put a hand over her mouth and glanced toward the living room. "Listen. We need to have a talk. A proper one, I mean. About these companies your dad asked you to send your CV to."

Maya's insides tightened. "Why?"

"You know why," Yvonne said, raising her eyebrows. "I can tell your heart's not in it."

Maya's mouth went dry and she swallowed. Then the doorbell rang, signaling Sam's coming to rescue her from her discomfort. "That's him. I'll see you later."

She grabbed her blanket and opened the door, unable to resist giving him a hug on the doorstep.

Sam kissed her and gave Yvonne a smile. "Hey, Mrs. B."

She laughed. "It's Yvonne, Sam."

Color streaked his cheeks. "Yvonne."

"You two have fun," Yvonne said, waving, and closing the door after them.

Sam took her hand as they went down the drive to his car, and she leaned up to kiss his face where the flush was still apparent. "You're so cute."

He raised his eyebrows as they climbed in. "Cute? I was hoping you were going to say handsome and sexy."

Maya smiled as they set off. "Those things too."

A little seed of guilt sowed itself into the back of her mind. Had it been unfair of her to suggest that fake-but-actually-very-real kiss earlier? Sam had only discovered his long-term girlfriend's deception, and finished with her, barely twenty-four hours ago. Perhaps she should have kept her distance a little longer. But it had seemed such a natural progression.

A warm feeling erupted as she remembered how he'd told her that he used to be in love with her. She'd nearly told him that she'd felt the same, but it had been too overwhelming, and now she was worried about doing or saying anything that might be too full on for him.

They still hadn't discussed the revelation of the lie in any detail; she'd had to hotfoot it to her class after their snogging session on the terrace.

"By the way," Sam said. "I caught Brodie today, and apologized for being a dick at the race night."

Maya flashed him a soft look. "Thank you. What did he say?"

Sam smiled. "He was very gracious."

Once they arrived at the Tavern, Sam grabbed his waterproof sheet and they made their way into the woods, past the nook, and out into snow to reach their spot. Maya liked that she thought of it as "theirs," as did he, even though they'd only been there together once before.

They spread out the sheet and sat on it, opening Maya's large, thick blanket to snuggle underneath. Sam put his arm around her shoulders to tuck her in to his side as they did some star spotting.

"Which one's that?" Maya asked. "Ursa Major?"

He grinned. "I have no idea."

Maya chuckled, rolling her eyes. "Come on, Leonard. You need to up your game on the first date."

Immediately she regretted calling it a date, when she'd not long had a word with herself about not rushing him.

Lifting a hand, he turned her face toward him, his fingers lingering on her cheek. "Is that what this is? Our first date?"

She swallowed, wishing she could reach out and grab the words in order to stuff them back into her mouth. "Not if you don't want it to be. It's too soon for you."

"Too soon?" He raised his eyebrows. "I've been waiting eight years for a first date with you."

Warm, delicious sensations flooded her as he drew her closer.

"I'm sorry that you thought I was an evil bastard who led you on, then fobbed you off." He grimaced. "And then went off with your friend. I hate thinking about it."

"Then don't." She brushed her lips against his. "It doesn't matter right now. And for the record, I'm sorry too. That you thought I'd rejected you." Grasping the front of his jacket, she met his eyes. "You know now that I'd never think you weren't good enough, right?"

Sam nodded. "I do. I should've known, back then too. But I already felt so insecure about us." He squeezed his eyes as if in discomfort. "Stupidly, I asked Cat about you when I got to the pub and told her what you'd said on the phone. Now I realize she used that against me."

A hot spear of anger pierced Maya's gut, and all she could manage was a grunt.

Sam glanced down. "I can't believe she took me in. Well, maybe I can. I just can't believe how much my own insecurities fueled it."

Maya kissed his cheek. "It's not your fault. It's hers."

"You sound like Liv." He sighed. "My instinct had been to call you before you left for uni. But Cat told me you'd specifically asked me not to, and I didn't want to come across like some crazed stalker."

What an evil mastermind she was. Or, is.

Flashing her a soft smile, he touched the charms on her bracelet. "It was my idea to get you the moon charm, after you told me you liked it." He swallowed. "You liked that other one too. The star."

Smiling, she was flooded with warmth that he'd remembered. "I knew it was your idea."

Rubbing his face, he flashed her a weak smile. "I wish I'd told you then. How I felt, I mean. On your birthday. Then none of this would've happened." He sighed. "But I hadn't quite plucked up the courage. I was too insecure, and worried about what your dad might think. I suppose giving you the charm was my way of conveying my feelings without actually saying it. But the message was probably diluted with it being a group gift."

Shaking her head, she leaned over to kiss his cheek, enjoying the brush of his beard against her lips. "The message was lovely. I knew it was something significant." Glancing down, she stroked the little moon. "I just lost sight of that message in all the hurt."

Sam put his arms around her and drew her in, kissing her with an intensity that made her heart burst into life and her entire body come alive.

He leaned them both back to lie under the blanket as they looked at the stars. "I promise that I'd never hurt you."

"I promise that I'd never reject you." She snuggled into his chest, listening to the rise and fall of his breathing, and she could sense how much her saying that meant to him.

The significance of his reaction to what had happened between them, in the context of the rejection he'd received at the hands of his father, wasn't lost on her. She wanted to kick Catriona's arse for taking advantage of his vulnerability. Maya's anger and protective instinct toward him made her own suffering at Cat's hands pale into insignificance.

The thought crossed her mind again, that if she'd stood up to Catriona at that point, rather than avoiding conflict, then she and Sam wouldn't have lost all this time.

Still, she was back together with Sam and things had worked out for them, in the end.

Chapter
TWENTY

SAM PLACED THE BOX INTO THE TROLLEY AND SCOOTED AROUND
into the next aisle to find Maya. She was searching through
some boxes of lights.

"Hey," he called. "Check this out." He came to a stop and
pointed proudly at what he'd found.

"Amazing!" She lifted her hands in the air. "You got the inflatable Santa. Hold on, let me cross it off."

Taking out the scorecard from their lights walk, she drew a line
through *inflatable Santa*. "Now we need the general lights, the
icicles, the inflatable penguins, that giant wrap thing for the
garage . . ." She glanced up. "Are you sure you don't mind us doing
this to your house?"

He grinned. This was fun. In fact, being with Maya was always
fun. "Course not."

She gave a contented sigh. "This is my best idea *ever*." She licked
her finger and put it on her shoulder, making a noise to imitate
putting out a flame.

Reaching over to tug her in, Sam smiled. "You certainly are hot stuff."

He kissed her, only meaning for it to be a brief peck. But the fire that burst inside galvanized him into running his mouth thoroughly over hers, exploring the softness and the heat and gently biting her lower lip. Her breath hitched, sending a wave of desire through his body.

Sliding in his tongue, he absorbed the way she responded, pressing close and threading her fingers into his hair with a delicious traction that set his skin alight.

Sam broke off when heat built a little too quickly in his body for a Sunday morning in the Glenavie Garden Center. He didn't want the evidence of that to strain too hard against his jeans and give any of the other shoppers a heart attack.

They'd been seeing each other for only under a week, but each time he was near her, the heat between them was more intense. That must be because whatever was brewing hadn't only been present a few weeks, but had started years ago and lain dormant until their unexpected meeting at that party.

However, he didn't want to rush her. They hadn't been together very long, plus he'd been in another relationship a few days ago. He didn't even know how they'd define things. Was it casual? Serious? Exclusive? For him it was serious, and he very much wanted it to be exclusive. Those were issues that he was keen to voice, as well as wanting to admit his craving for physical intimacy. But again, he didn't want to exert any pressure or hurry her.

Maya was blushing, and it was so adorable his heart throbbed. He brushed his lips over the dusky color staining her cheeks.

She smiled. "What time is everyone coming to yours?"

He checked his watch. "In about an hour."

"Cool. Let's find all the other items and get everything over there."

* * *

AFTER HELPING HIM TO DRAG THE LAST BOX OUT OF THE BOOT and into the garage, Maya sat on it. "Blimey. How are inflatables so heavy when they're mostly air, and not even blown up yet?"

Sam grinned. "Maybe we should've waited for Nico. His muscles have got muscles. It's what gives him his lady-killing persona."

"Hmm." Maya curled her lip. "I only have time for bearded ski instructor–naked butlers with fiery amber eyes."

"That's very specific," Sam said slowly, keeping a solemn expression on his face. "We might have difficulty finding him for you."

"That's okay." Maya shrugged. "I already found him."

Sam shot her a smile, warmth gathering inside him. "Found him, and got him." He sat next to her on the box, and took her hand. "Speaking of which. I was wondering how you'd . . . *define* us."

Maya rubbed her thumb over his skin, and it made him lose his train of thought. "Define?"

Clearing his throat, he nodded. "If, for example, we were out and about and someone I know stopped to chat. Let's say his name's Bobby. And I was like, 'Hey, Bobby, this is . . .'" He paused. "What would I say?"

She arched an eyebrow, giving him a deadpan look. "Maya. My name's Maya. I can't believe you've forgotten already."

Smiling, he shook his head. "I mean I'd be like, 'This is Maya, my . . . friend'? 'Girlfriend'?"

She pursed her lips. "Do you actually have a friend called Bobby?"

He couldn't help but laugh, and she joined in, the both of them getting more and more hysterical until Maya held her middle.

"Stop it!" she said. "My stomach hurts."

Sam wiped his eyes. "You started it."

"Wasn't my fault. It was Bobby's."

That got him going again, and it took another minute to stop.

"Okay," she said, taking a deep breath and clearly trying to keep the giggles at bay. "What definition do you prefer?"

He took her hand again, his heart rate picking up. "I like the sound of *girlfriend*."

"Me too."

The fact that she hadn't hesitated swelled his heart.

She smiled. "The only thing is, I'd like us to chat to Liv about it first, before it's properly official."

He gave her hand a squeeze. "Is this the equivalent of a guy asking his girlfriend's dad's permission to marry her? You asking my twin sister if you can be my girlfriend?"

"Well, not permission exactly. More like getting her blessing." She glanced down. "It's important to me, you know? She's my best friend, and I want her to know she can trust me." She swallowed, and met his eyes.

He knew exactly what she meant. Liv hadn't liked Cat. At all. And they'd started out as friends. Although this situation was entirely different, with Maya and Liv being so close and the fact that Maya wasn't manipulative as hell. There was no way that Liv wouldn't love their making things official. But it meant the world to him that seeking his sister's approval was so important to Maya.

Sam pulled her close, kissing her forehead and holding her against his chest. "We'll speak to her about it today."

"Thank you," Maya said softly. "Oh." She lifted her head. "Speaking of ski instructors–cum–naked butlers, have you got any more gigs coming up?"

For a moment he wasn't sure what to say. Would it make a difference to Maya's opinion of that job now that they were together, or at least, about to be together, pending Liv's stamp of approval? What if Maya didn't like the idea of her boyfriend parading around nearly naked in front of a load of women? There was no way he'd lie about it, but he didn't want to anger her.

"I . . . I've got one more booked, yeah," he said, aware that he was stumbling over his words. "It's been on the cards for a while, from before Ben's bonus and my pay rise. He also wants me to keep all the money from the one-to-one lessons with Emma, so I've got plenty to give Arran for the studio light and still have loads left over but it's too late to cancel the booking now and—"

Maya squeezed his hand. "Whoa there." She stroked his face. "What's up? You're freaking out."

Taking a breath, he tried to form his words a little less quickly. "I don't want you to be mad."

Maya studied him with a curious air. "Why would I be mad?"

"I don't know," he said slowly, mulling it over. "I suppose I just assumed that's how a girlfriend would react."

Maya hesitated, then something seemed to click for her, and she gave him a reassuring smile. "I'm not mad. I don't mind, same as I didn't mind when I was just your friend." She cleared her throat. "Remember that there's a lot of stuff that Cat did that you shouldn't take for granted any girlfriend would do. It's just what Cat would've done. Okay?"

He nodded, relief warming his insides.

Maya leaned in to kiss his cheek. "The one thing I *do* mind, is that I still think you're overdoing it. I'd like it if you could speak to Arran, get it all out in the open now that you don't have to worry about Catriona finding out. Hopefully, once you've given him some money for the light, he can manage without any more cash.

But if he can't, we'll help him together. Then you don't need to do any more butler gigs. Not unless you want to."

A weird sensation overwhelmed him. Not a bad one, but alien nonetheless. Was this too easy? She wasn't acting jealous or possessive, plus she seemed to be putting his needs first.

Sam took a breath. This was a good thing. No, a great thing. He just needed to get used to being in a functional relationship. The problem was it was uncharted terrain for him.

The other night at their stargazing spot, she'd said that she would never think he wasn't good enough. But the real problem was, *he* still wasn't sure he was good enough. Not in a financial manner, at least, not any longer. He'd made his own way in the world and was proud of it. But her family was so different from his, and his relationship baggage was revealing that he was damaged goods. What if Maya reflected on that and decided he wasn't worth it? He glanced at her, absorbing the affection in her eyes, and told himself to stop being so paranoid.

Liv's voice sounded from the driveway. "Miss Maya, what a delight!"

He lifted his gaze and she was walking toward them, Elise in tow.

The two of them entered the garage and had a kind of three-way hug with Maya, which he got pulled into.

Once they broke it up, Liv gave him a separate cuddle. "All right, bro?"

Sam gave her a squeeze. "Great, thanks."

Even in the last few days, he'd felt the sibling bond strengthening. Not that he'd ever considered it weak, but now he could see it had been under strain from the weight of his issues with Cat. At the time he'd been oblivious, and he couldn't believe he'd not sensed it before. Though perhaps he had, albeit subconsciously.

He and Liv had spoken on the phone every night since the split, and Sam had told her everything that had been happening with Maya. Although most of the time she'd already known, because Maya often got in there first, and he loved that about them.

Liv released him, and he gave Elise a kiss on the cheek. He could see what Maya meant when she'd confided to him that she was worried about Elise. Her eyes were tired, and he was sure she looked thinner than she'd been the last time he'd had a proper conversation with her. With a jolt, he realized that had been when her husband was still alive.

"How are you?" he asked.

Elise smiled, but her blue eyes seemed dull. "I'm fine, thank you. You look well." She gave him a nudge. "Your new woman suits you."

He rubbed the back of his neck. "I'm a lucky man."

A very brief flash of sadness passed over her face, but then it was gone. "You both are."

Sam opened his mouth to reply, but then Arran's voice sounded from the driveway. "Ladies and gentleman . . ."

Sam turned, and Arran was standing at the end of the driveway, arms raised. "The muscle has arrived."

He moved his arms to the side to point at Nico as he rounded the corner. Nico rolled his eyes and gave Arran a shove, which Arran utilized to comic effect by throwing himself off to the side, into a pile of snow that Sam had shoveled off the drive earlier.

Everyone laughed, though Sam couldn't help but notice Elise's laugh died down as she locked eyes with Nico.

Nico pulled Arran out of the snow. "There's plenty of muscle here already. And that's just Liv." He came over to kiss Liv's cheek. "How's my favorite black belt?"

Liv shifted fluidly into a karate stance. "Good, thanks."

Nico hugged Sam and Maya, then gave Elise a nod. "Right," he said, rubbing his hands together. "Who's in charge of this outfit?"

Sam pointed at Maya. "This gorgeous specimen right here is the project manager."

"Too right," she replied, coming over to give him a kiss. "About the project manager bit, I mean." She pouted. "I'd describe myself as more striking than gorgeous."

Smiling, Sam kissed the top of her head.

"Okay," she continued. "I've got a plan in mind. But . . . we'll need to try all the different permutations to make sure it's the best one."

There was a chorus of groans and eye-rolling.

"What?" she asked, eyes wide and palms up.

"The accountant strikes again," Liv muttered, shooting Maya a grin.

"Ah, you bloody love it," Maya said. "Right, team, let's go."

❄   ❄   ❄

SAM HANDED OUT MUGS OF HOT DRINKS TO LIV AND ARRAN, WHO were sitting on the garden bench. Arran took his, blowing out a deep breath that puffed into condensation.

Liv accepted her mug from Sam. Sighing, she rubbed her shoulder.

Sam frowned. "What's up with your shoulder?"

"I think I was too gung ho with that big box," she said, stretching it.

"Here," Arran said, putting his mug onto the arm of the bench and then massaging the back of her shoulder.

"Ow!" Liv said.

"Sorry," Arran said, wincing. "Don't know my own strength." He continued, but this time with no yelping from Liv.

Sam went to stand with Maya, who gave him a nudge. "What's with those two?" she asked.

Sipping his tea, Sam frowned. "What two?"

Leaning closer, she muttered from the side of her mouth, "Liv and Arran."

"Nothing," he said, watching them and wondering what Maya was talking about.

She narrowed her eyes. "Hmm."

Elise came over and linked arms with Maya. "You do realize, that after trying every permutation, we've ended right back up at your original idea."

"I know," Maya said with a grin. "But it means we've proven that this is the right one."

Elise smiled. "Fair enough."

Sam checked his watch. "Who wants to eat before it gets dark and we have the official switch on?"

There was a chorus of yeses, and he led everyone inside to where he'd laid out some soup and sandwiches on the kitchen table. As everyone sat, Sam absorbed how much happier the atmosphere in the house seemed. Not just from having his friends inside, but from the lack of Cat's presence. Again, it was only now that her influence was missing that he fully realized how suffocating it'd been.

Maya slid her hand onto his knee and shot him a concerned expression. "All right?"

Nodding, he leaned in to give her a kiss.

"Aw," Liv said from his other side. "You two are *adorbs*." She put her hands under her chin and fluttered her eyelashes.

Sam laughed, glancing across at Elise, Arran, and Nico, who were chatting over their food across the table. He gave Maya's hand a squeeze. "Is now a good time for the talk?"

Maya nodded.

"What talk?" Liv asked, picking up a sandwich. "I already know about the birds and the bees."

Maya laughed, and Sam rubbed his temples.

"There's no way we're talking about that," he said.

Maya scooted her chair closer to Sam's, putting her arm around him and leaning in to face Liv on his other side. "We've decided to be official. Boyfriend and girlfriend. Would that bother you?"

"Bother me?" Liv replied, grinning. "I think that's bloody awesome! And it's about time." She leaned in to kiss Maya's cheek, then Sam's. "Utterly delightful news, Miss Maya, and dear brother of mine. I hope I shall be buying a wedding hat forthwith."

"Steady," Sam said, raising his eyebrows. "Don't scare her off when I've just snared her."

Maya laughed, giving his shoulders a squeeze. "Snared? I'm not a bear."

"No?" He tickled her sides and put on a baby voice. "Not even a teddy bear?"

"Argh! Stop it! I'm ticklish," Maya said, trying to wriggle away from him.

"Yeah, I know." He grinned. "That's why I'm doing it."

"Ugh," Liv said, lifting her glass of water. "I've changed my mind. It's fast becoming more sickening than adorbs." But the smile still played on her face, and Sam could tell his twin was delighted.

"You know," Liv continued, "I don't understand why either of you thinks that I'm surprised about this." She met Sam's eyes with a wink. "Why do you think I suggested that Maya apply for the ski center job? Or start giving you lifts into work when your car broke down?"

Sam's mouth fell open. "You sneaky little—"

"Hey." Liv held up her hands. "Don't start. You used to ask about her *all the time* when we were seventeen, eighteen. I can't believe I didn't realize something had happened between you."

Maya gave him a nudge, grinning. "Used to ask about me, eh?"

Heat rose in his cheeks and she kissed each one in turn.

"Who's blushing now?" Maya asked.

Liv laughed. "You'd better watch it too. Because you were always asking about him as well."

"Aha!" Sam said, reaching out to tickle Maya again, but she squealed and dodged out of the way. Laughing, he turned to the others. "Eat up, it's getting dark and the big switch on is coming."

It didn't take long for the food to be demolished, and then they were getting their outerwear back on and heading outside.

He held Maya's hand as they crossed the threshold, and she shot him a look when Arran shifted behind Liv to massage her shoulders as they walked. Sam shrugged. Arran was like that with everyone.

They gathered in front of the house, and Sam went into the garage to flip on the switch. There was a chorus of *oohs* and he hurried back out, closing the garage door behind him to get the full effect and taking up position behind Maya, circling her waist.

The night was clear, the dark skies studded with stars as the backdrop to their display. A huge wreath hung just below the peak of the roof, sparkling with multicolored lights, and they'd erected a glittering archway around the doorframe below. Matching white lights surrounded every window, and white-light icicles dangled from the gutters. They'd decorated all the tall bushes and small trees in the front garden in the same twinkly hue. A display of sparkly ice-skating penguins stood on the lawn in front of the living room window, and the garage door was draped in a large red bow, as if it were a wrapped present. A small Santa's sleigh with a red-nosed reindeer had pride of place on the low roof above the living room window, and the inflatable Santa himself was on the grass next to the garage, waving at them and bobbing around in the breeze.

Sam reached into his pocket and took out his phone, snapping a few pictures.

"Are you going to post it on social media?" Maya asked, turning to face him.

"Kind of," he replied, opening the e-mail confirmation he'd had for their entry into the Christmas lights competition and revealing it to her.

Maya screamed and threw her arms around him. "Yes! That's brilliant."

Nuzzling her neck as he held her tightly, anticipation built in his core. He didn't want her to leave with the others. He wanted her to spend the night with him. As she leaned back to meet his gaze and kiss him, he tried to read her. Did she want that too? Or would it be too soon for her? Perhaps it wasn't fair of him to ask—they'd had their first date only a few nights ago.

The others were all chatting and admiring the lights. Elise gave Liv a nudge. "I need to head back to relieve Mum and Dad. Do you want a lift home?"

Liv checked her watch. "Yes please. I've still got some stuff to do for work tomorrow." She gave Sam and Maya a kiss, and Elise followed suit. As they headed away, Liv stopped to give Arran and Nico a hug, but Elise hung back, giving them a wave instead, and they left the driveway for Elise's car.

"Thanks for the feed, mate," Arran said, circling Sam's shoulders with a squeeze.

Sam smiled as he shook Nico's hand, addressing Arran. "Feel free to return the favor sometime."

Arran grinned as he kissed Maya's cheek. "Nah. You're a much better cook than me."

Nico gave Maya a hug, and then the two men left, disappearing around the corner and leaving Sam alone with Maya and his fast-building libido. If he were honest with himself, it'd been building ever since their not-very-fake fake kiss. Scratch that, it'd been escalating ever since he'd laid eyes on her in Kirsty's living room.

Maya cuddled into his chest. "Can I stay for a bit?"

He kissed the top of her head, relief that she'd suggested it taking the edge off his tension. "I'd love that."

He took her hand and led her inside, where they took off their boots. Sam's nerves flared as he watched her unzip her jacket. *Why do I feel like a teenager?* Perhaps because the woman of his teenage dreams was alone with him in his house.

He cleared his throat. "Tea? Or coffee?" He turned and went into the kitchen before she could answer, busying himself in there as she shot him a bemused look from the table, where she was clearing the plates.

Maya loaded everything into the dishwasher while he made a pot of tea, still aware that she hadn't said she'd wanted any.

Taking the pot and mugs over to the table, he glanced at her. "I'm afraid my tea isn't as good as Liv's."

Maya took a seat next to him. "Don't worry. Nobody's is."

Sam lifted his mug to take a sip but aborted the process when he realized it was too hot. Glancing up, he saw Maya was frowning at him.

"What?" he asked.

Leaning over, she took his mug from him and put it on the table. "What's wrong?"

"Nothing." His mouth was dry, but the tea was still too hot to aid in that predicament. "Why would anything be wrong?"

She smiled. "You're nervous."

Sam bounced his leg. "No, I'm not."

Glancing down at where his leg was bouncing like a bunny on

a trampoline, she placed a hand on it and stilled the movements. "Talk to me."

Come on, Sam. Talking isn't so hard. "I just . . . I wondered whether you might want to stay over tonight." He rubbed his beard. "I mean, we don't have to do anything, not if you don't want to. But it'd be nice to sleep together." His eyes widened as his pulse spiked. "I mean sleep as in *go* to sleep. Nothing else. Unless you want to, which would be nice."

Nice? He closed his eyes, willing his stupid mouth to stop moving.

Maya was still smiling, so at least he hadn't scared her off with that immensely unromantic monologue. Talk about not being smooth, he had less game than a misogynist at a feminist rally. She lifted a hand to run her fingers through his hair, and Sam felt like he'd settle for her doing that all night.

"What do *you* want?" she asked. "What do you *really* want? Not what you think I want to hear."

Swallowing against his sandpaper-dry mouth, he took her hand, playing with her charm bracelet. "I'd love to do . . . stuff." He glanced into her warm eyes. "But only if you're definitely ready. I don't want to rush you."

He almost startled when she got up and then climbed onto his lap to straddle him. Leaning toward his ear, she let her lips brush his skin, sending a delicious sensation into his core. "Ready? I was ready in that boot room, eight years ago."

Sam tried to voice his escalating emotions, but she was kissing his neck, and it made his brain short-circuit. He took a breath in an attempt to kick-start his cognitive processes, but then she bit his skin gently, and all that came out of his mouth was a groan.

Maya lifted her head to meet his gaze. Her eyes were like dark liquid pools of desire.

She brushed her lips over his. "Is this what you're nervous about?"

"Kind of," he breathed against her mouth.

She sank more deeply onto him, drawing him in, and sliding her tongue against his. The fluttering sensation of his nerves was fast being dissolved by an intense heat that gathered low in his belly.

Maya broke off to rest her forehead against his. "Don't be nervous. As long as this is what you want and it's not too soon for you, then I'd love to."

Sam pushed his fingers into her hair, tugging and tipping her head back to expose the long line of her neck. He dipped his head to kiss the skin there, licking and sucking until she let out that little moan, the one he remembered from the boot room all those years ago. It stoked the fire burning within him.

He let her face tip down and meet his gaze. "It's what I want." He paused, getting lost in her eyes for a moment. "I feel like I've wanted this forever."

Maya slipped her hand down and over his jeans, onto where he was as hard as a rock. He sucked in his breath.

"Me too," she whispered. Sinking into their kiss again, she teased his mouth with her tongue until he couldn't stand it any longer.

"Here?" he breathed.

"No. I don't think a little kitchen chair is the right spot for our first time." She climbed off and took his hand, tugging him to his feet. "Let's go to your room."

Leading him along the hallway and up the stairs, Sam felt as if this were too good to be true and any moment now, he was going to waken and have to come to terms with the disappointment that it had just been an amazing dream.

Maya paused on the upstairs landing. "Which room is yours?"

For a moment he wasn't sure what to say. Would it be weird for her to be in his bedroom after he'd shared it with Cat up until recently? Not that anything had happened in there for as long as he could remember, but still.

He pointed to each door in turn. "My room, or the spare room?"

Maya pulled him toward his bedroom, pushing the door open. "Hey. I'm not going to the general dumping ground."

She spun around and kissed him as they neared the bed, then pushed his chest to lower him down on it. Stepping toward him, she dipped her head and kissed him again slowly, spiraling his heart out of control, before standing straight and lifting off her woolly jumper.

Sam gripped the edges of the bed, unable to tear his eyes from her movements.

"I've got a confession," Maya said, keeping her gaze locked with his as she took hold of the bottom of her T-shirt.

"What?" he asked, staring at where she was lifting the shirt.

"I made the unfortunate decision of going for thermal underwear." She pulled the T-shirt over her head to reveal a thermal vest, then stripped off her jeans to display the matching knickers.

Sam couldn't help the laugh that escaped his mouth, and Maya jumped on him, knocking him back onto the bed to lie on top of him.

She grinned. "I hope you aren't laughing at me, Leonard."

He drew her into a kiss. "I'm laughing *with* you, not *at* you."

Pouting, she let her hair shower over his face. She smelled like teenage dreams coming to fruition. "Are you saying my underwear isn't sexy?"

Sam spun her onto her back, pinning her in place with his weight. "No, that's not what I'm saying. You'd be sexy in a binbag."

He leaned down to kiss her neck.

"I'd look rubbish in a binbag."

Sam laughed hard at that pun, resting his face against her neck. This was already the most fun he'd had in bed in his life.

Lifting his head to meet her eyes, he slowly slid his hand under the vest, appreciating the raw desire displayed in her gaze.

"We've been here before," he said softly.

Her dark eyes held his as he explored underneath, running his hand over the soft swell of her breasts and teasing the hardening peaks with his fingers.

Shifting his hand back down, he slipped his fingers under the waistband of her underwear, his heart pumping and sending wave after wave of heat into his core.

"But this is uncharted territory," he whispered.

Sliding lower, he absorbed her intake of breath as he explored her soft folds, touching and teasing the sensitive mound of flesh beneath his fingers.

He forced himself to wait, biding his time until she let out that delicious moan, studying what to do in order to make her moan louder, more desperately. Then he brought her up to sit, dragging the vest and underwear off before easing her back.

She lay there below him, fully naked, and he paused to take in the sight of her soft, delectable curves in the silvery darkness. He'd pictured her naked a thousand times, but imagination had not lived up to reality. She was perfect, and he wanted to kiss every inch of her smooth, tawny-brown skin.

Maya bit her lip as he pulled off his top layer in one go, and he shot her a smile. "No thermals for me, I'm afraid."

She ran a hand onto his chest. "I've been wanting to do this ever since I saw you at Kirsty's."

Her admitting that she'd wanted him as long as he had her only served to drive him wilder, and harder.

Maya let her fingers trail back down to the fastening of his jeans, undoing the button and the zip, then grazing over the material that bulged where he was straining against it. The exquisite ache of her touch was almost unbearable.

She pointed at his jeans. "Take those off."

Nearly falling off the bed in the process, he did as he was told, then took up position straddling her as she leaned on her elbows, admiring him in only his underwear. Her appreciative gaze made Sam feel like he was about to leave said underwear without even using his hands, he was straining so hard against the cotton.

Maya gave him a slow smile. "I've seen all of this before. I want to see what's under there."

Swallowing against his dry throat, he slid a hand down to his waistband and eased the underwear off, one leg at a time. The removal of the fabric's constraint did little to ease the ache. Then Maya reached out to take him in her hand, and pleasure pulsed into his core.

He leaned forward to plant a hand on the bed next to her head and grip the sheets, uttering a groan as she stroked him over and over. It didn't take long for his already intense libido to become dangerously close to overwhelming, no doubt because it had been a long time for him. He couldn't even remember the last time he'd had sex. But moreover, he couldn't remember ever wanting someone this much.

Taking a calming breath, he took hold of her hand to halt her movements. "This is going to be over too soon if you keep that up."

Maya reached out and brought his head down to hers, kissing him with such abandonment and longing that it took his breath away.

Shifting his weight to the side, he grabbed a condom from the bedside drawer, breaking off to fumble with the packet. He rolled it on quickly before she offered to help, because another touch from her and it could be game over.

Maya was reaching for him again, drawing him in, shifting her position to guide him where she wanted.

He took a deep breath to regain some control, desperately searching for an extremely unsexy thought in order to put the brakes on his overexcitement. *Boris Johnson in a mankini.* Nailed it.

Fixing his gaze on the intensity of her liquid brown eyes, he gradually eased inside her. He soaked up every time she gasped, absorbing every moan as he thrusted. Gently at first, then harder as she spurred him on. She moved with him, coming up to meet him as he stroked in and out.

Sam lifted her arms to pin them above her head, entwining his fingers with hers as he kissed her, tasting her, remembering how he'd pressed her against that wall at age eighteen. How she'd wanted him and how he'd dreamed that they'd be moving on to what they were doing right now.

Suddenly those years of separation ceased to exist, and they were teenagers again, fulfilling all their promises to each other.

His conscious thought faded away, until there was only sensation left. The delicious friction of her body grazing his, the delectable softness of her heat surrounding him. The scent of her filled his lungs, and the sound of her breathy moans all served to drive him insane.

He needed her to come, and he could sense her getting close, the way her breathing was becoming ragged and her movements more urgent. Tiny ripples began to tighten along his shaft, and he leaned down to let his lips brush her ear, trying to control his voice. "I want to hear you call my name. And I don't mean my middle name."

She tried to smile, but her climax was clearly too intense. She arched her back, the waves of it beginning to roll over them both.

Sam didn't know how he'd held out until this point, but now he let it all go. Years of pent-up want and need that he'd buried, brought to life since he'd laid eyes on her in that gold off-the-shoulder top that had made him want to bite her bare skin until she'd begged him to rip the clothing from her body.

Maya clung to him as she was racked with it, calling his name over and over. God, he loved the sound of it.

Holding her tightly, he sank his weight onto her, covering her with his body, protecting her, finally making her his. A sense of unreality overcame him. The woman of his dreams, the love of his life, was here in bed with him, and they'd made each other fall apart at the seams.

He sensed their breathing slow into a satisfied sync, his head resting on her chest as she ran her fingers through his hair.

Her soft voice sounded next to his ear, soothing him, her tone tentative. "Did you mean what you said the other day? That you were in love with me back then?"

Lifting his head, he kissed her thoroughly, attempting to extinguish any doubts with his mouth before his words took over. "I meant it," he murmured against her lips.

His thoughts drifted for a moment, onto a silver symbol of that love. Not the moon charm that he'd gotten her from the ski team, but its sister star that still lay in a little black jewelry box in his bedside drawer. Tucked where Cat would never have found it and where he now imagined his love had been locked away, waiting to be let out again. *Should I tell her?* He'd bought it at the same time as the moon, knowing that she'd liked them both, but the star had been from him alone. His intention had been to give it to her that night, when he had been going to ask her to be his girlfriend. He'd had it in his pocket the whole evening.

Meeting her gaze, he decided to keep it secret a little longer. Christmas was coming, after all. "Of course I meant it. You were my first love."

There was no denying that particular emotion was snowballing wildly, to the point that Sam began to question if he'd ever stopped loving her. But it was too soon to admit that.

Her eyes shining, her voice caught. "You were mine too. I'd liked you for ages, but being around you made me tongue tied. Until we worked together."

Sam realized that was the reason she used be quiet with him at school, not that she was aloof. It seemed so obvious now.

Pulling him into a lingering kiss, she trailed her fingers down his back. "I'm pretty sure I just died from a pleasure overload and now I'm in heaven. Do you think it was even better because we waited so long? The buildup of anticipation?"

Sam leaned on one arm, stroking her hair. "I can confirm that all my years of pent-up Maya-related energy went into that, so maybe." He raised his eyebrows. "That does *not* mean I'm willing to wait another few years to do it again, by the way. I'm pretty sure I'd die if I thought we weren't moving on to round two soon."

Maya laughed. "Wow. That's intense."

He grinned. "Tell me you disagree."

"Nope," she said, sighing. "I cannot. For 'twould be a massive lie."

Sam rolled to the side to dispose of the condom, then brought her into his chest, spooning her and wrapping his arm over her front. He nuzzled her neck. "Stay over with me."

She shivered under his touch. "Yes please."

Pulling the duvet over them both, Sam felt he was cocooned in a warm ball of contentment. The only tiny nag at the back of his mind was that Maya still hadn't faced the demons of her family's expectations, and her future in Glenavie still hung in the balance. She'd sent CVs off to those big-city firms to appease her father, and he knew her father's approval meant a lot to her. What if one of them turned into a job? One that took her away from him?

An icy needle dug into his heart at the thought that she might leave him, but he pushed it away, taking slow, deep inhales of her scent and letting it infuse his lungs, soothing him to sleep.

Chapter
TWENTY-ONE

SURVEYING THE END OF THE BOOT ROOM, MAYA WAS BEGIN-
ning to regret taking on this reorganization project. Especially
when everyone else was busy with their classes and couldn't help.

On a sigh, she realized the task would be a lot easier if she
could keep her mind on it rather than being distracted by delicious
flashbacks from the previous night. And the what-ifs of the morning's events, if she and Sam hadn't slept in and been in a hurry to
get to work.

A tiny seed of worry planted itself into the back of her mind.
Was this happening too quickly after his long-term relationship
had ended? It was fine for her—she didn't have a recent relationship trauma to get over; her ending with Rich had been more of a
gentle fizzling out. In any case, there had never been any drama
between them. Maya was careful to cultivate a drama-free zone
where her relationships were concerned, glossing over any minor
disagreements rather than having to endure any serious debates.

She chewed her bottom lip. What if Sam needed more time to
process the loss of his (toxic) relationship? Plus, work through

whatever damage it had left? Maya hadn't intended for the previous night to be when things moved on for them, as evidenced by her shortsighted choice in underwear. However, once she'd realized that was what Sam wanted, she'd let her libido run away with her.

What was more, she still hadn't spoken to her dad about them. Instead, she'd chosen the coward's way out and asked her mum to tell him, then she'd avoided speaking to him about it since. If she shied away from it, then maybe there wouldn't be any fallout.

Lifting another set of boots, she got back to work. The sound of the boot room door opening and closing a number of yards away became apparent. Then there was a pause and a scraping noise, before Sam's voice rang out.

His tone carried an edge of urgency. "Maya?"

"Down the back," she called, her heart rate picking up.

What was wrong? Last time they'd had a conversation in this particular room, the bombshell of Cat's deception had dropped, and Maya wasn't sure she could handle any further revelations.

He appeared around the corner, helmet, gloves, and goggles in hand, with his ski jacket hanging open and a hungry look in his eyes.

Maya dropped the boots she was holding as he closed the gap between them, the contents of his hands falling as he lifted them into her hair, pushing her against the wall and ravaging her mouth with his.

Maya's heart rate spiraled as he dragged his lips onto her neck.

"I nearly wiped out on the black run because I kept thinking about this," Sam whispered in a husky tone as he kissed and gently bit her skin.

He must have come straight off the slopes to find her, and the thought of that sent her head spinning.

Sam slid one hand down over her chest, causing her to shiver with anticipation, then pushed it under her top. Thank God she hadn't gone with the thermals today.

He trailed his fingers upward, leaving a wave of goose bumps in his wake. Then he brushed his touch over the thin material of her bra, causing the sensitive flesh underneath to ache. Maya arched her back, needing to bring him closer.

Lifting his head to mold his gaze with hers, he ran his hand to the fastener of her jeans, pushing them down along with her lacy underwear. *Thank you, underwear gods, for my better choice in knickers today.*

Keeping his eyes locked with hers, he sucked his fingers, making her heart pound in her ears and an unbearable heat pool low in her belly. Then he trailed his fingers between her legs, teasing, rubbing, and dipping them in and out. Her pulse accelerated, the delicious sensation building.

Maya took hold of his face as her breath came in ragged bursts. "What if someone comes in?"

He smiled, moving his mouth close to her ear so that his lips grazed her skin. "Then you'd better hurry up."

Liquid heat shot into her core, and he ramped up his movements, responding to her moans until her climax began to roll over his fingers. She tried to breathe his name rather than calling it out, lest anyone outside the room hear her cries.

Maya collapsed against the wall as the waves slowed, Sam holding her steady and kissing her softly.

"I've got a confession," he murmured.

"What?" she asked, trying to focus on him through her post-climactic haze.

He smiled. "I blocked the doorway with one of the shelves."

Maya paused to take in what he'd just said, her thought processes still foggy from the amazing orgasm he'd just given her. She managed a laugh. "You could have told me that before."

He kissed her neck. "It was more fun this way."

"So, you're telling me that no one can get in?" she asked, glancing toward the bank of boots that shielded the view of the doorway.

"That's right," he murmured against her skin.

"Good." She pushed him back a little, causing him to arch a brow in surprise. Then she tugged off his ski jacket, and a smile spread across his face as she unfastened his ski pants and dragged them down, along with his underwear.

Maya took hold of his jumper to pull him back in.

There was raw need in his voice. "We can go to my office if you'd prefer."

It was clear he wanted no delay and was only asking for her sake.

Maya shook her head. The thought of having to wait a few extra minutes to get out of the room and upstairs was unbearable.

She met his eyes for emphasis. "Now."

His gaze darkened and he took her face to kiss her roughly, then reached down into his trouser pocket to grab a condom and roll it on.

Maya raised her eyebrows. "You were skiing all morning with that in your pocket?"

Sam shrugged, smiling as he stripped off her bottom half and lifted her to straddle him against the wall. "This was premeditated. I told you I couldn't wait to have you again."

He drove into her against the wall, catching the gasp that escaped her lips with his mouth.

She held his head against her neck as he moved more and more urgently, clearly slaking the need that had been building all morning. Maya pushed aside the little voice inside that told her she was doing it again—letting her desire for him run away with her when she should slow matters down for his sake. But when they both wanted each other this badly, what harm could it do?

❄ ❄ ❄

"FOR GOODNESS' SAKE," YVONNE SAID, GLANCING OVER FROM THE dishwasher. "Can nobody load this thing properly except me?"

"Sorry, Mum," Maya said, rising to help with the reloading process. "They skipped the 'how to load a dishwasher to Yvonne Bashir's satisfaction' module at university."

Yvonne swatted her with a tea towel. "None of your cheek."

Maya glanced up, taking in that Hana looked awful, sitting at the dinner table and pushing the practically untouched food around on her plate while Omar read through a medical magazine, oblivious to his surroundings. There was a stomach bug going round the community, and poor Hana had been chucking her guts up all day.

Hana stood and took her plate over to scrape it into the food bin. "I'm just going for a lie down."

Yvonne frowned. "Still feeling off color, sweetheart?"

Hana smiled weakly. "I'm sure I'll feel better in the morning." She turned and left the kitchen.

Omar put down his magazine, as if he were just entering the room. "Have you heard back from any of those firms?"

Maya closed her eyes briefly, imagining that doing so might force back the nausea that appeared whenever he mentioned it. "Not yet."

He frowned. "I might chase Perry and Pearson for you. My old friend from university is a partner there, so perhaps underlining your affiliation to me will help."

Maya's heart mimicked the *Titanic*, sinking to the bottom of the ocean and taking Kate Winslet's shiny jewel with it. The reality of the situation hit. If she succeeded in securing a job there, it would entail moving over a hundred miles away to Edinburgh. Over a hundred miles from Sam, and the ski resort that she loved so much. *And I don't think the resort is the only thing I'm in love with.*

"That's okay," she said quickly. "I don't want you doing me any favors."

Omar shook his head. "Of course I'm going to do you some favors. You're my daughter and I want the same success for you as your sister."

Can't he stop mentioning Hana for two bloody minutes?

The doorbell sounded, signaling a reprieve.

"I'll get it," Maya said, hurrying from the kitchen and down the hallway.

She opened the door, imagining running out into the night, toward Sam's, and was met by the very welcome sight of his handsome face.

Maya threw her arms around him, nearly knocking him off the doorstep.

"What a welcome," he said, kissing her cheek.

"Thank God you're here," she replied. "You've provided an interruption to Dad's latest railroading." She ushered him in, realizing with a jolt that this would be the first meeting between her father and Sam since they'd started seeing each other.

Sam frowned, taking off his snow boots. "What's happening?"

Keeping her voice low, Maya led him along the hallway. "Dad's going to call his friend's firm in Edinburgh to ask them to employ me."

Sam's eyes seemed to widen for a moment, and then he smiled

as they entered the kitchen and he caught sight of Yvonne and Omar.

Yvonne glanced up from her dishwasher audit. "Hi, Sam. Would you like a cup of tea?"

"That would be great, thanks, Mrs. B."

Shaking her head with a smile, Yvonne fetched the mugs. "It's Yvonne, sweetheart."

Color rose in his cheeks, and Maya leaned over to kiss both of them, her heart melting.

Sam cleared his throat. "Yvonne. Hi, Dr. B."

Omar gave him a curt nod. "Hello, Sam. How's your mum?"

"Good, thanks. She and Angus are getting on well. He's moved in."

"That's fantastic," Yvonne said. "They're such a great couple."

Sam glanced at the floor. "Liv and I are really pleased for them."

Maya took his hand and gave it a squeeze, aware that he was still wary of Angus. Not because he was a bad guy, far from it. But Sam had confessed his concerns that Angus might not stick around, and she could tell he still had trouble believing that people weren't going to up and leave.

She led him to the table to take a seat.

Omar folded his magazine. "What brings you here this evening?"

Yvonne shot him a look, and Omar shrugged. "Just asking. Making conversation."

Sam laughed, though Maya detected a nervous edge behind it. "Maya left something at work, so I was just dropping it off."

Maya realized she'd never asked why he was stopping by; she'd been so pleased to see him. "What did I leave?"

He fished her woolly gloves from his pocket and handed them over. Smiling, she met his gaze—he could easily have given them to her the next morning. He'd just wanted an excuse to see her again that day. Maya took his hand again, scooting her chair closer.

Yvonne came over and handed out mugs.

Omar lifted his, blowing on it. "Your mum tells me that you two are an item."

Maya nearly spat out her tentative sip of tea. "*Dad.*"

"What?" he asked, taking a drink. "Isn't that what you youngsters call it anymore?"

Yvonne rolled her eyes, a smile on her face.

Sam glanced at Omar, rubbing his neck. "That's right, Dr. B." He shot Maya a soft look that nearly made her swoon off her chair. "I'm a lucky guy."

Nodding, Omar set down his mug. "She's a clever cookie, our Maya. Destined for big things, and big places."

Maya narrowed her eyes at her dad. Was he firing a warning shot at Sam? Intended to give him a heads-up that she wouldn't be his for long because she'd be moving on? That was not the signal she wanted sent to the man who'd already suffered rejection with her, even though it hadn't been of her doing.

She shifted her chair right against Sam's, bringing their entwined hands possessively into her lap.

Sam shot her a glance, clearly aware of the intention to reassure behind her movements.

"I know," Sam said to Omar, the hint of a waver behind his voice. "She's one of a kind."

"*Anyway,*" Maya said, flipping her hair in order to cover her discomfort. "Enough about my attributes for one evening."

"Sam," Yvonne interjected, and Maya nearly kissed her mother for sweeping in. "Would you like to come for dinner at the weekend? It'd be nice to all eat together. And hopefully by then Hana will be feeling better."

"I'd love to, thanks, Mrs. B. I mean—Yvonne," Sam finished quickly. If he'd clocked that her dad hadn't extended the same courtesy of requesting to be called by his first name, then Sam didn't let on.

They finished their tea with Yvonne making small talk and Omar interjecting with short responses, and then Sam stood. "Thanks very much for the tea, and the dinner invite. I'll leave you good people to it."

Maya followed him out of the kitchen, closing the door behind them. She took his hand again as they walked down the hallway to the front door, leaning in for a kiss. "Sorry about Dad."

Sam put his arms around her. "He just wants what's best for you." He kissed her again, but there was a sad look in his eyes, and Maya regretted that she'd told him about her dad's resentment. But she had felt it better to forearm him, and it made the fact that he'd turned up out of the blue even more heartwarming.

"Hey," she said, lifting her hands to his face. "You know that was all bluster, don't you? All the 'my daughter is set to jet off and save the world' crap?"

Bumping his nose against hers, he smiled. "It's just that sometimes I think he's right. Maybe you belong away in a big city somewhere, crunching numbers for a big firm and raking it in, not stuck here with me mucking around on the slopes."

Maya pulled him in, kissing him so deeply that she hoped he could taste what she really wanted, and the way in which he was imprinted upon her heart. "I'm going nowhere, buddy. So get used to it."

He smiled against her mouth, and guilt stabbed in her chest that she hadn't told her dad how she really felt about her future.

She pulled back to meet his eyes. "You know what's weird?"

"What?"

"It's weird how this isn't weird at all. We loved each other, then we hated each other. Now we've only been friends for a few weeks, but last night felt as if it was meant to be."

Sam reached over to squeeze her hand. "I know. I kind of feel like the last eight years never happened." He grinned. "And for the record, I didn't hate you. I just didn't like you that much. But unfortunately for me, I still fancied the arse off you."

Maya laughed. "Same."

Sam's phone buzzed, and he lifted it out of his pocket. "It's Vicky. She's all settled in Inverness." His face fell as he seemed to catch himself. "You remember me mentioning my friend Vicky? She took the kids' classes before you did? And the message is really from both her and her fiancé, Gary. Do you remember me saying that they moved to Inverness?" He was speaking so quickly that she had to concentrate to catch the individual words.

Maya raised her eyebrows, trying to keep up with his fast-moving speech and attempting to fathom why he appeared panicked. "Yeah, I remember. I've heard she was a great teacher." Taking both his hands, she met his gaze. "Are you okay? Was there something to worry about in her message?"

Sam hesitated, appearing thrown. "No, everything is good. They're doing great."

Maya nodded, trying to work him out. "Then why are you so panicky?"

Sam took a breath. "I just didn't want you to get the wrong idea. You know, about me getting a text from a woman."

Maya looked at him for a moment, still lost. "Get the wrong idea . . . about a friend messaging you?"

He glanced down. "Yeah."

She raised her eyebrows, things falling into place. He thought she'd be jealous. "Sam. There's nothing wrong with friends messaging each other."

He lifted his head to meet her eyes again.

She smiled. "So don't expect me to give you a commentary every time Brodie and Ben message *me*, because I can't be arsed."

Sam laughed, and it sounded very much like relief. "No problem. I'll see you tomorrow, okay?" He gave her another kiss, then stepped away to open the door, and she waved him off into his car.

Shutting the door, she headed quickly into her room, pulling out her phone to video call Liv.

She appeared on-screen, pushing her glasses up her nose. "Good morrow, Miss Maya."

"Miss O, good morrow to you too. Listen, I need your twin psychic ability."

Liv raised her eyebrows, smiling. "I don't think that's a thing, Maya."

"Sure it is," Maya replied, flashing her a grin. "Sam was weird just now. He had some sort of panic attack because he got a text from his mate Vicky. He seemed to think that I'd be upset about it?"

Liv raised an eyebrow in a knowing manner. "That's because if he ever mentioned any women apart from Mum and I, or got any calls or messages from a person identifying as a woman, then Cat used to go apeshit."

"Really?" Maya asked, her eyes widening. "Why?"

Liv shrugged. "All part of her controlling personality. She got jealous if he was even around any women."

"That's intense," Maya said slowly. She'd been right about the baggage. Not that it made her doubt being with him; nothing would change her feelings for him. It was more that she was questioning how to deal with it. "But why would he think I'd have an issue with it too? I'm nothing like Cat."

"I don't think it's a conscious thing," Liv said, her tone reassuring. "He just doesn't have a good frame of reference. She's been his only long-term relationship. They both saw other people casually for a really short period on one of their longer breakups, but nothing that would've given him any real baseline of normality." She smiled. "He just needs time to adjust to the non-crazy."

"Okay," Maya said, taking a deep breath. "I can give him time." She bit her lip. "Although I am a bit worried that we've rushed into this relationship, when I should've given him some space on his own first."

"He's an adult, and he felt ready. More than ready, once he realized the real story."

"Still. I wonder if we should encourage him to get some counseling. I don't want to say or advise the wrong thing if he's struggling."

Liv studied her, a soft look shining in her eyes. "That's a great idea." A big smile broke out over her face. "Hey, have I told you recently how awesome you are?"

Maya smiled, her heart swelling with love for her friend. "Not as awesome as you, Miss O. You're the only one of us who has their shit together."

Liv bit her lip and averted her gaze for a second, then glanced back at the screen with a soft smile. "You're the best sister-in-law ever. Christmases from now on are going to be amazeballs."

The weight of responsibility felt heavy on Maya's shoulders, but it made her all the more determined to help.

A strange sound from the hallway took her attention, and when she tuned in to it, it sounded like someone retching. "Sorry, Liv, I need to dash. I think Hana needs some help."

"No worries. Love you."

"Love you too."

She hung up, and paused. The sound was still apparent, and it was consistent with Hana being sick in the bathroom. Maya went down the hallway and hesitated outside the door, giving a knock. It was slightly ajar. "Hana, I'm coming in." She slipped inside.

"Don't!"

"Too late, I'm here now."

Hana was clutching the toilet bowl, shivering. Her normally formidable form seemed so vulnerable and fragile that it made Maya freeze for a split second, her heart pierced with empathy.

She grabbed a towel and put it around Hana's shoulders, crouching next to her. "Here. You can wipe your face on it too."

Hana's voice was hoarse as she pulled it around her shoulders. "Thanks."

Maya put her arm around her sister. "Shall I go ask Dad what might help the stomach bug? He's been treating loads of people with it."

"No," Hana said quickly. "That's okay."

She seemed to wipe away a tear, and Maya's heart rate accelerated. "Hans, what's going on?"

The tears began to openly fall and Hana's voice broke. "It's not a stomach bug."

Panic punched Maya in the gut and she tugged Hana in, not bothered that she could get vomited on. What if it was something sinister? Her worry spiraling, Maya tried to assess her sister's tearstained face. "What is it?"

Hana must've sensed Maya's anxiety. "It's nothing serious." She took a breath. "I'm pregnant."

Maya's mouth dropped open, her panic doused with delight. "That's brilliant! I didn't know you and Rosie were trying."

Hana shook her head. "We didn't want to put pressure on it by having people know." She snuggled further into the towel, and into Maya, glancing away. "We decided to try artificial insemination last year, and it wasn't happening. So, we got referred privately for IVF because we figured it was best not to waste time."

"Awesome," Maya whispered, the thought of being an auntie and going out shopping for the coolest baby clothes in town playing on her mind. She was brought back to earth with a jolt as she realized that Hana was still crying. Was she upset because they'd needed IVF? It would be typical high-flying, putting-herself-under-pressure-to-be-perfect Hana if she viewed that as some sort of failure, which, clearly, it was not.

Maya gave her a squeeze. "Why don't you seem happy about it? Is it because you feel so ill?"

Hana shook her head. "Rosie and I had a big bust-up."

Maya frowned. Rosie was the loveliest, most placid person on the planet. "How come?"

Hana glanced down. "It was all decided. She's let her career take the back burner for the past few years so that we could be near my workplace and I could make partner. Moving out to the country was meant to be the initial move in Rosie's job beginning to take center stage, and I was going to be the first one to have a baby."

Maya nodded. "Sounds like a solid plan. Rosie's supported you climbing the career ladder, now it's her turn to shine."

Hana rubbed her face, wincing. "Except I had a crisis of confidence and told her I wasn't happy about switching into the career back seat."

Maya hesitated. "But why?"

Hana looked up. "Because I'm such a driven freak that I couldn't let go. We had a huge argument and I got in the car to drive here. She wanted to follow me but I told her not to."

Maya sank farther onto the floor, sitting with her legs out and bringing Hana into her body for a proper hug. "You push yourself too hard."

"I know," Hana whispered. "But I don't know how to stop. And now I'm doubting that I can be a good mum."

Maya sighed. Why hadn't she realized this before? That Hana was as damaged by their father's driven attitude as she was, just in a different way.

"First of all, you'd make an excellent mother. And second, you need to let go of what you think Dad might say about it." She was aware that was probably the most hypocritical thing she'd ever said, when she hadn't been able to do the same herself. "You need to do what will make you happy, what's best for your family. You've achieved brilliant things, but you work to live, not the other way around. Anyway, it's not like he'll be disappointed. He'll be delighted to be a grandfather."

Hana nodded. "I know you're right, but it's like I can't let go of work. As if I'll be losing what defines me."

Maya's heart beat harder with sadness. "It *isn't* what defines you."

They sat in silence for a few moments, Maya stroking Hana's hair.

"I'm sorry I grassed you up to Dad," Hana said, her voice quiet. "About your ski job. I think I was trying to deflect the heat off myself somehow." She sighed. "I know it's messed up, but I think I was jealous, in a way. Your career doesn't seem to have the same hold on you as mine does me."

Maya gave her a squeeze. "That's because I don't like my career." A stab of regret pierced her being. Perhaps she shouldn't be confessing that to Hana, not when her sister had already betrayed her. "Anyway, it doesn't matter that you told him. At least you got me out of doing it myself."

Hana managed a weak laugh. "Do you want to switch careers? Work at the resort permanently?"

Maya fell silent, unsure whether to say anything further.

Hana's voice was small. "You can tell me. I promise not to break your confidence again."

Maya's breath caught. She'd heard that one before, but this time felt different. Something about Hana's raw vulnerability, a quality that she didn't normally display. "Yes. I want to leave accountancy, and be a ski instructor full-time."

Lifting her head, Hana met Maya's eyes. "I'll support you. When you tell him."

Maya's heart tripped, and she swallowed the emotion gathering in her throat. "Thank you."

Helping Hana off the floor, Maya guided her into her room to lie down, then went in search of a receptacle. She placed it by the bed alongside a glass of water, noticing that Hana had dropped off to sleep. She must have been exhausted.

Maya wandered downstairs, plagued with worry for her sister.

She poked her head around the living room door, and Omar was in there, alone. She wanted to tell her parents about Hana in order to enlist their support. In general, for what she was going through, and for her dad's medical opinion on what might help the sickness. But if she did that, she'd be breaking Hana's confidence, and she couldn't undermine that, especially when Hana was so vulnerable.

Clearing her throat, she addressed her dad, deciding the only way forward was to tell a white lie. "Have you got any information I can give to a friend about morning sickness? She's having a hard time of it."

Maya realized that it would be easy for him to put two and two together if Hana continued to be ill rather than recovering as would be the case for a bug, but hopefully Hana would feel able to tell them soon. She blew her fringe out of her eyes. "It's difficult for her to get going in the morning, because she feels so sick."

Omar looked up from the TV. "I'll send you a link to a patient information website that she can use." He paused. "Which friend is it?"

Shit. "Well, it's more a friend of a friend. Not anyone you'd know."

Omar raised his eyebrows, looking at her for a second, then lifted his phone. "I'll text you the link."

Chapter TWENTY-TWO

RAKING THROUGH HIS WARDROBE, SAM PULLED OUT A FOURTH shirt, stripping off number three and replacing it with the latest attempt. As he buttoned it, he studied his reflection in the mirror, and sighed. None of his clothes seemed suitable. He just didn't possess anything that said, "I'm good enough for your awesome daughter."

Unbuttoning number four and going back to number one, he checked the time on his phone and noticed a text from Liv.

Have you checked social media this afternoon?

Frowning, he messaged back.

Which one?

All of them.

Whatever this was, it didn't sound good. Opening the first icon that his thumb found, he went into Instagram, scrolling through the most recent posts on his feed. He was considering calling Liv to ask what she was talking about when he spotted it. Underneath a picture that Maya had posted of her and Rowan smiling on the slopes, Cat had commented: Nice to see that stealing other people's boyfriends suits you.

A cold, heavy weight settled into his gut as he scrolled Maya's profile. Cat had trolled pretty much everything on there, and when he checked Facebook, it was the same.

Feeling sick and not wanting to see any more, he threw the phone onto the bed. *Shit.* This was all his fault. Nothing had happened between Maya and him while he'd been with Cat, but Cat would want to deflect the heat off herself in case her lies came to light in the community. She wanted to discredit them in advance. Why on earth had he been involved with her for so long? Now his inertia in shedding the burden of Catriona had consequences for Maya.

Deciding that shirt number one would have to do, and that Maya had made a mistake in getting involved with him, he grabbed his phone and made to head for hers.

❄   ❄   ❄

MAYA OPENED THE DOOR, AND FROM THE DULL HUE OF HER EYES, he could tell that she'd seen the social media trolling.

Stepping inside, he brought her into a hug. "I'm so sorry."

She buried her head in his neck, and his protective instinct overcame him.

"It's not your fault." She lifted her face to kiss his cheek. "I've blocked her now."

Sam held her face. "Still. I'm sorry that you were affected by it."

She smiled brightly. "Come on. Dad's made curry and it smells *delish*."

As Sam followed Maya, and the scent of dinner, along the hallway, his heart accelerated. He hoped he could make a good impression on Dr. Bashir.

Yvonne was dishing up, and Omar sat at the table with Hana next to him. Hana appeared pinched and pale. Maya had told him that her sister was pregnant but going through a difficult time emotionally, and Sam had promised not to tell anybody. But him being trusted with the responsibility of a secret the rest of Maya's family didn't know was another factor in his escalating nerves.

Hana shot him a weak smile and made to get up to greet him, but he crossed around the side of the table to save her getting to her feet, giving her a hug where she sat. "Nice to see you."

"You too," she replied, clearly trying to stretch the smile across her face.

Omar reached over to shake Sam's hand. "Don't worry, she's not contagious anymore."

Sam let out a short laugh that sounded a little high pitched.

Hana was aware that Sam knew. Maya had been keen for that to be in the open in order to be aboveboard in keeping her sister's confidence. His heart swelled at the knowledge that Maya would protect the trust of those who didn't always do the same for her. He gave Hana a reassuring smile.

Taking off his jacket, he turned to where Yvonne and Maya were bringing the food over to the table. "What can I do to help?"

Yvonne shook her head. "It's all in hand. Take a seat next to your girlfriend." She shot Maya a grin, and Maya rolled her eyes.

Sam did as he was told, sitting next to Maya and across from Omar, grateful for the fact that Maya had enlisted her mum to work on her dad.

Yvonne sat at the head of the table. "Dig in, everyone."

The curry was as tasty as it smelled, though Hana mostly pushed hers around her plate, Maya shooting her the odd anxious look.

"So, Sam," Omar said, studying him across the table and making his heart rate spike. "What are your career plans?"

Maya took Sam's hand under the table. "Ugh, Dad. This is pretty boring dinnertime chat."

Omar raised his eyebrows. "I'm getting to know him, Maya."

"Then ask him what his favorite TV show is, or what sports he likes," Maya shot back.

Sam gave her hand a squeeze. "I recently had another promotion, and I'm the assistant manager now. So, once I've settled into the role, I'll see."

Omar nodded.

Smiling, Yvonne swept in. "What are your family doing for Christmas, Sam?"

His shoulders relaxed at the change in subject. "Liv and I are going to Mum's. Well, Mum and Angus's," he corrected himself.

It would be the first time in years that there had been four people around their Christmas dinner table, and he was sure it would be a much better atmosphere than when his dad had been there. Though he couldn't shake the feeling that one day, it might end up the three of them again, if Angus bolted.

At least now he didn't have to worry about Catriona's wrath, not where Christmas was concerned. She'd always been resentful of him seeing his family around the festive season and tried to block those plans, even when he'd been more than willing to see her family in addition. It was as if she just didn't want him to see his mum and Liv at all, and only be around her and her family. Come to think of it, her attempting to block him seeing family and friends had been an all-year-round exercise.

Glancing at Maya, he knew there was no way she'd behave like that.

Yvonne lifted her glass. "We usually have a little Christmas Eve party here, and we'd love it if you came."

A warm feeling settled in his chest. "That would be great, thank you."

Omar sipped his water. "So how much does an assistant manager at a ski resort make these days?"

Yvonne shot him a hard look. "Omar."

"I'm not being rude. I just want to make sure everything is . . . secure." Omar's gaze penetrated Sam, causing his heart to feel like it was trying to bury itself in his stomach. "Your future needs to be so, if you're planning on settling down."

"It *is* rude," Maya said, her mouth drawn into a thin line. "That's not the sort of question you ask anybody. Especially a dinner guest."

Sam took a breath, realizing that last time he'd been here, Omar had given him a cloaked warning not to expect anything long term with Maya. And now he was making barbed comments about needing a secure future? *Oh shit*. It dawned on him that Maya had mentioned seeking medical advice from Omar about morning sickness. What if he'd put two and two together and reached five—making the assumption that his younger daughter was pregnant, rather than his older one? And now he was sounding out Sam because he didn't think he was a good enough prospect to be the father of his grandchild.

Suddenly, Sam knew exactly how Hana felt, pushing the food around his plate with a nauseated feeling and trying to communicate to Maya with his eyes what was going on.

Omar continued tucking into his dinner, clearly not fazed by any of this. "There comes a time where you have to put family first. Do what you need to do to provide for them."

Oh God. Sam caught Hana's eye across the table, and she shot him a pained look. She'd caught on too. He couldn't correct Omar though, not without breaking Hana and Maya's confidence, and Hana clearly was too fragile to have a discussion about her pregnancy or the fallout with her fiancée.

Maya blew her breath out through pursed lips. "Whatever, Dad. We're not even thirty yet. Plenty of time to think about all that stuff."

Sam gave her hand a squeeze and shot her a look that he tried to make read "your dad thinks I've got you pregnant," but it must have come out as "I'm terrified" instead, because she just gave him a supportive smile. Though, to be fair, those two sentiments were rather similar.

Somehow, Sam managed to get through the rest of dinner without passing out from intense stress and was the first to help with the tidying up. Something he would've done anyway but was even more keen to now, in order to avoid any further grilling.

Maya kept shooting him worried looks, and he could tell she still hadn't realized what the misunderstanding was. As they loaded the dishwasher together, he leaned in, keeping his voice low. "We need to talk."

Frowning, she nodded. "Okay. But I hope you're not dumping me because my family is a nightmare." She glanced across the room at where Omar had his head buried in a medical magazine. "Well, one of them is anyway."

"No," he replied. "It's not that."

They finished, and Maya made their excuses, leading him out of the kitchen and up to her bedroom, shutting the door behind her.

They both sat on the bed, Sam taking her hand and letting out a breath he felt that he'd been holding for years. "Your dad thinks you're pregnant."

Maya let out a snort. "Yeah, right." When she realized he wasn't smiling, her eyes widened. "Oh shit."

"Yep."

She rubbed her forehead. "That's what all that 'secure future' crap was about. Oh man. I should've just googled that information rather than asking him. I'm as bad as those people who go on the town Facebook page to ask what time the next bus is."

Sam laughed, feeling that it could be a shade close to hysteria and clamping his mouth shut again. "My mission to win your dad over is *not* going the way I'd planned."

Maya pulled him into a hug. "It'll be okay. We'll work through it."

Sam kissed the top of her head, hoping that she was right and that he wasn't driving some sort of irreversible wedge between her and her father.

"Hey," she said, lifting her head. "Did you speak to Arran? About your second job and taking a step back?"

"Yeah," he said, brushing the hair out of her eyes. "You were right. It felt good, and he's fine without the extra money now he's got the last of his equipment. Things are taking off for the studio."

Her face relaxed, and he sensed that she was relieved. Having a girlfriend who looked out for him and worried about him was a new experience.

She smiled. "You're welcome to do a bit of private naked butlering, if you want. For me. My pay rates are pretty good."

Bringing her closer so that she was practically on his lap, he smiled. "Oh yeah? What would I get for it?"

She pushed her fingers into his hair, drawing his head down

into a kiss that knocked the breath out of his body and made him forget about the disapproving father and secretly pregnant sister.

When she broke off, he had to take a second to reorientate himself. "Wow. That's pretty much the best pay packet I've ever gotten."

Maya laughed.

There was a knock at the door, and the disapproving father–pregnant sister situation came home to roost in Sam's mind.

"Come in," Maya called.

Hana stuck her head around the door with a sheepish expression on her face.

Maya gestured her inside, and she closed the door behind her, leaning against it.

"I'm sorry, guys. I'll fix things." Hana addressed Sam. "Maya's convinced me to stop being a wuss and call Rosie to sort things out. Once I've checked in with her that it's okay, I'll tell Mum and Dad."

Sam hadn't seen Hana for a long time prior to this, but she appeared so much more fragile than her usual forthright self.

He smiled. "Don't worry. I've not been chased off the premises quite yet."

Hana returned his smile. "Dad'll come round. Anyway, I'll leave you guys to it." She gave them a wave and left, closing the door again.

Maya lay on the bed, drawing him down next to her with his head on her chest. Closing his eyes and breathing her in, he really could imagine that everything was going to be okay.

She stroked his head. "I need to ask you something."

Nestling his face into her neck, he sighed. "I hope it's nothing bad, because my heart can't take any more after that dinner."

She laughed, and he absorbed the gentle sound of it through

her chest. "No, it's not bad." She paused. "I was thinking it'd be a good idea for you to get some counseling."

Lifting his head, Sam shot her a bemused smile. "I don't know what I was expecting, but it wasn't that." His smile slipped a little. "Do you think I'm that messed up?"

"No." She kissed his forehead. "You don't need to be messed up to get counseling. It just helps us all work through things better."

Laying his head back down, he breathed in her scent again, wishing he could bottle it and carry it around with him because it soothed his soul. "Why do you think I need it?"

She pushed her fingers through his hair, and the tension began to leave his body. "I think it'd help you find your feet, generally and also relationship-wise, after all the stuff with Cat. There're behaviors of hers that I think you don't realize were warped, and it's affecting how you react to things, causing you stress where there doesn't need to be. And maybe there's still stuff to work through after your dad."

Sam closed his eyes, feeling as if he could drift off to sleep. He could see what she was saying, but it really wasn't necessary. He had Maya now, and that was all he needed. "I appreciate it, but I don't need counseling. Once things get sorted with Hana, everything will be great."

Chapter
TWENTY-THREE

FLICKING THROUGH HER PHONE, MAYA CALLED UP THE STAIRS to Hana. "Are you ready? I've got a plastic bag for the car, just in case."

"Coming." Hana descended the stairs, still looking awfully peaky. "Thanks for driving me to the appointment. I don't think I can manage the journey without having to pull over and vomit."

"No problem," Maya replied. "This way we can continue traveling while you puke in a bag instead."

Hana smiled, and for the first time since she'd gotten home, it seemed to reach her eyes.

They climbed into the car, and Maya gestured to the pile of plastic bags at Hana's feet. "There you go. I've all the best bags for life there. You can take your pick whether to go upmarket with Waitrose or slum it like the rest of us with Aldi."

Hana managed a laugh, and Maya felt that was progress.

On the drive over, she shot Hana a look. "Did you speak to Rosie last night?"

Hana nodded. "We made a bit of headway. I apologized for being a selfish cow and explained what you and I had discussed about my warped sense of self being tied into my success. She understood, and we're going to work out a plan, which means she can get her teeth into being a country vet like she always wanted, but also to share the maternity leave if I want to return to work a little earlier and her have some time with the baby."

"Sharing the maternity leave sounds like a great idea. You'll both benefit from bonding with the baby that way."

"That's what Rosie said. Anyway, I hope I'm not holding you back by getting you to come home from work early to take me to the GP."

They were on their way to the surgery they were registered at, a different one from their father's place of work.

"It's no problem. I don't even have any classes on a Monday. I've just been doing some various projects around the place to help spruce things up."

Hana smiled. "You love it there, don't you?"

Warmth spread through Maya's veins. "I really do."

"It's great to see you happy. You always sounded so miserable when you talked about work before."

"Yeah," Maya said, sighing. "I just need to convince Dad."

"Maybe we don't need to convince him. Just tell him that's how it is, deal with it."

The thought of that filled Maya with dread, but the edge was taken off by Hana using the word *we* rather than *you*, giving her the reassuring feeling that her big sister was in this with her. Just like Maya was invested in the pregnancy and Hana letting go at work.

Pulling into the doctor's surgery car park, Maya turned to Hana. "Maybe you should take a bag with you. Just in case."

Nodding as she unbuckled, Hana picked up the Waitrose one.

"Ha!" Maya said, grinning. "I knew you'd go for that one."

Hana stuck her tongue out as she left the vehicle, and Maya laughed, taking out her phone to check her social media.

She was distracted by a text from Sam, saying he hoped Hana's appointment went okay. It was a shame her idea about counseling hadn't floated. The more she thought about it, the more it felt like the right move. She should've realized it wouldn't be that easy. Sam didn't have a grasp on the extent of the damage Catriona had done because he had no baseline to measure it against. Plus, it was clear to her now that all of those issues were built on the foundation of the abandonment issues left by his dad. There was a lot to unpack. Perhaps if she left it for a while, then came back to the idea in the New Year, he might be more receptive.

Maya smiled as she spotted a photo that Rowan had posted on Insta, of all the women on the instructor team. She scrolled the comments, pleased that it was such a cool group. But then her delight ran cold as Cat appeared in the comments. Be careful of the second one on the left, she'll steal your man in a heartbeat.

Maya swallowed. Blocking Cat may have prevented her from commenting on Maya's own social media, but it didn't stop her from appearing on Maya's friends' stuff.

Sinking back into her seat, she wondered whether she could ask everyone she knew to block Cat too, but surely that was impractical. Nausea rose in her gut as she realized getting rid of Cat wasn't going to be easy.

She wound the window down, needing some fresh air in her lungs. The delicate icy structure of the snowflakes falling past represented the fragility of her happiness. Every time things seemed to be looking up, something else came along to derail the situation.

Lost in her thoughts, she startled as Hana climbed back into the car.

"What did the doctor say?"

"I've got a prescription for some anti-sickness tablets. Hopefully they'll help." Hana buckled in. "What's wrong? You look a bit pale. Hope you're not coming out in sympathy for me."

Maya didn't have the heart to voice it, so she handed Hana the phone, pointing at the comment in question.

Hana's face soured. "That little bitch. She always was a spiteful cow." She glanced up. "Don't worry about it. She'll soon get bored and piss off."

"I hope so," Maya said, starting the car. Though she wasn't sure that would be the case. "Come on. Let's stop at the chemist on the way home, then we'll be back in time for dinner with the parentals."

"Thanks for all of this," Hana said.

Maya smiled. "You've already thanked me. The last one is still valid, you know. They don't have an expiry date."

Hana laughed weakly. "You're always looking out for me. Even though that's meant to be my job, as the older sibling." She touched Maya's hand. "This pregnancy has got me thinking. I'm going to do better. You can rely on me."

A lump formed in Maya's throat, and she nodded, unable to speak.

They managed a trip to the chemist and home again, and were just pulling on the drive when Hana grabbed the Waitrose bag and heaved her guts up into it, having to abandon it and work her way through a couple of others.

"Whoa there," Maya said, rubbing her back. "This is a three-bag event. That's the equivalent of ten on the Richter scale."

Hana tried to smile as her retching eased, and Maya continued to rub her back until she was done.

They climbed out and Maya disposed of the bags, whose duties were one hundred percent over rather than being for life. Then she took Hana inside.

Omar's car was on the drive, signaling his return from work.

"Honey, we're home," Maya called out as they entered the hallway.

She went ahead into the kitchen, where their parents were making dinner, and gestured for Hana to sit while she got her a glass of water. Hana's plan had been to tell Yvonne and Omar about the pregnancy once they got home, but the poor woman clearly needed a few moments to recover from chucking her guts up.

Omar glanced over from peeling potatoes to eye Maya as she passed the water to Hana, who was sitting with her head in her hand.

"I'm glad you're home," Omar said. "We need to talk about this ski nonsense. I'm beginning to think my previous suspicions about Sam leading you astray were correct."

Maya's gut tightened, and she nearly sloshed the water out of the glass. "Leading me *astray*?"

"That's right. Just like last time."

She took a breath, her heart rate accelerating. "He wasn't influencing me last time, or this time. Will you give me some credit? I can make my own decisions. I don't need a boyfriend to make them for me."

Her dad shook his head. "That's not what I mean."

Maya was having difficulty summoning her usual shield of humor. "What *do* you mean, then?"

Omar put down the potato peeler, and Yvonne shot him a warning look. He hesitated. "I'm just worried. That you're going to abandon your career in haste and settle for a second-rate job. Especially when you might be in a certain . . . condition."

Yvonne tilted her head in confusion. "Condition? What do you mean?"

"Oh God," Maya said, rubbing her temples.

Omar glanced at Yvonne. "I didn't want to worry you, but Maya asked my advice on morning sickness."

"Dad," Maya said loudly.

Yvonne's eyes widened. "Maya, are you okay?"

"Yes! Yes, I'm fine, I—"

"So you see why I'm worried," Omar said. "Now she'll feel tied to this place and this relationship when an offer from Perry and Pearson comes through the door."

Yvonne frowned. "Do you want to work at Perry and Pearson?"

"No," Maya said. "I—"

"*No?*" Omar replied. "I went to all the trouble of calling James, and this is how you repay me?"

"I don't want to be an accountant, Dad," Maya said, aware her voice was rising but unable to stop it. "I want to be a ski instructor."

"I knew it," Omar said, pointing at her. "You've had your path muddied by this man, and this pregnancy."

"Stop it!" Hana shouted from the table, her head buried in her hands. It was clear it'd taken all her reserve to even speak, never mind shout, after that last bout of vomiting. "Stop," she whispered. "Maya isn't pregnant. I am."

There was a moment's silence, and then Yvonne threw her hands in the air, grinning widely and letting out a shriek as she quickly crossed the room to hug Hana, and then Maya, who was still standing by Hana's side. "Oh my goodness! I'm going to be a grandmother. Omar! We're going to be grandparents."

Omar's mouth was open as he darted his gaze from one of them to another.

Yvonne stroked Hana's head. "Oh, no wonder you've been so ill, my poor love. Shall I make you some ginger tea?"

Hana smiled weakly. "Yes please." She grasped Maya's hand. "I just need to take one of the anti-sickness tablets that Maya took me to get."

Omar closed his mouth again. "You were asking for advice for your sister. And you took her to see the GP?"

"Yes," Maya said, not meeting his gaze. Hana squeezed her hand.

Omar cleared his throat. "Congratulations, Hana. That's wonderful news for you and Rosie."

The fact that he didn't apologize for all the crap he'd just said, plus the clear difference in reaction to Hana's pregnancy compared to Maya's suspected one, wasn't lost on her. She gritted her teeth, trying to keep a lid on her anger. *Like I always do. Give them what they want, don't complain.*

Omar crossed over to kiss Hana's cheek, then moved back to the potatoes. "Take your medicine, Hana. We'll get you on the mend. We need to make sure you get some fluids into you. I thought you looked dehydrated." He glanced at Maya. "And this is good news for you too, Maya. I'm pleased that you'll soon be on your way into a big accountancy firm, without this sort of tie holding you back."

Holding me back? Being on the slopes and with Sam had made her the freest she'd been in years.

"Is Rosie coming soon?" Omar continued.

Something snapped inside Maya. Her anger at her father for his accusations toward her was one thing, but her protective streak over Hana was the final straw. "Rosie might have been here already if it wasn't for the pressure you've put poor Hana under."

Omar's eyes widened. "What do you mean?"

Maya glanced at her sister, who nodded in silent permission as she took her medicine, clearly still struggling with the emotionally charged atmosphere when she felt so terrible. "Hana had a crisis of confidence about taking time off work and loosening the reins on her career in order to become a mother," Maya said, her heart racing at saying it, but the need to support her sister driving her on. "Because she has this constant and intolerable pressure to be the best and maintain a high-flying professional lifestyle."

Yvonne took a seat next to Hana, cuddling her.

Omar glanced between his daughters. "And you think that's because of me?"

Maya rolled her eyes before she could stop herself. "Of course it is."

"Oh, sweetheart," Yvonne said quietly, stroking Hana's hair. "Everything's going to be okay."

Omar was silent. Maya watched her mum comfort her sister, her temper simmering down. It was replaced by a sickening churning in her gut. A wave of dizziness washed over as she took in the look of shock on her dad's face, and her head began to throb.

She squeezed Hana's shoulder. "I'll leave you guys to discuss it before dinner." Exiting the room, she headed upstairs for a lie down. Conflict gave her a headache.

❄ ❄ ❄

THERE WAS A KNOCK AT THE DOOR, AND MAYA OPENED HER EYES. She must have drifted off after she took that painkiller.

Yvonne's voice sounded from the other side of the door. "Maya? Can I come in?"

Sitting up, she rubbed her eyes. "Yeah."

Her mum entered the room, coming in to sit on the edge of the bed and kissing her forehead. "Thank you for supporting your sister, even though you two hadn't been getting along."

Maya shrugged. "Just in training for my mission to bring about world peace."

Yvonne smiled, stroking Maya's hair. Then her smile faded. "I'm sorry that you didn't feel able to tell me you didn't want to be an accountant any longer. I should have pushed you a little harder when we spoke about it."

Maya sat forward. "It's my fault. Trying to avoid the issue, as usual. Plus I didn't want to ruffle feathers between you and Dad."

Yvonne sighed. "I need to step up. I didn't realize what Hana was going through, at least not the extent of it. Too busy getting my physio business off the ground. And now I've let you down too."

"No, you haven't," Maya said, hugging her. "It's not your fault. We're all complicit, including Hana and me. We need to voice the things we're feeling more."

An awareness that she'd managed to confront her father in order to protect her sister, but that she still hadn't been able to do the same for herself, enveloped her.

Yvonne rubbed Maya's back. "I'll have a word with your dad. Try and work on him a bit more, and we'll get him onto our page." Easing back, she smiled. "Dinner's ready, if you feel like eating with us."

"Sure," Maya said, feeling anything but. She lifted her phone off the side and noticed that an e-mail had arrived, so she checked it. The hairs on the back of her neck rose as she realized it was from Perry and Pearson. "Ugh. Terrible timing."

"What is?" Yvonne asked as she rose from the bed.

"I've got a bloody interview at Perry and Pearson. A vacancy's come up and they want to do it via Zoom this week." Maya climbed off the bed, and shot her mum a look.

"What do you want to do?" Yvonne asked.

Maya sighed, pocketing her phone and rubbing her face. "I don't know. My brain is still fried from having to have an actual confrontation earlier. You know how much I love those."

Smiling, Yvonne reached for the door handle. "What does your gut tell you?"

"Apart from that I'm starving?" Maya asked, following her mum down the stairs. "That I don't want to work for Perry and Pearson. But that I equally don't want to let Dad down by declining the interview when they're clearly offering it because Dad contacted one of the partners."

Yvonne spoke in a low voice. "Do you want to keep it to ourselves until you decide?"

Maya shook her head. "If Dad hears about it from his friend at the firm and realizes I didn't tell him, it'll cause trouble."

Yvonne took her hand and squeezed it.

They entered the kitchen, and Maya kept her eyes off her dad, instead returning Hana's smile. She took a seat next to Hana, out of Omar's eyeline, and they started eating. The elephant in the room (as in, the recent shouting match) remained ignored in true Bashir fashion.

Flashing Hana a side glance, Maya touched her hand. "Feeling any better?"

She nodded. "A bit, thank you." Maya could sense that she meant emotionally as well as physically. "Rosie's coming at the weekend," Hana continued.

"Brilliant," Maya said, relieved to hear it. All these arguments were seriously throwing off her groove. Speaking of which, she decided to come clean about the interview. She took a deep breath. "I just got an e-mail from Perry and Pearson. They want to do a virtual interview later on this week."

Omar snapped his gaze up. "That's excellent news."

Maya remained silent.

"You *are* going to accept the offer of an interview, aren't you?" Omar said. Yvonne touched his hand and shot him a gentle frown.

Maya sighed. "I don't know."

He opened his mouth, then closed it again when Yvonne's frown deepened. Taking a sip of water, he cleared his throat. "Perhaps a compromise would be to do the interview, and then see how you feel? They might not offer the job, but it'd keep your options open."

Maya studied her food. She didn't feel the need to keep her options open; she only wanted to continue teaching her kids how to ski. Glancing up, she took in the earnest expression on her father's face. But it *would* be a compromise, and perhaps meeting him halfway would be a step in the right direction. "I'll accept the interview, then we'll see."

A smile spread across Omar's face. Maya couldn't help the good feeling it gave her to finally cause that expression to display on his features.

❄   ❄   ❄

PRESSING THE BELL, SHE LISTENED TO IT SOUNDING WITHIN. THE door opened to reveal the sight of Sam's handsome face, which infused her with comfort.

Stepping inside and closing the door, she wrapped her arms around him, burying her face in his neck and inhaling his scent. Memories of that afternoon flooded her mind, from when they'd stripped each other naked and had mind-blowing sex on his desk.

The lock he'd installed on his door when he'd gotten that office had been an excellent investment.

Maya tipped her face to kiss him, appreciating the now-familiar graze of his beard. "I needed to see you."

Frowning, he rubbed his thumb over her cheek. "Is everything okay?"

"Yeah," she sighed. "Things just blew up at home so I needed some sanctity."

Sam put his arm around her shoulders to lead her into the living room. "Liv's here too. She popped in on her evening walk."

Maya smiled. "Two twins for the price of one. Excellent."

Sam kissed the top of her head as they entered the room, and Liv stood to greet her.

Settling onto the sofa next to Sam, Maya snuggled into his side to address Liv, who was in the armchair across from them. "In a nutshell"—she mimed the outline of a nutshell around her body—"Hana is pregnant and she had a crisis about what it meant for her career. Dad thought *I* was the one who was preggers and was a dick to Sam about it . . ." Sam squeezed her hand and Liv raised her eyebrows. "Then Dad had a go at me about working at the ski center and sacrificing being an accountant due to my *condition*." She caught Sam wincing at that point and opted not to add that Omar had commented on Sam leading her astray. "Hana stopped the argument by telling them she was the one up the duff and not me, then I made it all awkward again by telling Dad that it was his fault that Hana had been upset in the first place." Taking a breath, she smiled. "And they all lived happily ever after."

Liv laughed, shaking her head. "Wow. Fun times in the Bashir household."

"Yep," said Maya, resting her head back onto Sam's shoulder.

He lifted his arm around her.

"Oh wait, I forgot to add that I got an interview with Perry and Pearson, and had to make a compromise with Dad that I'd do the interview, and see what happens after that."

Sam seemed to stiffen next to her, but when she glanced up at him, he gave her a smile.

"Which ones are Perry and Pearson again?" Liv asked.

Sam cleared his throat. "The Edinburgh firm."

"What'll you do if you get the job?" Liv asked.

Sam shifted in his seat.

"I don't want it," Maya said, settling back against Sam. "But I feel like I can't turn the interview down when Dad contacted them personally." She fiddled with her charm bracelet. "Perhaps I won't need to worry about the next part, if they decide they don't like the cut of my jib."

Sam kissed her forehead. "I doubt that."

"Might be a way of letting your dad down gently," Liv said, smiling. "One step at a time, eh?" She put her hands on the arms of her chair. "Right. I'm off to wrap Christmas pressies. I'll leave you two lovey-dovey lovebirds to it."

She stood, and Maya and Sam each gave her a hug before seeing her off at the front door.

Closing the door, Sam took hold of her, kissing her in a lingering manner that made it seem as if he hadn't seen her in days. When he broke off, he rested his forehead against hers.

Maya kissed the tip of his nose. "What is it?"

He smiled, but his eyes didn't light up as they usually did. "Nothing." He ran his hand down her arm to touch her charm bracelet. "What do you want for Christmas?"

Maya kissed him. "You."

He raised an eyebrow. "You've already got one of those."

She shrugged. "Then I've got everything I need."

Sam brushed his thumb over her cheek. "I already got you the moon. So maybe I can get you the stars."

Smiling, Maya took his hand to lead him back into the living room. "I've got you something already. And it's also moon and star related. Kind of."

"Intriguing." He laid her onto the sofa, climbing on top of her to kiss her neck. "If it's from you, then I'll love it."

Her body tingling from his kisses, Maya pushed her fingers into his hair as he pulled up her top, dragging his mouth down her chest and then her abdomen. He lifted his head to meet her eyes as he unfastened her jeans. "I think I know what might help you relax after your bad day."

Smiling, Maya lay back. This almost made a bad day worth it.

Chapter
TWENTY-FOUR

SAM SKIED THE LAST OF THE RUN, ARRIVING AT THE BOTTOM and seeing his class off. Maya should have heard back about her interview by now. They'd told her the decision would be made by Monday lunchtime, and it was now a couple of hours into the afternoon, so that should mean contact had been made with the candidates.

Pulling off his helmet and goggles, he took a breath. Ever since she'd told him about the interview, his anxiety had been gnawing at him. He didn't want her to leave, that was for sure. But the knowledge that she was in the running for what sounded like an excellent job, plus her father being keen she take it and even knowing one of the partners at the firm, made Sam doubt himself. And doubt his motivations. What if he *was* holding her back?

If he weren't around, would Maya still feel as strongly about working at the resort? His heart told him she would, but there was something niggling at the back of his mind. Their relationship was so fresh and new, and they couldn't get enough of one another. Their lunch breaks were filled with each other, and they spent little time eating lunch during them. What if, further down the line, once all that wore off, she realized she'd made a mistake? Passed up a good opportunity? What if she came to resent him for it?

Moving toward the terrace, he leaned against the fencing. How would he live with the guilt if he ended up holding her back? The feeling that she was too good for him had been snowballing. The trolling by bloody Catriona didn't help either. Maya had been in tears about it at the weekend, and Sam was beginning to wonder whether he should contact Cat and say something, but would that worsen her behavior? He wasn't sure what to do, and if he were honest with himself, the option of letting Maya go had crossed his mind, as excruciating as that was to contemplate.

Letting out a breath, he decided to stop catastrophizing and go find Maya. At least once he knew what the interview outcome was, it might help him to decide what to do.

He was heading inside and pausing just beyond the back entrance to decide where to search first, when she came through the door that led into the stairwell. Her eyes appeared red and her cheeks flushed.

Sam's insides tightened as he closed the gap between them and took her into his arms. "What's happened?"

"Can we talk in your office?"

"Course we can."

He took her hand to lead her upstairs and through his office door, taking off his jacket and sitting her on a chair. Sam pulled another chair up close and held her hand.

Maya gave him a weak smile. "I was offered the job."

Making a mammoth effort not to reveal how far his heart sank at that statement, Sam plastered a smile onto his face. "Well done." *I can't even be genuinely pleased for her. What kind of a douchebag boyfriend does that make me?* Did that make him like his father? *He* had always held his mother back, standing in her way with his psychological abuse when she'd gotten that promotion at work, and saying it would be selfish of her to take her attention away from the family. He'd emotionally blackmailed her into declining the position, thereby limiting Tara's career progression, and ultimately her pay. That had meant the three of them were harder up than they should have been once he left.

Forcing his smile a little brighter, he tried to infuse some warmth into his tone. "That's great news. Like you said, it gives you options."

She shook her head. "I called Dad to say I'd got it but I was thinking of turning it down. Despite his promises about how we'd compromise and cross that bridge, he was *not* happy about it."

Sam's insides turned to ice. "Did he mention me again?"

Maya glanced away, and that said it all.

Taking her hands, he gave them a squeeze. "Let things cool off a bit, and have a think about it. When do you need to let them know by?"

Maya frowned, meeting his eyes. "The end of next week. But I already know what I want to tell them."

She said that, but only a minute ago she'd been telling her dad she was "thinking of" turning it down. That meant, subconsciously, she must be considering it.

"I know," he said. "But let's not rush into anything."

Her frown deepened, but she nodded, and that cemented his suspicions.

He gave her a hug. "Everything will be okay, I promise."

❄ ❄ ❄

STICKING HIS HANDS IN HIS POCKETS, SAM MADE INTERESTED noises as the shop assistant ran through everything that was included in the hamper they'd made up for his mum's Christmas present. They could have been telling him that they'd filled it with hard drugs for all he knew; he wasn't taking a word in.

Angus's voice sounded behind him. "Great minds think alike."

Sam turned as the shop assistant was finishing, and Angus clapped him on the back. "I was going to get your mum something from here. I'd better make sure it's not the same as the stuff you've got."

Sam shot him a smile. "How do you know the hamper's not for you?"

"Because it's got all her favorite things in it." Angus smiled. "If it was for me, it'd be filled solely with whiskey and oatcakes."

"Good choices," Sam said, passing some money over to the shop assistant.

"Hey, while I've got you on your own, I wanted to ask something."

Sam frowned. "Oh yeah?"

Angus glanced down. "You can give me your honest opinion here, by the way, and I won't be offended. Do you mind that I'm having Christmas dinner with you? Because I wondered if you might prefer it to be just the three of you."

Sam opened his mouth, a little taken aback. Of course he didn't mind. Why would Angus think that? *Probably because I was funny about him moving in and then I've been pushing him away ever since.* Before he could think what to say, someone jostled him from behind, making him stumble forward a step, where Angus caught his arm.

"Steady on," Angus said, frowning behind Sam at whoever had nearly knocked him over. "Watch where you're going."

Sam turned to find Catriona's father standing there, giving him a dead eye. *Oh shit.* "Hi, Ian."

"Don't 'hi, Ian' me." Ian glared at Sam, then Angus. "And I'll walk where I like. It's not as if there was anyone worthwhile standing here anyway."

There was a moment's silence.

"Listen," Sam said, not wanting a scene in this poor woman's shop. "I don't know what Cat's told you, but—"

Ian stepped forward. "She told me that you cheated on her, that's what."

Sam took a breath. Getting into a fight with his ex-girlfriend's dad wasn't going to do much to tone down the reputation that Cat was fast spreading about him around town. And the main thing that worried him was what Maya's dad would think. There was no way Dr. Bashir was going to take kindly to his daughter's boyfriend getting into fights.

Before he could think what to say in order to de-escalate the situation, Angus stepped in, putting his arm across Sam in a protective manner and squaring up to Ian, who was at least a couple of inches shorter.

Angus narrowed his eyes. "Don't believe everything you hear, Ian. Now, you'd better pay for your stuff and get out of here, before I have to help you out myself."

Ian glanced up at Angus, clearly taking in his stocky physique, which was large in contrast to his own, rather rotund, form. He shot Sam a look, finally seeming to work out not only that he couldn't take either of them in a fight, but that two against one wasn't a favorable ratio.

Ian shook his head and backed off, quickly paying for his things and hotfooting it from the shop.

Angus turned and flashed a bright smile at the shop assistant, who was watching them rather wide eyed. "Sorry about that. We'll get out of your hair too." He grabbed Sam's hamper and nodded at him to get the door.

Sam obliged, holding it open as they went out onto the street.

He glanced at Angus as they walked. "Here, let me take that."

Angus shook his head. "I've got it. Where's your car?"

They went over and loaded the hamper into the boot. Sam shoved his hands into his pockets. "Thanks for sticking up for me."

He'd half expected Angus to shrink away and leave the vicinity once Ian had kicked off, but to his surprise, he'd not only stayed, but come through for him. Sam could handle himself in a fight, but there was no way he wanted to make life any worse for Maya by doing so. He could tell that no matter what he might have said to try to get Ian to realize that Cat was the one in the wrong, he would never have believed it.

Angus clapped him on the back with his weather-beaten hand. "Anytime. Right, I'd best be off." He made to head away.

"Wait," Sam said as Angus halted and turned back. "I'm looking forward to you being there. At Christmas, I mean."

Angus smiled, his eyes lighting up. "Me too. See you soon."

Sam gave him a wave as he left, climbing into his car and then pausing after starting his engine. The town gossipmongers were bound to spread this one about, despite the situation having been de-escalated, and he was foolish to think that Omar wouldn't hear about it. Then Maya would get a hard time from him because of it, and she was already upset enough.

As he sank back into his seat, it seemed his heart was sinking faster, right down to his feet. Would Omar ever forgive Maya if she declined the job offer? Would their relationship be irreparably damaged? Sam had been abandoned by his own father, and now he was driving Maya's away from her.

Guilt stabbed him so painfully in his chest that he had to lift a hand to rub it. The right thing to do was becoming clearer, but the agony that accompanied the plan was such that he had to take a series of deep breaths in order to stem the feeling that he might pass out.

Chapter
TWENTY-FIVE

T HINGS HAD BEEN CHILLY IN THE BASHIR HOUSEHOLD, AND not temperature-wise. Luckily, Rosie had arrived with her good-natured warmth, and she and Hana were back on track. Their displays of affection were at least going some way to providing good vibes in the house.

Maya could tell that her mum was doing her best to work on her dad, but he still wasn't really speaking to Maya, and she hated it. This was why she avoided these sorts of issues at all costs. Life had been better when she used to sweep things under the carpet.

Hadn't it?

She recalled the daily humdrum misery that had been her office life, and compared it to the excitement that built as she traveled the mountain road to the ski center, then the thrill of seeing the children's faces as they mastered their lessons on the slope.

Sighing, she lay back on her bed. She had a few days left until the deadline. Then her time would be up and she'd have to give her decision to Perry and Pearson, and face the consequences. The idea of it hanging over her until then was almost too much to bear.

The doorbell rang out downstairs, and she sat up, sure that she could hear Sam's voice. Footsteps sounded on the stairs, and her heart lifted as she got to her feet.

She opened her bedroom door as he reached the landing.

Throwing her arms around him in delight, she guided him back into the bedroom, shutting the door behind them.

He didn't hug her back. "I hope you don't mind me coming up, your mum let me in."

Maya released him, bringing him to sit on the bed, where she sat cross-legged next to him. "Course I don't mind. You're a sight for sore eyes."

He glanced away. "How're you feeling?"

"Stressed," she said, but immediately regretted admitting the whole truth when his face fell. She took his hand. "But better for seeing you."

Sam gave her hand a squeeze, visibly swallowing. "Listen. I came over because I think—no—I *know* what we need to do."

Maya nodded, feeling hopeful, which was a pleasant change from the last few days. "What's that?"

He kept his eyes off her. "Just hear me out on this one." Taking a breath, he glanced at the ceiling. "You should tell Perry and Pearson that you're taking the job."

Her heart tripped over itself and plummeted to her feet. "Sam—"

"Wait." He flashed her a weak smile that didn't meet his eyes, his voice wobbly. "Take the job, move to Edinburgh, and get settled in." He cleared his throat. "You and I will have a break. So that you can explore this opportunity, and really get to know whether it's for you or not."

Maya tried to calm her hammering heart by taking a couple of deep breaths. "You . . . you want to break up?"

Sam blinked, still not looking at her. "It's for the best, Maya. I think we got into this too quickly, when you were still deciding what you wanted for your future. I can't be the one to hold you back, or you'll end up resenting me." His voice cracked. "Like the way my mum resented my dad. And I don't want to damage your relationship with *your* dad either."

Maya's mouth was so dry she couldn't even swallow.

Trying to form the words to tell him that this was a mistake, it hit her—what she'd been worrying about ever since their first "fake" kiss. Sam said they'd gotten into this too quickly. That was exactly what she'd been concerned about—not with regard to herself, but rather for his sake. He hadn't had the chance to get over Cat yet. And as toxic as she was, it had been a very long relationship, spanning years on and off. Sam didn't feel able to proceed with counseling, so it meant that more than ever, he needed time. Time to heal. It had been selfish of her to have gotten into a relationship with him so soon. Even though she and Hana had made up, Maya couldn't shake the feeling that there was some truth in her sister's assessment. And regardless of whether she took this damned Edinburgh job or not, breaking up might be the best thing for *him*.

The realization stabbed so painfully in her heart that it took her breath away. She loved him too much not to agree to this, if there was a chance this was the right path for him.

Finally, she managed to force some words out, but her voice sounded strange and distant. "If that's what you want."

He nodded, blinking fast as he glanced toward the window.

The pain in Maya's chest was tightening with each passing second, balling in her throat and pricking at her eyes.

Sam's voice was strained. "I'll leave you to it. Let you e-mail your reply." Leaning over to give her a brief kiss on the cheek, he stood and left the room, closing the door behind him.

Maya listened to his footsteps descending the stairs, and then the sound of the front door opening and closing, signaling his exit from the house, taking her heart with him.

❄ ❄ ❄

HANA GAVE MAYA A NUDGE. "WHAT ABOUT THIS ONE?"

Maya blinked. "Pardon?" She focused on the clothing in the shop window, having been staring but not seeing for the past few minutes.

"The jumper, with the stars on it. Do you want that one? It's very you."

Tears filled Maya's eyes. Anything related to stars reminded her of Sam. Anything at all reminded her of him. Last night she'd cried because her mum had said the word *spam* and it rhymed with *Sam*.

Spotting her distress, Hana pulled her in for a hug. "Aw, sis. I thought shopping for your Christmas present would cheer you up."

"Me too," Maya replied into Hana's shoulder. Even though she'd thought nothing of the sort and had come along only to show she appreciated her sister's efforts. Nothing could cheer her up. Not even a free holiday to Whistler with unlimited cocktails and scones and Mr. Darcy plus all the Hemsworth brothers for company.

Liv and Elise had advised her to tell Sam that she wanted to get back together. But it wouldn't be right. She'd already put him under pressure, made him rush things. He needed time, and now she was wondering if it'd be better for him if she *did* take that Edinburgh post, to give him some space. Plus, it'd please her dad. Her friends had been concerned that she was neglecting her own needs, but it was all her own fault anyway. If she'd faced up to Cat years ago, then none of this would've happened. *But the issue of not wanting to study accountancy would've remained the same.* She closed her eyes briefly, willing the thoughts out of her head.

"Come on," Hana said. "Let's go and meet Rosie. She should be finished in that shop, and we'll all go for cake at the new tearoom you told me about."

They moved off down the street, Maya wiping the tears from her face. And just as she thought that life couldn't get any worse, Catriona stepped out of a shop and into their path.

Cat's face fell for a split second before her masklike facade went up again. "Well. I *would* say nice to see you, but it isn't."

Maya drew her mouth into a thin line, staring at Cat, taking in every detail of her face. *This woman. She* was responsible for all her heartache. All her pain, and Sam's. The realization hit that not confronting Cat back then had resulted not only in her own heartbreak but also, more importantly, in Sam enduring years of emotional abuse at Cat's hands.

Maya's guilt swelled, overwhelming her to the point that she had to take a deep breath. Then it twisted, pushing up her heart rate as it morphed into rage.

She narrowed her eyes, giving Cat the coldest, most snake-haired Medusa stare of her life, and staying silent. She slipped her hand over Hana's, gripping tightly.

Cat appeared thrown for a moment, clearly having expected some kind of retort rather than silence. Then a smirk played on her lips. "I heard you and Sam split? Probably cheating on you. A cheater stays a cheater after all." She flipped her hair. "You're better off anyway. He always was a loser. You're probably thankful he got together with me instead of you back then."

It wasn't a snap of her temper, more a huge crashing blow. Like the biggest tree in the forest falling and smashing all of the other trees to smithereens.

"*What?*"

Cat's eyes widened for a moment. "I said—"

Maya took a step closer, still gripping Hana's hand, her pulse hammering in her ears. Screw nonconfrontational. Right now, she wanted all of the conflict. *Bring it on.*

"How *dare* you. You fucking *lied* to us, Catriona. Made up shit to force us apart, then kept Sam in misery for years. You took advantage of him when he was vulnerable, and what's more, it was deliberate. You exploited all of his insecurities. Do you know what a nasty piece of shit that makes you?"

Cat's eyes were as wide as saucers.

"Did you even like him, before I confided in you that I did? Or did you only decide to go after him because taking him from me created some sport for you?"

Cat tried to get a word in, but Maya raised her hand. "No. You don't get to have the floor. Stop writing shit about me on social media. Leave me alone, leave Sam alone, and leave all of our friends and family alone. I don't want any of us to have to see or hear anything from you again."

Hana was squeezing her hand now, willing her on.

Cat swallowed. She went for another hair flip, but it was more lackluster this time. "Haven't you heard of freedom of speech? I can say what I want."

Hana stepped forward, towering over Catriona. "Not quite, missy. I've seen those comments, and some of them are libelous. I'm the best lawyer in England, and I've wiped the floor with peers who possess ten times your intellect." She leaned in, narrowing her eyes, and Maya almost felt terrified on Cat's behalf. "*One* more word about my sister, in any forum or format, and I will *ruin you.* Do you understand me?"

Cat was gripping her shopping bag for dear life. She seemed to give a tiny nod, then turned and walked away quickly down the street.

"*Sis*," Hana said, turning with a wide smile on her face. "You were *fierce*. Well done." She held her hand aloft for a high five, which Maya delivered, although her hand was trembling, her heart still pounding from the encounter.

"What about you?" Maya said, linking her arm through Hana's as they began to walk, feeling as if she needed the support. The aftermath had left her legs like jelly. "Oh my God, I thought she was going to shrivel up, you were so scary."

Hana pursed her lips. "Don't mess with the Bashir sisters."

Maya managed a laugh as they neared the tea shop, and spotted Rosie coming toward them.

"Hey, fam," Rosie said, giving Maya a kiss on the cheek and Hana one on the lips. "How come you two are all smiley all of a sudden? That's an improvement to the downer vibe when I left you."

Maya rubbed her eyes, remembering her anguish. "Don't talk about it."

"Oops," Rosie said, wincing. "Sorry." She opened the tea shop door. "I'll buy the cake, on account of reminding you."

They entered and found a table.

Hana gave Rosie a nudge. "The reason we were smiling was because Maya butted heads with her arch nemesis and it was *epic*."

Maya smiled. "It was more of a double team, actually."

Rosie grinned at Maya. "Nice one. Was it that nasty Catriona cow that Hana told me about? Hope you sent her packing."

Maya blew out a breath. "Packed, house sold, and off to a small uninhabited island, hopefully." She looked at Hana. "By the way, was that true? About the libel stuff?"

Hana screwed up her face. "Not exactly. That stuff doesn't really stick. Not unless you can prove what was written on social media cost someone a job or such like." She morphed her grimace into a grin. "But Little Miss Cow Bag doesn't know that, does she?"

Maya laughed.

"Speaking of jobs," Rosie said. "What are you going to do about that Perry and Pearson position? Don't you need to tell them by tomorrow?"

Maya stared out the window, where a bit of a blizzard seemed to be starting, remembering how good it felt to stand up to Cat. Fair enough, it hadn't felt good so far with her dad, but still. Sam was worth all of it, and what's more, her happiness was too.

"I'm turning it down." Saying it out loud was such a relief that it cemented it was the right thing to do. "I'm turning it down, and telling Ben that I'm staying on at the ski resort permanently. And I'm going to wait for Sam to be ready for a relationship. I'll prove that I'm there for him, every day, until then."

Rosie blinked furiously, reaching for a napkin to dab her eyes. "That's the most romantic thing I've ever heard."

Maya glanced over at Hana, and was surprised to see her eyes were shining too. "You okay, Hans?" Hana never normally went in for anything mushy.

She blinked, rubbing her eyes. "No. Bloody pregnancy hormones."

Rosie laughed, circling Hana's shoulders and kissing her cheek. "Aw, sweetheart."

Maya leaned back in her seat. "We'd better order extra cake. I'm going to need the sugar rush to fuel my next confrontation. With Dad."

Rosie's eyes widened and she waved at the server. "Excuse me, miss. You're going to need a few sheets on that notepad."

Chapter
TWENTY-SIX

LISTLESS DIDN'T COVER IT. ONLY A WEEK HAD PASSED SINCE HIS conversation with Maya, and it seemed like an eternity.

Thinking of what had occurred as a "conversation" prevented him from facing the truth of what happened—he'd dumped her. Whenever that definition crossed his mind, he'd have to squeeze his eyes tight in discomfort. Never in a million years had he thought if life gave him a second chance with Maya Bashir, then he'd be the one ending it. But he'd had to, for her own good.

A lifetime without her stretched before him. Her off to Edinburgh, starting that new job and becoming a highflier, no doubt meeting some guy with status that Omar would frigging adore.

He rubbed his eyes, staring out the patio window at where the snow was spinning in the wind, mimicking his inner turmoil. Just when he'd been so close, so near to believing that she could finally be his, everything went to shit.

The doorbell rang, and he considered not answering it. But then it rang again, and clearly, whoever it was would have seen his car on the driveway and known he was in.

Dragging himself up, he went to the front door and opened it. Liv was standing there, snow blowing around her as she raised her eyebrows. "Let me in, doofus. It's bloody freezing out here."

"Sorry," Sam muttered, shifting to the side to allow her to pass and closing the door against the whiteout.

Liv shook off her clothing, then removed her jacket and snow boots. She glanced up as she walked past him toward the kitchen. "Is the kettle boiled? You clearly need a cup of my tea, stat."

Sam managed the tiniest of smiles as he followed her back into the kitchen, taking his seat at the table. He didn't even have the energy to ask if she wanted a hand. Though that was probably a bad idea anyway; Liv's tea was the best around, and no doubt his cursed hand would end up tainting it.

Busying herself with the tea, Liv brought a couple of mugs over and passed him one, taking a seat next to him with hers.

They both blew on the mugs and sipped in unison, and she met his eyes over the rim with a smile, which he couldn't help returning.

"What brings you here in this snowstorm?" he asked.

Liv put her mug down. "Twin intervention. You and Maya are both making me miserable by default."

Sam froze, tightening his hold on the mug with a painful twist in his gut. "She's miserable?"

Liv rolled her eyes. "Of course she is. She's in love with you and you broke things off with her."

He froze at the idea of her unhappiness, despite hearing that she might love him, and despite the recent sip of steaming hot tea.

Shaking her head, Liv touched his hand. "How did you expect her to feel?"

Swallowing, he tried to get his words out. "I thought that I was doing her a favor, and she'd be happier because of it."

She was silent for a moment. "Really?"

"Why else would I make myself this miserable?"

Scooting her chair a little closer, she took hold of his hand. "What if, deep down, all of this is about self-preservation?"

He studied her, trying to fathom what she was getting at. "I don't feel very preserved. More like my heart's been ripped from my body and trampled by a herd of elephants. Wearing stilettos."

Liv smiled. "Okay. I'm going to be blunt." She took a deep breath. "You were worried that she was going to choose this new job over you. A different life, over you. You have a massive fear of rejection that you've never faced up to. Because Dad left us, then you thought you'd been abandoned by your first love and that she didn't regard you as good enough. You were taken advantage of by a narcissist who exploited those vulnerabilities and cemented them so deeply over the last few years that you can't even assess the depth of the trauma." Pausing, she studied his face. "So, you ended it with Maya. Before *she* could do it to *you*, because you couldn't stand the thought of her rejecting you for real when you're so in love with her."

Sam stayed silent for a few moments, trying to absorb all of that. His sister's words had impacted him like a truck carrying a ton of bricks.

He blew out a slow breath. "Shit. Who needs a counselor with you around?"

Liv gave his hand a squeeze, and he attempted to process his racing thoughts. In his heart of hearts, he knew there was truth in her assessment.

He glanced up. "I really did think it was what was best for her. I don't want to come in between her and her dad. Especially when I know, *we* know, what it's like to lose that relationship." He squeezed her hand. "Plus, I don't know if I'll ever be good enough for her."

Liv shook her head. "Good enough has nothing to do with what you do for a living, Sam. You love her, she loves you, and you both put each other first. I've seen it. You're an excellent team. *That's* what makes you good enough. And as for her dad, he's not going to abandon her just because she makes a career choice that isn't his preference. It won't take him long to discover that she would've wanted to turn down the job offer anyway, even if you didn't work on the mountain too. And that you make her happy—it'll be reflected in her well-being, and he'll be delighted by default." Liv gave him a meaningful look. "Because he'll know that his daughter is with someone deserving of her."

Emotion pricked at his eyes. "I've really fucked this up, haven't I?"

"Not yet. But you will have done, if you don't rectify it by accepting the trauma of the past and making a decision to work through it. *With* Maya."

Lifting a hand, he tucked his sister's hair behind her ear. "How come I'm the messed-up one, when we've both been through the same shit?"

She shook her head, averting her eyes. "I haven't been emotionally abused by my girlfriend for the past number of years." Leaning closer, she gave him a smile. "Remember, Sam. Not everyone leaves. Dad was an arsehole, but you aren't. Mum isn't. I'm not. Well." She grinned. "Sometimes I am."

He couldn't help but laugh at that. "*Sometimes?*"

Liv punched his arm. "Watch it. Also"—she shot him another meaningful look—"Angus isn't."

Knowing exactly what she was getting at, he nodded. "You're right." He cleared his throat. "Maya said that I should get counseling. I didn't understand why at the time, but now I'm starting to think it'd be a good idea."

Liv nodded. "You should. I did, a few years back."

Sam's eyes widened, his heart squeezing painfully. "I didn't know that."

She shrugged. "Sometimes I wouldn't tell you stuff, when you were going through a difficult patch. Didn't want to overload you."

The realization of just how much distance Cat had wedged between him and his family, especially his twin sister, hit home, and he was almost winded by it. What else had Liv kept from him, in order to protect him? As someone who viewed *himself* as the protector of the family, it was a hard pill to swallow. Though perhaps one of the lessons that Maya had taught him was that it was good to share the burden. And letting his sister in to do that felt right. "Did you work through your stuff with Dad?"

"Yeah," Liv said, smiling weakly. "It helped. You'll see."

Sam let go of her hand so he could hug her tightly. "I'm so sorry. I've not been there for you, I know that now. These past few weeks I've felt like we're closer than ever, and it was only then that I realized there was any distance between us."

She gave him a squeeze. "It's okay, Sam. I'm just glad to have you back."

"Listen." He released her in order to look her in the eyes, determination in his heart. "No more keeping stuff from me. I want to know everything, all right?"

Liv nodded, her eyes shining, and he kissed her forehead.

Her voice was wobbly. "All that will have to wait, because you've got somewhere to be."

He frowned. "Where?"

Raising her eyebrows, she gestured toward the front door. "You need to head out into that blizzard, and go get the love of your life back."

Chapter
TWENTY-SEVEN

MAYA JIGGLED FROM ONE FOOT TO THE OTHER WHILE WATCH-ing the whiteout from her bedroom window. Why was the theme tune to *Rocky* playing in her head? She half expected Hana to produce a bottle of water to squirt in her face and Rosie to dab her brow with a small towel.

"Right. You're clear on what you want to say?" Hana asked. "Preparation is key in the courtroom."

Rosie ruffled Hana's hair. "We're in your parents' house, not the courtroom, sweets."

"I know," Hana said, shooting her a grin. "But still."

"I think so," Maya said, trying to quash her nervousness. No doubt it'd all go flying out of her head and she'd end up shouting random phrases like *love skiing* and *hate accountancy* rather than putting together any sort of fluid sentence. But perhaps the point would still be made.

Rosie squeezed her shoulder. "Are you sure you don't want us to come down with you? We can be silent, just sit in moral support."

Maya shook her head. "I need to do this myself. No crutches."

Hana took hold of her in a tight hug. "I'm proud of you."

She hugged Hana back, love for her sister rising inside and causing her throat to constrict and tears to prick at her eyes. Her voice came out on a wobble. "Stop it. Don't make me feel feelings when I'm in the battle zone."

Hana laughed as she released her. "Go get 'em, tiger."

Maya pursed her lips and saluted, making them both laugh in an attempt to soothe her nerves. *Humor defense, again. But that's not going to work with Dad. Not this time.*

She turned and left her bedroom before she could change her mind, going down the stairs and past the living room, where they'd asked Yvonne to stay until Maya was done in the kitchen with Dad.

Her mum had asked to be there for the discussion, but Maya wanted to do it alone. So Yvonne had been tasked with settling Omar at the table with a cup of tea and his magazine, in ignorant bliss that Maya was coming to trample on his day. Well, probably his week. Perhaps even a number of months.

Entering the kitchen, she felt as if there should be cameras on her for this showdown moment. Her dad looked up, and, as predicted, all coherent thought left her brain.

"Hi," she said.

"Hi."

She cleared her throat. "We need to talk."

Omar gestured at the seat across from him, and she took it, feeling like one of his patients with him appraising her across the table.

"I'm glad you've come to speak to me," he said. "There are a few things I want to say."

Maya almost stopped him to launch into her monologue. But she decided it might be best to let him exhaust his side first. Hopefully then she'd be better able to keep the floor.

"I know you think that I drive you and Hana hard, but I only want what's best for you. For you to be self-sufficient. That's why I want you to take the Perry and Pearson job. In order for you to achieve that security." Omar paused, studying her face. "Just look at your sister. A partner in her firm, the youngest they've ever had. And she and Rosie are engaged to be married, with a beautiful house and now a baby on the way."

Maya hesitated for a second. "I know all of that, Dad. You've given me the same spiel a thousand times." She sighed. "The career thing isn't really what makes Hana happy. Not fully. She likes being a lawyer, and she's excellent at it. But it's her life with Rosie that makes her truly content. And she nearly let her career ruin that when she had a crisis of confidence about easing up on the workload."

Omar darted his gaze down at the table. "I didn't mean for that to happen. I told your mother as much, and I've apologized to Hana." He snapped his eyes back up. "In any case, it doesn't alter that you're abandoning not just a good opportunity, but your whole career. Everything we worked for you to achieve."

His use of the word *we* was very telling.

"My career is my own business. It's for me to decide. I'm an adult. You chose your career, and I'll choose mine."

Omar clenched his fist, and the sight of it caused her pulse to spike.

His voice rose. "It's more complicated than that, Maya. You're my daughter. It's my responsibility to set you on the right path, otherwise what kind of father does that make me?"

"Dad—"

He scraped his chair back to stand, making her jump. "We weren't as lucky as you, when I was growing up. Making their way in this country was hard for my parents, even as professionals back in their native land. They had to work twice as hard as others to reach the same goals."

He left the table to pace the room, causing Maya's nausea to intensify.

"I don't want you to have to struggle. I want a secure future for you." He stood still, giving her a hard stare. "I don't understand why you can't grasp that."

Tears pricked at her eyes, and a word flashed across the back of her mind. *Selfish.* Look at what her voicing her desires was doing to her father. She took a deep breath, her resolve wavering.

Omar came over and sat next to her. "You need a steady career. Not just a job. Something with a ladder to climb. Financial security and status."

Maya found herself nodding, muted into silence by her guilt. Just like the last time they'd had this conversation, when she was eighteen.

He lifted a hand to tuck her hair behind her ear. "Then you'll be happy."

Happy? Her breath caught. For a while there, she had been. On the slopes with her kids, spending time with Sam. Probably the happiest she'd ever been.

The spark of her determination stopped spluttering, and caught alight.

She met his gaze, her voice quiet. "Happiness for me doesn't come from job status, or how much money I'm making. Sure, having a steady career means stability and less stress, but that career needs to be one I don't hate." She paused to let that sink in, taking in the way his eyes widened. "Hating your job leads to unhappiness. No matter how much money or status is associated with it." Swallowing hard, she forced herself to continue. "I made myself miserable for years, studying a subject I didn't really care for.

Working in a career I had no passion for. It sucked the life out of me, until there was no joy left." Her voice cracked. "And I did it all to win your approval."

Omar took a sharp breath, opening his mouth, though no words came out.

Maya swallowed again. The nausea was building, making her feel light-headed. But she had to finish this. All her intentions of fueling what she wanted to say with anger were extinguished, because there was only sadness left. "I'm not Hana. I never have been and I've never measured up to her in your eyes, though goodness knows I've tried."

He snapped his gaze onto hers, but she didn't waver.

"I love skiing. I love teaching it. Being at the resort makes me so happy that sometimes I feel like I'm floating. And I'm really good at it. I can help people access the joy that it brings me, and that magnifies my own joy exponentially. I'm spreading happiness. And it pays more than enough to keep me stable." She leaned forward. "This is *me* talking. Nobody else. I think you know me well enough to realize that I'd never let a man influence these decisions for me. I'm my own person, and an intelligent one at that. I'd be making this change, whether or not Sam was in the picture."

Maya hadn't told Omar that she didn't yet know whether Sam wanted to remain in her particular picture or not. She reached over to take his hands. "I'm going to tell Perry and Pearson that I'm very grateful for the opportunity, but being back home has made me realize this is where I want to stay, and I want a career change."

Finally, she stopped talking, feeling that there was nothing else left to say. Except one thing. "I love Sam, Dad. He puts me first and loves me for who I am. Not for who I *could* be."

She let go of his hands, absorbing the shocked expression on his face and the guilt eating her up that she'd made him sad by saying all of that.

She stood. "I'll give you some space to think."

Crossing the room to the kitchen door, she opened it and turned back, trying in vain to keep her voice steady. "I love you. And I wouldn't change you." Her voice cracked as tears began to fall. "I hope you feel the same about me."

Leaving the room quickly, before she began to openly sob, she shut the door behind her, leaning back against it for a moment.

The living room door was open a crack, and her mother, sister, and sister-in-law were clearly in there listening, judging by the scurrying footsteps that were apparent on the other side. Maya managed a tiny smile as she walked down the hallway, brushing the tears from her cheeks and opening the door. "I'm going for a walk to clear my head."

Hana rose from the sofa and gave her a hug. "Good job, sis," she said quietly. "You did yourself, and me, proud."

Rosie smiled from her seat on the sofa. "You were great, kid."

A tiny bud of pride grew in Maya's chest.

Yvonne got to her feet, closing the gap to stroke Maya's hair. "I'll go in and have a chat with your dad. Help him come to terms with what you said." She kissed Maya's cheek, her voice soft. "Thank you for what you said to him at the end. He does love you as you are, and so do I. I just need to help him express it better."

Maya nodded, rubbing her eyes. "Thanks, Mum." She cleared her throat. "I'm going now before I cry like a baby." Managing to flash them a smile, she made for the front door to put on her boots and jacket, listening to her mum enter the kitchen and the start of a murmured conversation between her parents.

Opening the door to a blast of cold and billowing snow, she blinked. "Blimey. It's like being on the slopes."

She stepped outside and walked down the driveway, pulling her hood over her woolly hat and pausing on the pavement to look left and right, trying to decide which direction to go in.

The desire to walk toward Sam's was too strong, so she set off that way. Though she was unsure whether she'd go and ring his bell or not, because he might still need space. Maybe she'd just walk past and have a look at his place, if she could manage it without seeming like some kind of crazy stalker. At least the sight of their glorious Christmas lights might cheer her up a little.

A figure became apparent through the snow a few yards away, and she glanced up, wondering if it was one of the neighbors. But she recognized that red jacket, and the handsome face under the cute beanie.

Her heart lifted; was he coming to see her? Why else would he be in this vicinity in a veritable snowstorm?

Pushing down the urge to run toward Sam and throw her arms around him, she closed the gap, slowing to a stop.

"Nice evening for it," she said, getting lost in his amber eyes. "Come here often?"

He smiled, with the snowflakes swirling around him, and it was the most beautiful thing she'd ever seen. "I only come here when I'm looking for my hot girlfriend, to whom I owe a huge apology, in order to grovel on my knees that she take me back."

A starburst struck her insides so forcefully that Maya thought it must surely be visible for him to see. "On your knees? I think you'd end up with frostbitten legs."

Sam reached out to hug her close. "I'm so sorry about my impulsive reaction. I didn't want to break up. I thought that I was doing the right thing." He glanced down. "If I'm honest, and after a bit of amateur counseling by Olivia Holland, I did it because I thought I wasn't good enough for you. I was scared you'd be the one to end it, and it was an avoidance tactic from my apparently mammoth rejection issues." He took a breath, lifting his gaze to hers again. "Whatever you need me to do to prove that I'm worthy after my stumbling at the first hurdle, I'll do it."

Maya grasped the front of his jacket and pulled him in, kissing him, absorbing the graze of his beard, the heat of his mouth, and the tiny bursts of cold as the falling snowflakes became part of their kiss.

She broke off to hold his face as she spoke. "You don't have to do anything. Not a thing. Because I love you and of course I want you back." She kissed the tip of his nose and smiled at how cold it was. "I'm not going anywhere, Sam. You *are* good enough, and you're stuck with me. I was planning on telling you that, once you were ready. Plus that I'll wait around as long as it takes for you to be ready for a relationship. Because I was worried we'd rushed it and you needed time to get over what happened with you and Cat. That was the only reason I accepted you finishing things." She searched his face, taking in the emotion shining in his eyes. "We don't have to be official again until you're ready. I'll wait."

He tugged her back in to kiss her, taking her breath away. "I want it to be official. I've never been surer of anything in my life. Maya, I've loved you since I was eighteen, and I'm locked in."

Despite the arctic conditions, Maya had never felt warmer. "Me too."

Sam gave her a tentative smile. "I've been thinking about what you said, about the counseling. I'm going to go for it. It's my responsibility to face my issues, not yours to fix them." He cleared his throat. "I wondered whether, if my counselor thinks it's a good idea, we could get some couples counseling too? I don't want any past baggage getting in the way of us moving forward."

Maya nodded, pride swelling within her that he was brave enough to face his demons. "Of course we can."

His smile broadened, making his eyes shine. "If you want that job, then take it. I'll move to Edinburgh with you. They've got a dry ski slope, after all."

Maya pretended to gag. "A *dry* slope? Do not speak such filth to my ears."

Sam laughed, pulling her closer.

Shaking her head, she smiled. "I'm turning the job down. Which is what I would've done, whether you and I were together or not. I hate accountancy, and I love skiing. I want to be content in my career." She shot him a meaningful look. "As well as in my private life."

He ran a gloved thumb over her cheek. "I just want you to be happy, and I'll do whatever you need me to, in order to make that happen."

"I *am* happy," she said. "As long as I have you. You don't hold me back, Sam. You set me free."

He blinked hard, his eyes shining. "What about your dad?"

"We've just had a heated discussion. I nearly bottled it. But then I realized I couldn't keep on sacrificing pieces of myself to make others happy, because soon there'd be nothing of me left." She sighed. "I told him some hard truths, then left to walk it off, and here we are."

Frowning, Sam searched her face. "Are you okay?"

She shrugged. "Yes. No. But perhaps I will be."

She cuddled him, resting her head against his chest. She wanted to breathe the scent of him forever. "I left him with Mum for her to cultivate what I'd sown."

Sam stroked her hair. "What do you want to do?"

Maya hesitated, taking a couple of deep breaths. The idea of going over to Sam's and cuddling with him on the sofa was tempting—the desire to hide away in a safe bubble with the man she loved. But she knew what she had to do.

"I need to go back."

Sam tipped her face up to meet her gaze, giving her a reassuring smile, and it was apparent that he agreed. "I'll come with you. Let's start as we mean to go on. As a team." He kissed her nose. "I'm your support buddy."

Maya smiled as he put his arm around her and they turned to walk back toward her house. Not that it was very visible, in the whiteout.

"I appreciate that," she said.

Sam cleared his throat. "You should probably know that I'm planning on applying for the support buddy position on a permanent basis."

Maya grinned. "No need to apply. Position filled as of now."

"Wow." He glanced over with a smile. "Shortest interview ever."

Maya laughed as they went up the driveway. "There's no point beating about the bush. You're a shoo-in for the job." She reached the doorway and grasped the handle. "Time to face the music."

They brushed snow from themselves in the porch, then removed their outerwear to head toward the kitchen.

Yvonne and Omar were sitting at the table, holding hands. The sight of that infused a little comfort into Maya's veins.

"Sam," Yvonne said. "Hi." She glanced at Maya.

Maya had told her mum that Sam had ended things because he wanted her to feel free to go for the Edinburgh job. Maya gave her mum a smile, taking Sam's hand, and Yvonne returned the expression.

"Come and have a seat," Yvonne said.

"Thanks, Mrs.—I mean, Yvonne," Sam said, taking a seat across from them as Maya climbed onto the one beside him. He took Maya's hand again as Yvonne poured the two of them some tea from the pot. "Hi, Dr. B."

Omar managed a smile, and Maya dared to let her small seed of hope grow bigger. "Nice to see you. You two been for a walk?"

"Yeah," Maya said. "But then we got attacked by a yeti and figured it was best to retreat."

Omar laughed, taking Maya by surprise. He shook his head. "I'm not sure if I've ever told you this, but your sense of humor reminds me of my mother's. She was as quick witted as you."

Sam squeezed her hand, and Maya swallowed. "I don't think you have told me that. I wish I'd known her."

Omar nodded. "Me too." He glanced at Yvonne, who shot him a supportive smile. "She always did what was best for us, both her and my father. That was why they moved to the UK when my brother and I were small. To make a new life." He cleared his throat. "They struggled to fit in, and elevating their social standing helped. It was impressed upon my brother and me how important that was. To be a person of good standing in the community, and I think I've let that color my guidance of you and your sister."

Maya's breathing hitched in surprise; her dad hadn't voiced that before. Sam pulled her close, and she took hold of his knee.

Omar met Maya's eyes. "Realizing that what I've actually done is to make you unhappy, that you put yourself through misery for me . . ." His voice tailed off. Yvonne leaned in to kiss his cheek, and he gave her a weak smile. "I feel terrible," he said, his voice quiet. "I don't want you to be like Hana. I love you for who you are. My clever, quick-witted, kind daughter who reminds me of my mother. And I love Hana for herself too, my fierce lion with a heart of gold, who makes me think of my father. I want happiness for you both, and whatever you need to do to be happy, I'll support you."

Maya reached across the table to take her dad's hand, hardly able to believe what he was saying. Her voice broke. "Thank you. I can't tell you how much that means to me."

He squeezed her hand with a smile. Maya left her seat to go around the table, and Omar stood to give her a hug. She cuddled him tightly as he kissed the top of her head.

Maya pulled back to give him a wink. "Unfortunately, you do realize that this turn of events means I'll be staying in town, close by. *Ergo*, you'll probably end up feeding me every night."

Omar laughed. "We'd love that."

He looked at Sam as he released Maya and she went back to her seat. "I'm sorry if I made you feel unwelcome before. My judgment has been off, to say the least. I appreciate you giving me a second chance." Omar sat next to Yvonne, taking her hand.

Sam squeezed Maya's shoulders, smiling at her father. "You don't owe me an apology, Dr. B. I know you only want what's best for Maya, and that's what I want too."

He cleared his throat, and Maya could tell whatever was coming next was emotional for him.

"*My* father didn't care enough to give me or my sister any guidance at all. He didn't even care enough to stick around. So, the fact that you're so driven to make life as good as it possibly can be for your daughters, well." He paused, his eyes shining. "That's excellent in my book."

Something shifted in her dad's gaze, and Maya could tell that sentiment had hit home. She leaned over to kiss Sam's cheek.

Omar blinked, his throat working. "Thank you. I really appreciate that."

Sam glanced at Maya. "Maya is the best instructor I've ever

worked with. She really bonds with those kids, and they have such an amazing time with her." He met her dad's gaze again. "And I know she won't have told you this, because she's too humble. But it was due to her efforts that we doubled the money raised for the children's hospice at the charity sled race this year. The difference that money will make to those kids is down to Maya." Sam kissed her forehead. "Plus, she saved Ben from an accounts crisis that nearly turned his whole head gray."

Yvonne laughed, and Omar gave Sam a soft look. It was clearly dawning on her dad how much this man idolized her, and it was quickly dawning on her too. She wrapped her arms around his waist and leaned her head onto his shoulder, feeling like the luckiest person on the planet.

Omar swallowed. "She's very special, and we are so proud of her." He gave Sam a smile. "I'd appreciate it if you'd call me Omar."

Chapter
TWENTY-EIGHT

SAM SLID HIS PHONE INTO THE CENTER OF THE TABLE, AND MAYA shot him a puzzled look, trying to make out what was on the screen. "What's that?"

Arran, sitting across from the two of them, lifted the phone before she could grab it. "The winners of the Christmas lights competition are out!"

Liv leaned in from the seat next to Arran and studied the screen. "Who won?"

Maya grimaced. "Not the big house again."

Nico peered over Arran's other side. "Nope. It's that one near Sam's."

Maya snatched the phone from Arran, taking in the photo of Sam's neighboring underdog house with delight. "Brilliant!"

Sam gave her a nudge. "Look who came second."

Scrolling down, she spotted their house in second place, and the delight that swept through her was magnified by the fact that she thought of it as "theirs."

"It's us!"

"Awesome," Arran said, giving them both a high five across the table. "Good work, team."

Sam put his arm around her and gave her a squeeze. "Next year, we'll win it."

Joy infused her as she kissed his cheek.

Hana waved at them across the kitchen, and Maya took the signal to get out her phone and turn the music down. Glancing at Sam, she smiled. "Here comes the announcement."

"Thank God," he whispered. "Keeping it secret has been killing me." Maya laughed, quieting as Hana tapped her glass.

"Rosie and I have a little Christmas Eve party announcement." She held out her hand, and Rosie took it. Hana rubbed her belly. "We're having a baby."

The room erupted in cheers, and Liv leaned across the table to hug Maya and then Sam, giving them a wink. "Great news! You're going to be an aunt, and an uncle."

Sam shot Maya a grin. "Uncle Sam. That's got a ring to it."

"Ah," Arran said with a smile. "Christmas baby news is the best kind of news."

Sam gestured toward Arran with his beer bottle. "The other great Christmas baby news is that you get to have Jayce tomorrow night."

"Really?" Liv said, studying Arran with delight on her face. "I thought that Jess was having him Christmas Day?"

Arran cleared his throat, glancing away. "Something came up. A party she wanted to go to. So, she backtracked." He looked up with a smile. "Great news for me, and Mum and Dad."

"I'll bet," Nico said. "First grandchild at Christmas. Fiona and Abeo will be delighted."

Liv shook her head. "Can you imagine what Mum would be

like, Sam?" She rolled her eyes. "I'm terminally single though, so you and Maya will have to take the baton with that one."

Heat rose in Maya's cheeks as Sam laughed, squeezing her shoulders and kissing her red-hot cheek.

"I'll get on it," he said. He winked at his sister. "There's some mistletoe over there. Maybe you can find someone to kiss under it."

Liv glanced at Arran. "Nah."

Maya smiled at Liv, then looked at Arran. "What about you? Fancy kissing someone under the mistletoe?"

She raised her eyebrows, and Liv kicked her under the table.

Arran lifted his beer to take a sip, seeming oblivious. "Nope. None of that for me. It's just me and Jayce now."

Liv glanced away, and Maya felt guilty for having spoken.

Elise came over, Jack in her arms, and took a seat on Sam's other side. "What brilliant news. Congrats, Maya. And Sam." She tried to lift her drink, but Jack kept grabbing at it.

Nico held his hands out across the table. "Here. I'll hold him while you have your drink."

Elise raised her eyebrows. "Really? I thought a Porsche was more your kind of accessory."

Nico smiled. "Don't judge a book by its cover."

Sam nudged Elise. "Nico has the most baby-related experience out of all of us."

Elise shot Nico a wry smile. "Because he's got so many love children stashed away?"

Nico arched a brow. "Ha ha. No. Because I've got so many nieces and nephews, *not* stashed away, but under my care on a regular basis."

Elise's eyes widened. "You help out with childcare?"

Nico shrugged. "Yep. For all of them. From birth."

Elise studied him for a moment, then stood and handed Jack over the table. Nico placed him onto his lap, and Maya felt like they should start calling him the baby whisperer, because Jack seemed right at home.

Sam leaned in toward her ear, his lips brushing her skin and making her shiver. "I want to give you something. Upstairs." Maya raised her eyebrows and he smiled. "No, not *that*. That's coming later, back at mine."

Intrigued, she nodded and got to her feet, taking his hand to lead him out of the kitchen and up to her bedroom.

She shut the door. "What is it?"

He ran a hand through his hair. "I want to give you your Christmas present."

"Now?" she said, excitement rising at the thought of giving him the painting. She'd been anticipating the look on his face.

Sam nodded.

"Ooh," Maya said, rubbing her hands together. "Can I go first?"

Sam smiled. "Of course."

Practically running across the room, she lifted it out from behind some stacks of books, wrapped in brown paper.

Sam raised his eyebrows, coming over to kneel beside it. "Wow." He glanced up. "Yours is bigger than mine."

Maya grinned, clapping her hands in time to her speech. "Op-en it, op-en it."

Sam laughed, and tore a corner away, revealing the night sky underneath. Joy spread across his face. "Oh, I know what this is."

He shot her a grin and tore the rest of the paper off, staring at it with the stars from the painting seeming to become reflected in his eyes. "It's so perfect. I love it."

He stood and lifted her in his arms. "And I love *you*."

Maya kissed him as he set her down. "I love you too."

He took her hand to lead her over to the bed, where they sat. It occurred to Maya that whatever his gift was must've been on his person the whole time, but she had no clue what it could be.

Sam cleared his throat. "I feel I should point out in advance, that this isn't a ring."

Maya frowned, wondering why that needed to be said, then cottoned on when he brought out a little black jewelry box.

She shot him a smile. The box was small, so—earrings maybe?

As she opened it, her breath caught in her throat. The exquisite, perfect star charm that she'd coveted from her teenage years and that matched her twin moon.

Blinking back the overpowering emotions she felt, she met his gaze. "How did you find it?"

Sam took her hand, the look of love in his eyes intense. "I bought it when I got the moon charm from the ski team for your eighteenth birthday." He swallowed. "I was going to give it to you, that night."

Maya took a deep breath, passing him the charm so that he could secure it next to the moon.

Her voice wobbled. "It's perfect."

Meeting his eyes, she fought back tears of joy that he'd kept it, mixed with sadness that he hadn't been able to present it eight years previously. "I'm sorry that you never got to give it to me then. I feel like we wasted so many years."

Sam finished attaching the charm, and smiled. "I figure it's better this way."

She cocked her head, giving him a bemused look. "It is?"

Nodding, he took hold of her face to kiss her. "We were so young, and you were off to university in a big city with lots of new folks. Who knows what would've happened? Life might've driven us apart." He rubbed his nose against hers. "I figure, this way, we're future proof." His eyes were shining so intently that they appeared golden.

Maya leaned in, kissing him like it was their first and last time rolled into one.

Sam broke it off regretfully and smiled. "We'd better head back to the party, or everyone will get suspicious about what we're doing up here."

Maya laughed and stood, taking his hand as they went back downstairs and along the hall into the kitchen to rejoin their friends and family.

❄ ❄ ❄

HER BOOTS CRUNCHED THROUGH THE FRESHLY FALLEN SNOW as Maya ran for the tree line. The sparkle of the fairy lights adorning the foliage seemed to reflect off the falling snowflakes, giving the entrance to the nook an appealing glow.

She turned to grin at Sam as he caught up with her, grabbing her and lifting her off her feet, his deep throaty laugh warming her soul. He set her down and backed her up, pressing her against a tree trunk to kiss her, the soft touch of his lips and the gentle graze of his beard firing up every nerve ending in her entire body.

He shifted his mouth onto her neck, his hands roaming lower down her back. The sound of his breathing was a sharp contrast to the stillness and quiet of Christmas Day.

"Come on," Maya said gently. "We should get into the actual nook before this gets too out of hand."

"I'm always out of hand around you," he gritted out, lifting his head to mold his gaze with hers, his eyes dark with desire.

Smiling, she kissed him, then took hold of his hand. "We need to hurry, we haven't got long." They had just left his mum's place after a satisfying Christmas lunch and were on their way to her parents' for round two.

Sam gave her a look that was loaded with love, squeezing her hand as he led the way into the nook. "On the contrary. We have all the time in the world."

Maya's smile grew wider. She had gotten all she wanted for Christmas.

ACKNOWLEDGMENTS

Hello, lovely reader, and thank you for checking out my book. I appreciate your taking the time to not only add me to your TBR pile but actually read the bloody thing—a transition that we readers know is no mean feat!

I hope that this story has given you a smile or a laugh. If I can create even a tiny iota of joy for you, then that makes me very happy indeed.

This is the book where I stopped being afraid to use my sense of humor and found my true voice. I am so grateful to those who helped me on my journey. Firstly, my husband, Mark—my very own Scottish gent—who is an absolute gem of a human being and has been there for me every step of the way, cheering me on with overzealous enthusiasm. There are often times when acquaintances whom I've never told about my writing will say that they've heard I'm a writer and then ask lots of interested questions. It always turns out that my husband has shoehorned my writing and how proud he is of me into a completely unrelated conversation with them.

I also appreciate the support of my family and friends who were all unwaveringly enthusiastic and proud when I randomly announced that I was writing romance novels alongside my day job. My parents have done a sterling task in forcing pretty much everyone they know to read my books (sorry about that). And my children have supported me by making me notebooks and being patient when I disappear into my writing room.

My agent, Hannah Todd, is a fabulous person and absolutely awesome at what she does. I thank the universe every day for connecting me with her. Thank you, Hannah, and everyone at Madeleine Milburn for making this possible. Thank you, Liane-Louise Smith and Valentina Paulmichl, for your international work and all your guidance on scary tax forms and the like.

Thank you to Kerry Donovan for taking me on and being an utter delight to work with, as well as everyone else at Berkley for giving me the pleasure of being part of your team. And thank you to Belinda Toor, Audrey Linton, and the whole HQ Digital team for your expert advice and for welcoming me into the fold. Everyone has been brilliant, from the editing folks to the book-cover-design peeps (which, to be frank, is totally amazeballs).

Thank you to Natalie, my longtime friend who has read every one of my books from the beginning and given me confidence even when my skills were underdeveloped. And Laura, my lifelong friend who can deliver the best constructive criticism in a very kind way. Thank you to the group of beta readers—Kat McIntyre, Raven McAllan, Amy Craig, and Deana Birch—who read an early version and helped me to see that it really wasn't working. It was a painful return to the drawing board to start from scratch, but very much worth it in the end.

Thank you to my romance writer pals who read a later version and gave me invaluable advice—Katherine Dyson and Emma Jackson.

I also want to thank my fellow romance writers who have provided friendship, support, and advice: Jenni Keer, Lucy Keeling, Rachel Dove, Ruby Basu, Leonie Mack, Alison May, Janet Gover, and everyone in the Chick Lit and Prosecco Facebook group, headed up by the wonderful Anita Faulkner. The romance writing community is a true example of women championing women, and I am proud to be a member of it.

I would like to thank my Twitter writing friends in the Twoobs Twitter group for their support and the BookTok community on TikTok, where I can let my sense of humor roam weird and free.

Lastly, a tribute to the women whose books inspired me to write, to keep writing, and to find my voice. My author heroes—Sarah Morgan, Ali Hazelwood, Sally Thorne, Helen Hoang, Talia Hibbert, Tessa Bailey, Denise Williams, and Emily Henry, to name but a few. The work you do is invaluable in providing light and escapism in what can be, at times, a bleak world. Thank you.

Keep reading for a special preview
of Zoe Allison's next romance,

**WEDDING
ENGAGEMENT**

"THAT'S IT, CATHERINE, LEG NICE AND STRAIGHT," LIV INSTRUCTED, reaching out to point at her young student's posture. "And, Josh, remember to keep your thumb outside your fist, not tucked inside. If you strike someone with your thumb tucked in, then you might break it."

"Yes, Sensei," Catherine and Josh said in unison, immediately correcting their errors.

"Good," Liv said, adjusting the black belt tied around her waist and moving on to the next pair of students. The kids in her class had really come along in the relatively short time she'd been teaching them, and it delighted her to see it, especially after she had been unsure whether she could manage the commitment of becoming their instructor. But now she was pleased that her own sensei had talked her into it. *"Who better to instruct them than a black belt who's already a qualified teacher?"*

She continued around all of the students, giving them constructive criticism along the way.

Returning to the front of the class, she folded her hands behind her back. "Yame!"

The students ceased their movements.

"Line up," she told them, and watched as they moved quickly into position in front of her. "Excellent work today. Keep it up and we'll be right on track for the next grading." She bowed to signal the end of the class, and the kids followed suit, then filed out of the dojo to meet their parents.

Once she'd ensured that everyone had found and left with their parent or guardian, Liv went to the locker area to pull on her shoes. Just then, a buzzing noise sounded from her rucksack, and she lifted out her phone. The screen indicated that Arran was FaceTiming her.

Her insides did the familiar tumble at the sight of his name. *How long do we have to be friends before I stop feeling like a giddy schoolgirl whenever I see or talk to him?*

She connected the call and Arran's face appeared on-screen, causing her stupid heart to squeeze like an accordion playing a lovesick melody. His honey-colored eyes were unusually tight and he was frowning as he ran a hand over the loose coils of his dark, caramel-infused hair.

"What's up?" she asked, sensing the tension in his posture.

He sighed in a very un-Arran-like manner. "This is an SOS call. 'Help me, Obi-Wan Kenobi. You're my only hope.'"

She laughed. "I'll do my best. Though I have to warn you, my control of the Force is on the fritz."

He smiled; however, it was less bright than usual. "I've got a situation. I'm out of town getting some painting supplies. Jess called to say she can't pick Jayce up from his street dance class as planned, and I can't get back in time to do it. Her parents are away for the weekend and I just called mine, but, as usual, their mobiles are turned off." He rolled his eyes. "What's the point of having a fucking mobile phone if it's permanently off?"

"My mum and Angus are the same," she told him. "They say they're 'saving the battery.'"

He huffed out a breath. "Parents."

Liv shot him a smile. "*You're* a parent, remember?"

He rubbed a hand over his dark stubble, and she experienced a strong craving to know what it felt like. Against her mouth. *Down, girl.*

"Oh yeah," he said, almost absently. He flicked his eyes to meet hers. "But I'm way cooler."

"Sure you are," she said, giving him a wink. "Anyway, yes, I can pick up Jayce for you. Shall I take him home with me, or bring him to yours?"

Arran hesitated for a second, glancing away from the screen. "Thank you. I'm really sorry to ask for your help." He swallowed, returning his gaze to hers. "Again."

"That's what friends are for," she said, waving her hand dismissively. "Don't sweat it."

The defeated look on his face made it clear that he *was* sweating it. Copiously. She'd never known anyone as proud and reluctant to ask for help as him. And it didn't escape her notice that he hated even voicing the question, which is why she had jumped in to say yes before he'd outright asked.

"I thought it might make sense to call you, because I knew you'd be nearby," he said, as if still trying to justify the very legitimate action of asking a close friend for a small favor.

"Arran, it's fine," she told him, her tone kind but firm. "It wouldn't matter if I wasn't nearby, I'd still be happy to help. I'll nip across the road to the dance studio now and fetch him."

Arran's shoulders sagged with relief. "Thank you. If you head over to mine, I'll meet you back there ASAP."

She gave him a two-fingered salute. "No problem. How come Jess couldn't pick him up anyway? I thought this weekend was hers."

"Yeah, so did I," he muttered, before clearing his throat. "I'll tell you later."

Liv grabbed her bag, heading for the door. "I'll take him for a milkshake first, give you time to get your painting stuff and reach home."

This time his smile was more relaxed. "You're a lifesaver, ka-rate kid. I owe you one."

"You can pay me back in scones," she told him, eliciting a laugh from his lovely, soft-looking lips. "Give the teacher a quick mes-sage to say I'll be picking him up, so they don't think I'm trying to kidnap your adorable son."

"Will do." He raised his eyebrows in a manner that made her heart skip a beat. "And by the way, we need to get your scone addic-tion under control. You, Maya, and Elise have a problem."

She shrugged. "There's no problem. I can give them up any-time I want."

He laughed. "Yeah, right."

They ended the call, and Liv pulled her purple-framed glasses out of her bag to place them on, taking out her hair tie so that her dark wavy locks fell free. Then she made her way over to the dance studio. She knew Jayce's class would be finishing in around ten minutes, because sometimes she'd see Jayce leaving with either Arran or Jess.

Once inside the studio, she headed over to where the group of parents were waiting for their kids to exit, and she peered through the small window in the door to watch the class. The wee ones were having an absolute ball, performing moves that, in some cases, barely resembled what the teacher was doing. *So cute.*

A few minutes later, the class was dismissed. Liv kept watch for Jayce, hoping he wouldn't be disappointed that she was there instead of his mummy. Before long, his little face appeared behind a crowd of kids, big brown eyes wide and sandy curls bouncing. "Lib!"

"Hey, buddy!" she said, crouching down as he ran over and practically threw himself into her arms.

"Teacher said you were coming," he told her in an excited tone. "We going to play at your house?"

She ruffled his soft hair. "Not today, pal. I'm just picking you up as a favor to Mummy and Daddy."

He grasped her hand as she stood. "You taking me to Mummy's?"

She gave his hand a squeeze. "We're off to Dad's house. I think there's been a change of plan because Mummy's busy."

"Why is she busy?"

"I'm not sure, buddy. But we'll find out in a bit."

They exited onto the street. Jayce pointed down the road, toward the fifties-style diner. "Can we get milkshakes?"

"Wow. You read my mind," she said with a smile. "That was exactly my plan."

He threw his small fist into the air. "Yay!"

✳ ✳ ✳

"AND THEN WHAT HAPPENED?" LIV ASKED, MAINTAINING A SERI-ous expression as Jayce carried on with his tall tale.

"And then I rescued everyone from the dragon and saved the day," he said from the back seat, a proud look on his face when she glanced his way through the rearview mirror.

She returned her eyes to the road as she navigated the last turn onto Arran's driveway. "Wow. And this was definitely real, not a dream?"

"Wasn't a dream," he scoffed. "It really happened."

"Okay," she told him. "I believe you." She pulled up outside the house and exited the car to get Jayce out of the car seat. She couldn't even remember when she'd started keeping Arran's spare seat in the back; it had happened at some point since the New Year.

Jayce scrambled out of the car before she could help him, running past the grassy area lined by yellow daffodils and purple crocuses, and up to the doorway, where he banged his fist. When she reached the doorstep, Liv glanced back at the hills, the green of springtime making her feel as light as the fresh Highland air.

The door opened and Arran's smiling face appeared. He crouched down as Jayce barreled into him in his signature greeting. "Daddy! We had milkshakes."

"What? Without me?" Arran said, pouting his lips in an exaggerated manner that made her fantasize about kissing him. "What flavor did you get?"

"Chocolate!" Jayce yelled, running off down the hallway.

Liv laughed as she crossed the threshold. Arran held out his hand and she shook it, then gave him a side five and a fist bump. Despite the fact that they now performed these gestures pretty much every time they met, the touch of his hand still gave her goose bumps. *That's not how "just friends" is supposed to feel.*

"Have you got time for a cuppa?" he asked her.

"Sure. Always time for tea," Liv told him as she followed down the hallway.

"Excellent. Walk this way," Arran said, putting on a comical gait for her to imitate, which she did. It occurred to her that she had as many in-jokes and gestures with him as she did with her best friends, Maya and Elise. And yet up until the previous summer, while Arran had always been best friends with her twin brother, Sam, to her he'd merely been a casual acquaintance. A really hot acquaintance that she'd harbored a crush on for the past decade or so. Not that he'd ever noticed.

Arran set about making them some tea. "Don't judge me," he said, glancing up to meet her eyes.

She frowned as she took off her coat, then the jacket from her karate uniform. "Judge you for what?"

For a moment he was silent, and when she looked up, he was eyeing her vest-clad form with an odd expression on his face. He shook his head slightly, as if bringing his thoughts back to the conversation. "For my inferior tea-making skills. Nobody is as talented at brewing tea as you."

Liv smiled. She *was* renowned throughout their friend group for making the best cup of tea in the land. She blew on her fingernails, then pretended to polish them on her white vest top. "Well. One does try." She took a seat at the breakfast bar, looking behind her to where Jayce was sitting at his little red table, energetically drawing something that resembled a tiny stick figure battling a dragon. "What's the deal with Jess, then? Change of plan for this weekend?"

Arran glanced over at Jayce, then pushed a steaming mug toward her, leaning his elbows on the counter to bring himself closer. Liv's pulse rocketed as she inhaled his scent and struggled furiously to keep her eyes off how his biceps flexed under the close fit of his T-shirt.

"Yeah. She asked if I'd have him last night so she could go to this party with the boyfriend." Arran always referred to Rory as "the boyfriend," and Liv was sure it was because he still resented Jess having one.

He lifted his mug. "The deal was that I'd drop Jayce at street dance, then she'd pick him up and have him the rest of the weekend. But then she called to say they'd overdone it last night and she was too hungover to drive."

"Ah," Liv said, sipping her tea. "And by that time, you'd already reached the paint shop?"

"Yep," he said on a sigh. "I'm behind schedule on this commission. There's a specific deadline because it's a present for a wedding anniversary."

He took a drink, eyes down in a rather dejected manner.

She touched his hand. "Why the long face? I thought you loved doing this new line in portraits?"

"I do," he said, eyes still on his mug. "Problem is, I'm . . ." He paused, rubbing the side of his face.

"You're what?" she asked, studying him.

He cleared his throat. "I'm struggling. To manage it all." He met her gaze. "Don't get me wrong, I love having Jayce more often. But Jess keeps reneging on her weekends, and it's the only free time per month I get to paint."

She could tell admitting that was a big deal for him. "Are you in a position where you could give up your day job to concentrate on painting during the week?"

He shook his head with a wince. "Nah. Not yet. But I can't wait for that day to come. Especially since no one in the office appreciates my sense of humor."

"What did you do this time?" she asked.

He grinned. "I replaced everyone's desk photos with Leonardo DiCaprio memes."

She sighed, trying to suppress the smile threatening to break out over her face. "You're *so* immature."

He gave her a nudge. "I can see how desperately you want to laugh at my hilarious joke, karate kid. Don't try to hide it."

The corner of her mouth quirked.

"We have the same sense of humor." He waggled his fingers. "We are kindred spirits, you and I," he said in a mysterious tone.

That was the last straw, and she broke down laughing.

He joined in, but as the laughter died away, the tense expression made a reappearance on his normally relaxed face.

Liv watched him, hating seeing her lighthearted and playful friend so stressed, and wondered what she could do to help. "I'll babysit for you," she blurted out.

He frowned. "You'll what?"

"Babysit. On the Saturday that's meant to be Jess's. I'll come over after karate to watch him for the afternoon while you paint. I can stay into the evening too if you need it."

Arran stared at her, his jaw working. "No."

She waited for him to elaborate, but he stayed silent. "'No'? That's all you've got to say about it?"

He swallowed hard, lifting his mug to his lips. "No, thank you."

Liv huffed out a breath. "Why not?"

Arran shook his head. "This is my responsibility, so I'll handle it. You've got your own life to deal with."

She shrugged. "I'm not busy."

"That's because you're the only one of us that has their shit together," he said, shooting her a smile.

"Yeah, right," she muttered under her breath.

He cocked his head. "Pardon?"

"Nothing."

They both fell silent, and she willed him to change his mind, wishing she were an actual Jedi with the power to sway people's intentions. But he just sipped his tea with a determined look on his face.

She sighed. "You're so stubborn and annoying."

He grinned. "You love me, really."

"Hmm," she said, keeping her eyes on her tea.

"Any plans for tomorrow?" he asked, in a transparent effort to change the subject.

She decided it was best to let it go—for now. "Yeah. I'm meeting Elise at Maya and Sam's house tomorrow afternoon. Sam will be there too."

"Oh yeah?" he said. "What time? Sam's meant to be meeting me and Nico at Nico's sister's house tomorrow, after lunch." He paused, appearing to ponder for a second. "Sam seemed pretty eager to catch up. When Nico asked for a rain check—because he was babysitting his sister's kids—Sam said no and that we'd just meet Nico there."

She frowned. "Not sure what that's all about. But our thing isn't until midafternoon, so he must be seeing you guys first, then coming to us."

Arran arched an eyebrow. "Curiouser and curiouser."

She smiled. "Yes, indeed. Anyway, we'll find out what the story is tomorrow."

"Yep." He lifted his mug, and she clunked hers with his, savoring the warm honey tone of his eyes as she sipped her drink and tried to remind herself that no good could come from her attraction to him.

Photo courtesy of the author

ZOE ALLISON lives in Scotland with her husband and two children, having been brought up in a mixed-race family in Yorkshire. Growing up, Zoe enjoyed stories about falling in love. But rather than day-dreaming of being rescued by a knight in shining armor, she imagined herself fighting dragons alongside him, battling supervillains as heroic allies, or teaming up to dive into perilous waters and save the day. As an adult, Zoe became a doctor. However, as time passed, she craved a creative outlet to counter the soul-sapping burnout that her career inflicted upon her, and also to achieve the happy endings that were so often lacking in the real world. She wanted to create heroines who represent her and her values, as well as heroes who truly love women—men who find their true loves inspiring, want to connect with them as soulmates, and fully open themselves to their partners on an emotional level. And so, Zoe began to write romance.

VISIT ZOE ALLISON ONLINE

ZoeAllison.co.uk
🐦 ZoeAllisonAuth1
📘 Zoe.Allison.9279
📷 ZoeAllisonAuthor
🎵 ZoeAllisonAuthor

Ready to find
your next great read?

Let us help.

Visit prh.com/nextread

Penguin
Random
House